THE
ICEMAN

ALSO BY P. T. DEUTERMANN

THE CAM RICHTER NOVELS

The Cat Dancers
Spider Mountain
The Moonpool
Nightwalkers

THRILLERS

Red Swan
Cold Frame
The Last Man
The Firefly
Darkside
Hunting Season
Train Man
Zero Option
Sweepers
Official Privilege

SEA STORIES

The Commodore
Sentinels of Fire
Ghosts of Bungo Suido
Pacific Glory
The Edge of Honor
Scorpion in the Sea

THE
ICEMAN

P. T. DEUTERMANN

ST. MARTIN'S PRESS
NEW YORK

THE ICEMAN. Copyright © 2018 by P. T. Deutermann. All rights reserved.
Printed in the United States of America. For information, address St. Martin's
Press, 175 Fifth Avenue, New York, NY 10010.

www.stmartins.com

Design by Jonathan Bennett

The Library of Congress Cataloging-in-Publication Data is available upon request.

ISBN 978-1-250-18137-4 (hardcover)
ISBN 978-1-250-18138-1 (ebook)

Our books may be purchased in bulk for promotional, educational, or business use.
Please contact your local bookseller or the Macmillan Corporate and Premium
Sales Department at 1-800-221-7945, extension 5442, or by email at
MacmillanSpecialMarkets@macmillan.com.

First Edition: August 2018

10 9 8 7 6 5 4 3 2 1

This book is dedicated to the memory of all the American submariners who were driven out of Cavite in the Philippines in early 1942 and who then struck back at the Japanese from bases in Australia, at a time when no other American forces could retaliate for Pearl Harbor, especially those who remain on eternal patrol.

ACKNOWLEDGMENTS

I wish to acknowledge the extremely useful history book by Clay Blair called *Silent Victory*. I used it as my principal research reference for this story.

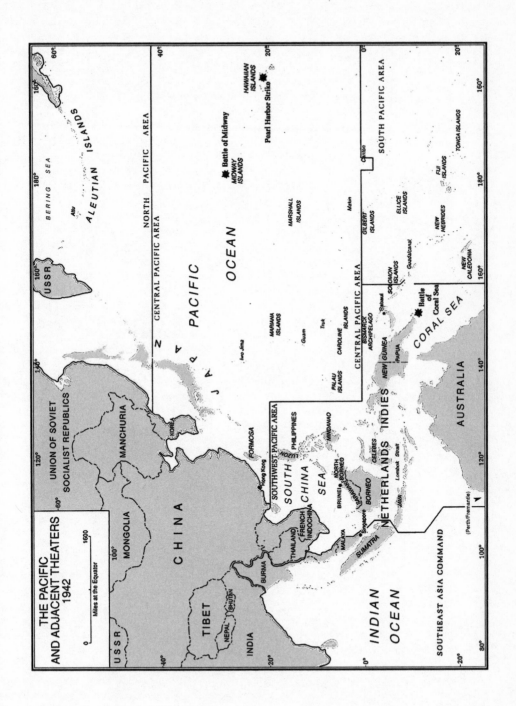

THE PACIFIC
AND ADJACENT THEATERS
1942

Miles at the Equator

0   1600

USSR

UNION OF SOVIET
SOCIALIST REPUBLICS

MONGOLIA

MANCHURIA

CHINA

TIBET

NEPAL

BHUTAN

INDIA

BURMA

THAILAND

FRENCH
INDOCHINA

KOREA

FORMOSA

Hong Kong

SOUTHWEST PACIFIC AREA

SOUTH
CHINA
SEA

MALAYA

Singapore

SARAWAK

BRUNEI

NORTH
BORNEO

BORNEO

Java

Lombok Strait

SUMATRA

NETHERLANDS INDIES

CELEBES

MINDANAO

PHILIPPINES

PALAU
ISLANDS

JAVA SEA

CAROLINE
ISLANDS

Truk

Guam

MARIANA
ISLANDS

Iwo Jima

PACIFIC

OCEAN

CENTRAL PACIFIC AREA

NORTH PACIFIC AREA

ALEUTIAN ISLANDS

Attu

BERING SEA

USSR

MARSHALL
ISLANDS

✸ Battle of Midway
MIDWAY
ISLANDS

HAWAIIAN
ISLANDS

Pearl Harbor Strike ✸

CENTRAL PACIFIC AREA

BISMARCK
ARCHIPELAGO

Rabaul

NEW GUINEA

PAPUA

✸ Battle
of
Coral Sea

CORAL SEA

AUSTRALIA

SOLOMON
ISLANDS

Guadalcanal

NEW
HEBRIDES

NEW
CALEDONIA

GILBERT
ISLANDS

Makin

Canton

ELLICE
ISLANDS

FIJI
ISLANDS

TONGA ISLANDS

SOUTH PACIFIC AREA

INDIAN

OCEAN

SOUTHEAST ASIA COMMAND

(Perth/Fremantle)

60°

160°

180°

160°

140°

120°

100°

-60°

40°

20°

0°

-20°

80°

100°

120°

140°

160°

180°

160°

20°

0°

20°

ANY TIME, ANYWHERE, ALWAYS READY, ALWAYS THERE.

Submarine Service motto

THE
ICEMAN

ONE

Malachi Stormes took one last cheek-flattening drag on his cigarette and then extinguished it in a butt kit. He exhaled through his nose and then depressed the talk button on the bitchbox. "Depth beneath the keel?" he called out.

"One hundred ten feet, Captain," the sonar operator reported from the sound room, one deck below. "Mud bottom."

"Can you hear that pilot boat yet?"

"No, sir. No prop sounds."

The submarine, an American S-class, was hovering at periscope depth eight miles offshore from St. Nazaire, and, theoretically, 2,000 yards west of the entrance to the new German minefield. The Germans had mined the Loire River approaches following the British raid on the *Normandie* dry dock and the nearby U-boat pens two months ago. The seaward entrance to the swept channel was marked by two black buoys, 150 feet apart. The safe channel course past those buoys and into the harbor was known only to the Germans. Malachi assumed it was probably a zigzag pattern of some kind.

"First light is when?" he asked.

"First light in forty-two minutes, Captain," the navigator, Lieutenant (Junior Grade) Dick Harris, answered.

"Very well," Malachi responded. He lit up another cigarette and peered down at the chart table in the middle of the conning tower. The space was crowded, damp, and cold, with only a hint of warm air coming up through the hatch from the control room immediately below. The frigid waters of the Bay of Biscay kept the temperature inside their steel cocoon at no more than fifty degrees, even with eight men crammed into the tiny space. The conning tower was under red-light condition in deference to Malachi's night vision in case he had to use the periscope.

They'd been hanging out in the outer Loire estuary off St. Nazaire for five days, submerging and then resting on the muddy bottom during daylight hours. After dark they'd come back up to charge the batteries and reconnoiter the harbor approaches. Daylight was too dangerous for lurking submarines in the shallow waters off the French coast. A scouting German bomber could actually see a submerged submarine if it lingered at periscope depth during the day.

Twice at night they'd followed small coastal freighters right up to the minefield entrance, where they'd been met by a pilot boat. The pilot would then turn around and lead the freighter between the buoys and into the swept channel of the minefield, using only its stern light as a visual reference. They'd watched carefully as the freighter went deeper and deeper into the field, staying right behind that dim stern light. Then the light disappeared, which meant that the pilot boat had made a turn. Moments later, each of the freighters had turned right, but to which exact course and at what distance into the field they could not measure. By watching two ships start the trip, they'd calculated the initial course into the field and guesstimated the distance to that first turn, but that was all they knew for sure.

This is insane, Harris thought, as he looked down at the chart. Nuts. Crazy. The navigation plot in front of him was based purely on a series of assumptions. Their current "position" was a dead-reckoning one, meaning they had assumed a known starting point on the chart out in the bay, and then drawn estimated position marks based only on the ordered courses and speeds into the harbor approach area, making no allowances for tidal and river currents. Harris knew there'd been no real fixes since yesterday at noon. The only physical points of reference right now were those two dimly lit buoys, and their position on the approaches chart was based on French resistance reports.

Crazy, he told himself again. We're flying blind and we're going to die here. He refused to look at the other men in the conning tower, not wanting them to see his own mounting fear every time he looked down at the chart. He was the navigator. If *he* didn't know where they were . . .

The approaches chart showed the assumed sea frontier of the minefield, with the putative swept channel laid out for a distance of a thousand yards into the field before that first turn. The rest of the field was drawn onto the chart with diagonal lines indicating simply dangerous ground. Malachi had positioned the submarine so that it could straight-line fire torpedoes down that initial leg of the safe channel. He was not interested in itinerant coastal freighters. He was waiting for a U-boat to come out to begin her patrol.

That's what this insanity is all about, Harris thought. Cozying up to the seaward edge of a minefield because the captain wants a U-boat. The red light on the face of the bitchbox lit up.

"Conn, Sound: I have faint screwbeats, bearing one three zero."

Malachi quashed his cigarette. "Conn: aye," he replied. "Open all outer doors forward. Make ready tubes one through four."

The fire-control officer, LTJG Mickey Houser, acknowledged the command and sent orders through sound-powered phones to the torpedo room, where torpedomen actuated the hydraulic outer doors and began charging the four firing-flasks with 3,000 psi air.

"Up scope," Malachi ordered.

The fire-control team tensed at their stations as the scope hydraulics began whining down below the control room deck plates. Malachi had briefed his plan daily for the past five days. They would let the pilot boat come into view. She would be visible by the white-over-red lights on her mast. Those lights would be dimmed in deference to wartime conditions, but the French harbor pilots knew that no one would attack a 30-foot pilot boat—they were small, insignificant targets. The soundmen had been trained extensively to recognize the sound of U-boat diesels. Steam-powered ships made waterborne noise, too, but the underwater acoustic signature of a German submarine's diesel engine running on the surface was quite distinctive. If that's what they heard, Malachi would wait for the pilot boat to turn off from the channel entry course to get out of the way of whatever was coming out, and then he'd fire four fish down the center of that channel. A logical plan, Harris had to admit. Except we don't really know where we are in relation to that swept channel. We're depending on those two buoys. What if the Krauts moved them from time to time? What if the buoys marked the first string of mines instead of just the entrance to the clear channel?

"Conn, Sound: it's that pilot boat. Same antique up-and-down steam engine. Can't hear anything behind him yet."

"Conn: aye. If he's coming to meet someone we'll stand down. Scan west as well as east."

"Sound: aye." The sonarman sounded a bit put out at being told to check both directions. Get used to it, Harris thought. Lieutenant Commander Malachi Stormes has zero empathy for the professional qualities of his people. He issues orders. We do as we're told. Right now if you please, Mister Christian.

Malachi walked the periscope handles around in a slow sweep, forcing Harris and the other men to move back out of his way in the cramped space. It was still pretty dark on the surface, but the captain always wanted a look. One night they'd crept in submerged to the edge of the field and he'd put the scope up only to find a German PT boat tied up to one of the buoys. The wooden-hulled PT boats weren't worth a submarine's torpedo, but they all carried some depth charges and bristled with cannon big enough to punch holes in the elderly S-boat's pressure hull. That's why I always look before coming up, he'd told them. Always. Especially when Sound says there's nothing up there.

He steadied the scope on the bearing reported by the sonar gang.

"Ask Sound if he's got any Doppler."

One of the team queried the sound-shack via sound-powered phone. "Slight up-Doppler on that steam engine," he reported. "Definitely coming out. No contacts to seaward."

Malachi glanced down at the bearing ring. The sub's head was 100, not the 130 he'd ordered. He bent over to the bitchbox. "Control, Conn: get her back on ordered heading and keep her so," he snapped icily.

A moment later they could feel the electric motors back aft

opposing each other to twist her head back onto 130. There were uncomfortable looks exchanged in the conning tower. Somebody in the control room below had a red face about now. The problem was that at bare steerageway, the boat's rudder had little effect. Stormes had to know that, Harris thought.

"Conn, Sound: harmonics on a bearing of one three two. There's something behind the pilot boat. Possibly *two* contacts."

Malachi returned to the optics on the periscope. Nothing. He ordered the scope up to full navigation height, which gave him another two feet above the surface. That finally allowed him to see the dimmed lights of the oncoming pilot boat, but the optics were fuzzy.

"Stand by to mark bearing." A one-second pause. "Mark!"

"Bearing is one three five."

"Can't get a range," Malachi said. "Steer one three five. Speed three. Down scope."

Harris cleared his throat. "Sir, that's *toward* the minefield. We—"

"Steer one three five, speed three. As soon as that pilot boat turns I will fire all four. Confirm settings. Torpedo speed: slow. Torpedo depth: ten feet. Spread is one degree."

The fire-control leader read the settings aloud back to him, then transmitted them electrically to the forward torpedo room. Then they waited. Up forward in the torpedo room, each torpedo guidance system was receiving running orders.

"Sir, torpedoes set as ordered."

"Very well."

Harris tried again. "Captain, we are closing the edge of the minefield. I have no nav data other than DR. Recommend slowing back down to bare steerageway."

"No," Malachi said. "Up scope."

Faces tightened in the conning tower. The navigation plotter, whose job it was to record the boat's position and track on the plotting table, put his pencil down. Prior to this the boat had been simply hovering in place, but now . . . he had no data other than a dead-reckoning calculation. "No fix," Harris reported dutifully.

"I understand and I have the pilot boat's lights showing target angle of two seven zero. He's turning around. I can see the buoy lights now.

We're at least five hundred yards away from the buoys. *New* bearing: standby—mark!"

Harris read the index markings on the opposite side of the periscope. "New bearing is one *four* zero."

Malachi swore quietly. The boat's heading was ten degrees off the swept channel's heading. And the damned periscope was fogging up again.

"Surface the boat," he ordered. "Decks awash. I need to see."

There was silent consternation in the conning tower. Surface in the face of oncoming enemy ships? But there was discipline aboard the boat and Control immediately brought her up from 60 feet to the surface and then adjusted the ballast tanks to let her ride with just the sail exposed, a delicate balancing maneuver between diving and surfacing but which raised the periscope far enough into the air to clear the lenses.

He took one more bearing and then decided to split the difference. "Firing bearing will be one three five. All other settings: no change. Prepare to fire."

The fire-control talker confirmed the new firing bearing, which was the course the torpedoes would take once launched. He read back the other settings just to make sure.

"Torpedoes one through four, ready," he announced.

"Fire one," Malachi ordered, followed by the remaining three in fifteen-second intervals. Once the fourth fish had thumped out of its tube, Malachi ordered the boat back down to 150 feet and made a course change to 270, due west, and away from the minefield at a speed of 5 knots. The relief in the conning tower was palpable.

Again, they waited. Malachi had selected a slow speed—21 knots—for the Mark 10 torpedoes because that gave them longer range—almost 4 miles, double the high-speed range. Without knowing how far back in the swept channel his targets were, he wanted a long reach. He ordered the torpedo room to begin reloading.

"Steady on two seven zero," the quartermaster reported. The boat drove west for a minute and then Malachi surprised them again.

"Prepare to surface," he ordered.

Then the sound shack had a question. "Conn, Sound: what's the run time?"

"I have no idea," Malachi said, as if that was the most natural response in the world. "Surface."

The klaxon alarm sounded and the boat's thirty-eight-man crew jumped to their valves, wheels, and hatches. The boat tilted up. Just as she broke the surface in a roar of compressed air and bubbles, they all heard a distant boom. Harris would have sworn that, for the briefest instant, the captain seemed to smile, but then his expression settled back into his normal stone face.

"Stable on the surface, main induction is open," engineering reported. "Lighting off mains."

"Very well, steer two seven zero, speed fifteen. Set four lookouts."

The conning team again flattened themselves against the steel sides as the maneuvering bridge watch personnel, one officer and four lookouts, came scrambling up the ladder, and then came the blessed whoosh of fresh air as the upper hatch was spun open. Then they heard a second boom, followed by a third, and then several more in quick succession. The men looked at each other in astonishment. *That* many hits on a blind-range shot?

"Unbelievable," one of the fire-control men muttered.

"Maybe," Malachi observed. "Or maybe all four fish hit mines, and those mines countermined other mines. *Or* we hit the first boat and the second one instinctively turned into the minefield. We'll have to wait for HQ intelligence to tell us. Mister Harris, get an attack report out while we're still on the surface. We'll run for an hour and then we'll have to get back down. The Huns will have air up pretty quick." Then he went below.

"Jee-zus," one of the other officers, LTJG Ben Hiller, whispered after Malachi was safely out of earshot. "How close did we come to that minefield?"

"I have no fucking idea, Benny," Harris said. "And that's the God's honest truth. I *still* don't know where we are, other than we're headed in the right direction."

Hiller closed his eyes. "I've had it, Dicky," he said, no longer caring if the enlisted in the conning tower heard him or not. "I want off this fucker. This guy's nuts."

That night the boat was ordered back to its base in Scotland. Upon arrival two days later they were met with a hero's welcome. The British admiral was on the pier, along with the American submarine squadron commander and a small group of staff officers. There was even a band, whose squad of wailing bagpipes against a cold, stiff wind coming across the slate gray loch. The wind turned the landing into a circus of missed heaving lines and much backing and filling. When the gangway finally went over, the admiral came aboard and shook Malachi's hand enthusiastically.

"Three U-boats, by God, sir. *Three!* Damn my eyes if you didn't sink the whole lot! Well *done*, Captain. *Very* well done, indeed. There'll be a mighty gong for sure. Now, come with me, if you please. There's a press conference on in half an hour. The Admiralty is over the bloody moon."

Lieutenants Harris and Hiller watched from the navigation bridge as the admiral, Lieutenant Commander Stormes, the squadron commander, and a clutch of aides trotted off to some staff cars on the pier.

"First thing in the morning, Dicky," Hiller said. "I'm putting in my letter. I won't sail with that nutcase."

"They'll surface you, Benny," Harris said. "You'll be finished in submarines, especially after this success."

"Suits me just fine," Hiller said, "just fine. I'll take my chances with the Germans *or* the Japs."

Harris wondered if he shouldn't do the same. Stormes was unlike any other submariner he'd ever met. Quiet but exuding a powerful physical presence. When he was moving through the boat men had to not just get out of the way but flatten themselves against a bulkhead to make room. He wasn't a screamer or any kind of a ramrod martinet, but when something was going on he was so fully concentrated that no one dared question him. He rarely slept, which meant that his brooding presence was felt throughout the day's routine.

He decided to have a sit-down with the boat's exec, but he knew he faced a difficult decision. If asked, he would not have been able to say what he was more scared of: the Nazis or Malachi Stormes.

TWO

At 0945, Lieutenant Commander Marty Brandquist was standing on the quarterdeck of the American submarine USS *Firefish*. Next to him was the chief of the boat, Chief Torpedoman Cory O'Bannon, commonly addressed as COB. The rest of the crew were scattered along the main topside deck of the boat, smoking cigarettes and waiting for the order to fall into formation. It was a gray July day in Fremantle Harbour, but with a stiff, warm breeze blowing in from the northeast bringing hints of the approach of antipodean summer. *Firefish* was tied up in a nest of four boats alongside USS *Otus*, their tender. They were awaiting the arrival of the new commanding officer, Commander Malachi Stormes, USN.

It had been four months since the American retreat from the Philippines, and the Aussies had bent over backwards to accommodate the US Pacific Fleet subs that had turned up without much notice, looking for a home and to put some distance between themselves and the approaching Japanese hordes. Australia in mid-1942 was convinced the Japanese were going to invade them next, which remained a distinct possibility. Singapore had fallen. The nearest Japs were in New Guinea, beginning a long slog through the jungles toward Port Moresby, at the southern tip of the island. The two biggest British ships in Southeast Asia, the battleships *Prince of Wales* and *Repulse*, had gone down in the South China Sea under a hail of Japanese bombs and torpedoes. Indochina, most of China, Korea, the Malaysian peninsula, the Philippines, Java, and Indonesia were in Japanese hands or about to be. Darwin, Australia's northernmost port, had been scouted twice by Japanese carrier planes, which meant something was coming.

"So, COB," Marty said, "what've *you* heard about the new skipper?"

"Not a damn thing, XO," he said. "That worries me a wee bit."

"None of the other chiefs know him?"

"LantFleet guy is all I know," O'Bannon said. "How about you?"

"Admiral called me downtown yesterday," Marty said. "Said his name is Malachi Stormes. Three striper. He's coming from one of the S-boats we sent up to Scotland right after Pearl. Class of 'thirty."

"Younger guy, then," O'Bannon observed.

Marty made a face. He was naval academy class of 1937. The issue of aging, super-cautious captains versus the number of ships sunk was officially taboo in the Southeast Asia submarine force, but a hot topic among the younger officers nonetheless.

The COB quickly changed the subject. "Haven't heard shit about LantFleet boats doing anything, so far."

"Well, this boat did," Marty did. "Stormes apparently cozied up to the entrance to a German minefield off St. Nazaire in France and sank three U-boats while they were transiting the swept channel outbound. Fired four fish straight down the exit channel. They don't know how many subs were actually hit, or whether they started evading and ran into their own minefield. Spectacular results, either way."

"He must have been shooting Mark tens, then," the chief said.

"Apparently, that's all they had up there in Scotland. All the Mark fourteens are being sent west."

"For our sins," the chief observed, disgustedly.

Marty sighed his agreement. The Mark 14 torpedoes had proven to be unreliable at best and downright dangerous at worst. It didn't help that the admiral currently commanding the western Australian submarines had been one of the Mark 14's principal designers when he was a three-striper several years ago. The topic of torpedo performance was another hot issue in the Pacific submarine force, with the admirals blaming the skippers for poor shooting, and the skippers blaming the torpedoes for running under their targets without exploding.

Marty was a fresh-caught lieutenant commander and the executive officer of *Firefish*. He'd been temporarily acting as the commanding officer ever since their skipper, Commander Montgomery Russell, had been relieved for not having accomplished a single sinking on *Firefish*'s first war patrol from Australia. He wasn't the first skipper to have been sent ashore for poor results on patrol, and the admiral's wrath was an often-discussed matter around coffeepots in the refugee submarines. *Firefish* was one of the new Tambor-class fleet boats, bigger and more capable than the aging S-class boats. Much had been expected of her, which had added to the admiral's ire. Russell was a soft-spoken Southern gentleman from the academy class of 1926, whose obvious concern for the crew's welfare had made him something of a father figure in the boat. He had not protested his relief, admitting to his exec in private that he didn't have the stomach for risking his boat and everyone's lives just to sink a freighter.

A sudden gust of wind made the flag on the fantail crack like a shot, making everyone topside jump. People were nervous, and while there was no immediate threat to Perth and Fremantle, located on the far west coast of Australia, the appearance of Jap carriers in northern Australian waters had brought the heretofore distant Pacific war home in a big way to their hosts.

"There's the car," the COB said. He turned to the other sailors hanging about the deck. "Fall in," he shouted. "Two ranks. Stand at attention."

The crewmen hustled into makeshift ranks as a beetle-backed black sedan made its way down the long quay toward the tender and then disappeared behind her great, gray bulk. They heard the four bells ringing out on the tender as the new skipper boarded the *Otus*, came down the accommodation ladder on the tender's outboard side, and then crossed over the quarterdecks of the two inboard submarines to get to *Firefish*. By the time he arrived at the brow, *Firefish*'s crew, dressed in a variety of working uniforms, was at attention in two ranks up and down the length of the sub's sloping topside deck. Every one of them was straining his eyes to get a look at the new skipper.

They saw a man of average height but with the build of a fullback.

He was wearing wash khakis and the brass hat of a commander, USN. It was his face that caught everyone's eyes. Commander Russell had been a smiling, pleasant officer with the quiet dignity of a Southern plantation owner, which in fact he was. Commander Stormes's visage matched his last name. Black hair, dark brown eyes under bushy eyebrows, and a face that was all planes and flint-like ridges. His eyes framed a beak of a nose over lips flattened in a steely, almost disapproving line. Look at this guy, Marty thought. Maybe I should have put everyone in dress whites.

Stormes stepped across the rattling brow, saluted the national ensign on the sub's stern, and then the apprehensive lieutenant who was standing the officer of the deck in-port watch. He stepped down onto *Firefish*'s steel deck and handed a thick brown envelope to the OOD. He then turned to Marty and the COB.

"Lieutenant Commander Brandquist," Marty announced. "XO and acting CO. Welcome aboard, sir." He didn't offer to shake hands, and neither did the new CO. Good thing, he thought, as he saw the new captain's hands. They were huge and scarred. "This is Chief Cory O'Bannon, chief of the boat. Welcome aboard, sir."

"Log my arrival onboard, XO, and note that I have assumed command. There will be no ceremony." He had a deep voice with the faintest hint of a Southern accent. "Is the boat ready for sea?"

"We're topped off on fuel and water," Marty said. "We have eighteen torpedoes, all Mark fourteen, which is our current quota, and a full allowance of five-inch for the deck gun. Fresh provisions are being delivered at thirteen hundred. We have one generator down for a bad exciter, but the part arrived yesterday. ETR is this afternoon. Otherwise, yes, sir, she's RFS."

"Very well," Stormes said. "We don't have sailing orders yet, but I anticipate going out soon. Send someone for my sea bag; it's on the tender. Tell the crew to resume their duties, and then I want you to give me a tour. I got a quick look at this class boat in Pearl, but now I want to get a really good look. No secrets, please. If some piece of gear is a perpetual problem child, I need to know about it. Understood?"

"Yes, sir," they said in unison.

"Very well," Stormes said. He made an opened-hand gesture that said "after you, gentlemen."

"When would you like to meet with the wardroom, Captain?" Marty asked as they headed for the forward hatch.

"Once we're at sea, XO."

THREE

They showed the new captain to his "stateroom," which was a tiny cabin just forward of the control room measuring eight feet by about five. It had a single bunk, a fold-down desk with a chair, and a foldout sink and medicine cabinet. There was a safe built into the desk; its combination and the instructions on how to change it were written on a shipping tag that had been taped to the locked-open door. Inside was a loaded .45 caliber semiautomatic pistol and a set of keys. There was a depth gauge, a lighted gyro compass repeater, and a speed indicator mounted on the bulkhead at the foot of the bunk. The "door" to the cabin consisted of a heavy curtain. A reading light equipped with an optional red lens was mounted on the bulkhead at the head of the bunk, along with a sound-powered telephone handset.

Malachi dropped his briefcase on the bunk and told them they'd start in after torpedo. They threaded their way aft along the main and only passageway, pressing past the sailors they encountered. The passageway was so narrow that it provided for one-way traffic only, so when two men met, the junior one flattened himself against the nearest bulkhead to let the senior one get by. The XO facilitated this little parade by saying "gangway" each time they entered the next compartment. By the time they reached the after torpedo room, the entire crew already knew that the new skipper was making his first inspection.

The Tambor class was the newest iteration of the Navy's efforts to create a so-called fleet boat—a submarine with long range, large fuel capacity, and a more lethal weapons suite than the prewar boats. They had six torpedo tubes forward and four aft, plus a large, 5-inch-bore deck gun on the weather deck. *Firefish* was 310 feet long and displaced 2,500 tons submerged, making her almost a third larger than the previous S-class boats. Her conning tower, called the sail or, sometimes, the shears, had been enlarged to accommodate all the principal fire-control equipment in one space so that Malachi did not have to communicate with control stations down below in the process of an attack, as he had in the S-class. The periscope array, the sonar console, the main dead-reckoning plotting table, and the torpedo data computer, called the TDC, were now all in one place, directly under the captain's eyes. The boat was fully air-conditioned to deal with the hot and humid water conditions of the South Pacific, which meant that the crew could operate submerged and still wear their uniforms. On the surface she could do almost 22 knots; submerged, just under 10, but that for no more than thirty minutes.

Like all submarines, *Firefish* was double-hulled. The outer hull was shaped principally for hydrodynamic streamlining and contained the ballast tanks by which she submerged and resurfaced, the propeller shafts and rudders, and the diving planes, fore and aft. The inner hull, called the pressure-hull, contained the equipment and the people who made her go. From the keel up there were three levels. The bottom level contained tanks for fuel, compressed air, and water plus the two massive battery compartments, one forward, one aft. The main level contained everything else—the torpedo rooms, living quarters, a galley, crew's mess, officers' wardroom, the control room, the radio room, the engine rooms, and the motor room. The third and final level was called the sail, a steel projection rising above the main external deck amidships. The sail contained the conning tower, which was the main command and control space, and above that, a navigation bridge for surface operations. The conning tower room was within the pressure hull; the navigation bridge was not.

The submarine was driven by four direct-current electric motors tied to two propeller shafts. These could be powered either by the batteries or four generators coupled to four large diesel engines, hence the term "diesel-electric propulsion." On the surface, they ran on the diesels, which needed copious amounts of fresh air to operate. Submerged, she ran on the batteries, whose capacity was measured in minutes-until-exhaustion. As large as they were, they had a finite capacity to run everything in the boat, including the main motors. When they were near to total depletion, the boat *had* to surface, light off the diesel engines, and recharge the batteries for several hours before she could safely submerge again.

Malachi stood in the after torpedo room, flanked by the exec, the COB, and the boat's third officer, Lieutenant Peter Caldwell, who doubled as the boat's operations officer. Four torpedoes were lashed onto loading rails in front of four stainless-steel hemispheres that were the back ends of the after torpedo tubes. He silently inspected every square inch of the cramped space while four torpedomen stood by, not quite at attention but visibly apprehensive. The interior surfaces of the compartment were tangled with cables, piping, junction boxes, ventilation ducts, torpedo handling gear, and instrument panels. Two men could not stand side by side with their arms outstretched without having to bend their elbows. Malachi stood stock still, moving only his eyes as he took in every piece of equipment in the space.

"Very clean," he said, finally. "That's good."

"I'm a perfect bastard when it comes to a clean boat," Marty said, in a matter-of-fact tone of voice.

"I'm a perfect bastard squared on that particular subject, myself," Malachi said. "Oil is unavoidable; dirt is unacceptable."

They retraced their steps, lifting their legs over the shiny, rounded hatch coamings that separated each compartment. At general quarters, every named space was secured by thick, vertical watertight hatches. For maximum strength against an invading sea, the hatches required a man of average height to fold himself almost to two-thirds his height to get through. They'd made it to the after diesel-generator engine room when a messenger caught up with the inspecting party.

"Officer of the deck sends his respects," the sailor reported, with an awkward salute, awkward because there wasn't room in the engineering space for a proper salute. "Admiral wants to see you, Cap'n. Over on the tender."

Malachi turned to the exec. "Other than fresh provisions—we're RFS?"

"Yes, sir. That and the generator."

"Fuel, fresh water, torpedoes, gun ammunition, full batteries, full complement?"

"Yes, sir," Marty said. "Like I said, sir, RFS."

Stormes gave him a piercing stare. "Yes," he said, finally. "So you did. My apologies."

The tender was the 6,000-ton USS *Otus*, a former civilian freighter that had been acquired by the US Navy just before war broke out and converted into a Navy engineering repair and support ship. She wasn't technically a purpose-built submarine tender, but rather an internal combustion engine repair ship. She'd been stationed at the Cavite base in the Philippines, but had had to run from the advancing Japanese juggernaut along with her brood of submarines. The Japanese had caught MacArthur's entire Army Air Force on the ground right after Pearl Harbor, dooming his Army and forcing him and his staff to evacuate ignominiously all the way to Australia.

Malachi cooled his heels in a steel straight-backed chair outside the admiral's office. He rubbed his forehead, where the weight of the gold braid on the bill of his cap had made a dent. He'd been promoted to full commander after the big deal made by the Royal Navy over his killing of three U-boats. Most of his classmates were still lieutenant commanders, although the war and the Japanese killing machine had put some life into the Navy's historically glacial promotion system.

The boat looked good, really good, he thought. She should—she was just a year old—but still. The exec had to be pretty good and he'd liked the way Marty had stood up to him when he'd questioned the boat's readiness for sea. Now he was going to formally meet his boss, Rear Admiral Britten, the officer who'd removed Malachi's predecessor for lack of results at sea. Britten was fifty-nine years old and looked it. He was the personification of Old Navy: rigid, authoritarian, a teetotaler, and a workaholic who never seemed to stand down. His main office was in downtown Perth at an insurance company's corporate headquarters, which the Australian government had graciously turned over to him after getting a look at *Otus*'s small cabins. As a commander of fleet units, however, he'd appropriated the *Otus*'s captain's cabin as his flag quarters and broken his two-star flag on her foremast. He was an admiral. Admirals rated a flagship.

The past few months had been something of a blur. The surreal awards ceremony at Whitehall palace in London. The orders to Pearl, literally halfway around the world. It had taken him two months just to get to Hawaii. Then the frantic time at the sub base in Pearl, where he was introduced to the Tambor class boats, attended endless briefings, met Admiral Robert H. English, the commander of all submarine forces in the Pacific, made a formal five-minute call on Admiral Nimitz, fresh from his victory at Midway, and then spent time with the clutch of sub skippers who happened to be in port.

These had been no casual, relaxed drinking sessions, or sea-story telling nights at the Officers' Club bar. The sub skippers were all billeted in downtown Honolulu at the Royal Hawaiian Hotel on Waikiki beach. Pearl Harbor still reeked of fuel oil, seared steel, and corpses, whose bloated remains kept popping up from the muck of the harbor bottom. The sight of capsized battleships, a virtual galaxy of nighttime welding arcs at the shipyard, and the spectral upper works of the cremated *Arizona* sucked the life right out of what had once been a pleasant duty station. The O-Club itself was closed for renovation after having hosted several hundred badly burned sailors in the days right after the sneak attack. The shock was still palpable, hanging over the whole island of Oahu like the smell from the harbor.

"The admiral will see you now," an impossibly young yeoman announced.

Malachi went through to the admiral's inner office. Britten was sitting at his desk with his service dress blues uniform coat still on, as if ready to have his portrait taken. Malachi approached the desk. He did not salute—only the Army saluted indoors.

"Commander Stormes, reporting as ordered," he announced, standing almost at attention.

"Have a seat, Captain," Britten said. The admiral's tone was faintly imperious and not the least bit friendly. There was a single chair positioned in front of the admiral's desk. Malachi felt like a student summoned to the principal's office as he sat down. The flag cabin was warm; an overhead fan was trying hard but not succeeding. *Otus* was *not* air-conditioned.

He must be sweating in that coat, Malachi thought. He himself was wearing service dress khakis, a much cooler uniform. They were badly wrinkled from his seeming endless trip across the world, though.

The admiral was looking at Malachi's uniform. "Where's the DSO?" he asked.

"I didn't know where to put it," Malachi said. "I have the medal, but there's no ribbon."

"I'm told you flirted with the seaward edge of a German mine-field to get those U-boats. Is that true?"

"The field was buoyed, Admiral," Malachi replied. "Or at least the entrance to the swept channel was. We didn't just blunder in."

"That's good, Captain," the admiral said. "The Japanese do *not* buoy their minefields. If we think there's a minefield somewhere, we stay far away, understand?"

"Seems like a good plan, Admiral," Malachi said, as neutrally as he could. He hadn't liked that word "flirted."

"You are class of 'thirty, correct?"

"Yes, sir."

"Young for command of a fleet boat," the admiral observed. "Most of your skipper contemporaries out here are class of 'twenty-five through 'twenty-eight. Class of 'thirty are still execs."

"I was early-promoted because of the U-boat sinkings," Malachi said. "I had a year in command on an S-boat before coming back to the States. I don't feel particularly young."

"Indeed," the admiral said.

Malachi said nothing. The admiral's meaning was clear: you show-boated over there in the Atlantic, made a name for yourself, and now you're in command before it's appropriate for your age or experience. Damned upstart that you are.

"Were you submerged during that attack?" the admiral asked.

"Decks awash," Malachi replied. "The water is cold there, and our periscope was often fuzzy due to condensation. If you got it higher in the air the humidity would burn off and then you could see. I needed to see."

The admiral frowned. "That's not how we do it out here, Captain. Our doctrine states that all attacks are to be made submerged. Our priority is large warships, especially carriers. We do not engage escorts, either."

"Is this doctrine written down, Admiral?"

"We're working on that, but I believe I've made myself clear—preservation of the force, such as it is, is paramount. Same with torpedoes. There's a critical shortage after the attack on Cavite, and it's going to take some time to get production numbers up."

"I understand," Malachi said. "Do I have sailing orders?"

"Yes," the admiral said. "I want you to take *Firefish* out as soon as possible. I'd like to give you three days to get used to her and your crew used to you, but now that we're about to invade some island in the Solomons, they're screaming for submarine support. Assuming you're RFS, leave for the Solomons tonight. Captain Collins is my chief of staff. He'll give you a prepatrol brief before you depart this afternoon."

Malachi nodded. He'd hoped for a short break-in cruise before going on a full-up war patrol, but a real war patrol would do just as well.

"Any questions for me, Captain?"

"Yes, sir. The torpedoes. We had only Mark tens in the Atlantic. They worked fine, but I heard a lot of complaints about the Mark fourteens when I was in Pearl. Can someone on your staff fill me in?"

The admiral's face darkened. "There's nothing wrong with the Mark fourteen fish, Captain, and don't let mess-deck scuttlebutt tell you anything different. The so-called torpedo problem has more to do with incompetent or timid attack geometry and lackadaisical maintenance than the torpedo itself. I assume you've been briefed about the new exploder?"

"Yes, sir, in detail," Malachi replied. The admiral was talking about the super-secret magnetic exploder. He didn't think it prudent just now to bring up all the negative comments he had listened to from other skippers he'd met in Pearl. There was universal distrust among the officers who'd actually tried to sink ships with the magnetic exploder. Malachi also knew something the admiral might not know: the Brits had discarded their version of a magnetic exploder a year ago because it simply didn't work. But since Admiral Britten had been one of the proponents of the magnetic system at the Bureau of Ordnance, this was probably not the time.

"Well, the policy here is that we primarily use the magnetic exploder, sending the torpedoes *under* the enemy ship so that the warhead breaks the ship's back."

Malachi fully understood the principle of the magnetic exploder, having done a lengthy tour of duty at the Naval Torpedo Station in Newport. The flaw in the argument was that if the magnetic exploder didn't work, the contact exploder couldn't be counted on as a backup because the fish was running *under* the target. Besides that, if the torpedo itself was running deeper than set, as most of the Pearl Harbor skippers thought it was, the magnetic exploder couldn't work because the target's magnetic influence was too weak.

"Beyond that," the admiral continued, "we make all attacks submerged. We have too few submarines to cover this huge operating area, so preservation of the boat is as important as sinking Jap ships. Got it?"

"Yes, sir," Malachi replied.

"Okay. Now, if you've no more questions, I'll call in Captain Collins and he'll give you your sailing brief."

Malachi stood up and left the office. Welcome aboard, shipmate, he thought. But not very.

FOUR

By 2100 that evening, *Firefish* was cruising on the surface at 15 knots, on the way to a patrol area off the island of New Britain, some 2,500 miles to the northeast of Australia's west coast. They'd sailed at 1600, secured from the sea detail, and then made several dives, stabilized at ordered depth, surfaced, and then another dive as the new captain got a feel for his boat. He'd found some holes in the crew's training, such as when he ordered the diving officer to hold her at decks awash, a maneuver designed to leave as low a silhouette as possible while remaining on the surface and able to use the diesels. The diving officer lost depth control and the boat submerged suddenly, causing the main air induction valve to slam shut, just about breaking everyone's eardrums. The main induction piping provided air to the diesels. In an orderly submergence, the diesels were first shut down, then the valve closed, and only then would the ballast tanks be flooded to submerge the boat. If the diving officer "lost the bubble," as it was called, and opened the ballast tanks before shutting down the four engines, the main induction valve would close automatically, and then the engines would try to suck all the air out of the boat.

Malachi didn't say a word through all of the ensuing drama. He stood in the control room like a specter at a feast and watched his people recover from their mistakes. He knew part of it was a case of nerves with a new CO onboard, but he was more interested in seeing how well they pulled together to overcome a problem. He kept his face a blank mask, aware that the entire control room team was watching him as hard as he was watching them. When he sensed they'd had enough, he told the exec to secure from drills and to feed the boat. He took his meal in his cabin, and then had the exec gather the officers, less the diving officer and the OOD up on the navigation bridge, for a meeting in the wardroom.

Firefish had eight commissioned officers aboard. Malachi, the executive officer, and the third officer formed the executive triumvirate. Below them was a chief engineer, a torpedo officer, and three lieutenants (junior grade) who held various duties such as communications, supply, gunnery, first lieutenant, and main propulsion assistant (MPA) while they worked on qualifying for the coveted golden dolphins pin. They gathered in the tiny wardroom space, which allowed Malachi and four other officers to sit, while the rest stood against the bulkhead.

"My name is Malachi Stormes," Malachi began. "I'm originally from eastern Kentucky. I'm Annapolis class of nineteen thirty, courtesy of NAPS and a year and a half of being a torpedoman aboard a battleship. I've been in submarines for ten years. When I was ashore I was assigned to the Newport torpedo station as a consulting engineer. My last sea duty station was as CO of S-fifty-seven, which was based in Holy Loch, Scotland. I had the good fortune to trap three U-boats in the swept-channel of a minefield and kill them all. The Royal Navy made a big deal out of that, which is, I think, how I got command of *Firefish* at such a young age.

"This boat is much more capable than my S-boat. I regret that your previous skipper was relieved for lack of results. I've never met him, but I've been told he was a prince of a guy." He paused for a moment. "For what it's worth, I will aggressively seek results. Understand that I am *not* a prince of a guy. I'm all about business, all the time, which I define as killing Japs and their ships wherever I find them. I'm not especially friendly. Don't take that to mean that I don't like you or that I'm dissatisfied with your performance. You will know when that's the case, although if you're trying your damnedest and things still go wrong, you won't hear me bitching. My personality was shaped by becoming a part-time night-shift hard-rock miner at the age of thirteen down in a coal mine in Floyd County, Kentucky.

When I finished high school I went full-time. The work was dangerous and the people around me were tougher than plow steel. If the
mine didn't kill you, one of them just might. After awhile, deep coal
takes the friendly right out of you. So don't take it personally.

"Now, regarding the torpedoes. I've heard all the stories, and I understand probably better than you do the politics involved, by which I
mean the notion in Washington that what they call the 'so-called' torpedo problems are the result of incompetent fire-control teams, over-
cautious skippers, and improper torpedo preparation and maintenance,
and that there's nothing wrong with the fish themselves.

He looked around the table. "Some of that has to be true. You
know it, and I know it, but I'll tell you a dirty little secret. The Mark
fourteen was tested with its magnetic exploder against a real ship target and with a real warhead only twice. The target was an antique
sub, and she was anchored. The first torpedo did not work. Second
one did. Success was declared with a failure rate of fifty percent.
Think about that. Additionally, the depth-control running mechanism on the Mark fourteen is shaky at best and just plain defective at
worst. I know these things because I spent a lot of time at Newport,
and every time I raised these issues I was shut down by the Gun Club
in Washington.

"So, I mean to make some engineering changes to our torpedo
load. We are going to disable the magnetic exploder and we're going
to fire all fish in contact-exploder mode for a while. We are going to
fire every torpedo at the shallowest setting possible, every time, every
target. I allow that we'll see some porpoising, and that the Japs will
see our fish coming. But if we get in close and shoot like we mean it,
that won't make any difference.

"Finally, I'm told that SubPac doctrine is to attack submerged if
at all possible. That makes sense during broad daylight. But here's the
thing: when I grew up in Kentucky, the hunting laws said you had to
hunt deer in the daytime only. But if you needed meat on the table,
you went out at night when the deer were up and about. In the Lant-
Fleet, the Germans control the air near and in Europe, so during the
day you went down and stayed down. At night you came back up,
stuffed some amps in the can, and waited for a target to drive by.

Because most boats just waited, there weren't many enemy ships sunk. I decided that as long as we had to be on the surface anyway, we should go hunting rather than sit around waiting. I plan to do that out here. Hunt on the surface at night, maybe even attack on the surface at night. Instead of settling for the best attack geometry the gods hand us, I intend to use our twenty-two-knot speed to set up the geometry I need to get hits."

He leaned back in his chair and plucked a cigarette out of his shirt pocket. He waved it at them as a signal that they could smoke if they wanted to. No one did, apparently.

"I believe in training, which means I believe in drills. We will drill all the way to the northern Solomons, with a focus on doing things at night. High-speed runs, followed by careful submergence and then setup for a torpedo attack. High-speed runs, followed by a decks awash partial submergence and then setup for attack. High-speed runs followed by a crash dive at flank speed. In that regard, how deep has this boat been?"

"Three hundred feet is test depth," Marty Brandquist said, promptly. "We've done that once on sea trials, and again off Pearl on the way out after some valve repairs."

Malachi nodded, taking a deep drag on his cigarette. "We will submerge to three hundred feet tonight, and we will stay down there until we find every leak or potential leak in the boat. Then we'll see what she's really capable of."

Marty raised his hand as the other officers tried not to look at each other. "Sir, PacFleet regs say test depth is an annual test."

"Those are peacetime regs," Malachi said. "*Daggerfish* went to five hundred feet off Bungo Suido last month, not by choice but that's how she made it back alive to Pearl. They didn't stay dry, but all the Jap depth charges were going off at one hundred fifty to two hundred feet. She's a year older than we are. Second question: has the boat been depth-charged?"

There were heads shaking around the table.

Malachi smiled. "Me, neither, but I 'spect we're gonna be. Okay. That is all. XO, I need a detailed familiarization tour of the conning tower. Now would be a good time."

The following morning the boat submerged at dawn nautical twilight. Malachi ordered a depth of 250 feet and then stationed himself in the control room. He'd instructed the exec to put a chief petty officer in each of the major watertight compartments. Then he ordered the boat to general quarters, which included all hands manning their regular battle stations except for the chiefs.

Marty reported that the boat was at GQ and that everything was buttoned up.

"Very well," Malachi said. "Diving officer: make your depth three hundred feet."

The diving officer ordered the two men operating the diving planes to begin the descent to 300 feet. The back edges of the bow planes tilted up and the stern planes tilted down, forcing the boat, moving at a sedate 3 knots on the battery, to dip deeper into the ocean. The diving officer gave quiet orders to move water in the various ballast tanks from bow to stern to keep the dive under control.

"Passing two sixty," the diving officer announced. Throughout the sub a small chorus of noises started up as the pressure from the sea began to squeeze her steel hull. Malachi ignored them. His S-class boat had been riveted together. This one was welded together. Metallic crackling and groaning gave evidence of the pressure hull's deformation but also its flexibility. The circular hull was designed to do this, to "give" under pressure. Rigidity would mean a crack, and a crack could mean an unrecoverable flood.

"Passing two eighty."

Malachi nodded. "Very well. Settle out at two ninety, ballast drift to three hundred."

The diving officer acknowledged. Aim for 290, make fine adjustments to level off at 300 feet.

The temperature in the boat began to climb as the entire pressure hull literally began to change shape, deforming in response to the 18,720 pounds per square foot of seawater pressure at this depth.

"Stable at three hundred feet," the diving officer announced, finally. His voice betrayed the strain he was under. A mistake here could cause the boat to go out of control and either broach, or worse, much worse, go deep.

"Very well," Malachi said. He then walked over to the coffeepot at the forward end of the control room and casually made himself a cup. The control room was crowded with people, every one of them watching the depth gauge. Two hundred fifty feet was deep and also the informal operating limit, the depth where there was or should be no danger of a hull collapse due to depth. Three hundred was entering into uncharted territory. His S-boat had been limited to 200 feet.

"Come left to course three zero zero with ten degrees rudder," Malachi ordered. The conning officer relayed the order to the helmsman, who was sitting next to the planesmen. The boat could also be steered from the conning tower.

This was a thirty-degree course change. Flying submerged straight and level at three knots gave the diving officer a steady reference by which to control the boat's depth. Changing course added some new vectors to the situation.

"Coming to course three zero zero," the helmsman announced. Malachi watched the depth gauge to see if the diving officer could maintain depth control as the boat changed course. The needle dropped, registering 310 feet.

"Diving officer, maintain your depth at three hundred feet, if you please," Malachi said softly.

The diving officer said nothing, then gave some orders to the ballast tank controller, who moved water via the sub's elaborate pumping system to bring the bow up enough to return to three hundred feet. The diving officer's forehead was covered in perspiration, but, as Malachi observed, his concentration was complete.

"Continue left to course two seven zero," Malachi ordered. He was standing in a corner of the control room, which gave him a fine view of everyone involved in the maneuvers—the ballast tank operator, the planesmen who controlled the diving planes, those big steel fins deployed on either side of the bow and stern when the boat submerged, and the diving officer, who had to keep a mental picture of the forces acting on the boat at depth and then make fine adjustments to keep her stable, all the while pretending not to hear the creaking and cracking of the hull under the relentless assault of 300 feet of depth.

"Steady on course two seven zero," the helmsman called, his voice cracking just a little, along with the hull.

"Very well," Malachi said. He waited for a full minute. "Make your depth three fifty."

The silence in the control room became, if anything, more intense. The air vents and small electric servo motor noise were more noticeable. Malachi closely watched the exec, who swallowed visibly, his Adam's apple bobbing up and down a couple of times.

"Make my depth three hundred fifty, aye, sir," the diving officer said. For this exercise, the exec had chosen Lieutenant Caldwell to be the diving officer.

The planesmen once again in concert manipulated the large brass wheels that sent servo signals to the fore and aft diving planes at either end of the ship. There was, however, no wild spinning of the wheels. Tiny increments, now, with the bow planesman watching the hands of the stern planesman to make sure they moved in synch. The diving officer ordered two hundred pounds of ballast water moved from one tank to another, and then reversed his order as the sub started to descend too fast.

"Passing three twenty," the diving officer announced.

"Very well."

"Passing three thirty."

"Passing three forty."

At this point the diving officer gave orders to flatten the dive by moving ballast water from fore to after tanks. The whine of the ballast pumps seemed unusually loud in the tense control room.

"Steady at three hundred fifty," the diving officer said, although his voice gave Malachi some doubts about whether the diving officer was all that steady just now. The hull noises were no louder than before, but there seemed to be a lot more metal protesting.

"Very well," Malachi said. He told the executive officer to query the chiefs stationed throughout the boat if there were any leaks. Then he waited for a full two minutes before ordering a course change. As the sub banked slightly to make the turn, the hull made more urgent noises, small clanks, ticks, and even animal-like sounds as the welded joints in the sub's plated hull protested the increasingly aggressive

pressure from without. Malachi glanced over at the water temperature gauge and was interested to see that the temperature had changed
ten degrees colder from 300 feet. A deep layer, he thought. Need to
remember that.

The course change was uneventful this time, as the diving officer
did a better job of ballast control. The two planesmen had finally realized that if they adjusted their planes more carefully, the boat
wouldn't depart from ordered depth when changing course.

"We're flying, gentlemen," Malachi observed. "If we're going to
maintain depth control, we need to bank a little, just like an airplane.
Air is a fluid, too. Mister Caldwell, are we stable at three fifty?"

"Yes, sir," Caldwell replied. Malachi could almost hear the unspo-
ken "are we there yet, Dad" in Caldwell's voice.

"Keep her so," Malachi said. "XO—leak reports?"

"None so far, Captain," the exec said. He was wearing a set of
sound-powered telephones and talking to the chiefs stationed
throughout the boat.

"Very well. Diving officer, make your depth *four* hundred feet."

This time there were some audible intakes of breath in the control
room. They were already 50 feet past the boat's official test depth.
The temperature in the control room rose even more. As the hull
deformed, it compressed the air in the boat. They were definitely in
the dangerous part of the boat's performance envelope. They were
headed 100 feet below test depth, the depth at which the builder guar-
anteed the hull would hold together. Past that, they were descending
into an environment where the words should and would applied, and,
as everyone knew, the builder was not along for the ride just now.

Malachi knew that the term on everyone's mind right now was
crush depth. That number was an estimate, but every submariner
knew exactly what it meant: the depth at which the hull simply could
not withstand the pressure, measured in hundreds of pounds per
square inch, and collapsed, changing shape in a single white hot instant from a circular hull into a flat steel billet and then dropping like
a dull blade into the abyss, with every living thing onboard long since
vaporized.

As the diving officer began the descent, the XO suddenly grabbed his earphones. "Sterntube seal on the port shaft is blowing green," he announced.

"Mark your depth," Malachi said calmly.

"Three sixty," the diving officer said. His voice was up an octave.

"Hold at three sixty," Malachi ordered. "XO, what are they doing about it?"

"Lining up drain pumps to the port shaft alley. Jimmy says they can hold the flooding, but just barely."

"Jimmy being?" Malachi asked, as if they were talking about the laundry schedule.

"The chief engineer, Captain," Marty said, swallowing again, his eyes wide.

There was a loud, metallic snapping noise from somewhere outside the control room. Everyone except Malachi jumped, but nothing else happened.

"Let me know when they have it under control," Malachi said. "In the meantime, Mister Caldwell, maintain ordered depth and get ready for a course change."

"*Now*, sir?" the diving officer said, his fear overcoming his training to respect and obey any order given by Malachi.

"Especially now, Mister Caldwell," Malachi said. "This is where we're going to hide when the going gets tough, and it will get tough. Look around: we're all warm and dry. Think four Jap destroyers topside looking for us, and not finding us because we're underneath a thermocline layer. They'll be dropping depth charges here and there to show their boss they're sincere, but setting them for two hundred fifty feet, three hundred at most. Noisy, but not effective. Maintain ordered depth. Conning officer, come to course two two zero with standard rudder."

The conning officer had trouble finding his voice, but then relayed the order to the helmsman, who, apparently made of sterner stuff, acknowledged the order and put the rudder over fifteen degrees. The last course changes had been made slowly, carefully, as if the helmsman knew how delicate the sub's attitude was at these depths. There was a depth gauge in the conning tower, too, so the four men up there were all too aware of where the boat was operating. Almost immediately, the bow began to settle as the sub banked slightly into the turn. The diving officer was not reacting.

"Trim, Mister Caldwell," Malachi said sharply. "Right now. Your pumps can only move water fore and aft at this depth. You can't quickly dump any weight."

The diving officer froze up, and then did as he had been trained. "I've lost the bubble, Captain," he announced. For all his training and qualification, he didn't know what to do, and the fact that the depth gauge needle was just about to pass 400 feet wasn't helping. As if to scare him even more, the port shaft began to make a screeching noise as its seals came under even more pressure.

Malachi stepped in at once. "Blow negative for thirty seconds," he ordered. "Forward planes, up ten degrees. After planes, neutral."

The planesmen acknowledged in unison. The negative tank was a large ballast water tank just forward of the control room. If you were on the surface and had to get down fast, you flooded the negative tank and the sudden addition of tons of seawater weight would drag the bow under in a big hurry.

Nothing happened for another thirty seconds. At just past 400 feet, the compressed air that was attempting to push ballast water out of the negative tank was contending with 175 pounds per square inch depth pressure. As it expanded from the ballast air storage tanks, it cooled, threatening to ice up the external ballast nozzles unless they got upstairs quickly.

"*Full* power," Malachi ordered. The big DC motors aft responded at once, making the entire sub tremble and doubling the volume of that squealing port shaft. The squealing was annoying, Malachi thought, but it had the benefit of obscuring the creaking and cracking noises coming from the hull at 400 feet. He smiled to himself. Some of the crewmen saw that smile, giving birth to a rumor that the only time you'd see Malachi Stormes smiling was while approaching crush depth.

The boat responded to full power even as the batteries dumped amps like a waterfall. Fortunately there were no Japanese destroyers waiting topside, so they should be able to recharge. Should. Would.

"Diving officer, you got it?" Malachi asked, calmly. The boat was driving upwards at a ten-degree up-bubble, passing through 300 feet and gathering speed as she shed fathoms. Caldwell obviously wanted to say yes, but it was equally clear to everyone watching that he absolutely did *not* have it. The shaft wasn't squealing so much now, and everyone could almost feel the hull relaxing.

"Make your depth one hundred feet," Malachi ordered. "Maintain three knots. Secure the blow. XO?"

"I have it," the exec announced, and then began giving orders to slow the rate of ascent and trim the boat back to something more like a normal angle of attack as they headed up. Malachi went to the coffeepot and fixed some of the sugar-laced asphalt that passed for coffee in the submarine world. Then he started forward, toward his tiny cabin.

"Take her up to periscope depth and take a good long look, XO. Then we'll surface, trim down to decks awash, head northeast along the track at speed five. I want no wake. Secure from GQ and post four lookouts. Charge the battery for two hours, three if it's still all clear, and then we'll begin diving drills."

"Once we're up, do you want the radar continuous, Captain?"

Malachi had forgotten about the radar. *Firefish* had the new SJ radar set, which included a planned position indicator scope up in the conning tower. She also carried an air search radar, something he'd never seen before in a boat. This was a tactical luxury. "Occasional sweep," he replied. "Remember, Intel warns that the Japs can theoretically detect that thing twice as far away as we can detect a target. Don't turn it into a homing beacon."

"Aye, sir, I understand. Will you come topside?"

"No, XO," Malachi said, deliberately yawning, as if their excursion to the lightless realm of 400 feet had been a bit boring. "I'm going to take a nap. Call me when they get that seal repaired."

FIVE

Firefish arrived at the northern end of the Solomon Islands chain ten days after departing Perth, obtained a good radar fix on the channel between Buka Island and Bougainville Island, and then submerged to wait out the day, mindful of the large Japanese naval anchorage at Rabaul nearby. Marty Brandquist was already exhausted. The new skipper had drilled the crew and the boat like she had never drilled before. Standard dives, crash dives, deep dives, normal surface, emergency surface, partially submerged but still on the surface, gunnery drills, tracking drills, torpedo load and reload drills, engineering casualty drills, torpedo evasion, periscope celestial navigation, and a host of smaller evolutions. The drills had gone day and night, with the crew getting meals when they could or when there was enough surface air coming in to allow cooking. One night they sent divers over the side to repack that noisy stern seal, and then went down that night to 350 feet to see if the repair worked, as if going past test depth was nothing more than a routine maintenance procedure. Marty and the COB were having a coffee back in the after torpedo room.

"Does this guy ever sleep?" Marty asked rhetorically. The compartment was dimmed to allow the off-watch torpedomen to sleep underneath their two-ton torpedoes, with just a canvas curtain to give them some privacy.

"Had one like this back in the S-twelve boat," the COB said quietly. The two torpedomen playing cards up by the actual tubes were pretending not to eavesdrop. "Needed sleep but just couldn't manage it when we were out operating. Went Section Eight; XO had to take command and get him back to the base."

"I'm beginning to believe this one doesn't need any in the first place. Takes naps. Dozes in the conning tower when he can, but then he'll wake up and order the scope up, as if something had woke him up. *My* ass is dragging."

The COB grinned. As the chief of the boat, he was informally responsible for overseeing all the enlisted men aboard. Marty was the executive officer—second in command—formally responsible for the entire boat and its crew and senior to everybody except that all important officer, the Captain. The COB thought he had the better deal. "Be interesting to see what he does when a Jap comes along," he observed. "Much as I liked the guy, Old Man Montgomery would probably go hide."

"Those days are well and truly over, COB," Marty said. "We'll probably go and ram the bastard."

They both chuckled, and then the GQ alarm sounded. Marty made tracks for the conning tower, while the COB headed for the control room. By the time Marty got on station in the conning tower, the boat had been buttoned up and all stations were manned and ready. He had to admit, that happened in half the time it used to. Malachi was already manning the periscope, hunched over to keep the mast just above the water topside, and calling for Doppler readings on the sonar. Besides Malachi, there was the GQ officer of the deck, the fire-control officer, who ran the torpedo data converter, or TDC, a sonarman, a radar man, a helmsman, the torpedo-firing-panel operator, two plotters for the dead-reckoning tracer table, and the exec. Marty did not have any specific duties, other than to take care of anything that needed attention, either there or one deck down in the control room.

"What've we got?" he asked of no one in particular.

"A *maru*, a freighter, bearing one eight zero," Malachi replied, still staring through the periscope optics. "Maybe six, seven thousand tons, one escort, probably a DE. They're zigzagging, too. Base course seems to be northeast and coming our way, though, maybe eight thousand yards out now. Down scope. Make your depth two fifty. Come to course zero four zero."

"Make my depth two hundred fifty feet, aye, sir," the OOD replied. "Course zero four zero."

The term *maru* meant that the target was not a warship but rather a cargo ship or an oil tanker, all of whose names ended in the term *maru*. Malachi looked around the scope housing at Marty. "I plan to go down and let them run over on top of us. As soon as there's a Doppler shift I'll come back to scope depth and shoot both of them." He glanced over at the plotting table. "I need your best estimate of their base course, please."

The plotters huddling over the DRT table nodded but stayed focused on their developing track. The sonarman was feeding them continuous bearings to the target's propeller noises. The moment the two Japanese ships passed over them, the bearing would shift one hundred eighty degrees, which would be the signal to come back up and set up for the shot. Marty watched as the pencil marks went down onto the white tracing paper, a series of straight lines running almost parallel to one another, since all they had were bearings.

"Conn: I recommend coming left to course three three zero to resolve bearing ambiguity," Marty said.

Malachi thought for a few seconds. "I'll lose too much ground at three three zero," he said. "Make it due north."

The helmsman, who'd been listening, immediately announced that he was coming to course zero zero zero.

Then they waited. After a while they began to hear screwbeats, light ones from the escorting destroyer and heavier, slower beats from the much larger cargo ship. Mixed in with the propeller sounds was the occasional ping from the destroyer's sonar. Marty knew they were taking a chance with this approach: if the destroyer happened to pick them up, he wouldn't have to maneuver. He'd only have to roll depth charges to remove the submarine threat. "Do we have a layer?" he asked Sonar.

"Yes, sir, XO," the sonarman said. "Good layer at two twenty. Seven-degree differential."

Great, Marty thought. Sometimes the ocean would settle itself into layers of water that had different salinity and temperatures. The sound waves pinging out of a sonar transmitter would be refracted by the boundary between the two layers, thus masking the presence of the submarine. Marty glanced over at Malachi, who gave him a "I'm way ahead of you, Bub" look.

They waited some more as they listened for the Doppler shift. Like the rising pitch of a train's whistle approaching and then declining as it went away, the pitch of the screwbeats rose and then fell as the ships approached and then passed overhead.

"*Down*-Doppler," the sonarman reported. "Bearing now zero five five."

"Make your depth one hundred feet. Speed five. Helmsman come to zero five five."

The rumble of compressed air driving water out of the ballast tanks drowned out the sound of the screwbeats. The boat assumed an up-angle as she rose from the depths of the ocean to 100 feet. The sub was now behind both the main target and the escort, which meant that the escort destroyer couldn't hear any sounds made by the sub because of her own propeller noises. When the boat reached 100 feet, Malachi then ordered periscope depth, which was 60 feet. It took another two minutes to level off and stabilize the boat, after which Malachi ran the scope up.

"Stand by for setup," he called. "Target bearing is—mark."

"Zero five six," Marty announced. His job was to stand on the opposite side of the periscope to read off the bearing of whatever Malachi was looking at.

"Range is nine hundred yards and opening," Malachi said, and then raised the periscope handles to lower the mast. "Here's what I want: four fish, spread of two degrees, speed high, depth ten feet, contact exploder."

The TDC officer repeated the instructions and then fed the inputs into the computer.

"Open all outer doors forward," Malachi ordered. "Make ready tubes one through four. Up scope."

He stared into the eyepiece. The sunlight refracting down the optical tube framed his eyes in bright circles. "Bearing is—mark!"

"Zero five eight," Marty said.

"Agrees with TDC track," the fire-control officer said. That meant that the computer's predicted track agreed with Malachi's observed bearing, which in turn meant that the torpedo guidance systems were getting the correct instructions.

"Fire one," Malachi ordered. They felt the thump of the torpedo leaving its tube. Malachi fired the other three fish at ten-second intervals, took one last look all around to make sure there wasn't a second escort sneaking up on them, and then pulled the scope down.

"Time to first impact?" he asked.

"Ninety-five seconds remaining," the fire-control officer said. "Fish appear to be running hot, straight, and normal."

A minute and a half later came the first explosion on the predicted bearing. Then a second, followed by a third some thirty seconds later.

"Got something," Malachi observed. "Up scope."

He studied the situation on the surface. "The *maru* is settling by the stern. Big fire aft. I can't see the escort. Down scope."

He started to say something else when the sound of a really large explosion rumbled through the hull, followed by the crackling sounds of rending steel and the wet thump of boiler explosions. "How far away is that *maru* according to TDC?"

"Twelve hundred fifty yards. The escort was ahead of him when we first saw them, but I don't have a range."

"Come left to three four zero, and make your depth one fifty. Maintain five knots. I want to get two thousand yards off firing track before my next observation in case that escort retraces his own track."

The boat tilted slightly as the diving officer took her down to 150 feet and the helmsman brought her around to the northwest. The noises of the sinking faded and then there was only the whir of the fans in the control room.

"Maybe you hit both of them," Marty said.

Malachi shrugged. "It's possible," he said. "Two hits on the freighter, one on the tin can, then the tin can blew up. Or the freighter was an ammo ship and blew up and the tin can got the hell out of Dodge. We'll take another look when we get a mile sideways off the track. Do I need to tell forward torpedo to reload?"

"No, sir," Marty said. "They're on it, and tubes five and six are available."

After ten minutes and no further sounds from the surface, Malachi ordered periscope depth and then took a look all around. "A low cloud of black smoke to the east," he reported. "I don't see either one of them. Put up the air search radar mast."

The second mast went whining up behind the periscope. The radar operator turned the unit on and studied the scope. "No contacts," he reported.

"Down the radar mast," Malachi said. "Prepare to surface. How far are we from the nearest land?"

Marty consulted the chart. They'd established a good fix earlier that morning, so the dead reckoning track would be pretty close. "We're about seventy miles west of Bougainville and fifty miles south of Rabaul."

Malachi knew that Rabaul, a harbor on the northeast tip of New Britain Island, was a major Japanese navy and air base. If that cargo ship got off an SOS, there would be planes coming from Rabaul to investigate. He could surface for about twenty minutes, but then they'd have get down and out of sight.

"Surface and get on the diesels," he ordered. "Run at twenty knots to the estimated position of the sinking. Four lookouts, air search radar on the air every five minutes for one sweep only."

The klaxon horn sounded and the usual controlled stampede of men heading through the conning tower and up to the navigation bridge commenced. Malachi pulled Marty aside. "Remain in the control room and be prepared for a fast dive. I'm going to the bridge. If the air search radar generates a contact, sound the dive alarm immediately, and commence the dive, all right? No reports, just blow the horn and flood negative."

"Aye, aye, sir," Marty said. "How about the surface search radar? Want to take an occasional sweep with that as well?"

"Forgot about that," Malachi said, with a frown. "We had no radars on the S-boats. Yes, same deal. Intermittent radiation. Contact—blow the horn."

"Got it, sir."

Malachi grabbed his pair of binoculars and hustled up the vertical ladder through the conning tower hatch. Marty went to the plotting table and figured out a course back to the last-known position of the cargo ship. He called the OOD up on the navigation bridge and told him the course to take at 20 knots. The diesels erupted into their comforting growl and the boat heeled as it took off for that low, black cloud that was diffusing to the east.

Marty climbed down into the control room, where there was a lot of chatter about the attack they'd just made. The fresh air whistling down from the open hatches above was blowing papers everywhere, but the guys were excited. They'd certainly hit something out there. Marty went to the diving officer, LTJG Gary White, the navigator, and explained Malachi's instructions about making a crash dive the moment either radar picked anything up.

"A quarter of the Jap navy is at Rabaul, along with a couple hundred planes," he said. "They come out, we have to make like a sounding whale. Prep maneuvering for a fast shut down and shift to the batteries. Brief your planesmen."

"Got it, XO," White said. "I'll keep the GQ crew on station. Did we get that target?"

"We're going to find out," Marty said. "There were two ships out there. Now we can't find any."

Up on the navigation bridge, Malachi, like the four lookouts and the OOD, scanned the ocean ahead with binoculars for signs of the ships they'd attacked. The conning tower plotters reported they had about another half mile to go before they entered the area where the torpedoes should have impacted. Malachi was nervous about running at 20 knots on the surface on such a clear day. The sunshine almost hurt his eyes as he looked for signs of a sinking. The dirty brown cloud they'd seen when they surfaced had dissipated, and he also knew that the boat was creating a broad white wake behind them. A Jap plane would be able to see that from 15,000 feet.

"Oil sheen, dead ahead," called one of the high lookouts. "Four hundred yards."

"Slow to ten knots," Malachi ordered, and the OOD relayed the order down to the control room. Thirty seconds later he caught the rainbow glint of fuel oil floating on the surface. He slowed the boat to five knots, and they came left to avoid the main slick.

"Objects in the water, starboard bow," the other high lookout called out. He was positioned way up on the periscope structure, which gave him ten more feet of elevation.

Malachi saw them, too, as the boat slowed down on the edges of the oil slick, which looked to be a quarter mile wide. There were some charred crates wallowing in the oil, along with the lumpy shapes of bodies bobbing amongst the debris. They finally hit the stinking haze of the oil slick and it was strong enough to make their eyes water. The OOD pointed silently at a cluster of men floating in life jackets 50 yards out in the oil slick. Their faces were covered in the heavy bunker oil, and they made no sign that they'd seen the submarine as it cruised through the wreck site. Malachi knew there was nothing he could do for them, and that they'd probably refuse any help he offered. There was quite a lot of debris in the water now that they were on the edge of the slick, but it was so covered in oil as to be visible only as black lumps.

Malachi called the conning tower plotting crew and asked for a course to where the destroyer would have been. They reported that it should be 600 yards on the starboard bow. They cranked it back up to 15 knots and drove over to the estimated position, but found nothing. No additional wreckage and no oil slick. Malachi concluded that the escort had taken off for parts unknown, which meant that the Jap forces at Rabaul knew about the sinking. Time to go down for the day.

"Something in the water, Captain," one of the lookouts called down, pointing off to starboard. "Can't make it out, but it's pretty big."

Malachi made a hurried sweep with his binocs, fearing a Jap sub. Then he saw it. Dark colored. A familiar shape, bobbing gently in the water. He thought he saw tiny figures clinging to it, but he was looking into the sun. Then he recognized it: a bow. A destroyer's bow, floating vertically in the water. There *were* men surrounding it in the water, bobbing up and down like little dark corks in the seaway. There must have been twenty or even thirty survivors out there.

"Come left with ten degrees of rudder to course three zero zero," Malachi ordered, "and prepare to dive."

The men on the bridge looked at one another for a moment, and then the lookouts began to scramble down from their perches as the OOD passed the word to prepare to dive. The diesels cut off abruptly and then it was just Malachi left on the navigation bridge. He took another long look at the half-drowned men hanging onto the remains of their ship, and then he pressed the switch to sound the dive alarm. He went down through the conning tower hatch, stopping to pull the hatch down and firmly secure it. He could hear the rush of water flooding around the navigation bridge as *Firefish* went under in a roil of bubbles.

That night Marty brought Malachi the sinking report, claiming both the freighter and the escort, with visual evidence recorded on both sinkings. The message also stated their position in the general area of the huge Jap base at Rabaul.

"A nice start," Marty said while Malachi read over the draft message.

"Yes, it was," Malachi said. "Change the tonnage down to six thousand tons from eight. I don't think she was that big. And change the destroyer to destroyer escort. Otherwise, we'll go up at midnight to periscope depth long enough to transmit this, and then go back up again at zero two hundred and copy the fleet broadcast for an hour while we get some amps in the can. We should be getting more specific patrol area instructions just about now."

"Aye, aye, sir. I've put the word out to the crew that we got them both. Do we surface later and get a full charge on the batteries?"

"No," Malachi said. "I think the Japs will have some of those big Kawanishi seaplanes up in this area tonight, looking for a boat on the surface. Go to max conserve on the battery and stay down at two hundred feet."

"Should we stay in this area or head somewhere else?" Marty asked.

"For tonight let's head south, toward that big open passage through the Solomons. But only three knots. If it were my option I'd head for Rabaul and see what we could knock off on their logistics train. But . . ."

"Yes, sir. Big minefields around Rabaul."

"Exactly. So let's see what Admiral Britten has in mind now that we're in the assigned area. What's the date?"

"Seventh of August."

"I have an envelope in my safe that I'm supposed to open on the morning of the eighth and not before. That's all operations would tell me. Pass the word that I was pleased how people handled themselves today. Plotting, TDC work, shooting. All good. See you in the morning."

Marty headed back to the control room. A compliment. That was progress.

SIX

The boat was hot and stuffy the next morning, the result of no air-conditioning and minimal ventilation through the night to save battery life. Malachi stuck his head into the wardroom long enough to grab a coffee and a soggy donut and then headed for the control room.

"Captain's in Control," one of the enlisted announced. The men at the helm and the diving stations sat up a little straighter. Lieutenant Caldwell was the officer of the deck.

"Status?" Malachi said.

"Stable at two hundred feet, course one eight zero, speed three, no sound contacts. Battery is at fifty percent. There's a three-degree layer at one eighty feet. One motor on the line, most machinery is at max conserve, crew in their bunks unless they have the watch. Some indications of weather topside."

Marty slipped though the hatch into the control room, having been alerted by a watchstander that Malachi was up and about. "Morning, sir," he said.

"XO," Malachi replied. "Restore normal ops and get us up to periscope depth. I want to see this weather."

The XO began the process of getting more people up and about, restoring ventilation, and brought a second motor on line. Malachi climbed up to the conning tower so he could make periscope observations. The OOD went with him, along with the helmsman. Everyone else stayed down in the control room.

Ten minutes later they were at 60 feet, and everyone could feel that there was a large swell running upstairs. The planesmen had their work cut out for them just maintaining 60 feet. Malachi took a look and grunted. "Perfect," he said. "A good running sea, lots of white-caps. Overcast. Looks clear but run up the air and surface search radars, take two sweeps. If we're all alone, prepare to surface."

The presence of swells, wind, and whitecaps meant that aircraft would have a tough time sighting a submarine on the surface. If they could stay up for three hours undetected by minimizing their wake, they'd have the battery back to full charge. They could remain on the surface and start making progress to their assigned patrol area as long as the weather stayed nasty.

An hour later the bad weather had begun to take its toll on some of the crew. Heading south, the boat lay in the trough and with its round hull was rolling heavily. Submariners used to the dead calm of the depths were now starting to show a few green faces. Malachi laughed it off. After operating in the Irish Sea and the English Channel, this was nothing. The good news was that there was fresh air coming down and they were making a good 15 knots toward the lower Solomons. Malachi called a department head meeting in the ward-room for the opening of the sealed orders.

"Well," he began, after reading for a minute. "Looks like today we were supposed to have landed Marines on some place called Gua-dal-canal, down at the bottom of the Solomons chain. According to this they went in this morning to take a Jap airfield and also a small harbor called Tulagi. The Intel people are expecting a 'vigorous' reaction from the Japanese forces at Rabaul as early as today, and the way down to Guadalcanal from Rabaul is that big, inland passage. Our orders are to set up shop in suitable waters to take a shot at what-ever comes south from Rabaul. XO, we have charts?"

"I'll have to take a look, Captain. A lot of this area comes under the title of Oceania, which means whatever charts we do have are gonna be based on old, really old, information."

"We do have the most current HO charts?"

"Yes, sir, our chart portfolio is up to date. It's just that these are not normal operating areas for the Navy."

"Very well. Ops—anything on the fleet broadcast last night?"

"Not a word, sir," Lieutenant Caldwell said. "That's unusual, actually. There's always admin stuff. Since we're up on the surface, we're guarding the broadcast continuously now to see if we've missed anything."

"Very well, keep me informed. XO, let's take a look at those charts. We'll stay on the surface for as long as we can to get farther south and away from Rabaul. Occasional radar sweeps throughout the day, air and surface. Any *hint* of a contact, we get down quick."

The XO and the navigator came back to the wardroom ten minutes later with three Navy Hydrographic Office charts for the Solomons archipelago. The term "old" hardly described them. One of them, dated 1929, cited data provided by the explorations of Captain Edward Manning, RN, in 1792. Entire stretches of the passage running from Rabaul down to Guadalcanal, called New Georgia Sound, were marked simply with the words "dangerous ground." Malachi could only shake his head. "About all these tell me is here is water, here is land," he complained. "Half these so-called channels don't even have soundings."

"Yes, sir," Marty said. "Probably why the admiral instructed us to find 'suitable waters.'"

"Easy for him to say. On the other hand, if we can find some deep channels amongst the hundreds or so islands here, we could lay a nasty ambush."

A radioman interrupted them. "Got fresh traffic for us, Captain," he announced, and handed over a roll of yellow teletype paper.

Malachi took the roll and began to read it like an ancient papyrus scroll. Then the diving alarm sounded, and the boat tilted down. Malachi dropped the roll on the table and hurried to the conning tower. He had to wait for the lookouts and the OOD to tumble down through the hatch, slamming it behind them, as the boat slid under the surface. The familiar clamp of pressure in the boat indicated she was watertight and that the diesels' main induction valve was closed and locked out.

He told the diving officer to make his depth 200 feet, and then went up the ladder into the conning tower. "What've we got?"

"Air contact, sir, air, closing, eighteen miles."

"Helmsman, come right ninety degrees. Slow to five knots."

"Come right ninety degrees to course two six five, speed five, aye, sir."

Malachi knew that there was a chance, however remote, that the approaching Jap aircraft might have some kind of radar. If he'd made contact on *Firefish*, and, more importantly, tracked her, he could fly in to the last-known position of the sub and start laying down a line of depth bombs. Turn ninety degrees off his previous track and they were safe. He sent one of the plotters to the wardroom to retrieve the broadcast printout. The exec brought it up.

"Battery's at eighty-five percent," he reported. "We're stable at two hundred feet. Recommend slowing to three knots to conserve the battery."

"No, once this intruder is gone, I think we need to turn around and keep going southeast at five, at least. We're over a hundred miles away from the nearest point where I think we can penetrate that inner passage. We can come back up tonight and make twenty knots and recharge."

"In that case, I recommend we head south, not west."

Malachi gave him an exasperated look. "Do you know *why* I turned west?"

"No, sir, I don't."

Malachi explained it to him, realizing as he did so that he needed to establish a much better bond with his exec. Then he took the message roll and went below to his cabin, ordering the helmsman to come back to a southerly course and to maintain five knots.

He read the messages the radiomen had captured from the fleet broadcast for *Firefish*. The fleet headquarters in Pearl operated a powerful broadcasting station. In order to allow the submarines to remain radio silent, messages addressed to any particular submarine were collected onto a fleet-wide broadcast and transmitted three times a day. Each individual submarine was responsible for copying the entire fleet broadcast at least once a day, and then printing out the messages that pertained to them. The station in Pearl changed the encryption codes once a day, as did every submarine, also once a day.

Firefish's instructions were broadly stated. Get into that 250-mile-long channel between Rabaul and the Marine beachheads on Guadalcanal and do some damage. Malachi put a finger down on the chart of New Georgia Sound between the islands of Santa Isabel and Choiseul. "Let's go in here," he said. "That's almost twenty miles wide and probably too deep to mine. Then we'll see what, if anything, shows up."

They stayed submerged until dark, creeping along at a bare five knots. The younger sailors who'd been getting seasick were much relieved. During that time Malachi told Marty to have the forward torpedo room crew pull each of the six fish in the bow tubes and do what was called "routining" the torpedoes. This involved basic maintenance checks on the weapon's major systems, checking for fuel leaks, electrical grounds, free operation of the control fins, and the settings for the warhead.

In the eight months since submarine warfare had begun against Japan, though, over half of the magnetic exploder torpedoes fired had simply driven under their targets without doing anything. Since the torpedoes were steam-driven, they left a telltale wake pointing right back to where the submarine was lurking, making it easier for escorts to find them. The skippers were understandably not happy with such poor torpedo performance. The contact exploders worked better than that, although they, too, appeared to be defective far too many times. Some speculated that the torpedo itself wasn't running at the set depth.

Malachi had elected to disregard the orders about using the magnetic exploder, and had the torpedo crew deactivate the magnetic feature and set the fish for a contact hit. His crew was in full support. The admirals could issue all the orders they wanted, but they were safe on their tenders in Perth and Brisbane, while the sub crews were always going to be at the point of origin of that telltale wake. The exec personally oversaw the deactivation of the magnetic exploders and then the reloading of all six forward tubes. They'd do the four after torpedoes the next time they went down for the day.

The weather was still miserable when they surfaced but now they could make some decent speed on the diesels while charging the battery. In the eight hours they'd been submerged they'd traveled 40 miles. Now, assuming nothing turned up overnight, they'd make more like 160 miles, which would put them just outside of that 20-mile-wide channel into the New Georgia Sound. The exec put the bridge watches on two-hour shifts so they could come down and dry out from the thrashing seas topside. At nine that night he met again with Malachi to review the operations plan for the following day.

Malachi handed over some more messages that had come in, these detailing the progress of the landings on Guadalcanal, which, so far at least, hadn't encountered too much resistance. A second message informed them that another boat, the *Bluefish*, would also be operating in the New Georgia Sound, but much closer to Guadalcanal than *Firefish* would be.

"Make sure Perth knows where we're going to set up shop," Malachi said. "Make *Bluefish* info on that message."

"Yes, sir, I'll get right on it."

"And call me when we're ready to turn into the Sound. These charts with no soundings recorded give me bad dreams."

At dawn they went back down even as the weather cleared and the seas began to calm. Malachi picked a course into the Sound that went right down the middle between the two islands, and a running depth of 200 feet. He instructed the quartermaster to take fathometer soundings all the way in so they could begin to construct a useful chart of the area. Halfway into the Sound, the sonar operator picked up the propeller noises of several large ships approaching from the southeast at high speed.

"How close, Sonar?"

"Not close, Captain, but they're by God hauling ashes. Twenty-five, thirty knots. Sound like cruisers and destroyers, and their bearing is changing too fast to track."

Malachi considered coming up to periscope depth to take a look, but if they were going that fast, there was no chance *Firefish* could set up a shot at them, so why risk detection? Especially if the Japs had air cover from their strips at Rabaul and Buin. The fathometer was reporting that the depth beneath the keel was 3,000 feet, so he ordered the boat down to 300 feet. He noted with satisfaction that the previous drama about going to test depth seemed to have vanished. "I wonder what that gang has been up to," he said.

They came back up at nautical twilight and the navigator took star sights with the periscope to get a real fix on their position. They were out in the middle of the Sound, islands all around them, good, deep water, and clearing weather. The fleet broadcast brought them news of what that Jap cruiser formation had been doing down near Guadalcanal: sinking four Allied heavy cruisers, damaging a fifth plus two destroyers in one of the most lopsided defeats for the American Navy in history. The broadcast reported almost eleven hundred American sailors killed in action.

"Vigorous reaction indeed," Malachi said as he passed the message around the wardroom table. "I wish we'd been a day earlier."

"They'll probably be going back," Marty pointed out.

"Then let's see if we can plot out exactly what track line they were running today. How far out in the Sound—right up the middle? And then let's park on that track and see who shows up. There's no way we can get a shot off if they're driving by at thirty knots—but if we're *on* the track, we can shoot at their bows and maybe do some good work for Jesus."

"We do that, the entire battle line will run right over us," Peter Caldwell said.

That produced a moment of silence until Malachi nodded. "Yes, they will, which will allow me to fire stern tubes at them once they pass overhead."

That silenced the table for real.

SEVEN

At 2100 they were out in the middle of New Georgia Sound, equidistant between Bougainville and a group of islands called the Shortlands. The night was dark and clear with only a sliver of moon, and the seas had subsided to the usual deep ocean swell. Malachi perched on the navigation bridge bullrail, sipping some fresh coffee and cupping a cigarette so that it wouldn't show in the darkness. Two lookouts were high on the periscope tower, and two more on the navigation bridge, along with the officer of the deck, LTJG Billy Sullivan, the torpedo and fire-control officer. The battery was fully charged, so the diesels rumbled along quietly at six knots as the sub ran an east-west racetrack pattern to stay close to their best estimate of where an enemy task force might run. If indeed there was one headed down to Guadalcanal tonight.

Malachi heard the electric motor for the air search radar whine into life, make two sweeps, and then stop again. A moment later the surface search radar did the same thing, only this time he saw the red light on the bitchbox come on.

"Conn, Radar: we have surface contacts bearing three four six, range twelve miles, course and speed unknown until we get another mark. Looks like a column, though."

He reached for the talk switch. "Conn: aye, take one more look in three minutes, and then we'll dive. Pass the word: battle stations torpedo in five minutes."

He looked up at the lookouts and motioned them to get below.

"Mister Sullivan, pass the word to Control to prepare to dive. In the meantime, come left to three four six."

Although he couldn't hear it, he knew the crew would already be hustling to their general quarters stations, if only to avoid the usual mad scramble through all those knee-knocking hatches. He stepped on his cigarette, pitched it overboard, and told the OOD to get below, leaving him alone on the bridge. It was an exciting feeling, knowing a Jap formation was headed his way. He'd seen pictures of those Jap cruisers. They were beautiful the way a king cobra is beautiful: black, sleek, and bristling with guns and torpedoes. They routinely ran around at over 30 knots, and were rumored to have some of the best optics in the world for their fire-control systems. If they were running 30 now, they'd be on top of *Firefish* in exactly eight minutes. By doctrine, he should be going deep right now, but the radar gang needed that second look to be able to compute their course and speed, vital inputs to the TDC. He heard the surface search radar antenna crank around twice.

"Conn, Radar: enemy course and speed is one seven zero, thirty-two knots."

From the tone of the radarman's voice it was clear he'd done the math, too, and was now anxious for Malachi to give the order.

"Conn: aye," Malachi said, and pulled the dive alarm. He dropped through the conning tower hatch even as he heard the two radar masts coming down into their fairings. He tripped the holdback latch, dropped the round steel hatch, and dogged it firmly in place. "Hatch is closed," he called down into the conning tower as the boat slanted down. "Make your depth sixty feet."

The exec was already in the conning tower by the time Malachi landed on the deck. "Sixty feet, we might collide if those are heavy cruisers, sir," he said, obviously alarmed. "They draw thirty, thirty-two feet."

"I know that, XO, and I won't stay here any longer than I need to. But I want to be pointing right at them when I fire, so I need to see. Radar: any idea of how many ships are coming?"

"Five, maybe seven, Captain," the radarman said. "The contacts were all bunched up since we're looking at them bow-on."

"Very well. Up scope. Based on a DR, how far away are they? And does sound have contact?"

"Based on their computed course and speed, they'll be on top in five minutes, Captain."

The sonarman raised his hand. "Screwbeats, bearing three four two, sharp *up*-Doppler."

"Open all outer door, fore and aft. Make ready tubes one through four forward, and seven and eight aft. Speed high. Running depth ten feet. Contact exploder mode. XO, if you can get a TDC solution using sound bearings and estimated speed, good, but I plan to fire a two-degree spread of four right down the throat at twenty-five hundred yards and then dive to two hundred feet. Once the main body passes overhead, I plan to fire seven and eight on the reciprocal bearing, and then get down to two hundred fifty feet and drive ninety degrees off attack axis."

"Aye, aye, sir," Marty said and then huddled with the fire-control team next to the plotting table.

Having issued his attack orders, Malachi reviewed the picture in his mind. Two thousand yards was a bit of a long shot, except for the fact that the boat's torpedoes and the column of targets would be closing each other at nearly 78 knots. They should intersect at about 750 yards, not quite half a mile. Putting in a spread command meant that the torpedoes would begin to diverge when fired, so that instead of running parallel to each other, they would spread out into a narrow fan to increase the chances of hitting something. He took a look through the periscope, but could see absolutely nothing.

"Mark your depth," he snapped. Then he realized he hadn't heard the stable-at-ordered-depth report.

"Mark my depth seventy-five feet and coming up to sixty."

Malachi swore. He'd wanted a look before firing, but they were too deep. And they were out of time.

"Captain, the lead ship is only three thousand yards away," Marty called. "We gotta shoot and get down, right now."

"You have a solution?"

"No, sir, not enough time."

The forward torpedo room reported tubes one through four ready.

Everyone in the conning tower was staring at him, as if willing him to give the order. And then he realized he could hear those screw-beats as a formation of twelve-thousand-ton cruisers bore down on *Firefish*.

"Very well. Fire one." He fired the next three slightly faster than the ten-second intervals normally used. "Flood negative, make your depth two hundred feet. Seven knots. Ten-degree down-bubble. Make ready eight and nine."

The noise of the approaching formation grew louder and louder as *Firefish* assumed an even steeper down angle, the thrashing of destroyer propellers intermingling with the heavier thumping of the cruisers. Malachi was confident he'd be deep enough by the time those cruisers went overhead. He also knew that his attack had been a definite case of winging it, but it was the best he could do against ships going that fast.

A large explosion shook the boat as it passed through 140 feet, followed by a second one. Then the maelstrom of big propellers rushing overhead drowned out all other sounds. He issued the new attack instructions for the reciprocal course and then waited for down-Doppler before coming back up.

"Fire eight," Malachi ordered. Ten seconds. "Fire nine. Blow negative!"

He'd done all the shooting he could do, while still keeping two fish ready at each end. Now he had to get the boat back under control, as he watched the depth gauge rotating at an alarming rate. The noise of the cruiser formation began to diminish as *Firefish* ran back along their track. He sent the XO down to Control to supervise the planesmen, who were obviously having trouble getting her back on an even keel as they sought out the safety of 200 feet. In the distance they heard what sounded like a metallic thud and the sonarman swore. "Dud, bearing one seven zero."

The boat leveled up, courtesy of the exec's quiet stream of orders to the diving officer, who'd apparently lost the bubble again in the excitement of having the Jap formation passing overhead. Five minutes later he got the stable-at-ordered-depth report.

"Make your depth two hundred fifty feet and come to course two seven zero," he ordered, and then lit up a cigarette. "Sound: any echo ranging?"

"Negative, sir. It mostly sounded like they just kept going."

"But we hit something," Malachi said. He walked over to the plotting table. "Not much data was there," he said. The plotters looked at him and shrugged. They'd had no time to set up a nice, clear plot, enter anticipated course, speed, and bearing information into the TDC and then wait for the computer to confirm that their info seemed reasonable and issue orders to the torpedoes themselves. On the other hand, he'd fired four fish directly into the teeth of that approaching column and registered two explosions.

"Okay," he said. "Lay out a course at three knots to get three miles away from where all that noise was, and then we'll come up, take a look, maybe creep back and see if there's a cripple."

The exec came back up into the conning tower. "When we do come up for a look, we need to get a contact report out to the Navy units down near Guadalcanal. Let 'em know they got company coming."

"Do we have a direct comms link with Guadalcanal?"

Marty frowned as he thought for a moment. "No, sir, I guess we don't. We can radio Perth, they can radio . . ." He stopped, having no idea of what the communications path with the invasion forces was.

"Yeah, that's something we have to figure out," Malachi said. "Add that as a question when we make our after-action report. In the meantime, reload, XO. Reload."

An hour later they came up to periscope depth. The moon was flitting in and out of view as a high cloud deck began to move in over the Sound, but there was a faint orange glow of a fire to the south of their position. "Something's burning," Malachi said. He swung the scope through 360 degrees to make sure there wasn't a Jap destroyer right behind them. "Get me two radar sweeps, air and surface."

The radar revealed three contacts to the south, about six miles away. Two small, one large. Air search had no contacts.

"Prepare to surface," Malachi ordered.

"We should at least *try* to alert the amphib forces at Guadalcanal of what's coming," Marty said.

Malachi shook his head. "We don't have a direct HF channel, and going through Perth to Brisbane, Brisbane to Pearl, Pearl back to whoever's in charge down there will take hours. Plus, I don't want to light up the Japanese HF radio direction finding net. The Japs have too many forces at Rabaul that could come out and hunt our asses down. No, I still want to see if we've got a cripple down there and sink him. Now, surface."

They were up four minutes later. The diesels lit off and took the opportunity to feed their hungry batteries. Malachi ordered another radar sweep, which showed the three surface contacts to the south were still there. The glow he'd seen earlier was gone.

"Take another single sweep in three minutes," he ordered. "See if they're moving at all. They may be setting up a tow. I'm going topside. Two lookouts this time."

Three minutes later, the conning tower plotters reported that the three contacts appeared to be moving northwest at three knots. They asked for a few more single-sweeps to confirm that.

"Yes, go ahead and do that, but single sweeps only." He called for the XO. Marty joined him on the navigation bridge.

"XO, I want to drive to a point three miles ahead of them on their current track. Once there, we'll submerge and begin our approach. How's the reload going?"

"Tube one is reloaded. Tube two in progress. Five and six are ready. Aft takes a lot longer—there's just no room."

"Okay, I have two already loaded aft. I plan to shoot four at the cripple, and keep two back for emergencies. I'm guessing one destroyer is towing, the other patrolling ahead, looking for us. I want to get into fifteen hundred yards and let 'em all go straight in at the big one. Then I'm going to go deep and go under them."

"Sir?"

"Yes, *under* them. The torpedoes will get there before we do. They'll know the fish came from ahead, but two of them can't do anything about that when they're married by a towing hawser. The first tin can will charge ahead to gain contact on us, but by then I mean to be deep and going deeper."

"That's really risky, Captain," Marty said. "If the can that's out front gets a contact, even a fleeting one, he'll tell the can doing the towing to roll a load."

"If he's still there, XO," Malachi said. "I want you to be the diving officer, because I'm going to call for a twenty-degree down-bubble and full power until all the noise is astern. Then we're going to come all the way back up and take a look."

Marty blinked as he absorbed the proposed geometry. Twenty degrees down-bubble gave them no margin for error. If a diving plane jammed, they'd power all the way to crush depth. And beyond. "Aye, aye, sir," he gulped. "I'll go below and set up the intercept point ahead. And I'll need COB."

"Good thinking," Malachi said. The chief of the boat was one of the best diving officers onboard.

The exec disappeared down the conning tower hatch. Malachi lit a cigarette well below the side bulkhead and then turned away from where the Japs were to take a deep drag. He looked at his watch. It was nearing 2300. He was pretty sure he'd damaged one of the big ships and that the enemy had left two destroyers behind, one to take her under tow and get her back into Rabaul harbor, or possibly one of the closer Jap bases at Buin or Kieta. The other one would act as escort.

He could just submerge now, drive back to the formation, and open fire, but it would have to be a side-on shot. He had, however, a personal rule about firing torpedoes so that they did not have to make a turn once they came out of the tube. The TDC was able to set the torpedo to turn to a specific gyro-controlled course once fired, thus allowing the submarine to already be headed outbound sooner. But there had been documented cases of torpedo rudders locking up while making that initial turn to the firing bearing and then conducting a circular run right back at the submarine. He had resolved to always get into a firing position so that the fish didn't have to make a turn when they came out. Yes, it put the submarine right in front of the approaching targets, but if they were in column formation, the tactic had the added advantage of sending a crowd of torpedoes into the dense column, lengthwise, thus upping the chances of hitting something.

"Conn, XO: recommend three three five at ten knots to achieve intercept position."

"Make it so," Malachi said, taking another drag. "And I need some coffee."

Ninety minutes later they were headed roughly south by east, submerged at periscope depth. Their final radar sweep confirmed that two contacts were close together, while the third was ranging ahead, executing a sinuous weave and obviously looking for trouble. They'd been able to establish a stable plot on the slow-moving ships, so there was no more need for periscope or radar observations. The boat was headed right for them, all outer doors open, torpedo settings entered and verified, and the plot solution agreed with the TDC.

"Two minutes to firing point," the TDC operator announced.

"Sound: target bearing steady? Up-Doppler?"

"Yes, sir, barely, but no changes. One of the targets is echo-ranging in omni mode."

"General search, then. Very well. Control, Captain: initial down-bubble is to be ten degrees until we've reached full power, then down ten more. Minimize ballast movement going down—use the planes. Begin to flatten the dive as we pass two hundred feet and *then* use the ballast tanks. Once all target noises are astern begin the ascent back to periscope depth and slow to three knots."

"Control: aye," the exec said.

"Sixty seconds to firing point. Torpedoes set for high speed, running depth ten feet, contact exploders."

"I concur. Fire when ready."

The first fish pulsed out of its tube, followed by three more. Once the final one took off, the sub's bow tilted down and the rumble of the propellers coming up to full underwater speed of 7 knots could be felt throughout the hull. Malachi glanced at the depth gauge: 100 feet.

"Run time is one twenty to the towing ship."

Malachi nodded and watched the depth gauge as the sub gathered speed and pointed down into the darkness. The underwater log registered five knots, then six, then seven, and then the nose dipped again, steep enough that men had to grab something to stay upright. Pencils rolling off the plotting table made startlingly loud noises, and one empty coffee mug went crashing to the deck. One hundred eighty feet.

Two underwater blasts in quick succession shook the boat, followed seconds later by a third.

Two hundred twenty feet. Catch her, Marty, catch her.

A sustained roar of underwater noises rose to a crescendo seemingly right above them and then moved aft.

Two hundred sixty feet, but the dive angle was finally flattening. Malachi, and everyone else in the conning tower, started breathing again.

Two hundred seventy feet, and the speed was coming down, too. From a far distance astern came the thumping bangs of depth charges going off. The groaning and grinding of steel under great stress could still be heard behind them, drowning out *Firefish*'s own complaints about being so deep. They waited, listening to the ballast pumps whining as they pushed trim water aft, and then the first blow forward to lighten the bow. Malachi checked the speed: four knots.

Two hundred fifty feet, and almost level.

"Control, Conn: maintain four knots until we're ready to level off at periscope depth."

"Control: aye," the exec replied. "She's responding well."

It look longer than he'd anticipated to get her stable and properly trimmed out at periscope depth and steady at three knots. It had been a violent maneuver, and they'd have to talk about the coordinated use of ballast water and planes when making a dive like that. But it had worked. The only depth charges they'd heard had been way astern, right where that destroyer would have expected *Firefish* to be.

"Up scope," he ordered. He took the obligatory 360-degree sweep to make sure he hadn't put the scope up right in front of an enemy destroyer. Then he began a slower sweep to the east, just as the moon popped out again. He finally spotted a low-lying cloud of what looked in the moonlight like white mist, drifting slowly to the south.

"No ships," he announced.

The exec had come back up to the conning tower. "There's still that one tin can," he pointed out.

"Yeah, there is. He's probably on the other side of that cloud. Run the surface search radar mast up, take a sweep."

They waited for the radar transmitter to warm up and then come on the air for a single sweep.

"One contact, zero eight zero, range twelve miles."

"Twelve *miles*?" the exec snorted. "Somebody's getting the hell out of Dodge."

There were grins all around.

"Time for us to do the same," Malachi said. "The Japs will know what happened by now and that there's a sub out here. XO, plot a course for where we think that cruiser went down at five knots. I want to make a periscope observation there. Then we'll surface and run to the east. That Jap task force will be coming back in about six, maybe eight hours. I don't want to be here."

When they got to the estimated position of the sinking, Malachi raised the periscope high to keep any fuel oil from fouling the lenses. At first there was nothing to see, but gradually objects in the water began to come into view. Boxes that looked like vegetable crates, an oil drum, and then a float plane, sitting on the water as if nothing had happened. Next came some life rafts, and then a clot of floating debris, surrounded by heads in the water. He wondered if they even saw the periscope as it sliced slowly through the remains of a heavy cruiser—and possibly the destroyer towing it.

"Down scope," he ordered. "Proceed east for thirty minutes. Then surface to recharge and get a good radar fix on the islands. We'll submerge again just before dawn."

EIGHT

They were able to get almost a full charge, but just at nautical twilight a periodic sweep of the air search radar picked up an incoming patrol aircraft, precipitating a crash dive. They slipped down to 200 feet and then made a 90-degree turn in case they'd been spotted and the aircraft dropped a bomb or even depth charges. In the event, nothing happened, but to Malachi it meant that the Japs were out looking for them. They used a formidable seaplane called a Kawanishi H8K2: four engines, 20mm cannons, machine guns, a crew of ten, a range of 4,400 miles, and the ability to drop 1,500-pound bombs or torpedoes.

Malachi was pretty sure that one of the reasons a Kawanishi had come their way was that *Firefish* had come up on a high-frequency (HF) radio net to report the night's action while on the surface. This had triggered a hit on the Japanese HFDF network, called HuffDuff. Both sides maintained HF listening stations scattered over literally thousands of miles of their respective territories. If a ship at sea began transmitting on a specific frequency and one of the stations heard it, that station would "flash the net," and all the other stations would tune to that frequency and take a bearing. The central station would then plot all those bearings, and where they met was the location of the transmitting ship, sometimes thousands of miles away. American submarines were acutely aware of the HFDF system and made no more than one HF transmission a day, or even every other day, unless they were in trouble. Japanese submarine skippers, on the other hand, were positively garrulous in the 2-to 32-megacycle frequency, which had cost some of them their lives.

Radio had also been able to copy the fleet broadcast from Pearl, which updated *Firefish*'s orders and gave news of what was happening down at Guadalcanal. The news was dramatically unpleasant as the Imperial Japanese Navy battered the US Navy in a series of almost surgical night battles around Guadalcanal. The admiral in Perth acknowledged *Firefish*'s previous attack on the merchant ship and its escort of the night before and exhorted her and the other sub farther south to attack those nighttime cruiser formations whenever possible.

"Well, then he ought to like tonight's report," Malachi said at a late-afternoon department head meeting. He'd been careful to couch it in as accurate terms as possible, not claiming outright that he'd sunk a cruiser and a destroyer but rather that the first attack had been by radar on what looked like a cruiser-destroyer formation, followed up by an end-around run and a second radar attack and then visual confirmation of wreckage and people in the water. Once they got back to base they'd debrief the attack in detail with the admiral's operations people and let them sort out what the probable results had been.

Most of the officers and crewmen had spent the day getting some rest after the previous night's exertions. The relative calm and safety of 200 feet made that possible, especially in an air-conditioned boat. The crews of the older S-class boats still operating in the Pacific had no such luxury, and their life was a miserably hot and humid hell of constantly sweating bodies and failing electrical equipment. "Ops, what was on last night's broadcast?"

It was a rhetorical question, because Malachi had already seen the messages, but he wanted the department heads to hear it from LTJG Caldwell, who went through the news from Guadalcanal, and then the daily intelligence estimate on what the Japs were doing.

"Kicking American ass, apparently," the exec said. No one smiled. Caldwell confirmed the exec's sentiments with the latest battle results around the lower Solomons.

"Our station hasn't changed," he said. "Nor have our orders:

penetrate New Georgia Sound and attack the cruiser formations going down to Guadalcanal from Rabaul every night. Preferably *before* they get there, is what I'm reading into the wording."

"We can't get them on the way down," Malachi interjected. "They leave Rabaul and Buin in daylight, with air cover that stays on top until almost sundown. By nightfall they're a hundred miles south from where we've been stationed. If the admiral wants us to attack them *before* they get to Guadalcanal, either *Bluefish* has to do it or we need to shift south about one hundred fifty miles."

"Should we say that in our next report to the admiral?" the exec asked. "I'm wondering if he appreciates how thoroughly the Japs own the daylight hours in these parts."

"No," Malachi said. "We've been given a station and an operating area. In my experience, if the admiral wants suggestions from his skippers, he'll let us know."

"Well, how about this, then," the exec said. "We're down to five torpedoes. Should we stay on station or go back to Perth to rearm?"

Malachi raised his eyebrows in surprise. "Go *back*? Are we out of fuel or food?"

"No, sir."

"Is the machinery all working?"

"Yes, sir. We've got some small mechanical and electrical problems, but nothing serious."

"Then we need to find a home for those five fish. *Then* we go back."

"We've been shooting a lot of fish, Captain," the exec persisted. "Salvoes of four at a time. If we shoot four more, we'll have one to defend ourselves with."

Malachi looked down at the table for a long moment. "We're not here to defend ourselves, gentlemen," he said, quietly. "I know torpedoes are in short supply, but nowhere in our orders does it say to bring torpedoes back to Perth. We're here to sink Jap ships. Which means that, tonight, once we surface, we run back out into the Sound and see what turns up, and then we shoot torpedoes at it."

He looked around the table at the worried faces. "Look," he said. "*I* wouldn't have stationed a sub up here at the north end of the Sound, for the reasons I've already mentioned. But I think we've bagged a *maru*, a cruiser, and two, maybe even three destroyers, so just possibly the admiral knows what he's doing, okay? But he depends on *us* to take the fight to the enemy. If we exceeded the authorized number of torpedoes on any one target, that'll become my problem, when we get back, not yours. That is all."

At midnight they were back out in the middle of New Georgia Sound, about 20 miles south of where they'd operated the night before. The moon was waning and the sea felt like it was waiting for something, oily calm but with a hint of a deeper swell uncoiling from somewhere to the east of them.

Malachi sat on his metal stool in the conning tower, trying to read the Fox broadcast scroll in the red light. Down below in the control room the diving officer struggled to keep the boat at "decks awash," which meant that only the sail, the structure that housed the conning tower, the navigation bridge, and the periscope support structures, was showing above the water. Riding at decks awash required a careful balance between air and seawater in the ballast tanks. A miscalculation could cause the boat to either broach—pop up on the surface in an unstable condition—or submerge, with the OOD and the lookouts still up there on the bridge and the main induction valve wide open. Malachi thought his diving officers needed more training, so he'd told the exec to stand watch with them while the boat was in this precarious, if tactically stealthy, condition. As few as five sailors going from the crews' mess to the forward torpedo room could upset the balance.

Malachi sighed as he read the broadcast. Once a week the headquarters at Pearl transmitted a fleet-wide intelligence estimate for the western Pacific. The news was generally grim. The Japanese were tightening their grip on the bulk of Southeast Asia while the Allies reeled from defeat after defeat. The American invasion of the obscure Solomons was the only sign that real resistance to the Japanese had begun, although the costs so far to the US Navy had been grotesque. Malachi heard the radar transmitter come up for the quarter-hour sweep, followed by the grinding noise of sea salt–soaked bearings up on top of the radar antenna mast. He cocked an ear.

"Radar contact," the operator announced. "Three four one, range twelve thousand yards."

"North?" Malachi said. He'd been waiting for the nightly run back to Rabaul from Guadalcanal. From the south, not the north.

"Yes, sir," the operator said. "I'll wait three minutes, then sweep again to see if we can get a course and speed."

"Prepare to submerge," Malachi said. The word went out over the sound-powered phone circuits. The diesels shut down and the big main induction valve closed with an authoritative thump as the OOD and the four lookouts came down the ladder from the navigation bridge. Malachi nodded when the conning tower hatch clanged down, and the klaxon sounded.

"Periscope depth," he ordered. "Speed three." Three minutes later the boat was leveled out at 60 feet. "Surface radar mast up," he ordered. A single sweep was taken, confirming the contact was still there. The radar mast was pulled down, and then the plotters laid out the tentative track.

"He's headed south, speed fifteen, based on only two marks," the plotter announced. "Last range, nine thousand yards."

"Sound, Conn: hearing anything?"

"Not yet, sir."

"Open outer doors on tubes five and six. We'll take another mark in three minutes. I'll make a visual observation when he's down to three thousand yards." He looked over to the TDC operator, who had entered the first two marks and then set the computer running. If the third mark and the computer agreed, they had a firing solution. Then they waited.

"What's the computed bearing and range?"

"Drawing left to three three five," the plotter said. "Five thousand six hundred."

"TDC agrees."

"Up scope." Malachi stared into the optics on the computed bearing as the scope cleared the surface. Even with red light, his eyes took some time to adapt. Whatever it was, it wasn't all that big.

"Conn, Sound: diesels on the bearing."

A sub, Malachi thought. A Jap sub on the surface running south on his diesels.

"XO, confirm that there are no other US subs in this area?"

"Affirmative, Captain. Only the *Bluefish*, and she should be two hundred miles south of us."

"Very well, *down* scope. Up radar mast. Take a sweep and then bring it down. This will be a firing observation. Torpedoes: speed high. Depth five feet. Contact exploders."

The TDC operator read back the settings as the radar operator reported his results to the plotting table.

"We have a stable solution, sir," the TDC operator said. "Firing time in one hundred eighty seconds."

"Conn: aye," Malachi said. "Fire on TDC orders."

The countdown began. The approaching Japanese sub, running in a straight line on the surface, fat, dumb, and happy, while the cogs, gears, and wheels in an American TDC spun down the clock, and two torpedoes, their circuits awakened, their gyros set, their warheads programmed, the tube spheres pressurized, waited for the big thump.

"Firing five. Firing six."

They waited for the hot straight and normal report from sonar.

"Circular run, circular run!" the sonarman shouted.

Malachi didn't hesitate. He didn't need to know which fish had gone crazy, only that they had to get down before it ran a 360-degree circle and destroyed them.

"Flood negative," he ordered, in a voice they could hear down in the control room. "Twenty-degree down-bubble, full power!"

The boat pitched over and began to accelerate.

"Time to intercept is thirty-five seconds," the TDC operator announced, still focused on the job at hand even with an errant torpedo circling back at them. One torpedo had malfunctioned; the other should still be heading for its target. Malachi was busy doing geometry in his head. The errant fish would execute a wide circle at the ordered depth. If the boat did nothing, it might hit them. If the boat jumped out of that circle and plunged beneath it, the fish would run over the top of them and keep running in a circle until it ran out of fuel. Thank God he'd disabled the magnetic exploders, because that device might sense the scrambling submarine's hull and go off anyway.

Another reason to *never* use the magnetic exploder, Malachi thought. *And* he realized, he hadn't lined the boat up on the firing bearing as he usually did, to prevent this very thing from happening. He waited for the sound of high-speed screwbeats, hoping they'd be deep enough not to hear them.

"Mark predicted impact."

Nothing. What the hell, Malachi thought. That was a perfect track. He looked at the depth gauge: 230 feet and rotating rapidly.

"Catch her, XO," he shouted down the hatch.

"Catch her, aye," the XO shouted back up the conning tower ladder. "Just like last time."

Malachi grinned. That little stunt of driving under the cruiser they'd just torpedoed had been good training after all. Then they heard the torpedo, a high whining noise signaling death approaching at almost 50 knots.

Above them. Definitely above them. A collective sigh of relief spread around the conning tower as the Doppler rose and then fell sharply. The crazy torpedo ran off into the dark to make another try.

"Leveling at two eighty," the XO reported. You hope, Malachi thought, as he watched the depth gauge sink to 300.

"Get back to periscope depth, speed three, once that fish quits running," Malachi ordered.

"Conn, Sonar: unidentified noises on the firing bearing. And that crazy fish is coming back. High up-Doppler."

"We're at three hundred feet, Sound. It's okay."

"Okay, aye, sir," the sonarman said, but he didn't sound all that assured. The creaking and cracking of the hull probably wasn't helping.

"Plot: continue the TDC track on that contact," Malachi ordered. He could have crash-dived and then kept going." In fact, he thought he could be down here with us, and for the same reason: evading a torpedo. He wondered if he should rig for silent running. Could the Japs go down to this depth? "OOD, pass the word: quiet in the boat. There may be another sub down here with us."

This was a different command from "rig for silent running," where machinery was turned off. It also alerted the sonar gang to begin a different search program. "Where's the layer?" Malachi asked. "Layer at two hundred forty feet, Captain," Sound reported. "Six-degree gradient."

The errant torpedo was coming back around one last time. Malachi wondered what the Jap sub skipper would make of a torpedo circling him in the darkness. First one had come right at him, then a second one was howling around like a hungry if blind banshee. They listened as the wild fish ran over the top of them and then went down-Doppler before finally exploding some distance away. With that problem out of the way, he still had to decide what to do.

He could go up to 240 feet and probe above the layer to see if he could hear the other sub. But what if he could? He couldn't fire at it because he had no idea of the target's track, and besides, the Mark 14 wasn't designed to operate at this depth. And, finally, he could end up colliding with the other boat as they both played an underwater version of blind-man's bluff.

He was at that point overcome by a sudden urge to get out of there, to disengage from this enemy contact and this whole weird situation before it got out of control.

"Make your depth two hundred sixty feet, XO," he ordered. "Come to course two three zero, speed five knots. We're leaving."

"Leaving, aye, Captain," the XO responded. Malachi ignored what sounded like muted cheers from the control room below, and gratefully lit up a cancer stick.

Two hours later they surfaced to get a last charge into the battery before daylight. The fleet broadcast informed them that their attack on the crippled cruiser had been acknowledged at Pearl. Ops sent back a report on the encounter with the Jap sub, noting they had two torpedoes and fifteen percent fuel left. Just before they went down for the day they received a message to return to Perth.

NINE

Two weeks later Malachi found himself cooling his heels in the admiral's office in downtown Perth. Their homecoming had been anticlimactic since they'd arrived at two in the morning alongside the tender. Even at that hour, their first duty had been to refuel the boat, fill up the potable water tanks, and begin taking on torpedoes. Food, mail, and spare parts would arrive today. He'd brought his captain's log, which contained daily summaries, and, where appropriate, details of his attacks in his own hand. In each instance, he'd left out the details of his torpedo settings, although he suspected he'd be questioned about that eventually. He had put in the extreme depths at which he'd operated.

There were two yeomen in the office, this time, both female. One was young and pretty, the other a chief petty officer whose no-nonsense expression matched her mannish frame. The young one had brought him a coffee, and then gone back to clacking away on her shiny new Underwood typewriter. The chief busied herself with reading reports and then filing them in folders for the admiral's perusal. He could hear voices in the inner office, but it didn't sound like an argument. The chief must have read his mind.

"That's the morning staff meeting, Captain," she said. "They'll be done shortly."

He nodded and closed his eyes. The transit back had been uneventful, with not a single ship sighting. It had given the crew time to rest, make repairs on troublesome equipment, and generally unwind from the patrol. They'd get liberty here in Perth, for which they would need their rest. He'd conducted some training sessions with the officers, including spontaneous crash dives and some more hours spent running at decks awash. They'd transited on the surface the entire way back once they cleared the Solomons. It had been somewhat surreal: a world war was going on all around them, but the ocean had been empty.

The door to the inner office opened and the chief of staff, Captain Collins, waved him in. He found the admiral standing, with his aide next to him, and the staff officers, all nine of them, standing in two ranks. The admiral gave him a big grin and a hearty handshake.

"Welcome back, Captain, and congratulations on an excellent patrol. A heavy cruiser, two destroyers, a seven-thousand-ton transport, and a frigate. That's pretty damned good for a first patrol. Please come to attention."

The admiral then pinned a Navy Cross on Malachi's shirt and shook his hand again. The staffies broke ranks and each of them shook his hand before filing out of the office. The admiral pointed to a chair, and then he and the chief of staff took seats. The latter began reading Malachi's daily logs.

"How's the boat?" the admiral asked, lighting up a cigarette and inviting Malachi to do the same.

Malachi was still trying to absorb being decorated with the nation's second highest medal. "The boat, sir? She's fine. We're refueled and rearmed, and we expect fresh provisions today. We've got the usual weeps and leaks, but nothing major."

"And you're *already* refueled and rearmed?"

"Yes, sir. The tender wasn't thrilled with handling torpedoes at three in the morning, but, well, remember Cavite."

"Yes, indeed, you did exactly the right thing. I'll speak to Bill Worth; he's CO of *Otus*."

The chief of staff let out a low whistle. "You went *under* that cruiser after you torpedoed him?" he asked, sounding a little incredulous.

"We did," Malachi said. "The escorts were heavy on our side, and they'd probably guessed from which direction the fish came. Slipping under the cruiser put us on the unengaged side, so to speak. In fact, they ran off depth-charging the area where we'd been."

"How deep did you go?" the chief of staff asked.

"Two fifty," Malachi said. "We did a twenty-degree down-bubble at full power, then leveled out and came back up to periscope depth on the other side. The XO had the dive."

The chief of staff and the admiral looked at each other. "That's pretty deep at twenty degrees," the admiral said.

"I've had her down to three fifty, Admiral," Malachi said. "She's brand new."

"But her test depth is three hundred, is it not?"

"Yes, sir. I wanted the crew to gain confidence that she's a deep diver against the time when we need to be really deep. I wanted them to hear what it sounds like, and also to force any potential leaks to show themselves. Three fifty is pushing it; three hundred is no longer a big deal in *Firefish*."

The admiral frowned and then blew out a long breath. "*I* think three hundred is a big deal, Captain," he said softly. "You have little margin for errors or sudden damage at that depth."

"Yes, sir, I know," Malachi said, wondering if the admiral wanted his medal back. "But the thermal layers I've been seeing are below two hundred where we've been operating. Those layers—"

"I know, I know," the admiral interrupted. "We have three other fleet boats operating out here on this side of Australia. I don't believe any of them have been routinely challenging three hundred feet. I need to think about this."

The chief of staff, who was sitting just behind the admiral's sight line, gave Malachi a warning look, as in "don't argue." Malachi tried changing the subject.

"I have a question, Admiral," he said. "How do we know that those ships I shot at actually went down?"

The admiral glanced back at his chief of staff for a second. "*We* don't," he replied. "But Naval Intelligence back in Pearl apparently does. They confirmed all the sinkings. I must simply presume we have spies where we need them. How many torpedoes did you expend?"

"We can carry twenty-four. We had nineteen onboard. We expended seventeen in all."

"And you brought home an impressive good bag. Let me warn you, though, if you shoot that many torpedoes and *don't* bring home a good bag, that will be problematical. We still are facing critical shortages of fish, and your next patrol you'll have even fewer. Okay, for right now, you'll be in for two weeks; make the best of it with the tender. Congratulations again on a fine patrol."

"Thank you, sir," Malachi said.

The chief of staff followed him out and then buttonholed him the corridor outside the executive suite. "One more question," he said. "I noted that you did not write down torpedo settings in your daily log. Does that mean what I think that means?"

Malachi hesitated, but then decided he might as well draw the line. "Yes, sir, it does. I disabled all the magnetic exploders, fired nothing running deeper than ten feet, and all set for high speed and contact."

The chief of staff just stared at him. "You do know the admiral's policy on that, right?"

Malachi stared right back. "I do, but I was stationed at Newport when those things were being developed, and I know they were never tested against a moving target, or in the Southern Hemisphere where we are now. The earth's magnetic field is not homogeneous. *Firefish* had to calibrate her magnetic compass every day on the transit down here from Pearl. They don't work, and they'll never work. The Brits and supposedly even the Germans have already shit-canned theirs, if it's any comfort."

"Those are decisions way above your pay grade, Captain," the chief of staff retorted.

"Undoubtedly, Chief of Staff, but I'm not alone in my opinion about the magnetic exploder, if what I heard in Pearl was any indication."

"From whom?"

"COs of boats that tried to use them."

"And yet Admiral English requires that they be used."

"I understand that ComSubPac sets the policy, sir, but he doesn't go out into Indian Country like we do."

The chief of staff's face hardened. "Admiral Britten's going to read your logs. He reads them all. Then he's going to ask. Better think long and hard about how you'll answer. You tell him you refuse to use the magnetics, you'll find yourself on the beach."

Malachi looked down at the floor for a moment. "I had a boss once," he said, finally. "He told me never to ask an official question if I couldn't stand *all* the possible answers. I had to think about that before I understood it. Can you recommend a good hotel in this town?"

The chief of staff opened his mouth to rebut that but then closed it. "We have the top three floors of the Benbow Hotel reserved exclusively for skippers," he said, finally. "It's a small hotel, but pretty nice. Ask the chief yeoman to get you set up, and think hard about what I said."

"Aye, aye, sir," Malachi replied.

That evening he found himself on the rooftop of the Benbow in downtown Perth, enjoying a cold beer while watching another three-striper who was apparently intent on getting himself blind drunk at another table. The bar was manned by two delectable bartenders dressed in shorts and midriff-tied blouses. He sipped on his beer and blew blue smoke into a sea breeze that was stirring the evening air. After what had happened between him and his father a long time ago, he wasn't much of a boozer. In Australia, that probably would be classified as a bit peculiar.

Another commander in khakis showed up, waved at the girls behind the bar, who immediately set to work fixing him a drink. He glanced over at the solitary drunk in the making, shook his head, and came over to where Malachi was sitting. He was tall and athletic-looking, with a full, black beard.

"Reed Burlington," he said, offering his hand. "*Sea Lion*."

"Malachi Stormes," Malachi replied. "*Firefish.*

"Oh, yeah, the new guy," Burlington replied. "Been hearing about you down on the waterfront. Bagged a heavy cruiser *and* you like to go deep."

"Grapevine's alive and well, I take it," Malachi said. One of the girls arrived and presented Burlington with a fruity concoction that reeked of rum and had tiny Aussie and American flags on skewers sticking out of a pineapple slice on top.

"Oh, hell, yeah. We're all professional gossipers. You came from the LantFleet?"

"I did, sort of. I had an S-boat, one of the antiques we sent over to

Scotland to help the Royal Navy with their Nazi problem. Had one good day over there, and got *Firefish* as my reward."

"Ri-i-ght," Burlington said. "You got the three U-boats in the minefield. Love to hear that tale."

A sound of breaking glass came from the table across the room. The other skipper had dropped his glass on the concrete floor.

"That's Pogue White," Burlington said softly. "Class of 'twenty-five. Going to be relieved for being too cautious on patrol. Guy from 'twenty-nine got his boat."

"I'd guess the heavy boozing didn't just start with that," Malachi said as he watched White swaying in his chair while one of the girls swept up the glass after bringing him a new one.

"You'd guess right," Burlington said. "But a lot of us skippers hit the booze pretty hard when we get in. I think that's why the admiral makes all the COs get a room here. You wanna get boiled, the staff here will help you out and pour you in your rack if they have to."

"One of those two?"

Burlington laughed like a pirate. "Perth's chock full of gorgeous women, and they all seem to like Americans. The Aussie men prefer drinking beer with their 'mites' to spending time with their 'Sheilas.' Thanks be to God. Welcome to bachelor Paradise."

"May not be here long," Malachi said. "Got into it with the chief of staff today. On the matter of the Mark fourteen magnetic exploders."

"Oh, *no*," Burlington said with mock horror. "The dreaded torpedo issue. Lemme guess: you deactivated all your magnetics."

"And set all fish for ten feet regardless of the target except for one sub I shot at. I spent three years at the Torpedo Station, a lot of it on the Mark fourteen torpedo. Know its inner workings and hidden mechanisms pretty well."

"Compared to the Mark ten it's a piece of shit," Burlington declared. "There's something you should know: if you have problems with the Mark fourteen, they're all of *your* making, and none of their lordships' at the Bureau of Naval Ordnance. Just so you know."

"So I was told in Pearl by every CO and prospective CO back there. They said ComSubPac apparently agrees with BuOrd."

"Admiral English is Old Navy. Bugles from the top hampers. Port your helm, if you please, Helmsman. Properly suspicious of newfangled gadgetry, like radar or air-conditioning in submarines, because when he was in the fleet, by God . . ."

Malachi smiled. "So was everybody in charge on Pearl Harbor day," he said. "Old Navy. And then, dead navy."

Burlington lifted the two little flags out of his glass and ceremoniously put one behind each ear. A moment later he had a fresh drink, which the impish bartender delivered with a flirtatious smile. Burlington lifted his glass in appreciation. "A four-devil mai tai: white rum, cherry-vanilla puree, Amaretto, Cointreau, and fruit juices. Topped with a dark rum float. Wonderful. You ought to try one. Makes chiefs of staff evaporate before your very eyes."

"Not much of a drinker," Malachi admitted. "No head for alcohol. One beer is about it. After that, headache city."

"*Damn*," Burlington said with real concern.

Malachi laughed. "That may change once the admiral reads my daily logs," he said. "The chief of staff as much as promised me that he would."

"Maybe, maybe not," Burlington said. "This was your first patrol, right? What was your bag?"

"Heavy cruiser, three destroyers, a *maru*, and a frigate."

Burlington whistled softly. "Hadn't heard about the other ships," he said. "With a couple of exceptions, our results out here have been dismal. I suspect he'll balance that with the mortal sin of disabling the magnetics," he said.

"Why isn't anyone doing anything about it?" Malachi asked.

"It's coming, I think. We just might need some modern leadership at the top. We also need to untether our patrol areas from Jap naval bases, where they have all the advantages. *I* think we should be out on the shipping lanes, where the odds are much better for us."

"Does this admiral ever talk strategy or tactics with his skippers?"

"One-way transmissions, mostly. He's an admiral. Therefore he *has* to know more than any lowly commanders or lieutenant commanders."

"Even though he's never made a war patrol."

"Bite your tongue, insolent dog," Burlington said, with a grin. "But *I'm* betting you'll get a severe talking-to and one last chance to cleave to the gospel or be damned, sir."

Malachi sighed. "I'm not going to put my boat, my crew, and myself at risk by using a torpedo that doesn't work," he said. "It's a steam fish. It leaves a big wake, pointing right back at me. I'll take that chance as long as I think *we* have a chance to sink something, but not to protect the reputations of the graybeards at BuOrd."

"Well said, Matey," Burlington said. "Just don't say that to the admiral. Instead you say, aye, aye, sir, three bags full, sir, tug your forelock, and then do what you want once you get out to sea. That's what most of us have been doing."

"You fudge the logs?"

"No, we just don't log the settings. I use the phrase 'as per doctrine.' I've done some damage, so no one's asking."

"That's what it takes to keep command out here?"

"Listen, you keep bringing back lots of tonnage sunk, they're not going to fire you. Nimitz wouldn't allow it. Now, you go out there and get skunked? Poof, you're gone. I say, big deal. You and your crew will still be alive."

Malachi wondered if that was the four-devil mai tai talking, but then, looking at the rakish Reed Burlington, that might actually be good advice. "They serve decent food here?" he asked.

"Don't know," Burlington said, finishing his drink. "I don't come here to eat. I come here for this—he raised his glass and then pointed with his chin—and also that."

"That" turned out to be a half dozen pretty young ladies who had just come out onto the roof lounge in the company of three more sub skippers. Two of the girls waved happily at Burlington, who mouthed a silent "bye, now" to Malachi and hurried to join them at the bar. Malachi thought briefly about joining the party, but decided not to. They were all going to get seriously drunk, and that was something he simply could not do. He left the lounge and went down to the hotel dining room.

He was shown to a corner table in the dining room, which was surprisingly full. It was an international crowd, with Aussies, Brits,

Dutch, and Americans contributing to the accented babble. Australia had become the principal refuge for the surviving Allied forces that had managed to escape the clutches of Imperial Japan. In addition to the American submariners, there were elements of the British army and RAF who'd gotten out of Singapore and Burma just ahead of the Japanese army, as well as Dutch survivors of the doomed American-British-Dutch-Australia naval task force, cornered and destroyed in the Java Sea. The bulk of the Australian army was deployed abroad with the British overseas armies.

"Excuse me, sir," the waiter said. "May this young lady join you? I'm afraid we're out of tables."

Malachi looked up in surprise and then rose to his feet. He made to pull back a chair, but the waiter beat him to it. The young lady in question was one of the crowd that had shown up on the rooftop. She was older than the rest, a tall, slender brunette with dark, smiling eyes and an air of inherited grace. She sat down, thanked the waiter, and asked for a whiskey when he had a moment. Her voice was low, almost throaty, but her accent was more British than Australian. He thought she was quite good-looking, although she did have some dark semicircles under her eyes.

"I'm McKensie Richmond," she said, offering him a slim hand. "Call me Kensie."

"Malachi Stormes," Malachi said. "US Navy. Didn't I just see you upstairs?"

"You did indeed," she said. "Uncle Reed said you really didn't drink and that that was why you'd left instead of joining in. I decided I'd like to meet an American naval officer who wasn't a drunk."

"'Uncle' Reed?" he asked.

She smiled, and it softened her somewhat aloof expression. Up close he realized she was actually older than he was. "Don't ask," she said. "I'd rather not remember that party. At least, so my friends tell me."

Malachi grinned. "Well, we're not all habitual drunks. In fact, most of the skippers aren't career drunks at all. It's more the nature of our business, I think."

"And what is your business, Captain? It *is* Captain, yes? We've been told that the entire top of the hotel has been requisitioned for submarine captains."

Malachi nodded. "Are you sure you want to know?" he asked.

She blinked and then her chin came up. "Yes, please."

"Okay. We leave here and drive for a couple thousand miles up into Japanese occupied Oceania. We lurk for days in iron coffins in the depths of the sea, coming up to ambush Japanese ships and their crews by blasting holes in their ships, burning them in their own fuel oil, and then drowning them in the wreckage. Then *we* go back down to endure being bombed by enraged escorting destroyers for a few hours, desperately hoping we've selected the right depth, course, and speed to avoid having a five-hundred-pound depth-bomb open up our hull and send *us* down to die by being crushed to death when our submarine implodes at crush depth."

He paused for a moment. Her eyes were wide.

"You asked," he said.

"So I did," she replied.

"So, oblivion from a bottle after four or five weeks of *that* is not entirely unwarranted, I would think."

She was staring at him now, a hand at her mouth, as were the people at the next table who'd overheard what he'd been saying. "I am *so* sorry," she began. "I didn't mean—"

He waved her apology away. "It's I who should apologize for being so dramatic," he said. "You folks only see us when we come in to unwind. I fully understand how you'd get a bad impression. The truth is, we really appreciate your hospitality. We're basically all refugees at the moment, and we thank *God* for you Aussies."

The waiter brought her Scotch at that moment, and she looked at it as if not sure she should accept it. She looked over at Malachi, who was silently laughing at her. She grinned, relaxed, took the drink, gave him a *salud*, and made a substantial dent in it. The tension broken, they ordered.

"Are you married, Captain?" she asked.

"No," he said. "Are you?"

"Goodness, no," she said. Then she hung her head for a moment. "That was indiscreet of me, wasn't it," she said. "That's the one question no one's supposed to be asking here in Perth these days, or so I'm told."

"It's a reasonable question," he said. "I think most of those guys upstairs *are* married, but they're also human. They've been stuck in a submarine for weeks on end. To have a beautiful woman pay them the least bit of attention is probably the best tonic for recovering from what we have to do."

She cocked her head. "That's quite philosophical, Captain. We've all heard the stories about what London's been like since 'thirty-nine. The blitz, I mean. There's apparently a sense that if you can grab some human solace, grab it. The next raid might put you in the ground."

"Why, yes," he said, giving her a rogue's eye. "I absolutely agree."

She giggled. "You Americans," she said. "You just come out and say it. A generous breath of fresh air."

"I've been told by expert Lotharios that your young men would rather spend time with their mates in a pub than with women. The skipper who told me that concluded that observation with a heartfelt *deo gratias*."

She laughed out loud and then finished her Scotch. "None of us knows what's going to happen," she said. "If you'd said a year ago that the entire British army in Malaya would surrender to a Japanese army invading Singapore on bicycles, we'd have laughed you out of the pub. Now we put a brave face on it, but with most of *our* army overseas with the Brits, this country is terribly vulnerable. The fact that you Yanks are here is actually reassuring."

"We're here because MacArthur got his ass handed to him in the Philippines and we needed somewhere to hide."

"Is that how this awful business is going to end?"

"Oh, hell no," he said. "The Japs made the biggest strategic error in history by sneak-attacking Pearl Harbor. On December 6 America was a nation of isolationists. On December 8 we became a furious nation bent on revenge. We *will* pursue this, all the way back to Tokyo, and we won't stop until they are *crushed*. They got a taste of what's coming this summer at Midway. They lost four carriers. We lost one. They can replace maybe two of those over the next eighteen months, during which time the United States will commission ten. The Japanese have no concept of what's coming."

"How long?"

"It's going to take three, maybe even four years, in my opinion. The Japs are tough as nails, utterly ruthless, and filled to bursting with a warrior ethos from the tenth century. The concept of surrendering when faced with overwhelming odds is not in their makeup. Death in battle is the supreme achievement for an honorable Japanese man. We will win this in the end, but it's going to be the hardest thing America's ever done."

"And you lot down there in Fremantle Harbour—the submarines— are beginning to make that clear to them."

"I must admit that, right now, we're probably just annoying them, but not much more than that. The only comfort to us is that we submarine sailors are the only ones who *can* annoy them right now, except for some Marines on some island called Guadalcanal."

She regarded him with a calculating look. "That's what my father says," she said. "He's a student of history. He says the Americans begin every war on the back foot. Then they recover. Then they come on like the bloody apocalypse. Like the Romans at Carthage, whose orders were to leave no stone left upon another and the entire land covered in a layer of salt for all time."

"Carthage is called Tunis now," he said. "I've been there, to the site of Carthage. It's acres and acres of jumbled building stones, brown weeds, scrub grass, and nothing—*nothing*—grows there to this day. Ah . . . here's dinner."

Malachi had a fish while Kensie took on a large beefsteak and a glass of red wine with obvious relish. "This probably came from my family's cattle station."

"Your family are ranchers?"

"Among other things," she said. "Iron and coal mining, trucking, sheep, road and rail construction, and various real estate holdings."

"Sounds like a regular empire," he said. "How do you fit into the scheme of things?"

"My principal duty is as a marriage prospect—into the right family, of course, in pursuit of yet another industrial alliance. Think medieval times. In the meantime, I'm a general surgeon and, I suspect, a huge disappointment to my father's plans for me."

"A surgeon," he said, admiringly. "I'm impressed. Forgive my ignorance, but is there an aristocracy here in Australia like there is in England?"

She laughed. "*We* would never call it such," she said, sipping her wine. "But there are some important families, the descendants of what you Americans call robber barons. Remember, a lot of the people in this country are descended from men sent out from England as convicts. Some of them made good."

"One way or another."

"Absolutely," she replied. "Some of us try for a veneer of civilization here, but Australia truly is a wild place, full of dangerous animals, ancient aboriginal tribes, tough men and tougher women, and a low tolerance for the affectations of Old Europe. We find it exhilarating."

He laughed out loud, again startling the nearby diners. "Sounds like where I'm from—the state of Kentucky. It's deeply Southern and proud of its mountains, deep coal mines, bourbon whiskey, endless caves, racehorses, guns, moonshine, and grotesque poverty disguised as flinty self-reliance. A man *knows* where he stands in Kentucky, and if he forgets or oversteps, some geezer up on a ridge with a Civil War rifle will correct that."

She had her chin in one hand while she listened to him, her dark eyes roving over his rough, almost grim face, aggressive jaw, and a Semitic nose that was almost too big for his face. From a distance she would have thought him a brawler, but his vocabulary and intensity told her that this was man with some layers. And history, probably.

"I met a so-called American Southerner a few weeks back," she said. "His accent was rather thick. Yours is definitely not."

"I came from a family of coal miners," he said. "When I got to the naval academy they made fun of my Kentucky accent and rustic expressions. A widowed teacher in Annapolis took pity on me and ironed all that 'grits and mushmouth,' as she put it, right out of me."

A young man in hospital whites pressed through the dining room, saw Kensie and made a beeline for their table. She uttered a low groan when she saw him.

"Doctor Richmond, there's been a train derailment. *Passenger* train, full of soldiers. Dr. King needs all hands on deck."

"I've had a Scotch *and* a glass of wine, Bennie," she said. "I should *not* be operating."

The young man just stared at her, making it clear that, one, they were overwhelmed at the hospital right now and, two, a piddling amount of alcohol, by Aussie standards anyway, was no excuse for not coming along. Right now would be nice, indeed. She made a face and turned to Malachi. "To be continued, Captain, if it suits you."

"Yes, ma'am," he said, surprising himself. "Suits me just fine."

She gave him a wan smile, got up, and then hurried after the hospital orderly. She moved with some authority and the confidence of a surgeon through the crowded dining room. Malachi admired what he saw.

TEN

The following morning the admiral called a skippers' meeting aboard the tender. There were only five boats in port, all in various stages of maintenance and preparations for their next patrol. They met in the admiral's cabin around the traditional long green felt-covered table. Malachi was surprised to find an armed Marine guard posted outside in the passageway. The chief of staff was there, along with the squadron commander's operations officer. The squadron commander, Captain Lockwood, was on the other side of the continent for a conference with General MacArthur and his staff in Brisbane. Reed Burlingame was looking none the worse for wear, but that was not the case with Pogue White, who looked badly hung over. Malachi shook hands with the other three skippers and then they all took seats. A steward came around pouring coffee and then withdrew. The admiral made his entrance a moment later, and everyone stood up.

"Morning, gents," he said. "Please be seated. Everybody met Captain Stormes of *Firefish*?"

There were nods all around. The chief of staff did not nod, Malachi noticed.

"*Firefish* really rang the bell out there on her first patrol. Confirmed sinking of a heavy cruiser, three escorts, and a *maru*. This was all up in the northern reaches of the Georgia Straits above Guadalcanal. Admiral English told me Admiral Nimitz made the comment that this was the *only* piece of good news coming from the current Solomons campaign. Our losses in surface ships there have been catastrophic—Nimitz's word. Those losses have had some consequences in the command arrangements here in the Southwest Pacific operational area."

Everyone perked up. This sounded serious.

"Vice Admiral Halsey has relieved Admiral Ghormley in Nouméa as Commander Southwest Pacific."

There were some low whistles around the table. Bill Halsey was a whole different kettle of fish from the somewhat overwhelmed Ghormley and everyone out there knew it, even submariners who had never worked directly for him.

"We here in Australia still work for Admiral Carpender under MacArthur in what they're about to rename as the seventh fleet. But make no mistake: Halsey is going to go on a tear just as soon as he can, and apparently he's already badgering MacArthur for the use of some of the submarines based in Australia. So it's possible our operating areas may change, at least until MacArthur decides to go to New Guinea."

"As soon as it's safe, you mean," Reed Burlington commented. There were some sniggers around the table. MacArthur's escape from Corregidor was still controversial among the few survivors of the Philippines disaster, in which his army had been captured, his air forces caught parked on the ground, and Dugout Doug, as he was called, safe in Australia.

"That will be enough of that," the admiral said. "He is the theater commander, and I will not brook any insubordinate comments about a four-star general. Now, the situation on Guadalcanal is becoming somewhat desperate. The Japanese navy controls the night, roaring down from Rabaul, bombarding the airfield there with impunity, and tearing up every surface ship formation we send against them. By day the Marines at Henderson Field control the Guadalcanal area using carrier planes taken from the *Lexington*, which was sunk back in May by a Jap submarine. This has led to an interesting situation. But first, let me tell you about the coast watchers in the Solomons.

"The Aussies have organized a bunch of civilians—plantation owners who lived in the Solomons before the war—who are operating clandestine radio stations in the islands. They report when Jap fleet units come down the Straits of New Georgia in daylight, headed for Guadalcanal. This gives our Marines warning and allows our naval surface units to get ready. So here's the pattern: the Japs show up at midnight and raise hell, but then have to get out of range of the Marine air at Henderson *before* daylight. The cruiser *Firefish* got was a damaged straggler from one of the night fights around Savo Island.

"It's that back and forth pattern that I think has caught Halsey's attention. They're calling the nightly Jap striking formation The Tokyo Express. They're calling the Straits of New Georgia The Slot. It's the most direct deep-water route to Guadalcanal from Rabaul, six hundred miles away. But we don't want to be operating *too* close to Guadalcanal because there are too many of our own trigger-happy forces there."

Everyone nodded. Malachi was probably the only skipper there who had *not* been attacked by friendly air or ships, who saw any submarine as a threat.

One of the other skippers raised his hand. "We work for MacArthur, as I understand it. They've divvied up the Pacific into two theaters of operation, the central Pacific run by Nimitz, the western Pacific by MacArthur. Does Halsey work for MacArthur, too?"

"No, he doesn't. He works for Nimitz. But he's been ordered to 'cooperate' with MacArthur wherever possible, and vice versa. So it's possible some of our boats could end up in the Guadalcanal operation."

"I think there's a bigger problem," Burlington said. "Right now ComSubPac has all the central Pacific boats concentrating on Jap bases or Jap-controlled harbors. That gives all the advantages to the Japs. We ought to be out on their sea lines of communication, where it's just us against some escorts. Make your presence known around a Jap naval base and they can send out aircraft, patrol boats, fishing boats, destroyers, even armed *marus*."

"I'm aware of your thoughts on this matter," the admiral said frostily. "Unfortunately, none of the people running the show seem to agree. Now, moving on—torpedoes."

Every one of the skippers' faces settled into an impassive mask.

"I needn't remind you that there is a critical shortage of torpedoes," the admiral said. "Which is why I have basically rationed how many each boat can take out on patrol. BuOrd promises that more are coming, but they can't—or won't—say when. I guess what I'm telling you is this: don't just 'take a shot.' Shoot only when you have a solid solution and you're well within range. Otherwise, wait for another chance."

He looked around the table. "One of the ways you can maximize the effectiveness of your torpedo load is to employ the magnetic exploder. Three Mark fourteens hitting the side of a heavy cruiser will inflict great damage, but one Mark fourteen magnetic running under its keel will cripple it every time."

"*If* it explodes," Burlington offered. "Most of them don't."

The other skippers held their breath. Malachi, watching the admiral's face redden, decided to keep his trap shut and see where this was going.

"Commander Stormes: you've just turned in a spectacular patrol. I haven't had a chance to read your CO's log. How did you employ your torpedoes?"

If he followed Reed Burlington's advice, this is where he would say: I followed PacFleet doctrine, sir. But that would be a bold-faced lie. He saw Burlington looking at him, a definite warning in his eyes. Sorry, Reed, Malachi thought, I'm just not as smart as you are.

"I spent three years at the Navy torpedo station in Newport," he began. "I was intimately involved in the development of the Mark fourteen fish. As you may or may not know, each torpedo is handmade. Literally, handmade. Master machinists fit parts together by hand. Cut propeller gears on a lathe. Fit springs, wire connections, flask connections, shaft bearings by hand. Cast propellers individually. It's all done carefully and slowly, so besides the fact that we lost so many of our fish at Cavite, *that's* why there's a shortage.

"I used to ask why we were not mass-producing torpedoes at General Motors or somewhere like that. Every time I brought it up, some graybeard from the production shop would tell me that this was how it's always been done. Think about that, gentlemen. Think about what that really means."

The admiral interrupted. "Captain, I asked you—"

"Yes, sir, I know," Malachi said. "But here's the thing: because they are handmade, and handmade with enormous pride and professionalism, they aren't properly tested. Not *really* tested, in bad weather, against a maneuvering target, with a real warhead, on some kind of instrumented range. Instead each one was fired *once* out of the window at Newport, with a water tank in place of the warhead, dutifully recovered, cleaned up, tweaked and peaked, and then sent to the fleet. That's not testing."

The expression on the admiral's face clearly showed that he was losing patience, but Malachi plunged ahead.

"The lower tail stabilizers would come back in damaged—meaning they'd hit the bottom. We had limited depth in Narragansett Bay, so that meant that they were running deeper than set. I suspected the depth-sensing mechanism was defective, but no one wanted to hear that."

"I *knew* it," one skipper said. "God*dammit.*"

"The contact exploder mechanism has a problem," Malachi continued. "Often it would not make the critical connection between the torpedo's face-pin and the electrical igniter. The Mark fourteen didn't get a new contact exploder. They simply used the one for the Mark ten. *I* think the problem is caused because the Mark fourteen runs a whole lot faster than the Mark ten and the contact exploder mechanism simply cannot take the impact at the higher speed. One test shot went off course and hit a pylon on the range at an acute angle. That one worked. I suggested we strengthen the face-pin. Not invented there, so no, we won't do that."

By now the admiral was listening. Malachi took a deep breath. "There's a lot more," he said. "And I haven't even gotten to the magnetic exploder."

"Captain," the admiral said, softly. "Please answer my question."

"I set all my fish for contact only. I set all my fish for ten feet, with one exception. I set all my fish for high speed, and I try to fire every fish so that it doesn't have to make a turn upon launch. And finally, I try to make the line of attack slightly oblique to the target. I shot at what I thought was a Jap sub, but missed. One of the fish made a circular run, the other apparently just missed because it was a hip shot— in a hurry. Otherwise, we hit what we shot at, and we sank what we hit. I'm new to the PacFleet sub force, but I understand that that is not always the case."

"Goddamn fucking right it isn't," said the skipper who'd made the outburst about the depth problem.

The admiral sat there looking down the table at nothing for a long moment. "And the magnetic exploder," he said, finally, as if waiting for the rest of the bad news. Malachi obliged him.

"It's a great idea, in theory, and there's no doubt that a fish going off under the keel is worth three banging on the side, especially with an armored warship. The problem with the Mark fourteen magnetic exploder is that it's dependent on two things we can't control: the magnetic field generated by the physical steel mass of the target, and the magnetic field generated by the earth itself. One is much stronger than the other."

Two of the skippers snorted at that.

"The stronger field is generated by the ship, of course," he said, as he watched the two COs blink in surprise. "The magnetic exploder doesn't look for a magnetic field. It looks for a sudden surge of magnetism *over and above* the background magnetic field of the earth. Like when we load it into a torpedo tube, for instance, which is why it comes to the boat in deadhead mode. Once you shoot it, the guidance system comes on and counts the revolutions of the propeller until it reaches a number that guarantees it's clear of the boat. Otherwise . . ."

"We know all that," Burlington said. "So what's the prob?"

"The problem is that the earth's magnetic field varies all over the planet. Strong in some places, weak in others, *and* it's constantly changing. That's what the term 'variation' means when you're using a magnetic compass. So the basis for the guidance system's decision to fire the exploder is a constantly varying, *unknown* quantity. The British gave up on theirs precisely because of this problem. Not to mention that the Germans were working on one of their own and realized that one defense against a magnetic exploder was to reduce the magnetic signature of their ships by deperming them. Just like we've been doing to defeat Japanese magnetic mines."

"And yet some of the Mark fourteen exploders have worked," the admiral said.

"Yes, sir, and that's to be expected. You fire enough torpedoes, you will from time to time get enough of a magnetic anomaly from the target hull to make it work. As long as the depth sensor hasn't put the fish forty feet beneath the target's keel instead of ten."

"If *you* know all this shit, why hasn't BuOrd addressed these issues?" Burlington asked.

Malachi just smiled. "You ever dealt with the Bureau of Ordnance?" he asked. "Basically it's like this: if they want any shit out of you, they will squeeze your head."

"Enough of that," the admiral said. "I've told all of you before, I will not tolerate insubordinate talk like that."

Malachi said nothing.

"This meeting is adjourned," the admiral announced. "I have to think about all this. Commander Stormes, you have deliberately violated SubPac doctrine and my policy in your operations."

"Which bagged a heavy cruiser, three escorts, and a *maru*," Reed Burlington observed.

The admiral's face went red. The chief of staff, sensing an eruption, intervened by standing up, which meant that everyone else had to stand up because, obviously, the meeting was *over*. The admiral glared at everyone for a moment, then got up and went into his inner cabin without saying another word.

"Well that was interesting," the chief of staff said. "Oh, by the way, I happen to know that the rest of you have also disabled the magnetic exploder from 'time to time,' as Commander Stormes so quaintly puts it. Stay close to your boats today, gentlemen. I anticipate a follow-on meeting coming soon."

Down on the tender's quarterdeck the five skippers gathered for a moment before going to their separate submarines.

"Your ass is a grape," Jack Carney, skipper of *Grayback*, told Malachi.

"Not with that bag," Burlington said. "You may get some kind of reprimand, in which case they may banish you to some distant sub squadron in the wilds of Australia. Oh, wait—"

The other skippers laughed and everybody headed to work. Malachi felt better as he crossed the nest of submarines to get to *Firefish*.

He could have done what the other skippers had apparently been doing—telling the admiral that, yes, sir, we have absolutely been using the magnetic exploders, and then disabling them once they got to sea beyond prying eyes. Throughout his career, he'd made an effort not to play any games with the truth. He'd learned that the Brits were a lot more relaxed about doing things that worked even if the Admiralty was demanding something different. There was one common thread, however, between the Royal Navy and the US Navy: results always counted. What was it Nelson had said: "No captain can do very wrong if he places his ship alongside that of the enemy"? You would be forgiven many mistakes if you got results. Reed Burlington was probably right: they wouldn't fire him after a patrol like that. He hoped.

ELEVEN

In any event, nothing happened, because later that morning a message came out from Pearl Harbor announcing several flag officer reassignments. Their admiral was being moved to Brisbane, on the other side of the Australian continent, where the other half of the American submarine contingent in Australia was based. His replacement was to be Rear Admiral Hamner W. Marsten. At dinner that night in the hotel, Jack Carney asked Malachi if he knew the incoming boss.

"I do, in a roundabout way," Malachi said. "He's a gun clubber—spent a lot of time at BuOrd. For a while they were calling him the Navy's Mister Torpedo. He was the principal impetus behind our favorite but defective Mark fourteen torpedo."

"Oh, God," Jack asked.

"Yeah, well, we're not going to get any sympathy from him on whether or not we use the magnetic exploder."

"More important question—will he know you?"

"I don't think so. I was a relatively junior officer at Newport. None of my suggestions and technical observations ever made it to Washington. But I've got a bigger problem—I will *not* use that damned thing."

"Damn, Malachi—you just gonna tell them that?"

"No," Malachi said. "Once I get back to sea, I will have it removed from the torpedoes and then I'm going to try to figure out how to make it work."

Jack stared at him. "Are you shitting me?"

Malachi shrugged. "You have to be careful handling the actual firing pistol assembly, but otherwise, it's just a piece of equipment like anything else. It's factory calibrated for a so-called notional magnetic field that's supposedly good anywhere on earth. I think that's its main problem."

"You gonna ask your torpedomen to remove the exploder? At sea?"

"No, I'll do it myself. At depth, where it's nice and quiet and also stable."

"They're gonna shit little green apples," Jack said. "It's one thing to turn the switch to deactivate it. I would think it's a whole 'nother deal to remove the damned exploder itself."

Malachi smiled. "Yeah, you're right. But the tender's got a torpedo shop, and they do it all the time. I may pay those guys a visit and refresh my knowledge."

"Watch yourself," Jack said. "That tender is an ants nest of scuttlebutt. Word gets out that you're proposing to screw around with the actual exploders, the bosses will hear it in twenty minutes."

"Point taken," Malachi said. "You done? If so, let's go to the roof."

"Sure," Jack said. "But I heard you didn't drink."

"You heard right. One beer maybe. But *I* hear there're other attractions on the roof. From time to time."

Jack grinned. Malachi signed his bill and then they headed upstairs. Kensie was not there that night, so Malachi ordered his single beer and retreated to a table in the corner of the roof. Wiggling ladies and horndog skippers up at the bar were pretending to talk about the weather. Malachi considered joining them but he'd been just a little bit smitten by the statuesque doctor with her sly smile. He didn't want to have her show up later and find him on the dance floor with one of the slinky toys at the bar, so he decided to just relax and enjoy the show.

Summer was coming on in western Australia, and the sea breezes from the harbor were turning the rooftop lounge into a comfortable oasis. There were no vent fans, hydraulic lines, periscopes, or any other reminders of *Firefish*. He'd met skippers of surface ships who viewed their commands with some affection. He'd never met another submariner who felt that way about his boat. Surface ships had weather decks, crew's lounges, big wardrooms, awnings, baseball teams, and breathable air all the time. A submarine was more like a big torpedo with scant space for sixty or so men, a purely killing machine.

His first duty station after graduating from the academy in 1930 had been the battleship *New York*, a coal-burning, 27,000-ton steel monster sporting ten fourteen-inch guns, several smaller caliber guns, and two torpedo tubes. Ensign Stormes was assigned as the ship's torpedo officer, as befit the most junior officer in the wardroom. After the first eighteen months, he was getting tired of the excessively spit-and-polish atmosphere in the battleship squadron, where crews of a thousand men and eighty officers were not allowed above deck unless in a formal uniform, and the daily holystoning of teak veneered decks would have made Lord Nelson feel right at home. The only exception to the strict uniform policy had been on coaling days, when the entire crew turned to in order to get tons and tons of coal into the bunkers down below, one one-hundred-pound sack at a time. The evolution covered the entire ship in coal dust, which then meant that the rest of the week was spent hand-cleaning every square foot of the superstructure and weather decks.

One night he met up with one of his classmates who'd volunteered for the submarine force, who regaled him with tales of adventures at sea, both during training exercises and the ones caused by the boat itself, whose every dive could be classified as an adventure. At least you go to sea, Malachi had observed. The Depression was on, and the capital ships stayed in port for most of the year due to the limited Navy budget. The whole fleet sailed for the annual Fleet Battle Problem, but that was about it. His classmate took him aboard his submarine, which was vintage 1921, warning him that although it was relaxed in comparison with the big ships, it might be a bit claustrophobic. Malachi reminded him that he had been a coal miner once upon a time. Claustrophobia was not one of his problems.

His reminiscences were interrupted by a light haze of perfume and two of the young women who'd been at the bar earlier, demanding that he come join the party and dance with them. Hell with it, he thought. Why not?

The next two days were filled with a swirl of meetings, inspections, shore-patrol reports, the pile of administrative paperwork that had been waiting for them to come back in, and more meetings. By the second night Malachi was ready for his duty beer, dinner, and then a good night's sleep. At ten-thirty, he was awakened by a call from the rooftop lounge. There was a woman up there who wanted to talk to him. Oh, God, he thought: that's what I get for "joining the party" the other night. The girls were fun but everyone except him had gotten so drunk that it had become boring.

"What's her name?" he asked, turning on his bedside table light.

"Dr. Richmond," the bartender replied. "Oh, and she's on her way down to your room."

"*What?*" he asked, but the bartender had already hung up. A moment later there was a knock on the door. He grabbed a bathrobe and opened the door. Kensie stood there in her blood-spotted scrubs, her hair a bit askew, dark circles under her eyes, and a look of total exhaustion on her face.

"I am *so* sorry," she said. "But I desperately need a hot bath and a bed. My ride back to Melbourne House broke down three blocks away, and there are no rooms available here. I happen to know that all the rooms here have two beds, so I went to the bar up top and asked them if you were in. They said yes, so I asked them to call you. Now you please say yes."

"Of course," Malachi said, gesturing for her to come in. "You look like you got shot at and missed, shit at and hit."

"It's been a *horrible* forty-eight hours," she said, sitting down on his rumpled bed. "I just want to forget about everything and sleep for about ten hours. Do you have any whiskey?"

"No, but I'll bet I can get some. Bathroom's over there. The water is mostly hot. Get your bath going and I'll see what I can do about a drink."

"A bottle, not a drink, my dear captain," she said, smiling up at him with weary eyes. He smiled back at her, helped her up, and gently propelled her into the bathroom. Then he called the lounge and asked for a bottle of whiskey, two glasses, and a bucket of ice. He called the front desk and asked them to bring up some more towels and a bathrobe for her.

An hour later she was ensconced in the other bed, the covers pulled all the way up to her chin. She'd consumed the top third of a bottle of Scotch and was now holding the empty glass between her two hands. Malachi had told her to cover up earlier when he brought in the extra towels, the bathrobe, and a glass full of whiskey. She hadn't really bothered, and beneath a thin film of water and suds he was able to see her in all her glory. She grinned at him. "The least I can do, mate," she said.

He laughed out loud and then went out. She'd come out thirty minutes later in her bathrobe and climbed directly into the second bed.

"So what happened?" he asked.

She lay there with her eyes closed. "The *fucking* Japs torpedoed a passenger ship just outside of Darwin," she said. "She was inbound from the Indian Ocean with a load of wounded soldiers from the Burma campaign. Darwin's hospital was overwhelmed so they sent half the casualties to us. It's over a thousand miles by rail. Burn cases. Shark attacks. Blast injuries. I think we lost half of them."

"But not for lack of trying," he said.

She grunted. "Most of them were hopeless. Burns, then six hours in the sea before Darwin could get boats out there. Infections. Amputations to get ahead of infections. Then the train ride. Hopeless, most of them." Then she began to cry.

He got out of his bed dressed only in his skivvies. He sat down on the side of her bed and pulled her to him and let her cry it out. Then she fell asleep. He laid her back down and pulled up the covers. Then, on an impulse that surprised him, he kissed her forehead. Her eyes opened. "Hold me," she said. "Please."

When he awoke the next morning he heard her in the bathroom. He looked at his watch: 0630. He lay back under the covers. He'd climbed into bed with her and then wrapped her up in his arms, where she proceeded to weep for a while and then they both fell asleep. For once he slept like a log with no visitations from his nemesis, The Dream.

She popped out of the bathroom a few minutes later, dressed in her rumpled scrubs from the night before. She came over to their bed and sat down. "You've been *such* a love," she said. "Thank you *so* much."

He put on a hardcase face. "Okay, sister," he said. "But the next time I find you in my bed I *will* have my way with you."

She looked down at him with those glorious eyes, dark circles and all. "God, I hope so," she said, kissed him, and then left for work.

Five days later they went back out on patrol.

TWELVE

The COB whistled softly when Malachi finally exposed the Mark 14 magnetic influence exploder within the torpedo's guidance section. It was actually fairly comfortable in the forward torpedo room, with the boat at 250 feet and stable as a billiards table. Malachi and the COB were the only ones present and the forward torpedo room hatch was closed. The COB, being a torpedoman himself, had been highly impressed with the skipper's technical knowledge of the fish and its guidance system. Malachi had wanted to extract the entire exploder mechanism, but its 92-pound weight and position in the warhead base made that dangerous.

"I'm not sure I can modify this thing here at sea," Malachi said. "I think the problem is twofold: one, the reference magnetic field stored in this machine is wrong for this part of the world, and, two, if the torpedo itself is running too deep, it might not be able to detect a sufficient magnetic anomaly to make it fire."

"What's that thing?" the COB asked.

"That's a thyratron tube," Malachi said. "Basically, when the pickup coil senses a magnetic disturbance, it sends some current to this tube. The thyratron then amplifies that current and trips a solenoid, which in turn fires the pistol into the warhead. If the signal isn't strong enough, the thyratron doesn't do anything—you get a dud."

"Does it have a battery of its own?"

"Nope—it has its own baby generator, right down here. Runs off the counter propeller shaft, which is driven by the torpedo's propeller shaft. It counts four hundred eighty turns of the propeller, and only then starts up."

"How could we modify this?"

"The reference magnetic field is stored in this coil right here. It contains almost five hundred *thousand* copper strands. That's the sensing mechanism. This resistor sets the value the sensor has to overcome to activate the thyratron. Change the size of the resistor and it might work."

"Or," the COB said, "fix the depth-control mechanism. Then all this secret shit might work."

Malachi smiled. "That might be the best approach, but we don't know what's screwing up the depth-control mechanism—it's a pretty straightforward system. Simple hydrodynamics."

The COB moved back to the torpedo guidance section, whose maintenance panel allowed them into the guts of the torpedo. He pointed to the module that controlled depth. "That's the same one they had in the Mark ten," he said.

"Yes," Malachi said. "So?"

"The Mark ten ran at thirty-three knots. This beast runs at forty-six when you set high speed. Maybe that's what's fooling the depth sensor."

Malachi sat back on his heels. The chief might be on to something, he thought. The depth sensor was designed to measure water pressure. As the depth increased, the pressure increased. The sensor then manipulated the horizontal fins on the back end of the fish to keep it at the desired pressure, which translated to an actual ordered depth. Was the slipstream of a 46-knot fish fooling the sensor designed for a 33-knot fish?

"Maybe I've been doing this wrong," he mused. "Maybe we *should* use the magnetic feature, but order the torpedoes to run at ridiculous depths—five feet, or even three feet."

"They'll porpoise at that depth."

"If they're running at that depth," Malachi replied. "But if they're running ten to twelve feet deeper, they should be stable."

"Be worth a try, Skipper," the COB said. "If that's all it takes to make the damned thing work, it solves a whole bunch of problems."

"Well I know," Malachi said. "We'll be in our patrol area in three days. I need to think, and then set up a firing template for the TDC operator. Okay, have the guys routine this baby here since she's out and then put her back in."

Three days later they arrived in their assigned area, just west of the Sunda Strait, between the islands of Sumatra and Java, and nervous host to the infamous volcano, Krakatoa. The rusting bones of the American cruiser *Houston* were somewhere down in this strait, the fate of her crew unknown. They surfaced at nightfall to recharge the batteries and refresh the boat's atmosphere. The night was dark but clear enough for the lookouts to be able to see the hellish glow of Krakatoa's rebuilding crater off to the east. Malachi climbed to the navigation bridge for a cigarette and a cup of coffee.

"Look at that damned thing," he said to the OOD. "You know its history?"

"No, sir," the OOD, LTJG Joe Brooks, the main propulsion assistant, said. "I think I've heard the name."

"Well, in 1883 that was a whole lot bigger than that little crater is now. When it exploded, the resulting ash cloud caused the climate around the whole earth to change, so bad that 1884 was called the year with no summer. There was famine in parts of Europe because the harvest was stunted by lack of sunlight. Los Angeles got thirty-eight inches of rain in the year after the eruption, and the sound of the explosion was heard all the way down in Perth, which is almost two thousand miles away."

"Wow," the OOD said.

"Yeah," Malachi said. "And we think we're significant."

An hour later, the bitchbox lit up. "Bridge, Control: we have a radar contact, bearing zero eight zero true, twelve miles and closing. Coming out of the straits. There may be more than one, but the radar's having some trouble differentiating."

"Dive alarm, Captain?" Brooks asked.

"No. I want to try something different. Call the XO up here."

Marty arrived a minute later, a bit out of breath for having climbed from the control room all the way up to the navigation bridge. "Yes, sir?"

"We have one, maybe more contacts headed our way, coming out of the straits. I want to remain on the surface when we attack, so you go to the conning tower and set up the approach. I'm going to stay up here. If I can see them I'll send you bearings via the TBT. I want the torpedoes set for high speed, magnetic exploder on this time, in addition to contact, and a running depth of three feet."

"*Three* feet? They'll porpoise all over the place."

"I don't think so. Set battle stations torpedo now, and leave the lookouts up here with me. Alert maneuvering that we may need full diesel power, and tell the diving officer to be prepared for a crash dive. Tell the radar operator to keep feeding me ranges and bearings."

"Aye, aye, sir," Marty said, and dropped back down into the conning tower. The GQ alarm sounded ten seconds later. The four lookouts topside asked the OOD what they should do—go to their GQ stations or stay there.

"Stay put," Malachi said. "We're going to make this attack on the surface."

Malachi checked the dimly lit gyro repeater on the starboard side of the bridge to see the course being steered: 090. Then he went to the target-bearing transmitter (TBT) and swung it around to that true bearing. The target-bearing transmitters were high-power binoculars mounted above a servo motor. Whenever the operator pointed them at a ship, the bearing of that ship was transmitted to the TDC in the conning tower in place of a periscope observation.

He saw nothing but darkness, but that was to be expected with the ships being nearly twelve miles away.

"Lead target now bearing zero eight two, range twenty-one thousand yards. Two more behind him."

"Conn: aye," Malachi replied. "That's too fast for a *maru*."

"Yes, sir. Still computing course and speed, but XO recommends coming right to one eight zero for initial intercept course."

"Make it so; increase speed to fifteen knots."

Malachi was working the attack geometry problem in his head and knew he had to get south in order to get in front of whatever was coming. If he had been submerged his maximum speed would have been about 8 knots. On the surface and on the diesels, he had 22 knots available, and he was charging the batteries the whole while. As the boat turned he felt the first puff of a breeze as she came up to 15 knots. He could have put on more speed, but those superb Japanese optics might pick up the boat's wake, even in the darkness.

"Targets now bear zero eight seven, range eighteen thousand one hundred yards. Total now is four. We have a computed course of two five five and speed of twenty-five knots. Recommend coming to two three zero at current speed."

"Make it so," Malachi ordered.

This was the point where the admiral would have ordered him to submerge immediately and write the formation off as a too hard. That speed indicated cruisers or destroyers, or both, running fast and dark out into the Indian Ocean.

"Conn, XO: do you intend to submerge once we achieve an attack position?"

And there was the critical question, Malachi thought. Approaching a cruiser-destroyer formation on the surface was extremely dangerous. If any of them spotted him, they would open fire immediately and possibly even try to ram him. He had the advantage of darkness and radar, and also the ability to run off into the night at 22 knots while seeding his wake with torpedoes. "I haven't decided yet, XO."

"Sir, do you want the gun crew topside?"

"No, I don't. If we have to get under quickly they'd be lost."

"Aye, sir." The XO's voice betrayed his concern. An attack on a cruiser line while surfaced was unheard of. Merchant ships, maybe. But never warships.

Speed was the key, Malachi thought. Soon they would start a zig-zag plan, which meant that at any moment the entire formation could turn away by as much as thirty degrees and leave him in the dust. Or, they could turn *toward* him and run right into him. Fifty-fifty chance, he told himself. Not bad odds. But if they did turn in his direction, the closing speed would be 40 knots. Two miles, every three minutes.

"Conn, XO: the bearing drift has stopped. We are on a collision course with the formation. Course and speed confirmed. Two five five at twenty-five knots. Intercept in nineteen minutes."

"And no zigzag?"

"Not yet, sir."

"Okay, here's my plan: If they turn away we can't catch them. If they zig toward us, we'll be right in front of them. I want a five-torpedo spread, depth setting *three* feet, speed high, contact exploders, two-degree spread. Open outer doors, make ready tubes one through six when the range gets to five thousand yards."

"XO: aye."

"Lookouts," Malachi called. "Lay below."

There was a brief scramble and then he was alone on the bridge. He glued his eyes to the TBT optics and strained to see anything. He really wanted a cigarette but could not risk that red ember being detected. He thought that one of the lookouts, a petty officer, had been just a bit white-eyed as he came down from his perch and disappeared into the conning tower trunk.

"How many minutes to intercept?" Malachi asked.

"Thirteen minutes."

Screw it, he thought. He sat down on the steel deck grates of the bridge, his sea boots wedged against the steel windscreen and his back up against the periscope tower. Hidden behind the windscreen, he lit up a cigarette. As he exhaled that wonderful first drag, he saw the smoke whip down through the conning tower hatch. He grinned and looked at his radium dial watch. Twelve minutes to intercept; plenty of time for the smoke.

After he finished his cigarette, he rubbed it out on the deck grates and stood back up, his lungs comfortably poisoned. He went back to the TBT and scanned the night. Still nothing.

"Conn, XO: they *are* coming right. Column formation. I think they've started their zigzag plan. Looks like a destroyer out front, two heavies, and one tin can behind. Current bearing is steadying on— zero niner one."

"Work up a solution for a head-on shot. Change course as necessary and slow to five knots before firing. Commence firing torpedoes when the range is four thousand yards. Once all the fish are away, come to due north and increase to flank speed. If I can get a visual I'll send a TBT bearing."

The exec repeated back his instructions. Malachi reviewed the attack geometry. He'd be firing at a range of 2 miles with the targets coming at him at the relative speed of 40 knots. The lead destroyer would see the wakes coming in and sound the warning. Hopefully the two heavies would turn to avoid and thereby present their broadsides to the incoming torpedo swarm. Five fish would take fifty seconds to get out of their tubes. By then the range would be only 3,000 yards, close enough for the lead destroyer to see him and open fire with his deck guns.

So, get the fish away, make the turn, run at 22 knots away from whatever was happening to the formation, and then crash dive if any of the ships opened up with guns. He felt the boat make a slight course adjustment and begin to slow down.

"Five thousand yards. Solution obtained. Radar mast coming down. You coming down, Captain?"

"Not yet," he said. "I want to watch."

There was no reply to that. A few moments later he felt the first fish leave its tube. He took another look through the big TBT binocs, scanning the night dead ahead. Nothing. A second thump, then a third. The targets were closing at him at almost 45 miles an hour. He looked again and thought he saw white in the water—bow waves or torpedo wakes? There was no way to tell.

He looked again to see if he could make out the torpedo wakes, but he could not. Then the boat heeled over as the exec began the turn. He heard the diesels open up to full power and felt the breeze stiffen up. They'd come left, so he had to look back toward their port quarter. Still nothing. He switched off the TBT and moved closer to the hatch, still peering through the navigation bridge railing.

Suddenly a large red flare blossomed into the night, followed by an enormous explosion that turned night into day and squeezed his eardrums a few seconds later. Behind the towering column of fire he saw the upper works of a Jap heavy cruiser, and then that was obscured by a red-hued waterspout that rose up along her starboard side to twice the height of her pagoda mast structure, followed by a second one farther aft.

The targets were drawing aft rapidly. Whatever they'd hit at the head of the column continued to disintegrate in a series of what had to be magazine explosions. The lead cruiser was visibly slowing down with a cloud of reddish steam enveloping her amidships, and then he thought he could see the shape of a second cruiser materializing behind the one he'd hit, sheering out to port to avoid the one ahead.

There were no more explosions. Time to quit the stage. He hit the dive alarm. Then he stepped into the hatch, climbed down three rungs, and closed the hatch cover over his head as the boat took its first, almost tentative lean forward as it sought the safety of the depths. She was still going pretty fast. He hoped the diving officer was using minimal plane settings, or they'd fly their way down to the bottom.

As his boots dropped onto the conning tower deck plates, he ordered a depth of two hundred feet. The control room acknowledged the order and the boat tilted down some more. With the captain in the conning tower, Marty went below to supervise the dive.

"Two out of four," he announced. "Not bad. Tell forward torpedo to reload what they can."

They drove north at 200 feet for fifteen minutes, and then Malachi called for periscope depth. "I want the radar mast up first to see how close they are," he said. "Then I'll take a look."

Five minutes later the radar mast whined its way to the surface. "Mast height two feet," he ordered. It wouldn't have much range because the antenna was low, just barely above the surface, but it should be able to pick up cruiser-sized targets that shouldn't be that far away.

They had to wait a minute for the radar picture to appear on the scope. There were three contacts, one small, two larger. "Targets are one niner zero, range five thousand, five hundred yards."

"Come right with ten degrees of rudder to course one eight zero," Malachi ordered. "Track all three until we can ID the cripple. Cease radiating the radar but keep it up there."

Malachi turned to the XO, who'd come back up into the conning tower. "So here's what I saw: the lead destroyer ate one or more fish and disintegrated. That allowed me to see the lead cruiser, pretty much bows on. He got hit twice on the starboard side and started blowing steam through his stacks. The second cruiser apparently saw that and sheered out to port—definitely a heavy, Mogami class. I never saw the trailing destroyer."

He was interrupted by the bitchbox. "Conn, Control: forward torpedo reports one tube reloaded, working on a second."

"Conn: aye, hold up after the second fish goes in. Prepare both fish for *magnetic* exploder function only."

Malachi saw the surprise in Marty's face. "I want to try something," he said. "Set running depth for twenty feet, speed *slow*. If they run true and nothing happens, then I'll use the stern tubes and a contact setting." He turned to the radar operator. "Now, take two hot sweeps with the radar, and then you guys get me to a point where I'm fifteen hundred yards off the ship that hasn't moved."

The plotters and the radar operator jumped to their calculations while Malachi lit up a cigarette and waited for the radar operator. The XO oversaw the plotters as they did their maneuvering-board work.

"Captain, the picture has changed," the radar operator announced. "One large pip is stationary; a smaller one has moved about five hundred yards away on the other side of the stationary pip. The other heavy is six miles southwest and appears to be opening."

Malachi nodded. "Okay, that's good. They've left their remaining tin can with the cripple. Give me a course solution to put the cripple between me and that destroyer at fifteen hundred yards."

The XO indicated he wanted to talk in private, so they moved over to a corner of the conning tower. "If these fish are running ten, twelve feet deeper than set," Marty said, quietly, "isn't twenty feet pushing it?"

"She'll be down in the water after taking two torpedoes. Their heavy cruisers typically draw twenty-two feet. Probably almost thirty now with a belly full of seawater. I need these fish to pass underneath, but close. Sound will hear it if they physically hit her, but if it's close enough, there should be a magnetic transient big enough to fire the exploder despite the incorrect base field setting."

"Or we could set them both for contact and just sink the bastard," Marty pointed out.

Malachi hesitated. He knew Marty wasn't challenging him, just reminding him that they could claim coup by doing what they had been doing: turning the magnetics off.

"I need to know if it's the depth control problem or the magnetic field problem that's making these things useless," Malachi said. "Our fish are nowhere near as powerful as those of the Japs, so if we can make these bastards work, we'll be doing good work for Jesus. I want to see if running a couple of these things close underneath will make them go off. Remember, we still have four fish aft that can finish this."

"That tin can will see wakes and come after us," Marty said.

Malachi shrugged. "Then we'll kill him first, and *then* finish off the cripple."

They didn't actually have much privacy in the tight confines of the conning tower, and Malachi was aware that the officers were listening. He scanned their faces. At least some of them seemed frightened. Why was that, he wondered. He had a weapon of great stealth at his command. The crew of that Jap cruiser were knee-deep in damage control efforts, and that tin can was probably getting ready for a mass casualty situation after seeing their sister ship disintegrating in a tower of fire. As far as he could see, he was in charge here.

"Captain, recommend course two four zero to get to a point fifteen hundred yards from the target."

"Make it so," Malachi said, finishing his cigarette.

It took fifteen minutes to get into position at 5 knots submerged. Malachi was tempted to surface. It had been satisfying to be able to actually see what he had wrought in the Jap formation, but there was that lone destroyer, who could still come after them at 36 knots.

"Up scope," he ordered. "Radar take another couple of sweeps and give me an exact range and bearing."

He peered through the optics and saw precisely nothing. The night hadn't gotten any brighter, and he was three quarters of a mile away from a ship showing no lights whatsoever. Probably because they had lost their generators. "Down scope," he ordered.

"Range is sixteen hundred yards, bearing one five five, sir."

"Come left to course one five five," he ordered. "Make ready tubes one and two."

"Settings applied. Doors are open. Tubes one and two are ready."

"Fire one." Wait ten seconds. "Fire two."

"Sound reports hot straight and normal."

"Very well."

The invisible cruiser was helpless. They might not even see the wakes approaching them at that ordered depth, but even if they did . . .

"Twenty seconds," the TDC operator announced.

A heavy blast shook the conning tower, followed by a second one ten seconds later. Both explosions carried a little more authority since they were happening much deeper than the contact torpedoes.

"Up scope," Malachi ordered.

Now he could see her. She was broken in half, sagging badly amidships, with a large oil fire shooting straight out of her after stack. We need to put a camera on these scopes, he thought, as he watched. The forward half of the ship, top heavy with that pagoda mast, capsized and disappeared. The back half was standing up out of the water, preparing for the final plunge.

"Got her," he announced. "Down scope and radar mast. Come to course one five zero, make your depth two hundred feet. Speed eight knots."

"What are your intentions, Captain?" Marty asked.

"I want to pass ahead of the target, because I'm assuming the tin can will be coming around behind her at full bore to find us. Then I want to turn south and get out of here while he pounds the waters where we just were."

They could hear the breakup sounds as the two halves of the heavy cruiser subsided into the shocked sea. Then they heard another, more frightening sound: the *swish-swish-swish* of a destroyer's propellers moving at high speed. The tin can had *not* gone behind the cruiser: he'd come around the bow instead and was headed right for them, echo-ranging furiously.

"Oh, shit," Malachi said. "Hang on, boys; it's gonna get noisy."

THIRTEEN

Malachi, who'd been watching the depth gauge, ordered Control to flood negative to the mark and to rig for depth charges.

"Conn, Sound: I think he's on us—he's gone to short-range mode on his sonar."

Malachi stared at the depth gauge, mentally urging it down. One hundred thirty feet. The boat was beginning to accelerate down. He felt her sag as the negative tank filled and dragged her bow down. One fifty. He knew the Japs usually set their depth charges for 150. If they could get down to 250 it would be noisy but relatively safe.

The swishing noises were getting louder as the Doppler of the pinging, audible through the boat's skin now, increased steadily. One seventy-five. The boat was still pointed down at almost twenty degrees.

"Make your depth two five zero," he ordered, because there was no way they were going to level off at 200 feet. "Blow negative."

Control acknowledged and slowly, very slowly, the bow began to level up as the depth gauge spun past 200. He asked Sound if there was any bearing drift on the pinging.

"Slight right, Captain, but he's gonna be pretty—"

A sharp explosion shook the boat, followed rapidly by three more, and then three more after that. Bits of dust and loose insulation started a fine rain from the overhead and one of the men in the conning tower made a frightened noise.

"What's the bearing to the sinking point of that heavy?"

"Two niner zero, Captain."

"Come right to two niner zero, speed five, and rig for silent running."

The pinging was down-Doppler now as the destroyer rushed overhead, but Malachi knew he'd be turning around for another run. He intended to head for the mass of disturbed water where the cruiser had gone down, through which the destroyer would hesitate to run because of survivors in the water. He hoped.

"Damage report?" he said.

"Small leaks and weeps, but nothing serious," the XO called back from Control. "I'm shutting off ventilation for silent running."

Malachi had already noticed. Technically, they were in the Indian Ocean on this side of Sunda Straits and the water temperature, even at 250 feet, was nearly eighty-five degrees. The conning tower, stuffed with men and electronic equipment, was heating up fast as the vent fans went quiet throughout the boat. Malachi donned a sound-powered phone headset so as not to use the bitchbox.

"Distant echo ranging to the east of us, Captain," Sound called. "Search mode. He probably can't see through his own depth-charge disturbance."

"God willing," Malachi said. "Search the area ahead of us. Take two active pings every three minutes. We're going toward the point where that cruiser went down. I don't want to run into a hulk if she turned turtle."

With the boat quieted for silent running, the creaks and cracks from the hull at 250 feet were now audible. They all jumped when they heard a series of thumping explosions that were, happily, well away from *Firefish*. Malachi breathed a sigh of relief, and switched to the JA sound-powered phone circuit, where he called the XO in Control.

"That guy will search for a while," he said, "and then he'll go back to the sinking datum to look for survivors. If we hang around, say out at about five thousand yards and wait for him to stop, we can creep in and kill him, too."

More distant depth charges pounded the sea, no closer than the last series. Malachi waited for the exec to reply, but then realized

which circuit he was on. There were doubtless many ears breathlessly
waiting for the XO's reply.

"Come on up to the conning tower," he said. "Let's look at the
plot."

A relieved exec said, "Right away, sir." The depth charging was
growing fainter, so Malachi ordered secure from silent running. A
sweat-soaked XO climbed into the conning tower and told most of
the crew there to go down and get some coffee. The ventilation came
back on, granting instant relief.

"Whaddaya think?" Malachi asked.

"I think the Japs have several fleet units at Batavia, just on the other
side of the Strait. We hurt them bad tonight, and I think they'll be
out with destroyers and those big-ass float planes now that they know
we're here. I recommend we declare victory and head to the other end
of our op-area for a few days. It's early—we have several hours of
darkness left, so we can run on the surface."

"Where's your killer instinct, Marty?" Malachi asked. "We weren't
sent out here to run away."

"Yes, sir, but we can always come back. But if we're still loitering
here in the morning, we can only evade at about four, maybe five
knots. The battery is no longer full after some of these maneuvers
tonight. If they sent air and a six-pack of tin cans out here, that could
make for a damned long day."

Malachi knew Marty was right. What he was suggesting made
perfect sense: get out of there, get a whole night's cruising away from
whatever the Japs did in the way of a reaction, and then sneak back
into the Sunda Strait approaches in a few days. Or—

"Is the Sunda Strait mined?" he asked.

Marty's eyebrow rose at the thought of taking a submarine through
the Sunda Strait. "It's much too deep to mine on this end," he said.
"But on the other side the water gets really shallow—sixty feet in
some places. The charts date to the seventeen hundreds, and the east
end is notorious for sand bars and volcanic reefs."

"Nuts," Malachi said. "I was thinking of sneaking through and
getting outside Batavia Harbor, see what comes out."

Marty didn't say anything, obviously at a loss for words.

"*That* dumb an idea, XO?" Malachi asked, his eyes twinkling.

"Um."

"Okay, okay, we'll do it your way. Get us out to five miles from this area, then we'll surface and make our creep."

Later that night they got off their attack report, claiming one destroyer and one Mogami-class heavy cruiser sunk with visual confirmation of both sinkings. They reported that the other cruiser had headed southwest into the Indian Ocean by itself, and that they intended to return to the straits in two days. The next day they received a congratulatory message from the admiral in Perth and a new patrol area off the eastern end of Java. They were ordered to lurk for three days on the western, or Indian Ocean, side of the strait, and then to go through the strait to the Java Sea. Their objective was to pick off oil tankers headed for or leaving the petroleum refineries around Surabaya.

On the first day off Lombok, they were driven down by constant aircraft contacts, probably from the big Japanese base at Surabaya. Malachi spent several hours familiarizing himself with the hydrography of the Lombok Straits themselves. Unlike Sunda, Lombok was wide and deep except for where some underwater pinnacles threatened the channel here and there. At 1,200 feet deep, the shallowest parts were unlikely to be mined, so they could probably do the transit submerged if they wanted to, relying on the radar for navigation.

He now had to consider the matter of torpedoes. The boat could carry twenty-four; their "allowance" for this trip had been eighteen due to the shortages in Perth. They'd already expended seven getting the cruiser and its escort. Getting the two magnetics to work presented a tantalizing opportunity: with their five-hundred-pound warheads, it took at least two Mark 14s to sink a warship. But if you could get that same Mark 14 to go off beneath the keel, it only took one. Big if. The final shots at the cruiser had been against a sitting duck target where Malachi could control the attack geometry.

Then he had an idea. What if they surfaced close in to a convoy at night and used that five-inch deck gun, firing incendiary shells, against gasoline and oil-filled tankers. Setting the highly flammable cargo afire with a few well-aimed shells was as good as torpedoing the ship. They could probably knock off two ships before the escorts realized what was going on, and then they'd have to dive and use torpedoes. That was the one good feature of a convoy, Malachi thought. From a submarine's perspective it concentrated the targets. The fact that it also concentrated the escorts was just a hazard of the game. Intelligence had warned that tankers especially were all being convoyed, which meant several escort destroyers and frigates for any sizable group. They also reported that the bigger tankers were armed with deck guns.

At night they surfaced and patrolled a line across the most likely shipping lane coming out of Lombok. At 0230, radar picked up four radar contacts heading in their direction. The contacts were smallish but they appeared to be in a line-abreast formation. The plotters in the conning tower made their calculations and reported the contacts were indeed in formation, and headed due west at 15 knots. They were almost 18 miles away.

When Malachi was informed, he ordered the boat to dive and go deep—250 feet. He'd recognized that formation. The Germans had used something similar when they went hunting for a submarine. Put four destroyers in a line abreast at a distance of eighty percent of effective sonar range for the water conditions at hand. Then they would sweep an area in a three-mile-wide swath using active sonar with each pass. Fortunately there was a good nine-degree thermal at 180 feet, so they should be safe enough if they kept reasonably quiet. But it was a disturbing development—until he realized what it meant. They were sanitizing the area. Something big must be coming out. He summoned the exec to the conning tower as the boat leveled out at 250 feet. He explained what he thought the current contacts meant, and that he wanted to move into the mouth of Lombok Strait once the sweep had moved past.

"Will they come back to meet the convoy?" the exec asked.

"They might, but I expect they'll wait for the convoy to come to them and then head west, or maybe even south. Either way, I want to get into the convoy if we can before they join up."

"Aye, aye, sir," the exec said.

"One more thing, XO—get the gun crew ready to go topside, and tell them to break out incendiary ammunition."

The exec just stared at him. "You mean to *surface* inside the convoy?"

"Yup," Malachi said. "I figure a convoy coming out of Surabaya will be tankers full of oil and gasoline. I mean to surface and fire incendiaries into them. Setting them afire from end to end is as good as sinking them. Then we'll submerge and start using torpedoes while the escorts go nuts."

There was a moment of silence in the conning tower as the attack crew digested this news. Then they jumped to their preparations. Malachi went down one deck and then headed forward toward the wardroom for a quick coffee and something to eat. They wouldn't go to battle stations until the destroyer sweep got much closer. As he approached the wardroom he heard Peter Caldwell, the ops officer exclaim: "Are you *shitting* me? *Surface* in a convoy?" One of the senior enginemen was passing Malachi in the passageway. When he heard the outburst in the wardroom he glanced at Malachi and grinned. Malachi drew the curtain aside and stepped into the tiny wardroom. Lieutenant Caldwell was on the sound-powered phone and went wide-eyed as he realized the captain *had* to have overheard him. He hung up the phone and then just stood there as if unsure of what to do or say.

Malachi let him suffer for a minute as he stepped by him and got some coffee. Then he sat down at the head of the table and pointed Caldwell into one of the side chairs.

"You have a problem with my tactical decisions, Mr. Caldwell?" he asked.

"No, sir, absolutely not," Caldwell said. "It's just . . . it's just . . ."

"Just what, exactly?"

"Sir, this is my first war-patrol boat, and Cap'n Russell told us our first priority was to keep the boat safe. That we were the only US forces out here who could do something to the Japs. So we did everything submerged, and if there were *four* escorts? We'd usually take a pass."

"And how many ships did you bag in those two patrols, Lieutenant?"

"Uh, damage to one, sir. The torpedoes just didn't seem to work."

Malachi gave him his best stone face and spoke through clenched teeth. "As I thought I'd made clear, our purpose out here is *not* to keep the boat safe. Our purpose out here is to destroy Japanese warships and the *maru*'s that keep their warships and their armies going. The Japanese have been butchering entire populations ever since they went into China, and that was eleven years ago. It's time somebody started butchering them, and that somebody is this boat, for one. My predecessor accomplished *nothing* in two patrols. So far I have sunk two heavy cruisers, four escorts, and one large freighter in one and a half patrols. That's almost forty thousand tons gone forever, along with a few thousand sailors. *That's* what we're out here to do, Mister, and if you're not man enough, feel free to let me know. But understand this: if you want off I'll put your ass ashore on Java, not Perth. Now go away before I lose my temper."

Caldwell was white-faced by this point. Malachi thought there might have been people out in the passageway eavesdropping. Not necessarily a bad thing, he mused.

The destroyer sweep passed overhead about an hour later without incident. *Firefish* headed inshore behind them toward the entrance to the Lombok Strait. They only had a few hours before dawn, so he wanted to close the convoy. If there was a convoy; those tin cans might just have been hunting. He ordered periscope depth as the sound of the sweep's pinging died away to the west.

"Put the radar mast up. Get a fix, and see if there's anything out there."

The navigator was summoned to the radar console, where he wrote down bearings and ranges to the landmasses surrounding the entrance to Lombok. Then the radar operator opened up the display to a greater range. "Christmas," he said softly. "Many, many contacts up in the strait. Range, eleven thousand yards to the lead ship."

"All *right*," Malachi said. "Start a plot on the lead ship. Are they in formation?"

"No, sir," the radar operator said. "A loose gaggle. Maybe twelve, or more. The pips are overlapping. Eight miles."

"Okay, troops," Malachi said. "I'm guessing there'll be a couple of escorts in that gaggle. Probably one ahead and one tail-end Charlie. I want to position the boat to the northern side of that crowd of ships. I intend to surface close to the convoy, get the gun set up, and start shooting into tankers. When I say close, I mean close: five hundred to a thousand yards. Point blank. I need hits immediately. We'll only have a few minutes before both escorts come after us, at which time we'll dive and drive *under* the convoy to the other side. Or, I might choose to stay on the surface and run through the convoy, shooting as we go. Get the plot going."

It took them thirty minutes of several quick radar observations, careful plotting on the dead-reckoning tracer table, and then repositioning of the boat to end up on the northern side of the crowd but still close in. Malachi told the torpedo officer, LTJG Sullivan, he wanted the 20mm antiaircraft gun also manned, with orders to shoot into the pilothouses of any ship within range.

Finally he put the periscope up to take a look. The night was dark but clear. Christmas indeed, he thought. There were over a dozen ships out there, not yet in any identifiable formation, but steaming west at about 12 knots. He could not identify any escorts, but he had to assume there were some. And there were three big tankers right in front of him. Filled with aviation gasoline, he prayed.

He could just start shooting torpedoes at them, but he wanted to try this gunnery gambit. Surface, start shooting immediately, set them on fire, then run into the convoy, shooting as they went. If one of the escorts showed up, they could crash dive and then run under the convoy, where the escort's sonar would be overwhelmed by all the propeller noises.

"Match our course with the convoy's course," he ordered, bringing down the scope. "Then let's get closer—we're still out at fifteen hundred yards or so. Get the gun crews ready. XO, make sure the chief understands: load and start shooting the moment they get up there. Aim into the hulls. As soon as they get a decent fire started, pick another target. We'll only have about two, maybe three minutes before we have to escape."

They made two more radar observations, trying to identify escorts, but it was still just a crowd of ships, chugging along while trying to keep from colliding. The second observation showed that they were starting to fall behind the convoy, but they were in to 700 yards.

"Battle surface—guns!" Malachi ordered, and headed for the conning tower hatch. The sub came up in good order. Malachi opened the conning tower hatch and climbed out onto the navigation bridge as the diesels lit off in a cloud of smoke aft. He saw the forward torpedo-loading hatch pop up and the gun crew coming up, each man cradling a five-inch fixed shell in his arms. After them came the 20mm gun team, each one of them carrying two ten-round magazine boxes. They ran to the ladders along the sail and climbed like a troop of monkeys to the cigarette deck, where the single-barreled 20mm gun was still shedding water. He looked back at the nearest tanker, which remained dark and unaware.

He was startled by the first shot from the five-inch, a heavy bark of ear-squeezing power from the short-barreled naval rifle. The shell apparently went over. Buck fever, Malachi thought; steady up and *aim* the damned thing! The next round hit the tanker low on the hull and a second later, it was no longer a clear *dark* night.

"Shift targets!" Malachi yelled as the tanker blew up amidships, throwing up a white-hot fireball of exploding gasoline a couple of hundred feet into the air. The gun crew swiveled the blunt barrel of the five-inch aft and opened fire on another tanker. The first round hit the water without exploding. The second hit the side of the tanker, also without exploding. The third drilled into pay dirt and the second target also blew up, this time with a red-orange blast of exploding fuel oil. Malachi was dimly aware of the 20mm gun behind him banging away, sending red tracers across the water at the third tanker within range, hitting the water, then the hull, and then the bridge at the back of the ship, sending red fragments ricocheting into the night air.

As the five-inch gun crew trained aft to take on the third tanker, Malachi searched the surrounding area, looking for the telltale shape of a destroyer coming with what was called "a bone in her teeth"— the huge white bow wave created by a tin can going 30 plus knots, bent on vengeance. He had no problem seeing: the first target continued to burn with the intensity of a blast furnace, clearly lighting up the whole convoy. There was a satisfying orange fireball erupting from the third tanker, followed by a much bigger explosion.

Then he saw it: the thin but deadly shape of a destroyer coming up the side of the convoy behind them. As he stared at it he saw gun flashes and then heard the ripping sound of shells going over, but not by much.

He yelled at the five-inch gun crew to get below, and then turned around to tell the 20mm crew the same thing, but they couldn't hear with all their gun noise. He picked up a set of binoculars and threw it at the gun captain, who turned to look at him in astonishment. Malachi gestured down vigorously with his index finger. The gun captain understood at once. He smacked the other gun-crew members with his hands and they all bailed out, scrambling down the sail ladders to the main deck hatch. Then he hit the dive alarm, after checking to see that the five-inch crew was clear of the main deck and the forward hatch was closed. More shells came slashing overhead, closer this time. He dived for the conning tower hatch and dropped through, slamming and dogging it behind him.

He slid down the ladder, landing on the steel deck plates with a bang and ordered a hard left rudder and full electric power. The boat was already slanting down and then she tilted dangerously to starboard as that rudder order took effect.

"Make your depth one hundred fifty feet and come to one eight zero," he ordered. That would take them under the convoy at right angles to the convoy's course. They could clearly hear more rumbling explosions as the three hapless oil tankers burned to death above them. Ninety seconds later came the depth charges, happily behind them as they slid underneath the chaos above.

"Shouldn't we get deeper?" the exec asked, looking nervously at the depth gauge—150 feet was within direct range of Jap depth bombs.

"I need to be above that layer so we can hear," Malachi replied. "I'm betting that four-pack split up when they came running—two to each side. I want to be able to hear if there're two escorts on the other side of this gaggle."

Above them the dozen or so *marus* chugged ahead, minus the three seared hulks behind them. A merchant ship's propeller sounds were different from a destroyer's—a regular, dull thumping noise from their single, low-speed screws. *Firefish* drove under the crowd at almost 8 knots, draining the battery rapidly. Finally they were clear and Malachi ordered the boat to slow down to 5 knots.

"Sound: anything?" he asked.

"No, sir. Merchie noise is drifting west and diminishing."

Malachi wanted to get up to periscope depth but he controlled that urge. "We'll keep going south for another twenty, thirty minutes. If no escorts show up, we'll take a radar look, then surface and run to get ahead of the rest of the convoy. We have an eight-knot advantage in speed on the surface."

"We'll be running right toward that division of destroyers," the exec pointed out.

"I don't think so, XO," Malachi said. "I think they were closer than we thought and came running when those tankers went up, and now they'll be trying to wrangle this group into some kind of formation so they can take stations and protect them."

He slipped down to the wardroom for a sandwich and some coffee. He was pleased with what they'd done. Three good-sized tankers destroyed—with no torpedo expenditure. If they didn't sink by themselves the Jap destroyers would put them down like sick cattle. The next big decision would be whether to attack the convoy on the surface or submerged. He looked at his watch. Ninety minutes to nautical twilight, when it would be too dangerous to be on the surface, especially if those tin cans had summoned supporting air. The other consideration was the battery: they could stuff some amps in the can when they made their run to get ahead, but would that be enough to get them through the daylight hours? The wardroom sound-powered phone chirped.

"Captain."

"Captain, Sound reports we have what sounds like two destroyers echo-ranging to the east of us. Recommend we keep going south and get deeper."

"Concur; make your depth two hundred feet, or whatever it takes to get below that layer. And slow to three knots."

The exec acknowledged. Malachi lit up a cigarette and sat back on his stool. If there were two destroyers out looking for them, he might not get to attack the convoy again. So be it—he'd taken down three tankers. Once the Japs went past in their search, he'd surface and concentrate on replenishing the battery. They'd get a contact report off just before sunrise on the convoy. Maybe there were other boats on their route. He yawned. The COB knocked on the wardroom bulkhead and stepped in.

"Sandwiches and coffee over there," Malachi said.

"Chiefs have their own supply, but thank you, sir. Need a word."

"Shoot."

The chief sat down in one of the wardroom chairs. He stared down at the table for a moment, choosing his words. "Sir, the crew's getting scared."

"Of what?"

"You, sir," the COB said.

FOURTEEN

"Okay," Malachi said. "I'm all ears."

"Part of the problem is the way we operated under Captain Russell. His whole emphasis was on keeping the boat safe. Attack if we could, but no unnecessary chances. He said things like he was 'husbanding' our resources. We were short on torpedoes, and the ones we were shooting often didn't work, but they always left a wake. And after Pearl Harbor, the only thing America had to throw at the Japs were the boats, so we had to preserve them."

"Go on."

"May I speak freely, Captain?"

"You're the COB."

"Thank you, sir. This thing tonight: surfacing and shooting up tankers with the guns, with four destroyers somewhere nearby. That's unheard of."

"Getting three tankers in one attack is unheard of, too, or so I'm told. You talk to the gun crew?"

"Oh, yes, sir."

"What'd they say?"

"They were scared shitless. On the other hand, now they're pretty proud—three of those tankers went to see the baby Jesus because of them. Then that destroyer started flinging rounds at us and we had to crash dive. They weren't sure they'd get back inside before the boat submerged. The last guy through the hatch was soaking wet by the time he got it closed. And the twenty-millimeter crew said you threw a set of binocs at them to get them inside."

"I assume they were grateful," Malachi said.

The COB laughed and shook his head. "Yes, sir, I'm sure they were. Then they started thinking about how close they came to being left topside during a crash dive. With a Jap destroyer coming in, offering a five-inch handshake. One youngster got so shook up he cried for an hour afterward."

Malachi nodded but did not say anything. The COB got up, fetched a cup of coffee for himself, refilled Malachi's cup, and then sat back down. "May I ask where you're from, Captain?"

"Floyd County, Kentucky. My father was a hard-rock coal miner. So was I, for a while."

"I've heard that's a tough business."

"It is."

"Often wondered why people do it."

"Because they have to, for the most part. No other kind of work in that part of the state. If you're born into that world your options are pretty limited. I first went underground at thirteen."

"*Thirteen?* That was legal?"

"The company usually doesn't ask if you look big and strong enough to do the job, or if your old man's a miner, as mine was."

"How'd you get out?"

Malachi grunted. "A sympathetic judge offered me a choice," he replied. "Prison or the armed forces."

The COB's eyebrows went up. Malachi could see that the chief really wanted to ask, but was too smart for that.

"Anyway," he continued, "I tried for the Army but they had demobilized after World War One, so I signed up in the Navy, became a torpedoman striker, then got selected a year later for the academy prep school. Graduated in nineteen thirty. Went into submarines after a few years on a battleship, and then spent three and a half years at the Newport Torpedo Station after my first boat. That's where I met the Mark fourteen."

The COB nodded, now understanding Malachi's knowledge of the troubled torpedo. "Back to the crew, Captain. *I* understand why we're really out here. I get it that we'll have to take chances if we're gonna get Jap ships. I guess what I'm trying to say is that you might want to talk to the officers and the rest of us along those lines."

"I explained this to the wardroom when I came aboard. I explained it earlier this evening to Mr. Caldwell. I would have assumed the word would be out by now."

"Well, yes and no, sir. After the first patrol, people sorta pulled into their shells. They're afraid of screwing up, and maybe they're finally figuring out what real submarine warfare's all about. They go into a bar in Perth, yeah, they're proud of getting Jap cruisers, but when someone asks about you, they say they don't really know you, other than that nothing scares you. You've got a name, by the way."

"Do I, now."

"Yes, sir. They call you The Iceman."

Malachi grinned. The Iceman, indeed.

"Guys in the conning tower said you sat down and had a ciggy-weed while we waited for the Jap cruiser formation to get closer. Coming in at pretty high speed, too. Said the XO was almost bat-shit when you finally called the dive."

Malachi shrugged. The Iceman. He liked it. "Well, COB, if it's any comfort, I don't have a death wish, and I'm not deliberately trying to do stupid stuff to show off or make a rep. But I am deadly serious about killing Japs and their ships. Emphasis on that word 'deadly.' That's not gonna change."

"Yes, sir, I understand, and I apologize if I've stepped over the line."

"Not at all, COB. It's your primary duty. Chief of the boat. You are closer to me in age and professional experience than any of my officers, so I want it straight every time, and my door's open to you anytime. Or my curtain, I guess."

They both smiled. "I appreciate that, Cap'n," the COB said. "I'll do what I can to make everybody understand what we're out here for."

"And I'll think about ways I can do the same, although I'm not ex-actly a chatterbox. But I'll try."

The COB got up to leave. "You know what did it, before this deal tonight?"

"Nope."

"The smell of cigarette smoke coming down the conning tower trunk when we were headed in for an attack. Everybody's grommet straining to the max and the skipper's up there, taking time out for a smoke. Thanks for listening, sir."

Malachi nodded and then called the conning tower to see where they were in relation to the convoy. The exec said he'd be right down.

Malachi poured out the remains of his coffee and lit up another cigarette. Gotta stop these one day, he thought. He remembered his father telling him that the only good thing about lung cancer was that it killed you much quicker than black lung did.

His father. George Mallory Stormes. Big man . . . really big man. Big drunk, too. Whenever he was part of a face crew, it was understood by the crew that Big George was in charge. Malachi closed his eyes for a moment, looking for the image of that bloody sixteen-pound hammer.

The exec came into the wardroom and plopped down into a chair. "You look beat, there, XO," Malachi said.

The exec nodded. "I am. Gotta learn to pace myself better."

"So where are we?"

"The convoy's well astern. We can't hear anything back there. Nobody's headed our way actively pinging. I think we're clear."

"Okay, come to periscope depth, but linger for five minutes at one fifty. Let Sound do a passive search above that layer. If it's quiet, I want to get a radar sweep, and then surface if we can. Turn back northwest, run at twelve knots so we don't make much wake, recharge as much as we can, and go back down when it's full daylight and hopefully before the Kawanishi flying boats come out."

"So we're *not* going to pursue the convoy, then?"

"No, I've decided that we'll go through the Straits as we've been ordered and take up a patrol area in the Java Sea. I need to study the charts some more, but I'm thinking north*east* of Surabaya. See if we can catch some Singapore-bound traffic. In the meantime, we'll go back down tonight and begin creeping back toward the Straits. Let everyone get some sack time, especially if they're as tired as you look to be."

"Aye, aye, sir," the exec said.

"One more thing, XO."

"Yes, sir?"

"The COB came to see me. Says the crew's getting scared. I need you to think of a way I can help deal with that. I'm not gonna change the way we operate. If anything, we're going to explore some even more unusual tactics. But I need the crew to understand that some of this wild shit is not just me. It's what the war requires if we're going to beat these bastards all the way back to Japan, and then burn them alive in their little paper houses. They also need to understand that it's going to take three, maybe four years to do it. The more ships we sink, the quicker this horror will be over, understand?"

The exec nodded his head. "It should have been me telling you that," he said. "That people are getting scared."

"You'd have a career to lose if I turned on you for saying that, which I would never do, by the way. The COB doesn't. Truth is, I need the both of you to talk to me about the people side of things. It's not in my nature to care, and that's *my* deficiency. There's history behind that which I can't share with any of you. So, go see if we can come back up and get some air in the boat and some amps in the can."

They surfaced thirty minutes later, after a careful air and surface search radar sweep. They had maybe an hour of darkness left. After that, the Japs would probably dispatch some Kawanishi flying boats out to the area to see if they could find and kill the submarine who'd hurt them badly last night. The ops officer got off an attack report to Perth, claiming the three tankers and setting out their intentions to move into the Java Sea. The boat filled with the smell of frying chicken as the cooks took the opportunity to cook while the boat was on the surface and able to vent the fumes. At dawn nautical twilight they went back down and continued their creep toward the entrance to the Lombok Strait.

Malachi met with the navigator and the operations officer once they were safely down and out of reach of the deadly flying boats. They studied the charts for Lombok and the areas around Surabaya. Malachi decided to go through the Straits submerged, using the surface search radar to navigate. He had a suspicion that the Japs would have patrol boats out after the attacks of the previous night. The Straits transit would take three hours at 8 knots, after which they'd surface on the other side to recharge until daylight drove them back down. Surabaya was an important Japanese base now because of the captured Dutch oil refineries, so he expected that there would be air assets and ships sanitizing the local operating areas.

The transit took longer than expected due to the strong current running through the Straits. They got only two and a half hours of recharging time on the other side before an air search radar contact drove them down. There was a sharp seven-degree layer at 140 feet, so they leveled off at 170 for the day, relatively safe from prying sonars. There'd been no reaction from Perth to their attack summary, but that wasn't unusual, given the scope of message traffic moving over the fleet broadcast system. Malachi directed the navigator to position the boat at the top of the channel between east Java and the island of Madura, through which any traffic for Singapore and points north would move. He didn't intend to go into that channel because he feared mines.

They surfaced after nightfall twelve miles northeast of the port of Surabaya. The battery was down to thirty percent after the hard push through Lombok, so the first order of business was to get back to a full charge. A few quick radar sweeps showed nothing within twelve miles of the boat, so Malachi had the navigator put them on the great circle track from Surabaya to Singapore. They would creep along that track, going back and forth so as to not get too far away from the Japanese base.

The fleet broadcast had a message from ComSubPac himself, congratulating them on their destruction of three tankers using the five-inch gun. One hour later another message came in from Perth, congratulating them on sinking three tankers but ordering them not to do that again. Malachi thought about framing the two messages side by side in the wardroom. Put them up on the mess decks so the crew could see what he had to deal with. Then he had an idea. He called for the ops officer.

"I want to build a read-board from the fleet broadcast," he told Lieutenant Caldwell. "Nothing that's super-secret, but war news. Jap ships reported sunk, but American losses, too. Anything on the war on the other side—in Europe. I want that put on the mess decks so anyone can read it."

"That'll make for pretty dismal reading right now, Captain," Caldwell said. "Between the Nazi U-boats and the Jap armies, things aren't going very well for the good guys."

"So be it," Malachi said. "I want people to understand what we're up against and how important it is that we take chances out here."

"Aye, aye, sir. Should I run it through the exec before posting it?"

"Yes, and make a copy for the wardroom if you can, too."

"Uh, sir, there's no way to make a copy of the broadcast. One of the radiomen would have to type the whole thing."

"Okay, then put it together, leave it in the wardroom for a day, and then post it on the mess decks. Put up a new one every three days if we receive enough interesting dope."

They stayed on the surface all night and encountered absolutely nothing. At dawn they went back down with a full battery and nothing to do. This pattern continued for the next two nights. No contacts, not even local fishermen. It was as if the Japs knew they were out there and were using a different route, the one from the Lombok Straits, to get in and out of Surabaya. Malachi toyed with the idea of going back into the Straits to see, but his orders were to patrol in the Java Sea, and that's what they were going to do.

The chief engineer reported that they had another ten days' worth of fuel, after which they needed to go back to Perth. The supply officer came up with the same estimate of stay time at sea. Malachi got the impression they were lobbying for a return to Perth. They'd bagged a cruiser, a destroyer, and three tankers, which was a spectacular patrol by Perth standards. Malachi simply nodded, noting that they still had some torpedoes left.

As dawn crept in on the third night on station, they took radar bearings on known land points to get a solid navigation fix just before submerging for the day. The protective layer had dissipated by now, so he ordered the boat down to 250 feet. One hour after they submerged, Sound reported echo ranging approaching from the direction of the Surabaya base.

"Multiple sonars in wide search mode," Sound reported. "Steady bearing, increasing Doppler."

Malachi went to the conning tower, where the attack team had already assembled. They had begun a plot on the approaching destroyers. Since all they had were passive bearings, the plot did not display a range to the incoming ships, only a wide cone of where they might be.

"It's almost like they know where we are," Malachi observed. He ordered the boat onto a course that would get them away from their last position on the surface but which would not present a full beam aspect to all those probing sound waves.

For the next ten minutes the pinging noises grew in amplitude, but then the bearing began to drift behind them. Malachi ordered the boat rigged for depth-charging and silent running, with the exception of ventilation. He slowed to 4 knots.

"Conn, Sound: I can't figure out what they're doing. They've slowed way down, and only one is pinging."

Malachi looked at the plot, which showed the fan of bearing lines pointing back toward Surabaya. With only one tin can pinging, they no longer had bearing information on the other three. Malachi ordered the bitchbox turned off and all comms to be done on sound-powered phones.

He called Sound. "Were all those sonars on the same frequency?" he asked.

"Pretty much, Captain. They may have shut down because they were interfering with each other."

Or, Malachi thought, they left one guy pinging and the other three listening for any returns on that same frequency. If so, this was a professional antisubmarine division. "Make your depth three hundred feet," he ordered.

"Conn, Sound: high-speed screwbeats approaching from zero one zero, up-Doppler, and I think I hear depth charges going in."

Before Malachi could answer the explosions began, punishing blasts that shook the entire boat and made people grab for a handhold. The blasts were above them and off to port, but books and charts flew off their tables.

"Passing two seventy feet," the OOD reported, as more thunderclaps erupted in the sea, still above them. Since the war had begun, the Japanese always set their charges for 150 feet. That certainly wasn't the case now.

"Conn, Sound: *new* screwbeats, bearing zero nine five, *up*-Doppler, steady bearing."

Time to turn, Malachi thought. "Come left with standard rudder," he ordered.

"Course, sir?"

"Just keep that rudder on for now."

"Passing three hundred, leveling off," the diving officer reported. "Permission to pump negative."

"Do not pump anything," Malachi ordered, glancing at the depth gauge—310. "Too much noise. Use your planes to get back to ordered depth. Helmsman, shift your rudder to right standard."

Another pattern of depth charges began going off, a little less powerful this time as the additional fifty feet dissipated some of their explosive energy, but still terrifying with their noise and lethal shock waves.

"Conn, Sound: number three is coming in now. They're definitely on us."

"No shit," Malachi muttered. Four destroyers, probably running a thousand-yard trapping circle, with one escort at a time turning into the circle to lay down a pattern on the hapless sub. "Shift your rudder," he ordered again.

He looked around at the white faces in the control room. So far the Japs were setting their charges for about 200 feet. Lots of noise and shock waves, but at 300 feet—.

Another series of blasts erupted outside, these much closer, close enough to throw the two plotters right off their feet and scatter even more gear onto the deck plates. The hull hummed in protest, and now they could hear the steel complaining. It was one thing to subject the hull to the pressure of 300 feet; it was another thing altogether to add to that the blast effect of a 500-pound depth bomb.

"Conn, Maneuvering: we have some leaks now. Can we come up in depth?"

"Only once," Malachi said.

"Conn, Sound: number four is coming in."

"Steady as you go, helmsman. Maneuvering: give me *full* power."

The hull vibrated at the sudden application of full battery power. Then they clearly heard the click of a hydrostatic fuze firing, followed by a nasty explosion just behind them followed by seven more in two-second intervals, ear-bruising blasts followed by the sounds of breaking glass down in the control room. Malachi felt the boat lurch up, and then settle into a nose-down attitude. The conning tower filled with white dust and the lights blinked. The hatch above them began a fine spray of seawater onto the ladder.

"Conn, Maneuvering: the after planes are not responding. Stuck at neutral."

"Better than stuck at down twenty," Malachi responded. This wasn't working, he thought. Okay, enough of this shit. "XO, open all outer doors, fore and aft. Make ready all tubes. Run depth *five* feet. Speed *high*. *Contact* exploders."

"Conn, Sound: another one's inbound, bearing one eight five."

"Conn; aye. Control: make your depth *sixty* feet. *Blow* negative. XO, set the torpedo course on manual control, and then boresight them. I intend to come up, find a tin can, and shoot straight at him. Then I'm going to find another one and shoot straight at him. Got it?"

"Yessir," the exec said, his face betraying the realization of how desperate the situation had become. He huddled with the TDC crew to make the settings.

With only one set of planes *Firefish* made an awkward ascent to periscope depth, helped along by the electric motors giving it their all.

"Slow to four knots," Malachi ordered. "Stand by all forward tubes."

When the depth gauge read 80 feet and the pit log showed 4 knots, Malachi raised the scope. He could feel the periscope assembly vibrating at this unusual speed, but he was pressed for time. Suddenly the scope broke the surface. He was staring at the back end of a of Kaba-class destroyer, with her distinctive tall mast all the way aft. He took a snap bearing, ordered the boat to steer that course, waited for the lineup, and fired a single fish as soon as she settled on that course. He estimated the range to be 800 yards, with the destroyer going away at 15 knots.

"Down scope," he ordered. "Give me full power again, and right ten degrees rudder."

The boat surged ahead and then leaned into the turn. A thunderous explosion shook the boat back on her port quarter, followed quickly by several more as the destroyer's depth-charge racks went up. After one minute, he slowed back down for another observation. He swung the scope through a 360-degree arc, knocking a couple of officers aside as he scrambled around the deck plates. He caught a quick glimpse of his first target, which was obscured by a large fire. Another destroyer was turning outbound. Then he settled on the third tin can, which was headed right for them.

"Bearing, zero five zero," he shouted. "Come to zero five zero. Angle on the bow is zero zero zero. Down the throat. Stand by tubes two and three."

He stared at the approaching destroyer, bow on with a magnificent bone in her teeth as she accelerated to ram them. She was no more than a 700 yards away. "Fire two!" he yelled. "Fire three! Right full rudder, make your depth two hundred feet. Flood negative to the mark."

"Captain, we have no stern planes!" the exec shouted as the torpedoes punched out into the sea. Flooding the negative tank meant they'd have a runaway dive on their hands, with only the forward planes to force the nose up once they started down.

"Do what I say, god*dammit*," he roared. "Tell maneuvering to hand crank the after planes to twenty degrees dive. Set the forward planes at neutral."

Instead of a sharp blast of a torpedo warhead they heard a loud clang ten seconds later, which meant one of the fish had hit but did not explode. The other was probably on its way to Surabaya. *Shit!* The Jap skipper had kept his cool and threaded between the two approaching wakes.

They could now clearly hear the approaching destroyer's propellers. He was close to being right on top of them and his sonar was pinging in the narrow beam, attack rate. Malachi swore and then concentrated on recovering from the dive. They actually heard the first depth charges hitting the water as the tin can passed overhead. The depth gauge read 180. He could feel the boat gathering speed with that lead weight in her belly, and then the depth charges started going off. Above them. Way above them. The Jap skipper must have set them to get a boat still at periscope depth, thank God, but the noise was still terrifying. The depth gauge was passing 250 and the boat was not responding to the planes.

"Blow negative, blow all forward ballast tanks," he ordered. "All engines stop. All back full emergency."

"Passing three hundred feet."

He could feel the screws biting in as Maneuvering reversed the electric motors, not waiting for the usual slow-to-stop and then reverse procedure. The entire back end of the boat began to shudder amid the noise of compressed air blasting the water out of the ballast tanks. Still no change in the dive angle.

"Passing three fifty."

Malachi glanced at the plane indicators. Forward was at rise twenty; the after planes had barely moved, but they were up slightly on a rise. Four men were slavishly putting everything they had onto a crankshaft back aft, but for every twenty turns they got only one degree of movement.

"Passing three seventy-five."

Somewhere in the distance another pattern of depth charges started going off, but that wasn't the threat now. If they couldn't get her leveled off and rising, they'd all be dead in a few minutes.

He called down to the Sound crew. "Give me a bearing to any destroyers you can still hear," he said.

"Can't hear much over the blow noise, but zero six zero is my best estimate, Captain."

"Come to course zero six zero," he ordered. The boat was still going down, somewhat slower now, but the rudder still worked, and she began a tortuous turn to the right. "How many fish left up front?" he asked.

"Two torpedoes ready forward," the TDC operator said.

"Prepare to fire both. Speed slow. Running depth five feet. Magnetic exploders on."

The TDC operator read back the instructions and made his call to the forward torpedo room.

"Passing four hundred feet," the OOD said. His voice cracked when he said the number. "Coming to zero six zero."

"Tubes five and six, ready," the TDC operator reported.

"*Fire* tubes five and six," Malachi ordered. Four thousand pounds of metal left the forward torpedo room. The chances of hitting anything were tiny, but getting rid of two tons from the front end might make the difference. He looked at the stern plane indicator. Five degrees of rise, and then he felt the boat start to level off. The noise of the ballast tank blow had subsided, so now they got to listen to the hull, which was not in a comforting mood at 410 feet.

Then she began to rise, and now the problem was to control the ascent so that the boat didn't pop up on the surface in front of three angry Jap destroyers. Malachi checked the after planes. Up seven degrees. Time for power.

"All stop. All ahead full power," he ordered.

Somewhere down below a fitting let go with a blasting noise as water blew into the boat, accompanied by a lot of yelling in the control room. He checked the depth gauge: 390. Finally, coming back up. In the far distance he thought he heard more depth charges booming away.

Then the boat began pitching over again and he had to pull the power off. They waited as the thrust came off, and then she started pointing back up. Malachi realized what was going on: the boat had momentarily achieved neutral buoyancy, so now she was seesawing. He needed to flood one of the ballast tanks aft to make her stand up and quit pitching back down. As he was about to give the order she pitched back down again. He waited, and sure enough, after a painfully long minute, the bow began to rise slowly. The commotion down in the control room seemed to have quieted down.

"Flood after ballast tank number one now," he ordered. That would add six thousand pounds of water aft and she should assume an up-angle.

She did, and then, no longer at neutral buoyancy, began to slide back down into the depths. The depth gauge dropped back off to 410 and seemed to be gathering speed. The steel around them sounded like it was cracking.

"All ahead *full* power," Malachi called down to Control. The after planes were now up to twelve degrees, which would finally give them some attitude control aft. The depth gauge began to unwind again as the boat struggled up out of these dangerous depths. He'd get her up to 250 and then flood something forward. Then he had to see if he'd evaded that four-pack. Three-pack, he reminded himself, with a quick grin.

He glanced around the conning tower at all the white faces. "Anyone got a cigarette?" he asked. Some jaws dropped and they all just stared at him.

Two hours later they were still picking up the pieces throughout the boat. Broken light fixtures, equipment cabinets dislodged, electrical connections ripped apart, and an amazing amount of loose paper covered the deck plates. Two watertight doors had jammed shut as the hull deformed at 410 feet, and the after planes' hydraulics were still inoperative due to broken hydraulic lines. The battery was down to twenty-five percent, and the remaining destroyers were still looking for them, although about two miles away. Malachi got her level at 260 feet and was headed in the away direction from the muted noise of the Jap destroyers. He prayed they didn't call for air support because he had a suspicion *Firefish* might be trailing a diesel oil slick from cracks in the fuel tanks. The exec had brought him a damage list, and while none of it was mortal, the sum of all the damage made them operationally ineffective. He was going to have to head for Perth, but he wouldn't be able to tell anyone until nightfall.

They'd have to run for it on the surface once it got dark, and they'd also have to keep those radars silent. He was convinced now that the Japs had detected all those surface search transmissions they'd made navigating with some kind of shore station detection locator network. They'd come straight at him, and they'd also known when to start the trapping circle. That meant they'd put up a network of listening stations on Java, separated by enough distance to give them cross-bearings, and therefore a precise location of the submarine emitting the signal. This would be important news in Perth, and maybe even in Pearl.

"Conn, Control: we're having trouble maintaining trim; we've just lost one of the trim pumps to a short. And there's a hydrogen gas buildup in forward battery; we're putting the smoking lamp out."

Malachi sighed and mashed his cigarette into his empty coffee mug. It was going to be a long damned day and an even longer trip back to Perth.

FIFTEEN

Two days after getting back to Perth Malachi was summoned to the downtown office complex to meet with the new admiral, Rear Admiral Hamner Marsten. They had received a nice reception upon arrival and many congratulations for the rich bag. Repair gangs from the tender were on hand to meet them and then swarm aboard to assess the damage and the scope of repairs. Malachi handed over his captain's log to Captain Collins, the chief of staff, who greeted him politely if not in a particularly friendly manner.

The trip back had been one of a series of irritating malfunctions resulting from all the depth charges and probably, in the case of some leaks, their excursion to 410 feet. The major problem was the frozen diving planes aft. He'd sent a diver over the side the night after the attack by the Jap antisubmarine warfare division to see if they could do anything out there at sea, but the shaft housing on both sides was bent completely out of alignment. To get back to Perth as quickly as possible, he'd broken with the transit rules of running surfaced at night and submerged during daylight. He'd run surfaced the entire way, with only one scare when a Kawanishi flying boat jumped them. The ensuing crash dive had turned into an interesting depth-control exercise, and fortunately the Kawanishi had apparently run out of depth charges and could only strafe the disturbance in the water where *Firefish* had disappeared. As a result, they got back a week earlier than anyone expected.

Malachi was still pretty tired after all the excitement, but he'd remained onboard to personally supervise the initial repair work. Last night he'd finally gone to the hotel, had a quiet beer with the other COs who were in port, and his first really good night's sleep in weeks. The other skippers had been full of questions and were especially concerned about the possibility that the Japs could detect their radars. When he told them about going down to 410 feet a hush came over the table. When he told them he'd taken *Firefish* down to 400 feet on his second day aboard, they looked at him as if he was nuts.

"*Daggerfish* went down to five hundred feet and survived," he reminded them. "She's the same class as *Firefish*. Now, I wouldn't want to linger for a long lunch at that depth, but I needed to know if four hundred was a tactical option."

"The admiral will see you now, Captain Stormes," the chief yeoman announced and opened the door to the inner office.

Hamner Marsten was a handsome man and, apparently, fully aware of it. His uniform was tailor-made, his hair styled, and he shook hands with Malachi with an entirely superior expression on his face. "Captain Stormes, great to meet you and congratulations on an outstanding patrol," he said. "Please have a seat and welcome home."

Captain Collins was also present, sitting in an armchair to one side of the admiral's desk. Malachi noticed that the office looked different from the last time he'd been there. There were now lots of pictures on the walls—most of them featuring Hamner Marsten.

"Another heavy cruiser, two destroyers, and three oil tankers— that's nearly forty thousand tons. Even better, they're all confirmed."

"I wasn't sure the tankers actually sank," Malachi said. "But they were certainly never going to carry oil again."

"The Japanese sank them for us," Collins said. "A destroyer torpedoed all three because they were derelicts."

"And you attacked on the surface with your five-inch gun?" the admiral asked, a note of incredulity in his voice. "What led you to try that?"

"They were basically unescorted," Malachi said. "We'd seen their escorts waiting farther out of the Lombok, and it looked like the convoy, which was just a gaggle at that point, was headed for a rendezvous before proceeding on to wherever they were headed. We used incendiary shells. It didn't take many."

"Amazing," the admiral said.

"If I may, Admiral: how do we know those attacks qualify as 'confirmed'?"

"That's one of the reasons for this meeting, Captain. To brief you about something called Ultra."

"This is probably the most secret thing you will ever know, Captain Stormes," Captain Collins said. "Naval Intelligence in Pearl has broken the Japanese naval codes."

"Wow," Malachi said.

"Wow, indeed, Captain," the admiral said. "That's how Midway happened. We knew where they were going, and when. And, as the chief of staff said, this is a secret that qualifies for any and all measures to keep. The next time you go out, *Firefish* will from time to time receive messages that only you may read. Not even the officer who breaks the encoded message can read it. He will sit on one side of the decoder machine and you will read the tape as it comes out and then destroy it, right there and then. Understood?"

"Yes, sir."

"These messages will be targeting messages. A carrier formation is expected to be at a certain place on a certain date. You be there, too. That kind of thing."

"That accurate?"

"The Japanese are rigid adherents to schedules," Collins said. "Once the fleet command issues an order, they stick to it like glue."

"Okay," the admiral said. "Now, when you went back in to finish off that cruiser, you used the magnetic exploders. Tell me all about that, if you please. And then I'm going to want to hear all about your going down to four hundred feet."

Malachi explained what he'd done with the two magnetic exploder torpedoes, as a test to see if he could make them work. The admiral listened intently but without comment. Then he related the "adventure" of going a hundred feet below test depth because of the jammed plane problem. The admiral had a question.

"I've heard that on your first week as CO of *Firefish* you took the boat to four hundred feet on purpose. Is that true?"

"Yes, sir, it is. I'd been told in Pearl that *Daggerfish* went to five hundred feet after a heavy depth-charging, but recovered. I wanted to know if four hundred was a tactical option if it was ever necessary."

"That's really deep, Captain," the admiral said. "How was it at that depth?"

"Noisy, sir," Malachi said. "Lots of complaining from the hull and we found a few imperfect welds in the process. But the depth charges were going off two hundred feet above us, if not more. That was comforting."

"Is it possible that some of your damage was caused by extreme overpressure on the hull and its fittings?"

"I don't think so, Admiral. The Japs sent out a specialist team of four destroyers. They set up a trapping circle and bombed the hell out of us. Their charges were being set deeper than the 'traditional' one hundred fifty feet, too. And they knew right where to find us. I think that was our fault—we'd been using our surface search radar a lot to confirm our position off Surabaya by getting radar bearings to known landmarks."

"You think they can detect it, then."

"Yes, sir, unless they're reading our radio traffic like we're reading theirs."

"That's *not* happening," the admiral said. "But you might be interested to know that a group of electronics wizards back in Pearl made a prototype receiver that could present a bearing to the antenna emitting a radar signal, so I'm thinking you're right on this one. I'm forwarding your report on to SubPac. Now, back to the magnetic exploder."

"Yes, sir?"

"The chief of staff here tells me that skippers here have been deactivating that feature on their torpedoes. Have you ever done that?"

"Yes, sir, I have. I'm relatively new to the Perth squadron, but from what I hear, everybody has. The thinking is that they're running too deep, which is the Mark fourteen torpedo's fault, not the exploder.

The second issue is the magnetic setting—this part of the world is not Newport, Rhode Island."

"Then why did *your* two fish work?"

"Because, I think, I had a stationary target—a disabled heavy cruiser. Ten, twelve thousand tons of steel, deep in the water after the first hits. I made a wild-ass guess at how deep she was after all the flooding, and then set the fish to run about three to six feet under her keel, assuming the Mark fourteen is running ten to twelve feet deeper than set. Both went off and she broke in half."

"Did you do anything else different?"

"Yes, sir. I make it a practice to, wherever possible, set up my attack so that the fish doesn't have to make any turns when it leaves the tube. That way you probably will never have a circular run. With that cruiser I maneuvered the boat until I had her physically aligned with the firing bearing. I could do that because the target was stationary."

The admiral sat back in his chair. "That's very interesting, indeed. You still think the magnetic exploder is a bad idea?"

"Yes, sir, I do. Combined with the problems with the Mark fourteen itself, it's too dangerous to use the magnetic exploders. On the other hand, even the contact exploders are having problems. I had one on this patrol that hit and bounced off. Personally, I think it has to do with the initiator pin—it's the same pin we used on the Mark ten, but this fish goes much faster. Much bigger impact."

"You seem to be a student of our torpedoes, Captain. Did you know that, when I was a captain, I was the manager of the Navy's torpedo program at BuOrd for four years?"

The admiral had a gotcha expression on his face when he said that. Malachi didn't care for that expression. "I was assigned as a mechanical engineer at Newport for three years," he said. "I'm intimately familiar with the Mark fourteen's development—and testing. Or should I say, the lack thereof."

The admiral's face darkened. He looked at the chief of staff, who had an I-told-you-so expression on his face. Malachi realized he'd walked into a little trap.

"Explain that remark," the admiral said.

"Only two test shots with the magnetic exploder were ever done against a ship-sized target, and that was only an anchored submarine."

"And the Mark fourteen torpedo sank that submarine."

"Two shots—first one failed, second one worked. That's a failure rate of fifty percent. By any engineering standards, that torpedo was not ready for deployment."

The admiral sat silent for a long moment, looking down at his desk. "You and I, Captain, are not going to get along," he said, "not with that attitude."

"Admiral, I've answered all your questions candidly. You asked me to explain my remark about the lack of testing on the Mark fourteen. I wasn't being impertinent. I'm new to this command, but listening to the more experienced skippers in Pearl on my way out here, the universal view is that that torpedo is not reliable, and since it leaves a big-ass wake pointing right back at the boat that shot it, it's down-right dangerous. If you want me to tell you what you want to hear, I'll be happy to oblige."

"Now that *is* impertinence, Commander Stormes," the chief of staff said.

Commander is it, Malachi thought. Not captain anymore. He waited for the admiral to say something, but he was busy looking through a stack of papers on his desk. Then he found what he was looking for.

"Are you aware, Captain, that we face a critical shortage of torpe-does out here?"

"Yes, sir, I am."

"Was it absolutely necessary for you to throw away two perfectly good torpedoes to get out of your little excursion to four hundred feet?"

"I thought so at the time, Admiral. I thought saving the boat and its crew was worth more than two torpedoes. And it worked."

"You have an answer for everything, don't you, Captain," the ad-miral snapped.

Malachi said nothing.

The admiral leaned forward and pointed his finger at Malachi. "I think you're letting your successes out there on patrol turn your head, young man. You think you're some kind of hot shit. But there are other skippers out here who are also successful at sinking ships, and they don't go taking the chances you've been taking. Let me put it this way: one more flagrant deviation from approved policies, tactics, or operating procedures and I *will* relieve you. Got that?"

"Yes, sir," Malachi said, with as little emotion as possible. There were lots of things he wanted to say, with "I quit" being one of them, but he held his tongue.

"You may go," the admiral said, turning his chair around to look out the windows of his office, as if no longer wanting to look at Malachi. The chief of staff gave Malachi a supercilious sneer on his way out.

SIXTEEN

That night at the hotel Malachi badly wanted something he almost never wanted: a glass of Kentucky bourbon whiskey. He knew better than to indulge, but he wanted it nonetheless.

He sat by himself in the rooftop bar, nursing his customary single beer and thinking about his unpleasant séance with the new admiral. He should have listened to Jay Carney, who'd told him to say nothing and then go do what you want once you get to sea. In his tenure as a skipper, he'd destroyed three German U-boats, two imperial Japanese Navy heavy cruisers, a clutch of destroyers, and four *marus*. By some accounts he was the third-highest scoring skipper in the Pacific submarine force since the war began, if measured in sheer tonnage sent to the bottom.

And yet his boss was mad at him, the boss's chief of staff was actively trying to get rid of him, *and* his crew was apparently afraid of him. His one-year-old boat was beat up; her hull possibly deformed by going down below test depth. Some of the other skippers, their ears ever attuned to the waterfront jungle drums, had been politely avoiding him after his testy meeting with the admiral.

"Penny for your thoughts?" a pleasant female voice asked, her words framed by just a hint of perfume as she walked up to his corner table. He stood up. Kensie was dressed in khaki slacks, a long-sleeved white blouse, and her hairdo was different. She looked demure and delicious at the same time.

"They're not worth even that much tonight," he said, surprised that he was glad to see her. "But I'd love it if you'd join me, Kensie."

"Actually," she said, "why don't you join *me*. It's my thirty-ninth birthday, and I've booked a table at Dannigan's. You'll like it."

"Absolutely," he said, finishing up his beer and still wanting a whiskey.

She drove a dusty Land Rover–type vehicle that the Aussies called a Ute, which showed both its age and its full-time occupation as a farm vehicle. Dannigan's was a combination Irish pub and steakhouse. The parking lot was full, always a good sign in Malachi's opinion. Inside, the place was noisy, filled with Aussies doing what they do best. The bar and dance floor area was on one side; the dining room on the other, but there was a steady flow of people moving from one room to the other. A harried hostess took them to a table for four back in one corner, next to a window that overlooked a large pond. The table was raised one step up from the rest of the dining area, and was obviously reserved for special customers.

"Others coming?" he asked, still a little startled by the amount of noise in the room.

"You'll see," she said. She snagged a passing waiter and ordered a whiskey for herself and a beer for Malachi. He didn't fight it, rationalizing that a second beer was better than a double Bourbon, which probably didn't exist on this side of the world anyway.

The drinks came quickly. Kensie offered him a salud and then began to scan the room. Almost immediately two men showed up at their table and plopped down in the two extra chairs. Both were in their late thirties and well ahead on their drinking for the evening. Kensie introduced them as two of the doctors with whom she worked in the hospital. Both politely shook hands and then tried to get Kensie to join them in the bar. She demurred, but when someone announced that it was her birthday, she was whisked away and onto the dance floor with about five men claiming her. The music was coming from one of those new Victrola's, which could stack and automatically play up to six LP records. The current stack was mostly fast jazz.

Malachi just sat back and watched the fun. She was being a good sport about it all, and not turning down a sip from many of the drinks pointed her way. It went on like that for another thirty minutes, with new table-hopping visitors arriving about every five minutes asking where was the birthday girl. He just pointed out to the happy mob on the dance floor. Malachi was a bit taken aback by how many people Kensie seemed to know, or who purported to know her. She finally saw him consulting a menu and broke it off, coming back to the table with a flushed face and totally out of breath. She grabbed his half-full beer glass and finished it in one big gulp.

"It's official," she burst out when she caught her breath. "I am too old for that anymore."

"You looked like you were having fun out there," he said.

"Oh, I was, in between fending off the gropers, humpers, and bumpers. But then I remembered I had a guest, and then it took some advanced shimmy-shimmy to get away."

He grinned at her. One year from being forty, and tonight was her first realization that middle age was looming. "I take it you're a regular here," he observed while looking over the menu.

"God, yes," she said. "Our ranch provides the beef and my father's company owns the restaurant. I recommend the filet—the big one. Get it rare."

"I'll try anything once," he said. "All our meat on the boat has been frozen since the first world war, I think."

They ordered and Kensie signaled for a second whiskey. Malachi ordered a second beer to replace the one Kensie had polished off. He knew if he went too fast he'd eventually join her on the whiskey train and that that might not end well. Even so, Aussie beer was a lot more authoritative than American, and he could already feel it.

"So what's happened that your thoughts are so depressing?" she asked. Her lovely eyes were brightened by the whiskey and the exertions on the dance floor, and for a moment he just stared at her.

"What?" she said.

He shook his head. "You're so pretty, that's what," he replied. "Lost my train of thought, I guess."

She grinned. "Well, thank you, kind sir. Now, out with it."

He told her about his meeting with the new Big Boss, having to speak louder than usual over all the noise in the dining room. The bar was getting even rowdier. He left out the operational details about the sinkings, saying only that their patrol had been successful by anyone's measure. He couldn't say anything about the torpedo problem, either, so he attributed it all to a personality conflict, ending with the old truism about Navy personality conflicts: the boss had a personality; the subordinate had a conflict.

She laughed out loud. He thought that nearby diners probably assumed he'd just told a dirty joke. "If the patrol was successful," she said, "and you badly hurt the Yellow Peril, then what's his problem?"

"I'm not sufficiently . . . respectful, I suppose," he said. "Someone asks me a question—talking Navy business, now—I'll answer it, straight up, whether that's in my best interests or not. Sometimes it's not what the boss wants to hear."

"Believe it or not, we doctors face the same problem from time to time," she said. "But in medicine we have one absolute metric that's bloody hard to argue with."

"What's that?"

"The patient dies. Or doesn't."

"Oh," he said. "Right. In that vein, we submariners have a similar metric: we either come back or we don't."

She blinked at that, but then the steaks arrived and they tucked in. Australian beef was different from American beef, but wonderful when compared to what came out of those frozen boxes marked "beef, miscellaneous cuts, USDA utility grade" that they'd been getting from the tender when they replenished. The Pearl boats, being only 2,500 miles from the US mainland, apparently fared much better than the exiles out in Australia.

They fell to and enjoyed the food, which Kensie now enriched with a glass of Australian red wine. As they were finishing up, an older man approached their table with a glass of whiskey in hand. He was in his sixties, almost six feet, round-faced with a red tinge to his complexion, eyes that almost glared, and a full head of gray hair. He was powerfully built and exuded an air of absolute authority. Kensie looked up.

"Oh, hi, Dad," she said. "This is Captain Malachi Stormes."

The big man extended a meaty paw. "Lambert Richmond," he announced in a booming voice. "Kensie told us about meeting you, Captain. Welcome to western Australia."

"Thank you, sir," Malachi said. He'd begun to stand up but her father had stopped him. "We Americans are really delighted to be here."

"So I've noticed," Richmond said, with a sly smile. "Giving all the local blokes a run for their money. *And* their Sheilas. Good on you, I say. Kensie, dear, why don't you bring the captain out to the station for a better view of western Aussie hospitality. Captain, do you ride, sir?"

Malachi grinned and shook his head. "Rode a mule once, and only once. I come from Kentucky coal country, Mr. Richmond. I rode trains, coal cars, and coal-skips growing up."

"We have plenty of accommodating horses at the station," Kensie interjected. "We'll just find him a nice husband-horse."

Malachi saw a flare of alarm in Lambert's eyes at her use of the word "husband"; then he saw her impish grin. Oh, boy, he thought; Kensie teasing the patriarch.

"I'll give it a try," Malachi offered, bravely.

"We have lots of vehicles, of course," Lambert said. "It's just that horses kick up much less dust. Gives you time to really see things out there in the bush."

"I'll sort it, Dad," Kensie said. "We'd both have to check our schedules."

"Good, oh," Lambert declared. He tipped his glass in their direction and then melted back into the cigarette smoke and the noise. Malachi and Kensie wandered out onto one of the screened porches overlooking the pond, or billabong as she called it. Normally he would have had a cigarette, but the rooms inside had made him feel like he'd already had an entire pack. They found a table in the shadows, lit only by the lights from the bar room, and sat down.

"Was your dad serious about my coming out to the station for a few days?" he asked.

She snorted. "If he wasn't, *I* am. The problem is getting enough time away to make it worthwhile. The Australian Navy is getting ever more involved in the Solomons campaign, which means our caseload is increasing monthly. I'm one of just six surgeons; the other half of the staff went into the field with MacArthur's blokes."

"I'm content to see you when we both can manage it, Kensie," he said. "You're an absolute delight to be with."

At that moment, the record player fired up an American band whose music was meant for slow dancing. She cocked her head for a moment, as if to make sure, and then asked him to dance. They joined one other couple who were barely swaying to the music in an open corner of the porch. She moved her body into contact with his, and suddenly he wasn't tired or depressed anymore. This was different from their time together the other night. This was a time for something much better than that.

"Back to the hotel?" he asked.

"I shouldn't drive," she said. "Well, I can, but . . ."

"I can," he said.

The trip back to the hotel turned out to be pretty funny, as Malachi confronted the Australian rules for driving on absolutely the wrong side of the road, and from absolutely the wrong side of the front seat. Kensie's giggling didn't help. When they were finally stopped by a Perth city police car, Kensie had to bail them out by declaring that it was her car, but she was too drunk to drive and that the Yank here, who didn't drink, was having trouble with the new driving situation. The cop just shook his head and waved them on.

Once in the hotel room she slipped into the bathroom ahead of him. He sat down on the bed he usually slept in, waiting his turn to pump bilges after two point two beers. She came out wearing nothing but her panties and motioned that the bathroom was all his. He went in, took care of business, hung all his clothes on the bathroom door, and came back out.

When he came out she was sitting up in "his" bed with the covers folded down to her waist. The overhead light was off, but the bedside table light was still on, casting a yellow light over her bare breasts and an expression on her face that clearly said: hurry up.

He did.

SEVENTEEN

The following morning the admiral called a skippers' meeting aboard the tender. There were six boats in port now, which made for a rather slim audience, and Malachi noticed that the staff officers outnumbered the commanding officers. The admiral reviewed several policy and matériel issues, shared some strategic planning news from Pearl, and then asked for questions or matters of interest from the COs. To Malachi's surprise, none of them had anything to ask the admiral. He himself had some pointed questions but decided that this might be a good time to just keep quiet.

"Nobody has anything at all?" the admiral asked.

Jay Carney, skipper of *Grayback*, finally raised his hand. "Admiral, is there any progress being made on improving the Mark fourteen's performance? Is BuOrd saying, or doing, *anything*?"

The admiral frowned. "The Bureau of Ordnance maintains that there's nothing wrong with the torpedoes and that operational failures are attributable to poor fire-control solutions or other operational errors. As a matter of fact, *Firefish* just sank a damaged heavy cruiser using magnetic exploders on two torpedoes, so it can be done."

"Anything special about the attack geometry?" another CO asked, looking over at Malachi, who suddenly realized that this line of questioning had some basis in his hotel bar talk with the other skippers.

"Captain Stormes?" the admiral said.

Malachi related the sequence and the setup, emphasizing that he'd tried to run the fish within only a few feet of the flooding cruiser's hull.

"How'd you know what depth to set?" the CO asked.

"I assumed they're running deep—maybe as much as ten to twelve feet deep. So I calculated the cruiser's normal draft, added ten feet because he was down by the bow, and set the running depth three feet below that. Truth be told, I wanted to know if the magnetic exploder would work if it came much closer to the target. It happened to work out, but I realize now that I can't with any certainty say which exploder did him in. Even worse, when I examined both exploder mechanisms, I couldn't see a way to disable the contact exploder in order to test the magnetic on its own."

The admiral perked up at that. "Are you saying, Captain, that you opened up a Mark fourteen and fiddled with the exploder circuits?"

"I did open one up, yes, Admiral. But I didn't 'fiddle' with anything. I was looking for a way to change the magnetic reference level to fit with where we are operating. I concluded that can't be done on the boat."

The admiral just stared at him. "You are telling me you opened up the guidance section of a warhead torpedo, *in* the boat, out at *sea*?" he said, his voice rising with every word.

Malachi knew he was deep in the muck, so, in for a penny, in for a pound, as the Brits used to tell him. "Admiral, I can disassemble a Mark fourteen torpedo's guidance system right down to its smallest components and put it back together, all in about an hour. *Where* I do that doesn't much matter, although I'd prefer the final assembly building at Newport to *Firefish*'s forward torpedo room. It's just a machine. It has defects. We need to address those defects, and the Bu-Ord response that it's all the operators' fault is bureaucratic, CYA bullshit. So if they're not gonna fix it, then the fleet'll have to."

The admiral looked around at the other skippers, who themselves looked like they wished they could just execute a nice little dive right about then. "Have any of the rest of you ever opened up a fish at sea? I'm not talking routining, I mean the guidance and arming section?"

Jay Carney said yes, that he'd opened the guidance section on all of his torpedoes once at sea in order to disable the magnetic exploders. Now the admiral looked like he was about to give birth.

"Admiral," Malachi interjected. "Routining the fish is something we do all the time at sea. And before you do anything, you open a port on the warhead and put the dowel in—I'm sure you remember, the wooden dowel that goes all the way through the firing train so that nothing, not even a static spark from a wrench, can fire the warhead? *Then* we check the fish out."

"All in order to *disable* a part of the guidance system that fires the goddamned warhead?"

"It doesn't work, Admiral," Jay Carney said. "Under real-world, tactical situations, the fucking thing doesn't work. And I believe it's causing the prematures, because there's no way the contact exploder can cause a premature."

The admiral took a deep breath and then started to calm down. "I'd heard rumors to that effect," he admitted. "Skippers deactivating the magnetic exploders. I just didn't believe them. But my predecessor didn't say anything about that." He turned to the chief of staff. "Did *you* know?"

Collins squirmed in his seat. "Um, I'd heard rumors, too, Admiral. But the only one who flat out told me he'd done it was Commander Stormes. Admiral Britten had made it clear that he wanted the magnetics to be used. He wanted to relieve Commander Stormes, but *Firefish* had just come in from a spectacular patrol and he thought SubPac would have a cow."

"Oh, right," the admiral muttered. "That reminds me. Commander Stormes, no, excuse me, *Captain* Stormes, if you will please stand up. He reached into the middle drawer of his desk and pulled out a small, white box that he opened. Inside was a gold star resting on a bed of blue felt. When the other skippers saw that they all stood up, too. The admiral came around the desk and handed the box to Malachi. "A gold star representing the second award of the Navy Cross medal for the exceptional results of your second patrol from Perth. Congratulations."

"Thank you, Admiral," Malachi replied, accepting the firm hand-shake. He appreciated the admiral calling him captain after the chief of staff's petty condescension. His rank *was* commander, USN, but his title was properly captain. The admiral went back to his desk and sat down.

"Okay, gentlemen," he said. "I'm going to stop here. I need time to think about this problem of the Mark fourteen. I'm recently pro-moted to rear admiral, and that was undoubtedly based in part on my getting the fourteen fielded in the first place. Which means I own some of this, personally. I will tell you now that I accept responsibil-ity for our current problems, and I'm going to get them fixed. And I agree with Captain Stormes: if the Bureau won't fix it, then, by God, we will.

"One more thing: it's obvious to me that this command has been operating on a if-you-don't-ask-me-any-questions-I-won't-tell-you-any-lies basis. That needs to stop right now. We're at war, and we haven't made it back up to zero from a large negative number yet. Don't any of you tell me anything but the cold hard truth, and don't ever assume that by doing that *you* might get in trouble. This busi-ness out here is going to get harder, not easier, especially once we start really hurting the Japs. Understood?"

There was a chorus of yessirs. The meeting broke up and the skip-pers congregated out in the passageway like they did the last time. One of the older skippers looked at Malachi. "Man, you got a pair of brass ones," he announced.

"The truth is the truth," Malachi said. "If you're gonna get fired for telling the truth, then why would you want to work here?"

The others laughed, but nervously. Jay Carney stepped up. "To-night I'm buying you a drink, pardner, and *this* time you're gonna drink it, by Godfrey."

If you only knew how much I'd like to do that, Malachi thought, as he went back to the boat. Maybe he'd stay aboard the boat tonight. The duty section would hate that, though. After a wonderful night with Kensie back at the hotel last night, he was feeling much better about everything. They'd made love twice, the first time in a hurried frenzy and the second, sometime in the middle of the night, with a lot more patience and attention to detail. They'd almost overslept except for passing voices out in the corridor talking about the admiral's meeting this morning. His meeting being sooner than her shift started, he'd gotten first dibs on the shower. She was facing a forty-eight-hour on-call shift, so they'd made plans to see each other the night after next.

The following morning two bits of news spread out like a grass fire through the nest of submarines alongside the tender. First, Captain Collins, the chief of staff, was being reassigned. He was being ordered back to Norfolk to take command of the Atlantic submarine refresher training program. On the face of it, those were excellent orders, but officers in the know could read between the lines: from chief of staff of one of only two flotillas operating in the Far East, the bright and shining tip of the spear, to a training command? There were lots of knowing looks. Malachi wondered how much that meeting had contributed to the chief of staff's sudden departure from the front lines. As far as he was concerned Collins wouldn't be missed.

The other news was more somber: one of the Perth boats, the *Catfish*, hadn't been heard from in ten days and was now presumed lost somewhere in the Coral Sea. Malachi shook his head and closed his eyes when he heard the news. This was the hell of it when the Japs managed to sink one of the boats: no one had any idea what had happened, or even where. The best they could say about *Catfish* was that she was missing in the Coral Sea, an area of 1.5 million square miles. The boat and her entire crew had simply disappeared. They all knew many things could kill a submarine: a minefield, a torpedo from another submarine, a circular running torpedo that comes back to see you, a well-placed depth charge, or even a major seawater leak at depth. The result was the same: the boat would just disappear.

Malachi asked Jay Carney if there'd be a memorial service. Carney told him that, since the war began, the Navy had made a practice of officially declaring the entire crew "missing in action" so that their dependents could keep receiving pay and benefits until the Navy could find out what really happened. Everyone in Perth knew what had really happened, but for that reason, there would be no memorial service.

He was doing paperwork amid the clatter of repairs onboard when a messenger from the tender knocked on the bulkhead and announced that the admiral wanted to see him. Malachi acknowledged, changed into a pressed uniform shirt, and then hustled over to the tender. The admiral came right to the point.

"I want you to figure out some kind of test we can make right here in Perth that would prove that these Mark fourteens are running deep," he said. "I want to use warhead fish, but set on safe, and it has to be somewhere that we can recover those fish because we're still short of assets. Your boat will be in for probably another ten days, so let's see if we can get it done quickly."

"Yessir," Malachi said. The admiral's phone rang. He waved Malachi toward the door and that was that.

It took two days to get everything coordinated. They ended up using two commercial fishing boats with a deep sea net strung between them. They anchored the fishing boats after the net was deployed in 120 feet of water, near a headland north of the city. The sea was calm with almost no wind. Behind the net the water shoaled all the way into a sandy beach, 500 yards away. It took a few hours to get the top of the net as close to the surface as possible, factoring in for the inevitable catenary, since the net, or the "target," was 200 feet across and hung down in the water 100 feet. They strung a line of fish-floats to mark the top of the net, with a red flag marking the center. The tender sent out their dive boat with four SCUBA swimmers and one hard-hat diver. An Aussie frigate was assigned to patrol offshore to keep prying eyes away, and Marines from the tender guarded the beach behind the net. The admiral and some of his staff were riding a harbor tugboat, which was stationed up in the vicinity of the two fishing boats. Everything was finally ready in the early afternoon.

Sea Lion got the job of firing the four test torpedoes. She took station 800 yards away from the red flag and then ballasted down to periscope depth. The torpedoes were set for high speed and a running depth of 20 feet. The warheads had been safed by removing both the contact and the magnetic exploders, replacing them with a bag of sand to restore the proper weight. Malachi was down in *Sea Lion*'s control room while Reed Burlington manned the conning tower. The plan was to fire four fish in sequence. One aimed three degrees left of the flag, one at the flag, one three degrees right of the flag, and one set for a running depth of 10 feet, which wouldn't be fired until the first three runs had been inspected by the divers.

Burlington called the tugboat on the radio and reported ready. The tug came back and told them to proceed. The first fish thumped out of the tube and ran in toward the beach. From the tug they were able to see the net jump, and a minute later the Marines reported that the fish had run up on the beach, its propellers still spinning. The second fish made a similar run, also ending up on the beach. The third fish broached and then commenced a circular run, causing Burlington to lay on full power to get out of the way. The torpedo made three circuits before giving up the ghost, somewhere behind the test site. Even without a warhead, getting hit with a 2,000-pound underwater missile going 46 knots was not good for watertight integrity.

The tests were halted to let the divers inspect the net and for *Sea Lion* to get back in position. Burlington came down into Control for coffee. "'Bout right for the Mark fourteen," he said. "One out of three is defective."

"Set for twenty feet and it still broached," Malachi said. "That is truly defective."

"I'm really interested in the final shot," Burlington said. "I set most of my fish for ten feet, and I'd really like to know how deep they're really going."

It took two hours for the dive boat to get into position and put divers over to inspect the net. When they got back up and were clear of the firing range, the admiral ordered up the fourth shot. Centerline, but at ten feet this time. The fish thumped out and ran hot, straight, and normal. It hit the net and screamed in toward the beach. About the time it should have punched out of the surf and run up the sand, it exploded, scaring the living hell out of the Marines on the beach. Malachi could hear Burlington cursing up in the conning tower. Gawd, he thought. What a circus.

Back in port the results were briefed in the admiral's office downtown. The two fish that had run normally, and supposedly at 20 feet, had punched holes in the net 35 feet below the suspension wire. A

15-foot deviation from ordered depth. The last fish had punched a hole at 22 feet, a 12-foot deviation. Not only were they running deep, they were running inconsistently deep.

The matter of the exploding "disarmed" torpedo was explained by the fact that the fish had hit a submerged boulder 50 feet out into the surf, still going 46 knots. "Maybe that's the way to make them explode," Burlington observed. "Take out both exploders."

"Okay, okay," the admiral said. "I'm forwarding this data to Sub-Pac back in Pearl. It's worse than we thought: if they all ran the same amount of depth deviation, we could simply compensate. But it looks random."

"We'd need to fire about fifty more torpedoes to get a scientifically reliable range of deviation," Malachi offered. "And, yes, I know that's not possible."

"Damned right it isn't," the admiral said. "We can't recover the one that went nuts, and of course the other one went off. We lost fifty percent of the torpedoes just doing a test."

"What a surprise," Burlington said. "Thing's a piece of shit."

As the admiral spooled up to retort, Malachi put up a hand. "Let me remind everybody here that these things are handmade mechanical devices. They are not 'pieces of shit' but rather insufficiently tested. Like I just said, it would take fifty fish to get reliable data. They fired *two* for the magnetic exploder, remember? We need to go after the Mark fourteen's problems, plural, in a sound engineering method. And then we need to get a manufacturing system up and running that can mass produce them to rigidly set standards."

"Well, I'll be damned," the admiral said. "Guess who's gonna write the report, Captain Stormes? And, by the way, I completely agree with you. Tomorrow too soon?"

Burlington started laughing. The rest of the staff officers weren't sure what to do, until the admiral grinned. Then they laughed, too.

Teach me to squeak, Malachi thought.

That night he stayed aboard the boat to compose the report. The admiral had been right in assigning him to do it—he was probably the most technically qualified CO out here to both describe the results of the testing and to make engineering recommendations. That being said, he knew what the reaction would be back in Washington, but now the Gun Clubbers had a new force to reckon with: four-star Admiral Chester W. Nimitz. A submariner, to boot.

Malachi wrote the report as if writing it for Nimitz to read, which he probably would now that people were starting to address the problems. The Bureau of Ordnance could trash one submarine's skipper's report, but if Nimitz's endorsement was as forceful as Malachi expected it to be, even BuOrd would have to do something.

The next night, Malachi phoned the hospital to see if he could talk Kensie into a dinner date. The operator said that Dr. Richmond was not available until further notice. When he asked what that meant, the operator sighed and repeated what she'd just said. Malachi hung up and went back to the boat. Not available? Or not available to *him*? Or, Christmas was a week away—had she gone off for a family function somewhere? Not that Christmas was going to mean much this year. About the only good news coming from the Solomons these days was that Halsey was now in charge and the Japs might be starving on Guadalcanal. The Aussies, on the other hand, followed the fate of the remaining British Army and the rest of the Empire. Earlier in the week the Japs had bombed Calcutta, and of course they were still picking up the pieces and treating the wounded from the bombing of Darwin to the north. Nobody was walking around saying Merry Christmas. Still, he thought. Something didn't sound right.

He changed into civvies and called for a cab to take him to the main hospital in Perth, where Kensie was assigned. He checked in at Reception. The young and uniformed receptionist seemed surprised to hear an American accent, as the US Army had established four hospitals in the Perth/Fremantle area for American casualties over the past year.

"I'm Commander Stormes from the submarine base," he told her. "I just needed to speak to Dr. Richmond if I could."

"She's been admitted, actually," the receptionist said. "She's in the intensive care section on the third floor, but they don't ever allow visitors, other than direct family."

"*Admitted?*" Malachi exclaimed. "What happened?"

"She collapsed during surgery," a stern female voice said from behind him. "Total exhaustion. Who's asking?"

He turned to see an older woman dressed in the wimple and white robes that British nurses, called Sisters, wore in the hospital. Her expression was as severe as her voice. Malachi explained who he was and that he hadn't known anything about her collapsing.

The Sister gave him a fierce look, but then relented. "You are the captain? The submarine captain?"

Malachi nodded, and the Sister's face softened a tiny bit. "Yes," she said, drawing him away from prying ears at the reception desk. "She's spoken of you often. She's recovering, but slowly, as these things must do. Worn out by two-day surgical shifts and a veritable flood of badly injured soldiers."

"Is she conscious?"

"Not really," the sister said. "She's sedated for the most part. They ease her out of it for an hour or so each day so they can feed her, and then back down she goes."

"Can I see her?"

The Sister gave him a disbelieving look. "Her father and mother are taking turns staying nearby on the ward. But it's direct family only in the IC station. Surely you understand."

He nodded. "Can you do this," he asked. "Can you tell her father that I'm down in the waiting room?"

The Sister gave him a calculating look. "Lambert Richmond is a very important man in western Australia, Captain. Are you saying he would recognize your name?"

"I think he would," Malachi said. "I know she would."

"Very well, I'll go tell him. But you may have a longish wait."

"I know how to wait, nurse," he said.

"It's Sister, not nurse," she reminded him. "Waiting room's over there."

"Yes, Sister."

An hour later, Kensie's father sought him out in the waiting room. "I've got a car waiting outside," he announced. "Will you come with me, Captain?"

"Certainly," Malachi said.

The car waiting out front included a chauffeur, who whisked them from the hospital to what Malachi suspected was the nearest pub.

Once inside, Lambert ordered a double whiskey. Malachi asked for a beer.

"Poor thing worked herself nearly to death," Lambert said. "Paused during an operation and asked the other surgeon if she could just sit down for a moment, then passed out. She'd been working two days on, a half-day off, then two more days on. Bloody stupid fucking hospital management."

"But they have lots of customers, don't they," Malachi said.

"Oh, God, yes," Lambert said. "British Army, our Army, they come by the boatload. Mind you, it was not like they were picking on her—the other docs are equally tired. But they *must* do something."

Malachi nodded. "Problem is, they can't just grow more surgeons in a couple of weeks," he said.

Lambert nodded. "I know," he said. "I know. Your lot have been standing up fully operational hospitals all over the city. One day, a vacant lot. The next, a fully staffed hospital. Reminds me that we're a bit of a colonial backwater here."

"How can I help you?" Malachi asked.

Lambert looked at him through whiskey-stained eyes. "Come upstairs," he said. "Margery is really upset. I need to take her home, do you see? But here's the thing: Kensie babbles once in a while and the name Malachi keeps surfacing."

"Absolutely," Malachi said. "Let's go right now."

Lambert hesitated. "There's one more thing, Captain," he said. "You've become important to our Kensie, but we both know what's coming. The Yanks are turning on the power. In a year, I think you'll all be gone. MacArthur's already talking about going north with his many minions. America is mobilizing, and then you lot will annihilate Japan. When? No one can say, but I dread the day that you leave, or, even worse, that you sail off on another bloody patrol and simply don't come back."

Malachi had no answer for that.

"She's my only child, Captain," Lambert said. "But she's asking for *you*, not Daddy. You're the first bloke she's, oh, God, what's the word? Really seized upon? But if you end up leaving her—"

"One thing at a time, Lambert," Malachi said, gently. "No one knows what's going to happen, or when. But right now, I want, no, I *demand* to help. I have a complicated personal past, but I've never been married, if that concerns you. Right now Kensie has my full attention. I promise you, I will never hurt her."

Lambert closed his eyes for a long moment. "*Bugger!*" he shouted, startling the other people in the bar. "*Bugger* this bloody war. God-*damn* the fucking Japs."

"Lambert, you keep yelling bugger, people are gonna talk."

Lambert opened his eyes "*What?*"

"Lambert, let's face it. You're not my type, mate."

Lambert stared at him for a second and then started laughing. "Right," he said. "Back to the hospital, then, Captain."

Kensie looked smaller in the hospital bed. She had one IV in, but otherwise looked relaxed and comfortable as she slept. The dark circles were back, however. Lambert explained to the Sister that the captain was going to take the family watch for a while.

"For the night, actually," Malachi said in his best captain's voice. The attending Sister took it all onboard and then Lambert and Margery left him to it. There were no chairs in the room, so Malachi liberated one from the central hallway. He scanned all the monitoring instruments along the wall before realizing that none of them was actually on. Then he figured it out: Kensie, being hospital staff and a surgeon, had been parked in an ICU more for privacy and personal care than what was available in the wards, filled as they were with military casualties.

He studied her sleeping face and asked himself if he was falling in love with this woman. She was lovely, tough, funny, a two-fisted drinker, a surgeon, and a hungry lover. But was this just one of those wartime romances, the mutual and somewhat frantic desire amplified by the knowledge that it could all blow up every time he went back out to sea? And with the dark secret in his past, was he even worthy of her or any woman? He was an American naval officer, a *commanding* officer, subject to orders that would brook no interference from personal considerations. Lambert knew the score. The whole sub squadron could be moved at a moment's notice to anywhere in the Pacific if it meant putting the Navy's fangs closer to the Japanese jugular. Australia had been the refuge of necessity after the boats had been bombed out of the Philippines, but Lambert was right: 1942 had been a disastrous year for the US Navy, but 1943 was around the corner and with it the coming avalanche of military power that was sliding down the building ways all across America. Lambert was right to be concerned for Kensie's heart.

"Sister, there's a man in my room," Kensie announced.

Malachi blinked and stood up. "Yes there is, Doctor," he said. "What are you going to do about it?"

She gave him a wan smile and then extended her hand. "*So* glad you're here," she said. "I think I rather fell apart. They'll never let me live this down."

He sat down on the bed and kissed her hand. "I came as soon as I found out," he said. "Your dad and I went for a drink, and then he left me here while he took your mother home. She was . . . upset."

"She was truly upset, I suspect," Kensie said. "To see me in a hospital bed rather than next to one. She and her family have really suffered in this war. She's a love, but this war has frightened her more than Lambert and I realized. Sometimes I think she's getting a bit dotty. My hours here haven't helped."

"Do you want to go home?" he asked.

"God, yes," she said. "This is ICU—I'm hardly critical." Then she hesitated. "Actually, no, I don't want to go home. I want to go somewhere else, where I can sleep and not worry about missing my shift. And where a nice man I happen to know will hold me in the night and give me no aggro if I happen to demand a whiskey at an inconvenient time.

"Wow," he said. "Tall order. I'll have to think about that."

She gave him an are-you-kidding-me look and he grinned. "Okay, all done," he said. "How do we get you out of this joint?"

"I need to get a doctor to discharge me," she said. "Oh."

"Atta girl," Malachi said.

EIGHTEEN

Malachi, the exec, and the COB were in the conning tower along with the OOD, the navigator, and one plotter.

"So that's Truk," the exec said as he peered through the periscope. "Happy new year, Truk. Although you don't look like much."

"We're on the other side of the lagoon from the main naval anchorage," Malachi said. "Even so, I don't much like being here. Down scope."

"From the intel briefs I understood this was the Jap fleet's main base," the exec said. "Ought to be some useful targets."

"Not our mission, apparently," Malachi said, handing the exec the single piece of paper that had comprised their sealed, secret orders, which were to be opened upon arrival in the assigned patrol area. The exec read them, and then shook his head.

"Report, but not attack?"

"Not unless it's a truly valuable target," Malachi said. "Think carrier or battleship. It seems there's some big operation coming down in the Solomons, so our job is to report any major force movements *out* of Truk. They don't want us to reveal our presence, which also might explain the light torpedo load."

The boat had left Perth with only ten torpedoes, one for each tube. It was obviously a strictly defensive loadout. The tender torpedo office had told them that the shortage was even worse than it had been, and that that was all they could have. That was one explanation, but, before he'd opened the orders, Malachi had wondered if the admiral was sending him a message: Don't want to use the torpedoes the way *I* want you to use them? We'll give 'em to someone who plays by the rules.

"Make your depth two five zero, and come to course two seven zero," Malachi ordered. "There are three passages out of this lagoon. One's too shallow for big ships, so our job is to watch the other two. If we see something significant, we wait until nightfall, surface and run fifty miles away from the lagoon, and then, and *only* then, send out the message. Apparently the Jap HF direction-finding net is improving."

"Just like their radar detection equipment," the exec said, remembering the pasting they'd taken off Surabaya. That news had hit the SubPac community hard and, inevitably, prompting some Doubting Thomases back at headquarters to question Malachi's theory.

The COB had come up to the conning tower to get a periscope look at Truk Lagoon just before the exec. "I still don't understand how us using our radar told the Japs right where we were," he said. "All they'd get was one bearing; how'd they know how far out we were?"

"By using more than one listening device," Malachi said. "Remember, a radar sends out a pulse of energy. If the pulse hits something, it reflects *some* of that energy back to the radar receiver. But since the rest of the pulse keeps going, your signal can be detected miles and miles farther out than your receiver's range. They can't know how far away that signal originated, but if you put up three listening devices with some decent bearing separation, you can get a passive bearing fix on where that radar is. That's how that destroyer division knew right where to go. *Has* to be."

"Stable at two hundred fifty feet," Control reported over the bitchbox. "On course two seven zero at five knots."

"Is there a layer?"

"No, sir, no layer."

"Okay, XO, here's what I want: get us ten miles away from that lagoon, and then slow to three knots and begin a big submerged circle around Truk. Conduct a passive acoustic search. If some big guys come out, we should hear them assuming we're near whichever passage they're using."

"And if we're not?"

"Well, then, we'll miss 'em," Malachi replied, impatiently. "I didn't say this was a smart way to use a submarine, did I. How many hours to full dark?"

"About seven, sir," the navigator said.

Malachi groaned and then went down the ladder and forward to his cabin. This was almost as bad as Pearl's latest great idea, using the subs to lay small minefields around Jap bases and choke points in the various southwest Pacific island chains. Now some genius had assigned a single boat, *Firefish*, to patrol the perimeter of a lagoon in the middle of nowhere that contained 800 square miles of anchorage and whose reef was 140 miles around. And if a Jap carrier happened by, the were *not* to shoot at him?

He closed the curtain, flipped off the overhead lights, and lay down on his bed. That was a signal not to disturb him unless something operational required it. As he closed his eyes he realized he was getting a little tired of the Navy's political games in Perth. He'd run two unusually successful patrols during a time when the Navy was still trying to get back on its feet after a long series of defeats. Now here they were, on their third patrol at the beginning of the new year, with him still at least partially in the doghouse back at Perth. So much so that they'd assigned him to picket duty off Truk with only enough torpedoes to defend the boat in case some Jap destroyer jumped them. And, oh, by the way, his crew was scared of him. The Iceman. He snorted in the dim light coming through the curtain from the passageway. Maybe he should do this milk-run bullshit patrol, go back to Perth, and hand the keys over.

Then he heard the general announcing system click on.

"General quarters, general quarters. Fire, fire, fire in the after torpedo room. Secure the boat."

Malachi made it to the control room just in time as all the watertight doors in the boat were being slammed shut and dogged down. The ventilation had been shut off immediately.

"Take her up to periscope depth," he ordered. "Where's Truk?"

"The lagoon bears two six five, range estimated ten miles. We're halfway around."

Malachi needed to put some distance between *Firefish* and Truk in case they had to surface, but the battery was depleted after a day submerged. "Then come to zero nine zero, five knots. Is everybody out of after torpedo?"

"Chief engineer says he *thinks* so, but they're still counting heads. The fire was in an electrical panel, but it's spread to berthing material and insulation. Bad smoke, sir. Repair party's about to go back in."

"Okay, they know what to do," Malachi said. "I'm going to go get a look around from the conning tower."

He climbed up into the conning tower and called for the periscope, only to find they weren't at periscope depth yet. The boat was still turning, and the air was already getting hotter. The exec had gone aft to oversee the firefighting effort. Malachi tried not to think of what would happen if the fire spread to the after torpedo tubes, but then was grateful they were carrying no reloads, because they would already be cooking by now. Then he remembered that all he had to do was open outer doors aft and flood the four tubes. He ordered Control to do that.

The big problem was that the fire, now burning canvas racks, bulkhead insulation, and bedding was consuming oxygen while filling the compartment with toxic smoke. Anybody who hadn't got out before the hatches were locked down would be a goner. He dared not restore ventilation, because then the smoke would fill the entire boat.

"Steady at periscope depth," Control reported. "Repair party is on scene."

"*Up* scope," Malachi ordered. He was careful to not just pop it out at full height, in case there happened to be Japs nearby. "Make your speed three knots," he ordered, to reduce the periscope's wake. It wasn't just Jap ships he needed to worry about this close to their main southwest Pacific base. A Kawanishi could kill them just as well as any Jap destroyer.

It was late afternoon, so there were at least a couple hours of full daylight left. The seas were mostly calm, with a light chop indicating maybe ten knots of wind. He walked the scope around through 360 degrees. The seas were empty. He thought about using the radar, but after the last patrol he had decided to be sparing with it. If the Japs had put up a radar detection net at Surabaya, they'd sure as hell have one here.

"*Down* scope," he called. "Sound, Conn: anything?"

"Negative contacts, Captain," the sonar shack replied. "Control, Conn: progress report?"

"Three men unaccounted for, Captain. XO's gone into the compartment. Maneuvering is getting smoke."

"Very well," Malachi said. He was itching to go back there, but that would mean opening four watertight hatches just to get to Maneuvering. The repair party should be in oxygen breathing apparatuses, and hopefully the exec had put one on, too, before entering the fire zone. If Maneuvering was getting smoke, it meant they hadn't totally isolated the after torpedo room. And if smoke was getting out, then air was getting in and sustaining the damned fire.

"Control: who's working the isolation of after torpedo?"

"Chief engineer, Captain, and whatever it is, it's really small. Wait one." A pause. "XO's back out. The fire is being starved of oxygen but it's still glowing. Request permission for the repair party to go in and fight it with CO-two."

"Permission granted. Any word on the three missing men?"

"Negative, sir. Too much smoke. Repair party is entering the space."

"Conn, Sound: I have screwbeats, bearing three five zero, slight up-Doppler. Multiples, I think. Something big."

Malachi sighed. Just what he needed right now. He turned to the radar operator. "I want to put the surface search radar mast up, but do not rotate the antenna. I want it pointed at three fifty true, energized for thirty seconds, and then pull it down. Got it?"

"Yes, sir, got it," the operator said.

"Conn, Control: repair party is backing out. When they opened the hatch, the fire reflashed."

"All right, ask the XO to call me here in the conning tower. In the meantime, open all outer doors forward."

The exec came in on a sound-powered phone. His voice sounded dry and stressed from the OBA air. In the background, Malachi heard the radar mast going up.

"XO, here's what I need you to do: go back in there in three minutes, when the fire's had a chance to use up that oxygen. I want you to go all the way aft to the torpedo tubes and manually fire one fish. The after outer doors are opening now. Once the fish is away, get out and call me. When I *know* you're back out I will close the after outer doors. Then I want two people to go back in. You go in and open the empty tube to the compartment like you were going to reload it. The second guy goes in and opens the suction valve to the main eductor in after torpedo. Then you both get out."

"What are you going to do, sir?"

"Once you're both clear, I'm going to reopen outer doors aft, which will flood that compartment and extinguish the fire. Then we'll close outer doors again and activate the eductor to get all that water out."

"Yes, sir, got it."

"Oh, by the way, there's a Jap formation coming our way, just for grins."

"Why not," the exec said, and then hung up.

"Control, Conn: the exec is going back into after torpedo to manually fire one tube. Tell me when he's back out, and then prepare to counterballast against a flooded after torpedo room."

"Control: uh, aye, sir."

Malachi looked around the conning tower space. The attack crew was in place, having nowhere else to go during a fire emergency. They all appeared to be digesting the news that the captain was going to intentionally flood the after torpedo room. "Don't just stand there," he said. "Prepare for an attack on the heavy coming our way."

The attack crew jumped to it, cranking up the plotting table and the TDC. The TDC operator started talking to sonar, which, at the moment, was their only source of information about whatever was headed their way.

"Conn, Control: XO's going in. They think they've found the air leak in an LP air line. Maneuvering is de-smoking now."

"Conn: aye, have the XO call me when he gets back out. Radar, what'd you get?"

"Five contacts, four destroyer size, one big bastard. Escorts are in a bent-line screen ahead of the big guy. They're out at ten miles and closing. Steady bearing, still three five zero."

"Okay, do that again in three minutes so we can get a course and speed. I want the big guy. Gonna fire all we got at him. Forward torpedo: set fish on contact exploders, running depth ten feet, speed high. No spread—all on the firing line."

They waited, and then felt the pulse of a torpedo launching from the back end and howling off to nowhere.

"Conn, Control: XO is back out." Malachi acknowledged and then immediately ordered the after outer doors closed. The sound-powered phone squeaked; it was the exec. "Captain, that fire is still getting air from somewhere," he said. "And it's spreading. I barely got out."

"Any sign of the three missing guys?"

"No, sir. Visibility in after torpedo is zero-zero. I had to crawl the deck plates to get to the tubes. If they're in there, they're long gone."

"I'm closing the after outer doors right now. You think you can go in one more time and open up that tube?"

"I can try, sir," the exec said. "I'll need a hose team to follow me in and keep me covered. The COB's here now—he'll go for the eductor valve under the deck plates."

"Okay, do your best, but stay alive. If you can't do it, then back out and we'll try something else."

"For what it's worth, sir, I concur with flooding the space," the exec said. "That flask handle was already hot."

Malachi hung up. The radar operator was trying to get his attention. "Conn, Radar: second sweep complete. Bearing remains three five zero. Range is now seven miles and closing."

"Based on that," a plotter said, "plot has the formation at twenty-five knots."

"Very well," Malachi said. They'd be on top in about five minutes. "Come to course three five zero," he ordered. "Prepare tubes one through six."

He desperately wanted to take a periscope look at the approaching formation, but really didn't need to. Steady bearing, decreasing range meant the formation would run right over the top of *Firefish*. The real problem would come when they fired all those fish and then tried to make the boat go deep, with the front end lighter by 12,000 pounds worth of torpedoes and the back end heavier with a flooded after torpedo room.

"Conn, Control: XO and COB are back out and the hatch secured. Tube ten air flask assembly is open to the compartment."

"Conn: aye," Malachi said. Now, he thought: decision time. Flood it now, and Control might lose control of the boat and pop to the surface right in front of the Japs. Or, let it burn, fire the six fish forward in the next three minutes, and *then* flood after torpedo. It was a tough call, especially when his orders were *not* to attack anything but rather to wait and report.

"Forward torpedo reports six tubes ready, settings applied," the TDC operator announced. "Time to fire is one hundred thirty seconds."

"Conn: aye," Malachi said. "Up scope." He just *had* to take a look. If it was a carrier coming, he'd attack. Anything else, he'd dive now and worry about them later. He squatted down as the scope came up. He dropped the handles and rotated the scope to look at 350 degrees true bearing.

"Conn, Control: Maneuvering reports the hatch to after torpedo is getting too hot to touch."

Malachi swore. If he waited much longer, the torpedoes might cook off even with the tubes flooded. He acknowledged the report, and then finally got the scope to focus on the near horizon. There were four contacts that he could see. Three small ones, and one much bigger. No, *two* much bigger. Two aircraft carriers, one slightly larger than the other, bows on, the distinctive shape of their flight decks clearly visible.

"Time to fire is fifty seconds," the TDC operator announced.

Two carriers in a down-the-throat shot. They were going 25 knots. His fish would be going 46 knots. A 70-knot closure rate. None of them would be able to turn in time to avoid. "Down scope. Fire all tubes in sequence, commencing *now*."

"Forward torpedo, aye. Firing one."

Malachi waited for the fifth torpedo to be fired, already feeling that tinge of uncertainty as the boat began to lose stability from the sudden weight loss forward.

"Six away," forward torpedo reported.

"Conn, Sonar: all appearing to run hot, straight, and normal."

"Conn: aye. All stop. All back one third. Open outer doors aft. Close outer doors forward."

They all had to hold on as the boat mushed to a stop and then began to go backwards. And downwards, as all that water came pouring into after torpedo. He'd decided to not try to fight the boat's instability, but rather to flood her aft and then let her do what she would want to do, which was to slide backwards into the depths. Depths being the operative word once those fish found their marks.

"All stop," he ordered, and then watched the depth gauge, as they accelerated backwards. For every foot they went down, the water would come in even faster. He had to catch her before this became a runaway.

"All ahead one third," he ordered. "Forward planes thirty degrees rise."

The depth gauge read 180 feet when the first booming sounds came through the hull on the bearing of 350. They'd hit something. Or else the escorts were dropping depth charges after seeing torpedo wakes.

"Passing two hundred feet," the OOD reported nervously. Malachi watched the horizontal level indicator, mentally shouting at the bubble to move back to the center, but it wasn't budging. The boat was still bow high and sliding backwards.

"Close outer doors aft and get that eductor going," he ordered.

"Passing two fifty."

The boat's attitude hadn't changed, and he thought he could feel that big slug of water back in after torpedo dragging them backwards. And down. "Flood negative," he ordered, in hopes of counterbalancing the extra weight all the way aft. "Blow all after ballast tanks. Blow safety tank."

"Passing two eighty."

Finally the boat started to flatten out and stop her descent. The rumble of compressed air disgorging into the after ballast tanks was dangerously loud, now that there were destroyers looking for them.

But he'd left the outer doors open long enough, he hoped, to flood that compartment and drown the fire. Now the eductor system would begin dewatering, although he realized that that might take as much as an hour.

"Steady at three hundred feet," the diving officer reported from Control. "Recommend pumping negative to fifty percent."

Good, Malachi thought. The diving officer understands our problem. From here on out it would be a balancing act, as the extra water aft was pumped out and they had to use the ballast tanks to keep the boat under some semblance of depth control. "Concur," he replied.

"Conn, Sound: I have pinging in a sector between three three zero and three five zero; no detectable Doppler."

Yet, Malachi thought. That's when he realized he was still going 350, his firing course, right back toward the destroyers. "Come to one seven zero," he ordered. "Use no more than five degrees rudder."

"Conn, Control: we're still too heavy. I can't maintain depth control."

Malachi glanced at the depth gauge, which had slipped down to 325 when no one was looking. Do what you might with plane angles and speed changes: if you have more weight *in* the boat than the boat itself displaced, the boat becomes a rock.

"Passing three four zero," the OOD announced, but quietly, as if not to alarm anyone. The familiar creaking and groaning sounds began to make themselves heard.

"Sound, Conn: what's the bearing of the pingers right now?"

"Conn, Sound: three two zero for the strongest signals."

"Plot: based on the little bit of dope we had about those carriers, what should the range be right now?"

The TDC operator looked at his wheels and dials. By doctrine, he'd kept the computer running on the original firing in case they needed to reattack. "Six thousand yards, Captain, but we only had two radar ranges, so that's a WAG."

Great, Malachi thought. A WAG—wild-ass guess. Better than nothing. "Open outer doors aft," he ordered. "Prepare to fire our remaining three fish: contact exploders, speed *low*, running depth six feet. TDC: force firing bearing to three two zero. Spread is four degrees. Remote fire from forward torpedo as quickly as possible. What's our course?"

"Passing one four zero, sir. Coming to course one seven zero."

After an eternity of seconds, they felt the thump of the first torpedo going out aft, followed quickly by two more thumps. "Close after outer doors," Malachi ordered.

"Passing three five five feet," the OOD said.

"Give me full power *now*. After planes twenty degrees rise."

They waited to see if the boat would respond. Malachi had just ejected three tons of weight from the after tubes. He may have let some more water in by re-opening the after outer doors, but he didn't think so. The chances of them hitting anything were nil, but those three fish just might distract the searching destroyers long enough for *Firefish* to get away. *If* she responded.

They waited, everyone in the conning tower fully aware of the throbbing propellers and the increasing protests of the boat's hull.

"Passing—no, *steady* at three six zero feet," the OOD announced, finally.

"Control, Conn: what's the battery state?"

"Twenty-five percent, Captain."

They were just holding her, but not rising. With the battery at twenty-five percent their fate was sealed unless something changed. He reached for the bitchbox. "Maneuvering, Conn: can you get HP air into after torpedo?"

"Well, it's already there, for the torpedo flasks, but we can't get in and energize that line."

"Steady on course one seven zero, Captain."

"Very well," Malachi said. "But you've got HP air available in after engine room, correct? For main engine start?"

"Yes, sir, and the HP air line runs from the after engine room through Maneuvering into after torpedo."

"Is there a tap in Maneuvering from that flask supply line?"

"Yes, sir, there is. We use it to blow down the switchboards."

"All right, this is what I want you to do. Connect a line to that tap. Then I want you to drill a hole between Maneuvering and after torpedo and insert that line into that hole, and then open up the HP air. We're nearly at four hundred feet. The pressure outside is about one seventy-five psi. The HP air is three *thousand* psi. The after outer doors are open. I need you to blast that water out of there, or we're going to see what it's like at *five* hundred feet. Gotchee?"

"Yes, sir," the chief engineer said. "We're on it."

Then they heard a distant boom, different from the thumping depth charges that had been going off for the past twenty minutes. Everyone in the conning tower looked at one another.

"End of run, boys," Malachi said. "There's no chance that one of those fish hit something."

The high-pressure air, fed from a compressor in the after engine room, worked. Two men had to hold the end of the blow-down line to the three-quarter-inch hole they'd drilled through the bulkhead, but the combination of the HP air and the eductor steadily blew all the water out of after torpedo. Suddenly the boat began to respond to the planes and the propellers, shooting up from 370 feet to 275 before they got her under control. Malachi ordered the after outer doors closed and then slowed the propellers down to 5 knots again. For the next two hours, they slunk away from the scene of the carrier attack, staying down at 275 feet.

Malachi was more than ready for darkness and the opportunity to surface. The air in the boat was becoming unfit to breathe as CO_2 built up. Once the outer doors aft were closed the fire-fighting party went back into after torpedo, which was a complete mess. Making matters worse, much worse, they found the three missing men, whose charred remains had to be literally scraped off the deck plates. Flooding the compartment had indeed snuffed out the fire. They found the source of the air that had reflashed it: a spare high-pressure air flask for the torpedo tubes. The fire had melted a brass valve, allowing the fully charged flask to feed a steady supply of oxygen to the fire.

Some of the men in the fire-fighting party became sick when they encountered the remains. Unlike their surface ship counterparts, submariners rarely experienced the sight, and smell, of wounded, burned, or maimed shipmates. Either everyone came out of a fight in one piece, or they all perished together in the dark depths of the sea. The boat's hospital corpsman, a chief petty officer, called the conning tower and recommended against restoring ventilation until they could surface. Malachi immediately understood why, because the boat's ventilation system constantly recirculated all the air onboard. He ordered the after torpedo room hatch closed and locked and any surviving vents taped off.

They surfaced just after sunset. Once the main diesel engines started up, fresh air was drawn into the boat in great quantities. Malachi considered doing a quick air and surface radar search, but decided against it with Truk nearby. He posted six lookouts instead and increased speed to 18 knots on a course for Perth. It would take a week to get back. Then he went below to his cabin to write an operational report, including his intentions to return to port. He told the exec to prepare a burial at sea ceremony for midnight. The exec said he would make it so, and then reminded Malachi that it was New Year's Day.

"Time passes fast when you're having fun," Malachi grumbled. "Happy goddamned new year."

"Happy goddamned new year, aye, sir," the exec said, as he drew the curtain and headed off to find the COB.

NINETEEN

They had only ten percent fuel left onboard when they pulled into the harbor at Perth. Malachi had timed the arrival for ten in the morning. The voyage back had been uneventful except for one emergency dive when one of the lookouts had spotted what he thought was a periscope just southwest of New Guinea. The line handlers had been out on deck early, fore and aft, as they passed the breakwater and approached the tender. They were dressed out in dungarees, white T-shirts, and clean, white Dixie cup hats. Several members of the crew were also on deck, anxious to see dry land again amid the prospects for some well-earned time ashore with Aussie beer and all those delectable Sheilas. Malachi allowed the exec to make the landing alongside USS *Trout*, which was the outboard boat on the nest of four boats alongside the tender.

As the exec grappled with the problem of maneuvering a close-coupled, twin-screw submarine alongside another one without colliding, Malachi scanned the decks of the tender. To his surprise, he spotted the admiral up on the bridge wing of the tender, waving at him. He straightened up and saluted. The admiral returned the salute, as did the second older officer standing next to him. Oh, shit, he thought. They'd brought someone in to head up the investigation into the fire and the deaths of three crewmen. Well, he'd been expecting that, but not a flag officer. The two officers disappeared into the tender's pilothouse door.

He'd sealed the after torpedo room for two reasons: the smell,

173

primarily, and also to preserve any evidence of what had started the disastrous fire in the first place. And then there was the problem of his patrol orders: report, but do not attack. That might be an even harder issue to confront than the fire. He had no idea if he'd hit either of the carriers with that down-the-throat, no-spread salvo of six torpedoes. There'd been sounds of torpedoes going off, but that could mean anything: they'd prematured or even hit an escort ship. Or run out to the extent of their fuel and detonated at end-of-run. His only defense would be that the two Jap carriers had presented him with an unheard-of opportunity. He could not believe that anyone would have approved his *not* taking that opportunity. Except maybe Rear Admiral Hamner W. Marsten, who had thought that he and Malachi were not going to "get along."

He'd given the bare minimum of details in the radio message he'd sent in after clearing Truk Lagoon. Fire in the after torpedo room. Attack on a two-carrier formation while fighting that fire. The decision to flood out the after torpedo room to smother the fire. The need to jettison the torpedoes from the after torpedo room in order to recover from an uncontrolled descent past 400 feet. The loss of three crewmen in the fire. His unilateral decision to return to Perth once all torpedoes were gone.

After that, he'd handwritten a lot more details into his captain's log. He'd wrestled with the idea of trying to justify disobeying his patrol orders to attack the carriers, but decided against it. They'd either approve or they'd disapprove. It would be interesting to see which. Then he'd written three letters of condolences to the parents of the three men killed in the fire. Two were just twenty years old; the third a graybeard of twenty-four. He hadn't realized his crew was quite so young.

The shrill sound of a police whistle indicated that *Firefish* had landed at least one mooring line on *Trout*, which meant that they were officially moored. As the exec used the engines to hold the boat snug against *Trout*, a crew from the tender slid the brow across. Back aft the American flag went up on the flagstaff as the at-sea flag was brought down on the sail. Malachi reluctantly climbed down from the bridge to the main deck and headed aft to meet the brass.

By the time he got back to the quarterdeck there were two captains waiting to come aboard. One he recognized as the "new" chief of staff, who had been in the process of replacing Captain Collins when *Firefish* had left for her third patrol. The other he did not recognize, but soon found out was the equally new squadron commodore, Captain Harold VanBuren, who'd taken command of the Perth submarine squadron while *Firefish* was off Truk Lagoon. Behind them were two commanders and a lieutenant commander, whom he assumed were staff officers. The second year of this war, Malachi thought, and the staffs are already propagating like weeds.

He introduced himself to everyone, and then led them to the forward hatch. The crew had spent the last four days cleaning and polishing, as everyone knew there'd be lots of visitors because of the fire. Malachi led the small parade of khaki back to the after torpedo room hatch, where the chief engineer was waiting.

"I decided to seal the space for the transit back to Pearl," he announced. "If there's evidence in there of what started this fire I wanted it to remain undisturbed. As you know, the after hatch is also the torpedo loading hatch, which lands in the space. I had the engineer use that to ventilate the space for the past few hours. But prepare yourselves. Three men were incinerated in there a week ago. There's a bottle of Vick's Vaporub right next to the hatch. I recommend you put a dab in each of your nostrils."

The two four-stripers, knowing what to expect, did just that, as did Malachi. The chief engineer had already applied some of the creamy, white goo that reeked of camphor and eucalyptus oil. The other staffies did not. Malachi nodded at the chief engineer, who undogged and then swung open the hatch. Despite the ventilation efforts, a wave of warm, wet, and fetid air bloomed into Maneuvering. The commander gagged and barely held on to his breakfast, while the two lieutenant commanders bailed out back into the submarine, slamming a hatch behind them. Malachi stepped carefully over the hatch coaming, a flashlight at the ready, as all the light-fixtures had been burned away. The engineer passed out flashlights to the two captains, and they began their inspection. The chief engineer had some men position a red-devil blower in the hatchway to direct the compartment air up the torpedo loading hatch.

"There were no reports of where the fire started?" the commodore asked.

"No, sir," Malachi said. "Control received a report of a fire in after torpedo, but no details. I asked if everyone was out and was told only that they were still counting heads."

"But Maneuvering shut that hatch immediately, right?"

"Yes, sir, I'm sure they did. That's standard procedure, especially submerged. They shut off all ventilation as well."

"And you ended up flooding the space to get the fire completely out," the chief of staff said.

"Yes, sir. There was an air leak somewhere that kept reflashing it."

The space looked the part. Charred insulation hung from the overhead and the bulkheads. The sailors' racks, which were strung up between the reload torpedo trays, had been turned into sodden, black lumps. Steel hydraulic lines had held up, as had most of the cladded cabling, which is what had allowed Malachi to operate the after outer doors and fire torpedoes. The overhead light fixtures had all melted, as had some of the copper piping. Charred and soaked papers, maintenance logs, toolboxes, and one forlorn coffeemaker littered the bilge area under the stainless-steel deck plates.

"Okay," the commodore said. "I've seen enough. If the torpedo tubes are undamaged, we can fix this here. If not, you're going back to Pearl to the shipyard. I've convened an informal investigation; Commander Harris here will conduct it, when he feels better. Meanwhile, I've told the tender to get a tiger-team in here and see if they can put this all back in order."

From the tone of his voice, Malachi could tell that the commodore had his doubts.

"And while all this was going on, you attacked an escorted carrier formation?" the chief of staff asked.

"Well, the damage-control team at least had the fire isolated," Malachi said. "And it wasn't like I had to do any tactical maneuvering to attack those ships—they were on a constant bearing, decreasing range from first detection. No zigzag that we could tell. We had a closing rate of nearly seventy miles an hour between my fish and their speed.

All I had to do was to fire everything I had and then deal with the problem of a fire that wouldn't go out."

The chief of staff nodded. "Well, you'll be pleased to know that both carriers were damaged and had to return to Japan for repairs," he said. "One was the light carrier *Otaka*, the other was *Shokaku*, who'd been heavily damaged in the Coral Sea fight and was just returning to operations. *Otaka* ate two fish, *Shokaku* one. They both limped into Truk. A destroyer escort turned in front of another fish and was sunk. Not bad, Captain, for what you're making it sound like an oh-by-the-way attack. Conducted on the shortest war patrol of the war, so far. Good work."

Malachi wanted to ask if the damage he'd inflicted on two carriers made up for his disobeying his operational orders, but elected to save that for another day. The commander went forward to Control to begin gathering up logs.

The tiger team, a thrown-together temporary squad of electricians, structural shipfitters, and torpedo tube experts arrived an hour later. A senior chief electrician was in charge. The first thing he did was to send for a quart of diesel fuel, which he dumped all over the area where the men had been killed. Now the compartment smelled of diesel oil, with which all submariners felt quite comfortable. That afternoon three tugboats showed up from Perth Harbour to rearrange the nest of submarines in order to put *Firefish* directly alongside the tender. This would allow the tender's crane to reach the sub's deck to remove damaged equipment. It also allowed the tender's diving team to inspect the boat's propellers, rudders, and outer door assemblies while standing on an underwater platform supported by the crane. One of the admiral's staff officers came aboard requesting the captain's personal log. He informed Malachi that the admiral wanted a debrief the following morning at ten aboard the tender. Malachi replied that he could hardly wait, prompting a knowing smile from the staffie.

He remained onboard until late afternoon, when the tiger-team chief came to see him. He reported that neither the boat's hull nor the torpedo tubes had been compromised. Everything else in the compartment would have to be ripped out and replaced. That would take at least two weeks, maybe three, if they had to wait for parts. He asked if ship's company engineers would be able to help, and Malachi said of course.

He then called in the exec and told him he wanted an all-hands meeting tomorrow morning at 0900. He then got a staff car to take him to the hotel downtown. The moment he stepped out onto the rooftop lounge he was ambushed by four skippers, all wanting to know what had really happened at Truk. His buddy Jay Carney was out on patrol. He didn't know two of the four skippers pulling up chairs, but after introductions were made and his legendary single beer produced, he told them his story. When he was finished they sat around silently for a minute before one popped the first question, and it went directly to the heart of the matter.

"Your patrol orders were to lay off Truk and report, but not attack any heavies leaving Truk. They even shorted you on your torpedo load. You expect they're gonna fang you for that?"

"Don't know," Malachi said. "They did give me an out, namely if a carrier or a battleship showed up. But my mission was to act as a sentinel for the Solomons. We failed at that, I think. On the other hand, I couldn't help thinking at the time that ComSubPac would ask: You had two Jap carriers coming straight at you, and you *didn't* shoot?"

"You could always say that your orders were to report but not attack any heavies *leaving* Truk," his questioner said. "These guys were headed into Truk Lagoon."

The others laughed and started making comments about sea lawyers.

"Our primary mission," Malachi said, "is to destroy Japanese shipping, military and merchant marine. We didn't sink either one of those carriers, and I don't think our Mark fourteen torpedoes *could* sink a Jap carrier. But neither of them will be available for whatever is happening down in the Solomons. If that's cause for my relief as skipper, then so be it. I'm satisfied I've done my bit. I'm just sad that I lost three guys."

"Hell, *yes*, you have," another skipper said. "Good God, Malachi,

Firefish is famous in SubPac. Cruisers, destroyers, *marus*, and now two carriers? They wouldn't fucking dare."

Malachi finished his beer. He hadn't eaten, but suddenly he needed sleep more than food. "I'm medium whupped," he announced. "We'll just have to see what happens tomorrow."

Up in his room, he'd taken a thirty-minute hot shower and then dropped into what seemed like an enormous feather bed. He was just drifting off to sleep when there was a knock on his door. It was nine o'clock. He groaned, found a bathrobe, and went to the door. It was one of the hotel's desk clerks. "There's a doctor asking for you," he said. "She says you know each other."

Malachi was having trouble keeping his eyes open in the doorway. "Tell her this, if you would, please: pretend that I haven't returned yet. To tell the truth, I'm exhausted. Tell her that, too. Ask her to come back tomorrow night, when I will most definitely want to see her. Can you do that for me?"

"Absolutely, sir. No worries."

Malachi went back to bed. A few minutes later he thought he heard the door opening, but he wasn't sure he was awake or dreaming. After a minute, a warm female presence was sliding into bed with him. She smelled suspiciously of medical alcohol. She put her arms around him and snuggled close. He tried to say something, but she put her fingers on his lips.

"Shush," she said. "I'm as tired as you are. Go to sleep. I will, too. Glad you're back in one piece."

If she was expecting a reply, she was disappointed. He was down at 250 feet and sleeping like a baby. She smiled in the darkness and wrapped herself around him for the night.

TWENTY

Malachi's meeting with the admiral started right on time. Present were the admiral, the chief of staff, Malachi's squadron commander, some engineering staff officers, and a warrant officer from the tender. The warrant, who was the ship's superintendent for the tender's *Firefish* tiger team, led off with a preliminary damage report summary plus his best estimate of how long it would take to get *Firefish* ready for sea.

"Everything that could burn *did* burn," he said. "Bedding, paperwork, technical manuals, cork insulation, gauge glasses, power tools, unarmored cabling, and maintenance supplies for the torpedoes. The hull, the loading hatch and the compartment hatch, armored cabling, steel piping, deck plates, and the tubes themselves are scorched but serviceable."

He offered to go into more detail, but the admiral asked him to just leave his report and thanked him. The warrant left the conference room.

"Now, then," the admiral said. He had three folders in front of him. "I've read the captain's log, *Firefish*'s patrol orders, and the intel reports from Pearl on damage inflicted on the carriers *Shokaku* and *Otaka*." He tapped each folder in turn as he named them.

"Let's get one thing straight right away. *Firefish*'s orders were to report Jap fleet movement, especially heavies, and *not* to attack and thereby reveal his presence. These reports were to be a part of surveillance network protecting Navy forces at Guadalcanal. The patrol orders were quite specific, with no exceptions mentioned in regard to making any attacks. I'd like to hear your reasoning, Captain, for disobeying the patrol orders."

Everyone else at the table seemed to go still. No more fiddling with notepads, coffee cups, or cigarettes, and no one making eye contact with Malachi except the admiral, whose gaze could only be described as flinty.

"There was one exception," he began. "Carriers or battleships."

The admiral picked up his message board and reread the patrol orders. He grunted when he saw the line about carriers and battleships. "Go ahead," he said.

"In the middle of our fire emergency," Malachi continued, "Sound reported a Jap formation, including at least one heavy, coming straight at us, steady bearing, rising Doppler. A quick radar sweep gave us a range of twenty thousand yards, plus the information that there were *two* heavies, plus escorts. We were, as you might expect, busy with the fire, so I had a scratch team in the conning tower start a plot and crank up the TDC. We were already at periscope depth in case the fire forced us to surface and abandon. I used the radar one more time to get a rough course and speed. They were not zigzagging. Coming right at us at twenty-five knots. The shot of a lifetime. The two heavies in a column; escorts out front in a bent-line formation. Like I said, it was the shot of a lifetime, and I instinctively believed that *everyone* in my chain of command would have crucified me if I *didn't* take the shot. So I fired every torpedo we had up front directly at that column. Down the throat, no spread. I waited for the plot to indicate a range, with a closing rate of about seventy miles an hour between my fish and the carriers, where the heavies could not avoid the fish. Then I went back to dealing with the fire we had going aft."

The admiral was silent for a moment. Then he lifted his head. "I'm Old Navy, Captain. In my view, you should have avoided the formation, got your fire under control, and then remained on station to carry out your mission and your entirely specific orders—*not* to attack, but to report the presence of *Shokaku* and *Otaka*, where perhaps one of our carrier task forces might have found them and put them down for good."

He paused, ostensibly to light a cigarette, but also to let his words sink in. "Lucky for you," he said, finally, "after I had sent a message to ComSubPac outlining my thoughts and concerns on this episode, Admiral English came back and reported that Admiral Nimitz himself thought that your attack on those two carriers was in the highest traditions of the submarine service, and the fact that you managed that while dealing with a dangerous fire onboard was positively amazing. He also pointed out that *his* orders to the Pacific Fleet submarine force state that the destruction of the Japanese fleet's heavy units, especially aircraft carriers, would always supersede any subordinate's orders to the contrary if the opportunity ever presented itself."

Malachi exhaled, but then realized there might be another shoe about to drop.

"Personally, I think this sets a dangerous precedent, in that the commanders of naval forces around Guadalcanal were counting on you to follow your orders. The decision by an individual commanding officer to depart from his orders can, and has in the past, put lots of other people in harm's way. That said, the fleet commander is reminding us all that our overarching mission is the destruction of the enemy's fleet, especially at a time when we are the principal means of doing so." He looked straight at Malachi. "You, sir, have dodged a bullet."

Malachi tried to think of a smart retort, but sense prevailed.

"Now, if you would be so kind, please tell us about fighting that fire and getting your boat back under control after an excursion to over one hundred feet below test depth."

That took almost an hour, with the other attendees seeming to be genuinely interested in the technical details of how *Firefish* had been saved. Malachi managed to resist every impulse to embellish the stark technical details with some clever riposte to the admiral's unwavering criticism of him as a skipper. He sensed that his squadron commander was aware of this, and approved. "Pick your battles" was the commodore's subliminal advice.

After the meeting, the commodore suggested they have lunch in the tender's wardroom. Over lunch the commodore asked about Malachi's prior service, and then told him about his own career. When they finished, they went up to the commodore's stateroom for coffee. And privacy, Malachi assumed.

"How's your COB?" the commodore asked.

"Steady Eddy," Malachi replied. "Solid, calm, the crew respects him. He and I talk often."

"And your exec?"

Malachi paused. "Marty's a good guy," he began. "Meticulous, high standards, fair. And apparently fearless, too. He was the key man during the fire."

The commodore sensed Malachi's hesitation. "But?"

"I'm not sure how to put this, but he's always reluctant to really push a tactical situation. It's not that he questions my authority or anything like that. But he'll try to talk me out of it if I want to do something really dangerous."

"You're saying he lacks the killer instinct, then," the commodore said.

"Well, yes, that's one way to put it, I guess."

"You don't appear to have that problem."

Malachi stared down at the table for a few seconds. "No, sir, I definitely do not have that problem," he said softly.

"I've never made a war patrol," VanBuren said. "I was a fresh-caught captain when Pearl happened, having just turned over my S-boat to Dave Chandler in San Diego. I was stashed on the SubPac staff while the whole world was still reeling from the attack. I'd served with Admiral English before, so he eventually sent me out here as a squad dog after three months at New London learning about the new fleet boats. Spent some time in Brisbane learning the southwest Pacific ropes and how we were supposed to work with MacArthur and his entourage. Have to admit, it feels a little funny to be the squadron commander when I've never done what you guys have been doing."

"Trade you," Malachi quipped. VanBuren laughed out loud. But then his face sobered.

"This admiral doesn't like you much," he said. "As I'm sure you're aware."

Malachi nodded.

"You're not the only one he doesn't like. Jay Carney made his shit list, as has Ray Calhoun, in *Scorpionfish*. Calls you guys young up-starts. In command before you were properly seasoned. *Much* too young. You all bear watching, et cetera."

"I guess I haven't been too smart about how I handle myself around him," Malachi admitted. "Jay advised me to smile, agree with every-thing he says, and then do whatever the hell I wanted once at sea."

"He's half-right," VanBuren said. "But the admiral does have a point—we can't have a bunch of totally independent operators running around the southwest Pacific theater, going wherever and doing what-ever, if only because one day one of you will torpedo an American boat."

"Area assignments are not the problem, Commodore," Malachi said.

The commodore frowned, almost as if he knew what was coming. "Okay," he said. "Shoot."

"First, the torpedoes are unreliable. Second, the admiral's blind faith in the Mark fourteen's magnetic exploder, backed up by BuOrd's refusal to admit there's *any* problem with the Mark fourteen, *invites* disobedience. None of us much likes being at the starting point of a dud torpedo wake in the presence of Jap destroyers."

"But for the past year," the commodore argued, "there are appar-ently innumerable instances of skippers making questionable tacti-cal decisions, boats abusing the torpedoes by not doing their required maintenance, skippers being too timid to take the war to the enemy or, even more disturbing, breaking down physically or emotionally under the strain."

"Are we now talking about the problem which cannot be named?" Malachi asked.

The commodore seemed taken aback for a moment, but then nod-ded. "I guess we are," he admitted. "The problem of age."

"We'd better stop right there, Commodore. It's not my place to discuss that issue, especially being eight years younger than the guy I replaced."

The commodore nodded again. "Okay, you're right. Now, one more thing. There's another Navy Cross coming for the carrier attack. The admiral is not enthusiastic, but I get the impression that this is coming from ComSubPac, probably in response to Nimitz's little reminder about why we're really out here."

"If I may, Commodore, I've got a better idea. My XO, Marty Brandquist, did some truly heroic things during that fire. Without him none of us would be here today. The Navy Cross is supposed to be about heroism, not simply sinking ships. How's about recommending that the medal coming to me be given to him, instead. I can write the nomination up and have it back here this afternoon."

"Well, I don't know about that," the commodore said. "If Admiral English nominates someone for a Navy Cross, I don't think any of us chickens out here in the boondocks gets a vote."

"We might if he knows the idea was mine in the first place."

The commodore snorted. "The admiral was right—you youngsters *do* bear watching. All right, write it up and I'll carry the water."

"Glad to be working for you, Commodore," Malachi said. "We skippers need a friend in court out here."

The commodore raised his index finger. "It's not us against the admiral, Captain. We're all in this together, and command is command, with all its authority—and ultimate responsibility. Don't forget that."

"Yes, sir. Absolutely."

Back aboard *Firefish*, the tiger team chief gave Malachi an update. Rip-out was complete. Tomorrow they'd begin by sandblasting the space, which would be followed by an alcohol spray to disinfect everything remaining. Then they'd rebuild it.

"Chief, we used HP air to blow all the water out the after torpedo room. We drilled a hole in the bulkhead and rammed a nozzle through it to introduce the pressurized air."

"Yes, sir, I saw the hole. Wondered what that was about."

"Any chance that hole can be repaired with a proper HP air-transit fitting? In case we ever had to do that again?"

"No, sir. That would be a ShipAlt, and only BuShips can authorize those."

"Okay. Worth a try."

"However," the chief said. "I may accidentally leave behind such a fitting, which, of course, you and your best welder can do with as you please, Captain."

In other words, Malachi thought: on your head be it if you do that. Unauthorized ship alterations undertaken in the fleet always carried some career risk. He thanked the chief and then went to his cabin to write up Marty's nomination for the Navy Cross. It took an hour to get all the details in order, and then he had the ship's yeoman type it up and get it over to the commodore's office. Then he cut a note to the exec, asking him to write up some awards for the fire-fighting team, and especially the man who'd gone into the burning space with him.

He yawned, not used to doing so much for lunch. The sub was relatively quiet, with at least half of the crew ashore and only small maintenance jobs going on out in the passageway. The tiger team was laying out spraying equipment aft but would wait until night, when most of the crew would be ashore, to actually do the spraying. He pulled the curtain and lay down on his bunk to check for light-leaks in his eyelids. Happily, there were none.

TWENTY-ONE

The next morning, after a surprisingly good night's sleep aboard *Firefish*, he and the other inport COs were summoned to a meeting with the commodore. They got an intel update from the admiral's intelligence officer on progress at Guadalcanal, and plans to begin the ultimate drive-out of all the Japanese forces still on the island. The ship losses from the calamitous sea battles of November were being replaced with new ships from back home. Then came some sad news: Rear Admiral English, ComSubPac, had been killed in an airplane crash in California, along with several other officers. The new ComSubPac was going to be Rear Admiral Charles Lockwood, currently commanding the American submarine operations being run out of Brisbane on Australia's east coast.

"That will be a big improvement," one of the other skippers said, and then looked around to see if he'd made a mistake in saying that. The commodore's expression made it clear that the comment was somewhat uncalled for.

"I'm sorry, Commodore," the skipper said. "That was disrespectful to Admiral English. But I know Admiral Lockwood, and he's going to be a whole lot more sympathetic to our complaints about the Mark fourteen. He might even do some more testing to refute the Gun Clubbers back in Washington."

"Don't get too excited, Captain," the commodore said. "Remember the old adage about the new watch officer not changing the setting of the sails for at least the first half hour of his watch."

"Yes, sir."

"Yes, sir, but—?"

"Well, I hope that's as long as he waits to get after these god-damned fish. One half hour."

Everybody laughed, including the commodore. They talked about other operational issues, matériel problems, people problems, and then the meeting ended. The commodore asked Malachi to remain behind. He asked for a progress report on *Firefish*, and then told Malachi that he'd sent the Navy Cross nomination to the admiral.

"He read it, thought that the medal was entirely deserved, and said he'd forward it to SubPac. I told him that you had offered to divert your medal to your exec."

"How did he react to that?"

"He said he'd include that information in his endorsement of the nomination."

"Might that not raise eyebrows at ComSubPac?" Malachi asked.

"It well might," the commodore said. "The proposed recipient of the nation's second-highest naval decoration implying that ComSubPac got the wrong guy?"

Malachi hung his head. He couldn't win.

"It was your idea, yes?"

"Yes, sir," Malachi replied with a sigh. "It absolutely was."

The commodore smiled sympathetically. "Don't worry about it, Malachi," he said. "I, too, know Charlie Lockwood, and he doesn't indulge in penny-ante bullshit like that. You just keep sinking those Jap cruisers. Now, new subject—I think you could do with a week's leave."

"But the repairs aren't finished, and—"

"Your exec is competent to supervise the repairs, is he not? The one you just recommended for a Navy Cross?"

"Well, of course he is, but *I'm* the captain."

"And *I* need you to get away from all this for a week, the repairs and the political machinations of perhaps too many staffs. Now, most COs would take leave, go to the hotel, get boiled every night, recover all day, and do it again until they get bored with the hangovers. Then we send them back to sea. But you don't drink, I understand."

"No, sir. I have a single beer, but, no, I do not get boiled. Ever."

"Good," the commodore said. "I like a drink like the next man, but getting drunk? I'm with you on that. So, maybe take a trip out of town? There's some beach resorts south of here. Or go inland; see the great Australian outback. I'm told it's spectacular, if a bit dangerous."

Malachi thought about it. Then he had a much better idea.

"Yes, sir, I'll do something of the sort. And thank you for thinking of it. Off Truk Lagoon, I was ready to pack it in, especially when I realized I'd disobeyed the patrol orders."

"You did the right thing, Captain. If two carriers came past my boat I'd throw potatoes at 'em if nothing else. As Chester Nimitz just reminded everybody, that's why we're out here. All of us."

That evening Malachi called Kensie from the hotel to see if she was free for dinner. The hospital operator said she'd get the doctor to call him back when she could. He was on the rooftop nursing his daily brew when one of the lovely bartenders told him he had a phone call at the bar.

"I can come down for dinner," she said, "but there's a hospital ship coming in tonight from Guadalcanal around ten o'clock, and I suspect we'll be busy for the next two days."

He told her about the commodore ordering him to take a week's leave, and wondered if she could manage a few days off so they could go somewhere.

"Go somewhere?" she asked with bright laugh. "We're in western Australia, dear heart. The nearest worthy 'somewhere' is three thousand miles to the east. But my family's country home has about sixty-five thousand acres and plenty of spare bedrooms in the main house. We could go out on horseback and see the countryside, and there's some fabulous trout fishing not a mile from the house. How's that sound?"

"Sounds wonderful," he said. "If your family wouldn't mind, that is." He still remembered his talk with Lambert Richmond.

"No worries, there, Captain. They're rather starved for company out there in the bush."

"The 'bush'?"

"Anywhere five miles out of a town or city is considered the bush by city folk. The back of beyond, as my Irish nanny called it, and, mind you, we're only talking fifteen miles out of Perth. Oh, shit, there's my SA coming down the hall. Get some rest for the next few days. I *will* arrange my escape."

TWENTY-TWO

Malachi had expected something along the lines of one of those big English country manors he'd seen when he'd taken a week's leave in Britain, but Richmond Station was completely different. The main house was single storied and about 150 feet long, surrounded by extensive porches on all four sides. There were four chimneys protruding through a metal roof, and the house was made entirely of wood. Three wooden log cabins, the guest cottages, flanked the sides and back of the house at a respectful distance, and covered walkways provided access to the main house. The ranch operations buildings were visible about half a mile away, and there was a large water storage tank between the houses and the barns. The house was situated on a low hill overlooking a ten-acre lake, surrounded by willows, which Kensie told him the locals called peppermint trees, as well as isolated groups of eucalyptus trees. A circular drive brought them to the front porch and then she turned left onto a larger circle that gave access to each of the cabins. There were several different kinds of bushes around the house but no lawn. The predominant color was brown. There were trees about, but it looked like some of them had had to struggle to survive.

"Looks more like Texas than England," he said to Kensie as she pulled the Ute up in front of the first cabin.

"The farther you get from the coast, the less water there is," she replied. "Father Time, that's my dad, tried to grow some of the more elegant, decorative trees here when he started up the station, but in the end, he went with what comes natural out here. Here we are, Captain."

The cabin contained two bedrooms, a living room/dining area, and a kitchen. There was a single bathroom between the two bedrooms, and a fireplace in the kitchen. There were porches on three sides in a smaller version of the big porches surrounding the main house. The cabin was compact but the walls were polished wood, as were the floors, which gave a warm gloss to the interior. Two large fans stirred the air up in the exposed rafters. They brought in Malachi's travel bag and then took a nap.

That evening they joined Margery on the front porch of the big house for drinks. Malachi had his usual beer; Kensie her usual Scotch. Margery fussed over Kensie for a few minutes until Kensie got her calmed down. Malachi got the impression that Margery wasn't entirely sure who he was or why he was there, but she quickly recovered her usual gracious and welcoming manners. She informed them that Lambert was away negotiating one of the biggest deals of his financial career, the acquisition of three anthracite coal mines north of Perth and the railroad that serviced them.

"There's coal in Australia?" Malachi asked.

"Oh, Lord, yes," Kensie said. "Most of it on the other side, but coal is just one of the minerals we've been blessed with. Some of the biggest iron ore deposits in the world are north of here about a thousand kilometers in an area called Pilbara."

"I forget how big this country is," Malachi said.

"Most of it entirely empty," Kensie said.

"Oh, right," he said. "The bush."

"The Outback, actually," Kensie corrected him gently. "It's a perfectly descriptive term. I'm a native and I haven't seen a tenth of it. Forty something *million* acres. Most of western Europe could disappear into the Outback without a peep."

"And probably wishes it could just about now," Malachi quipped.

They spent the next three days touring the farming and ranching operations and relaxing along some of the trout streams and ponds scattered about the nearby lands of the station. The summer heat was increasing, so they spent their afternoons in the library of the big house or in discreet bouts of afternoon delight back in the guest cottage. Malachi kept in touch with the boat through a daily phone call from the exec. There was talk they might be going out sooner than originally scheduled, but so far, nothing official. No serious liberty incidents, the new admiral making himself unpopular.

On the afternoon of the third day there was a small commotion outside as Lambert returned from his trip up north. Kensie went out to greet him, as did Margery and the house staff. Malachi lingered on the cottage porch, not wanting to intrude on the family. An hour later they joined Lambert and Margery in the main living room of the house for drinks. Lambert was pouring some champagne, celebrating, Malachi found out, the conclusion of the coal mine deal. He greeted Malachi with enthusiasm, pouring him a full measure of bubbly and then toasting the new acquisition. Malachi discovered that this was indeed good champagne, but he paced himself anyway. He didn't consider wine to be real drinking, but he did know it could creep up on you. Kensie showed no such inhibitions, matching Father Time glass for glass. She's bottomless, Malachi thought as he watched her fondly, and way out of his social reach.

After a wonderful dinner and even more wine, they all retired to the library to listen to Lambert describe the deal and the properties he'd acquired. There was to be a formal, celebratory dinner in two weeks' time down at the central bank in Perth. Everybody who was anybody in Perth would be there. Malachi realized he'd be at sea. For some reason he felt a pang of jealousy at the thought of Kensie loose among all those "anybodys." Dream on, he thought, and then sighed.

By the time they got back to the cottage Kensie had her blood up, leading to an almost violent encounter on the bed. Afterward he lit up a cigarette and offered her a drag. She actually took one and then coughed, making them both laugh. The fans drove the warm air up in the rafters down onto their bodies in a gentle, feathery massage.

"I got you a present," she announced. "Father Time brought it back. Where *he* got it remains a mystery. It's over there."

Malachi got up on slightly shaky legs and went over to the table next to the front door. A white box with a ribbon stood there. He picked it up and felt liquid inside. He opened it to find a bottle of

Woodford Reserve Kentucky bourbon. He stared at it for almost thirty seconds.

"Is it a good one?" she asked from the bed.

"It's an exceptional one," he said, trying now to hold back the memories that this bottle had unleashed. He was unaware that he'd begun to weep.

Suddenly she was by his side. "What, Malachi? What's the matter? What have I done?"

He put the bottle down on the table and turned to hold her. "*You* haven't done anything," he said finally. "You have been marvelous since I've met you. But I've been sitting on a secret, and I'm scared to death it's going to be a mortal one. The bourbon, and the reason I don't really drink, is a big part of that."

"Oh, Malachi, I'm *so* very sorry," she said. "I never meant—"

He put his fingers to her lips. "Get your robe on, and let's go out to the porch. And bring two glasses."

Out on the porch he cracked opened the bottle and poured them each two fingers. The sensuous aroma of barrel-aged whiskey rose in the night air. He raised his glass to hers and then they each took a sip.

"Wow," she said. She took another sip. "Just, wow."

"Yeah," he said. "They've been making this since the early eighteen hundreds. It's basically Kentucky corn whiskey, and in the States, that can only come from Kentucky." He took a deep breath. "It was my father's favorite, but he drank it to excess, which is why, one terrible and indelible night, I had to kill him."

Kensie dropped her glass, the sound loud in the shocked silence. She stared at him, open-mouthed.

He sighed and put down his glass. "Hear me out, my dear Kensie. It's a terrible story, but I feel I owe it to you to come clean. My crew call me The Iceman, the guy with no feelings and no fears. They're wrong about all of that, but I'm the way I am around people for a reason. Will you hear me out?"

"Of course I will," she said in a small voice, reaching out to touch his cheek. "Of course I will."

"My father was a deep-coal, hard-rock miner," he began. "Big man, powerfully built. He was a line supervisor who could swing a ten-pound maul with both hands and knock a railcar over. He was respected and he was feared. No one crossed him without getting hurt, sometimes seriously hurt."

He paused, looked at the glass in his hand for a second, and then finished it off. He poured himself another. He couldn't look her in the eye when he did that, and that made him put the glass back down on the table.

"He was a bad drunk. A really *bad* drunk. And when he got loaded, he took it out on my mother and me. Mostly my mother. She was as small as he was big, and she took great pains to please him and to mollify him. And yet, there were just too many times when he'd start shouting at her and then throwing things and then throwing her. As a kid I couldn't do anything but cower in the hallway. But eventually I grew up."

"One night I intervened. He hit me so hard I didn't wake up until the morning when he'd already left for the mine. My mother had a black eye. She told me it was nothing compared to the one I had. A neighbor's wife came to the back door and asked if he was gone. When my mother nodded, she came into the kitchen with coffee and some biscuits. Apparently they'd all heard it, and not for the first time. The houses were all close together, shotgun shacks, the miners called them.

"Over time I got bigger, and stronger. He got drunker and meaner. It got bad enough that he started coming home drunk, and I'd pay local kids twenty-five cents to act as lookouts to see what state he was in. If necessary, I'd get Mom out of the house to a neighbor's house. Usually she'd already made his supper, so he'd come in, sit down and eat, and then go out to the porch where he kept his jug of whiskey. I'd lay low, do my homework, and listen to him mutter and curse out on the porch. He'd usually pass out and end up sleeping outside, unless it was deep winter.

"When I finished high school I finally went to work in the mine, but I made sure I was on another shift. I didn't want to be down there with him. There came a day when he came up from the mine and got into it with two other miners. It was a brutal fight; coal miners don't back down from anyone. Two men were hospitalized, and my father was arrested and then fired. After thirty days he got out of jail, hit the local saloon, and then came home, bottle in hand. He blamed it all on us, my mother and me. The whole world was against him, and we didn't back him up, ever. More like that. He started to throw things, chairs, tables, pots and pans. My mother knew what was coming next and ran out the back door. He followed her out, shouting names at her and threatening to kill her. She made it to a neighbor's porch, and the neighbor, another miner, came out with a shotgun. My father backed off and then came back to our house. I was in the kitchen, picking things up.

"He started up on me, yelling incoherently, smashing his fist down on the stove and then punching out the kitchen windows. He picked up a straight-backed wooden chair and broke it to pieces on the kitchen sink. One of the chair legs hit me in the forehead and I went down on the floor, seeing stars. He stood over me, purple-faced, spittle coming off his jaw. At that moment, my mother came through the kitchen door and screamed at him to stop it. When he saw her he reached down for the chair leg that had hit me. I beat him to it and, still on the floor, hit him on the shin. I think I broke his leg. He howled, dropped the bottle, stepped back, and then fell down. He picked up the bottle and swung it at my head. He missed, but not by much. Then my mother tried to grab his arm. He smashed the whiskey bottle against the corner of the stove and tried to stab her with what was left of the bottle's neck. By then I was on my knees with that chair leg—rock maple, it was, and axe-handle heavy—and I hit him on the head with all the force I had."

Malachi paused to picked up his glass and take another sip, feeling the punch, but needing the alcohol to give him the strength to finish this story that had poisoned his sleep for so many years.

"When it all got quiet, deputies from the sheriff's office came. My father was dead on the floor, and I was sitting in a chair, crying, with that chair leg still in my hand. My mother was in shock. The deputies tried to talk to her but all she could do was shake her head. I was arrested and hauled off to jail. I didn't protest; how could I? I'd just killed my own father."

By this time Kensie was sitting there, staring at him, her small fist held up against her mouth. Malachi sat silent for a few moments, still sipping on that amber fire, knowing he should put it down.

"Well," he continued, "the sheriff was my mother's second cousin. He took over the investigation. He'd known all about my father; hell, the whole town knew. He interviewed all the neighbors personally. I guess he interviewed my mother, although she never spoke to me about the incident after that night. In the meantime, the drunks and the petty thieves in the jail had a good old time talking about my future appointment with Old Sparky, the electric chair at the state prison. Except, when I was brought up for a preliminary hearing three days later, the judge asked if I was sorry. I told him I was horrified by what I'd done, but that he was going to kill my mother and I couldn't just stand by and let that happen. Not anymore.

"Then the sheriff stood up and told the judge what he'd found out from the neighbors. That my mother was a battered spouse, an extreme case, even for coal-country Kentucky. That he'd beaten me, and others, more than once, and that what had happened was, in his opinion, a clear case of both self-defense and defense of my mother in the presence of a violent man deranged by whiskey. The sheriff recommended all charges be dropped.

"The judge elected to do something that was common in the South in those days: if I would agree to go into the Army, and by that he meant go far away and stay away, at least for the length of a hitch in the Army, he would dismiss the charges. I was so scared after all that electric chair talk that, of course, I agreed.

"The sheriff himself took me to Louisville, our state capital. We went to the Army recruiting station. The Army wasn't hiring, but the sergeant said the Navy was. So we went across the street to the Navy recruiter, and I was signed up. High school graduate, big and strong, no criminal record despite the fact that the sheriff took me up there. Well, of course, they knew what was going on even if I didn't, just like I didn't realize that my 'preliminary hearing' had all been staged. The sheriff gave me money to send a telegram to my mother care of the company store, because no one had telephones in those days. I never heard from my mother again. I got a letter from one of her sisters several years after, explaining that my mother blamed me for what had happened."

He looked at the bottle, but decided his head was swimming enough, and besides, he'd probably just lost Kensie forever. There wasn't enough whiskey left to take care of that problem.

"That's why I never married, or even tried to. That's why I have bad dreams and don't ever get personal mail. That's probably why they call me The Iceman, because I keep my own counsel and a definite distance from close and friendly relationships. Aboard the boat I don't sleep much, because I can't face the dreams. My chief of the boat told me my crew was afraid of me, especially when we found a target. My wardroom officers had all heard the stories of skippers getting fired because they lacked what they called the 'killer instinct.' They didn't produce, in terms of enemy ships sent to the bottom. Now they had a skipper who personified the killer instinct, and all I could think of was: I know where that comes from."

He turned in his chair to look at her face. He saw tears there, and it broke his heart. "That's how I was until I met you, anyway. And now, well, I guess I've lost that chance, too. Nor would I blame you. You are the first person I've ever told my story to. I'm really sorry to have disappointed you, but because I love you, I couldn't let this secret fester any longer. Please forgive me, Kensie."

She got up and came over to him and then sat down in his lap and pulled his head to her breast. "You're no killer," she said, finally. "Your father was a monster who caused his own death; you just had the unfortunate fate of being the instrument. You poor man, what a cross to bear!

"And as for the submarining," she continued, "you're an avenging angel, not a killer. What is it you Yanks are always saying? Remember Pearl Harbor? Every bloody day I see the results of what these yellow devils have done to our troops. Every *fucking* day. I'm with that noisy admiral of yours, Halsey, is it? Kill Japs. Kill Japs. Kill more Japs. And as for me, I'm Australian. Most of our forebears were criminal deportees from Old Blighty, banished to what the POMs considered a deserted island halfway around the world, and usually for some awful crime like pinching a loaf of bread from milord's pantry."

She pulled his head up so she could look him in the eye. "Let's go back to bed, Malachi Stormes," she said. "We both need to sleep on this. You were cornered into doing a terrible thing. You'll never just 'get over it,' and I'd be disappointed in you if you could manage to just forget all about it. But that catastrophe is part of *who* you are now, not *what* you are, and you needn't ever worry about me wilting in the glare of past troubles. Besides, right now I want to hear that 'I love you' bit again."

She got up and took his hand. "Bedroom's that way," she said.

"Where are *you* going?"

"I dropped my wee dram of that amazing whiskey," she said over her shoulder. "Now you're way ahead of me."

"I'm all done with that stuff," he said, wearily. "Much as I like it, I'm afraid of what it can do."

"Then I'll just have to take care of it for you, won't I."

TWENTY-THREE

Firefish departed Perth on the evening tide because of the recent sinking of the Australian hospital ship HMAS *Centaur*. Darkness would allow her to run surfaced at full speed through the night toward her patrol station off the Bay of Brunei, in the northwest sector of occupied Borneo. *Centaur*, a lighted and well-marked hospital ship, had been torpedoed by a Japanese I-boat off Queensland with the loss of four hundred medical personnel. This outrage marked a desperate change in the tactics of Japanese I-boats and also proved that they were concentrating in Australian waters. American subs were well advised to get clear of the Australian coast as fast as they could.

Malachi decided not to employ a zigzag plan, but chose a narrow weave instead. There was no moon and the sky was occluded with a heavy cloud cover as the northeast monsoon built into the southwest Pacific Ocean. Running at 22 knots all night meant they could make nearly 230 miles of their 2,200-mile journey. They conducted a post-repair shakedown of all the combat and engineering systems during the run north. The after torpedo room was essentially brand new and now smelled of fresh paint rather than death and destruction. They'd gone out for one day toward the end of the repair availability to test hull fittings, with a delightful excursion to 350 feet. One of the propeller shaft tubes had sprung a leak, as had one of the after torpedo tubes' outer doors. These were fixed again, followed by a second dive the next day, this time to 375 feet. The tender's repair personnel, who had been ordered to go along for the watertight integrity tests, had been visibly nervous as *Firefish* approached 400 feet of depth. The chief engineer helpfully informed them that she'd been to 410 and were still kicking. Cracking, groaning, and creaking, too. The symphony of the deep, the COB added, helpfully, to the chalk-faced repair team from the *Otus*.

They arrived off Brunei Bay nine days later, two hours before sunrise, having made an uneventful passage north from Perth. Malachi had run surfaced during the day when they were out of the primary shipping lanes, and submerged when not. At night, they'd run on the surface exclusively. Their mission was to interdict Japanese shipping between Japan and Brunei, where the Japanese had established a naval base, military airfields, and an important oil depot. The northwest region of Borneo was rich in oil resources, and the Japanese had been quick to occupy it on their push into Indochina. Malachi opened the patrol orders in the wardroom, with the exec, the COB, and the department heads present. This time there was no talk of "report but do not attack."

"Tankers, that's what we're after," Malachi announced. "*Out*bound tankers in particular, so that we deprive them of the ship and their oil cargo."

He read some more of the intelligence estimate for Brunei Bay. "Probably can't get into the bay itself," he continued, "because they've surely mined it. And there's one airfield dedicated to HK-eight model Kawanishi flying boats, which are the most dangerous aircraft we face. If one of those beasts catches you on the surface, they can bomb you, torpedo you, and then shoot up the wreckage with twenty-millimeter cannons. They can stay out for days if the weather cooperates. They can land at sunset and spend the night floating, and then resume their patrol the next morning. Our nemesis, if we're not really careful."

"Is the HK-eight big enough to have a radar signal detector onboard?" the exec asked.

"They carry a crew of ten, so it's a pretty big plane. It's possible. More importantly, there are two other airfields for regular fighters and bombers, so they can have twenty-four-hour coverage of this area from the air if they want to."

"Like after we sink our first tanker," the ops officer said. "So we're talking hide by day, attack by night."

"Pretty much," Malachi said. "And that means lots of radar. Talk to your operators about perfecting the quick sweep technique—for attacks: mast up, point the antenna to target bearing, on, off, and mast down. For search, one rotation, and down. Talk to the sonar guys, too—they'll be cueing you onto the best bearing. Okay, that's it."

Malachi indicated that the exec should remain behind when the meeting broke up. "XO, I need you to get us to an ambush position along the most probable sea route into and out of Brunei Bay. I've looked at the charts and it appears that the whole bay is pretty shallow, so I'm not sure how they get tankers in and out."

"And we're gonna let the empty ones just go by?"

"That's what the orders say," Malachi said. "If nothing else, they'll be riding high in the water; with a full load of oil they make better torpedo targets, not to mention the possibility of fire."

"Well, we can't shoot 'em in near the coast; the hundred fathom curve is way out at ten miles offshore."

"We can if we're on the surface," Malachi pointed out. He saw the exec trying not to cringe.

Nothing happened for three days, with the sea empty of everything but small wooden fishing boats. The crew used the time to "routine" the torpedoes, refurbish the backup air compressor in the after engine room, and study Japanese oil tanker silhouettes to determine their fully loaded keel depths. They practiced crash dives at dawn each day, and then settled out at 200 feet for the remainder of the day. On the fourth day of seeing and hearing nothing, Malachi was wondering just how major this Brunei base could be. They couldn't get close enough to get a periscope look into Brunei Bay itself, but the lack of *any* shipping was beginning to worry him. Had they come to the wrong place?

Thirty minutes before the morning crash dive practice, with the first lines of dawn breaking in the east, the radar operator took a long range, single-sweep of the northern horizon, being careful to turn the antenna by hand so as not to radiate toward the bay itself. Malachi was, as usual, in the conning tower to supervise the morning's drill. The operator straightened up in his chair.

"Radar contact," he announced. "Composition many. Range nineteen miles on a bearing of three two five. Radar off."

"Battle stations, torpedo," Malachi ordered, as he tripped the dive klaxon. "Make your depth one hundred feet."

He didn't really intend to attack anything inbound, but this was the quickest way to get the boat buttoned up and ready for action. Once all stations reported in, he started to give the order to come to periscope depth, but then decided to wait. The water offshore seemed to be extremely clear and he was afraid a passing flying boat would be able to see the shadow of the *Firefish* from the air. He finished his coffee and waited, along with the full conning tower team.

"Steady at one hundred feet," Control announced.

"Very well," Malachi responded. "Sound: set up a passive track as soon as you get noise spokes. Radar indicates a possible convoy approaching."

"Sound: aye."

The plotting team manned the table and began the laborious process of a passive sound plot, which involved a steady stream of bearing data from the sound heads beneath the boat. Malachi told the exec to stand down the torpedo rooms and to relax battle stations. This would take a couple of hours.

By late morning they had an estimated range from them to the convoy of seven miles; transferring the approaching ships' course and speed to the chart confirmed they were going into Brunei Bay, or at least the approaches to it.

"Now we have to decide about which track to sit on," Malachi told the exec down in the wardroom. "The northern one bound for Manila or Japan or the western track to Singapore. I'm favoring the northern one."

"I understood they've set up a pretty big naval base at Singapore," the exec said. "Those ships will need oil."

"Yeah, but Singapore can get oil from Malaysia or probably even the Middle East. They've invaded the Philippines, and that took a lot of troops and vehicles. Besides, some of these tankers could go to Japan by way of Manila, offload some of their oil, and then keep going."

"Should we go in tonight and scope out the anchorage? Get a ship count?"

"Let's see how the day develops," Malachi said. "They'll be there for a couple of days onloading, probably from barges, and that's time consuming. How old are the charts for this area?"

"British admiralty charts from the eighteen eighties. The sailing directions note that five rivers flow into Brunei Bay, so there's a pretty big silt delta offshore."

"Let's use our submerged time to do a little hydrographic work. See where the hundred fathom curve really is, sixty years on. If we do go in, I need to know where the water gets deep enough to go down to three hundred feet and still have room for more."

The exec nodded. "I'll navigate us in directly toward the coast at one hundred feet, and we'll take readings with the fathometer. When the water gets less than six hundred feet, we'll come to periscope depth, take a single bearing radar shot at the coast, and then mark the chart."

"Right," Malachi said. "Then go back out ten degrees higher on the compass, come back in and do it all again."

The radioman knocked on the wardroom doorframe and handed Malachi the yellow roll of the fleet broadcast for the day. He took it back to his cabin and lay down to get the day's fleet news and gossip.

By nightfall they'd discovered that the underwater silt delta had come out ten miles farther than the British charts showed, and that it was shaped like an arrowhead as it spilled out of Brunei Bay. Along the spine of the delta the water was only 80 feet deep all the way out to ten miles, where the drop-off began. At its widest point, the delta was eight miles wide. They annotated the chart with the new information, and then they could begin to scope out the best points to lay an ambush for an outbound convoy.

"Where are we now?" Malachi asked.

"We're twenty-two miles off the bay entrance," the navigator said. "Full dark thirty minutes ago."

"Okay, let's go up and get some fresh air. But first come to periscope depth and take a sweep."

Fifteen minutes later the radar operator raised the mast and did a single sweep from due south around to due north, keeping the signal away from Brunei Bay. Then he reported a contact. It was west of them, range seventy-eight hundred yards, appearing to be stationary.

"Classification?" Malachi asked.

"Haven't seen this before, Captain. It's bigger than a fishing boat, but not as big as a patrol boat or one of their sub-chasers. The skin paint on the scope indicates metal, though, not wood."

Malachi called Sound. They had nothing on that bearing or anywhere else, either. "Okay," he said. We still need to surface, but we'll do it on the batteries. Make no noise, and show no light. Then we'll creep over there and see what's what."

Once on the surface, Malachi went to the bridge, along with four lookouts. He'd told the exec to assemble the 20mm gun crew in Control. The night was dark, which meant a fully overcast sky. There was the usual southwest Pacific haze, but the wind, such as it was, was coming from the direction of the contact. The water was a sheet of shiny black glass.

"Five knots, and keep everything quiet. Send up the gun captain."

The gun captain was a red-faced Irishman named McReedie. He was the senior boatswain's mate in the boat, and looked the part. "Yes, sir?" he said when he approached Malachi on the bridge.

"Boatswain's mate, I don't know what's out there, but I mean to approach it on the battery to find out. I need you to get your crew up here now, quietly, and get that twenty ready to work. Again, *quietly*. If this is what I think it is, I'll definitely have some work for you."

McReedie grinned in the darkness. "Aye, Cap'n," he replied. "And what is it that we think this is?"

"I think it's a Japanese flying boat, landed for the night. Smell the air."

McReedie turned his broad face into the light breeze and sniffed. Then he grunted.

"I think that's wood burning," Malachi said.

"Beggin' your pardon, Cap'n," McReedie said. "That's charcoal."

Malachi's eyes gleamed. The Japs had landed their flying boat for the night and were making dinner. "God loves us, Boatswain's mate," he said.

"True enough, Cap'n. I'll go get my boys."

Malachi called the exec to the bridge, and a moment later the XO's head emerged from the dim red glow that was showing through the conning tower hatch. Despite the boat being on red lighting, he was practically blind as he climbed to the bridge. Malachi explained what he thought they had and that he intended to destroy it.

"Is that a good idea, Captain?" the exec asked. "They'll come looking when that Kawanishi doesn't return, which'll mean lots of airplanes searching our patrol area."

"The key is that we kill everybody on board before anyone can make a radio call. I've explained what I want the twenty millimeter crew to do."

"Yes, sir, but maybe we should post the five-inch crew as well. That way if they see us before we get into twenty range, we can at least start shooting at them."

Malachi thought for a moment. Five-inch shells would punch right through the skin of an airplane, and might not even go off. On the other hand, if they started the dance with five-inchers, especially from close in, the shock and surprise would be doubled.

"Okay, good idea. We're going in on the battery. Reset GQ; get the boat closed up. Send up the five-inch gun captain, and break out point-detonating ammo. I'd like to get into five hundred yards before opening up, maybe even closer. It's darker than a well-digger's ass out here tonight, so we might be able to get in really close."

"Not too close, sir—the five-inch ammo won't have time to arm."

"I think it's the noise that'll do what I want it to do. The twenty will take care of the real business."

A half hour later they were within 800 yards of the stationary contact. Everyone had been briefed, the guns were manned and ready, and the only problem now was that they couldn't actually see the aircraft. Malachi made a call down to the conning tower on a sound-powered phone and told the exec to get on the high-powered periscope and start looking down the bearing. "Your eyes are younger than mine," he said. "As soon as you see it, take a radar ping to get the range, and then tell me its aspect. In a perfect world, I'd like to pull up to it so we're broadside to each other."

If anything it was even darker than before. Malachi found himself straining his eyes to see anything out there, but all he got was the beginnings of a headache. He kept the phone in his hand. There was still a faint breeze coming from ahead. A seaplane sitting on the surface should end up with its nose pointed into the breeze, so this course ought to do the trick. He could still smell the charcoal. The phone barely squeaked.

"I see it," the exec said. "Target angle is one three five. Kawanishi. Plot says the CPA on this course will be about four hundred yards in three minutes."

Malachi relayed the information to McReedie, who was standing halfway between the gun mount and the bridge. He told him to train the twenty out to the port beam. "The five-inch'll go first. You should be able to see the bastards from the gun flash. Start at the nose and work your way aft, and then go back and forth. Into the hull first and then along the waterline. Tear it up—I don't want them to be able to get a message out."

The exec was controlling the five-inch gun from the conning tower, coaching them as to where to point the gun in the gloom, and to depress the barrel about three degrees. That way, the shell might hit the water near the flying boat, and maybe even explode.

"One minute to CPA."

CPA—the closest point of approach. After that the range would start to open. "All stop," Malachi ordered. The boat would coast into position. "Fire the five-inch *at* CPA."

"Thirty seconds to CPA."

Malachi relayed this to the boatswain's mate, who disappeared up into the gloom back to his gun mount.

The blast from the five-inch startled him badly and also blinded him with its flash, but not before he saw the Kawanishi, beam on, with Japs sitting in the open hatches around their hibachis, the source of that charcoal smell. There was no explosion from the five-inch round, but it didn't matter anymore, as McReedie's crew opened up, stitching the hapless sea plane from end to end in a continuous blast of 20mm shells, every fifth one an incendiary-tracer, starting a fire under the starboard wing. The five-inch crew, with something to shoot at now, opened fire again, and this time the shells *did* explode, just underneath the plane and then the fourth one in a fuel-filled wing that lit up the entire area in a bright gasoline fire. In the space of 120 seconds, the plane disintegrated before their eyes, leaving only a pool of flaming aviation gas.

"Cease firing," Malachi ordered. "All back one third."

The boat had begun to drive past the wreckage of the seaplane. Malachi picked up his binoculars and scanned the surface of the water illuminated by the burning gasoline. He saw faces.

"Boatswain's mate," he called.

"Leave 'em to me, Cap'n," the boatswain said. His brother had been killed on the *Arizona* at Pearl Harbor. He didn't need any further instructions. A thirty-second barrage from the 20mm solved the problem of talkative survivors.

"Come to course two seven zero and light off the diesels for twenty knots," Malachi ordered. "Two running, two charging. Secure from GQ. Good job."

They put twenty miles between them and the scene before slowing down to resume their normal night patrol. Malachi drafted an operational report about the tanker convoy entering Brunei Bay and that they had attacked a Kawanishi on the surface, and then sent it to Radio for encoding and transmission.

The cooks took advantage of fresh air to make a batch of cheeseburgers, a crew favorite but always a smoky business. A cook's favorite, too, because once submerged, cold cheeseburgers could be warmed up in the ovens. After dinner, the exec came to see Malachi in his cabin.

"XO," Malachi greeted him, "a good piece of work tonight."

The exec pulled a long face. "I'm uneasy about the last part," he said. "Shooting at survivors in the water."

"If that had been their version of a Catalina, a *life*-saving aircraft, I wouldn't have done that. And I won't do that to a troopship's survivors, either. But the Japs'll be out there tomorrow looking for that plane. I couldn't allow any survivors to be there talking about being attacked by a submarine."

The exec seemed to be choosing his words carefully. "That was part of my original reservation about doing this, Captain. What you're saying is completely logical, but I'm not sure *I* want to be a part of killing survivors in the water."

"Well, you were a part of it," Malachi said coldly. "We all were. Didn't have to convince McReedie, did I. This is *total* war, XO. Ask the Aussies, who just lost hundreds of doctors, nurses, and patients in the deliberate sinking of a well-marked and lighted hospital ship, the *Centaur*. Four hundred dead. I've seen intel reports that the Japs have been executing allied POWs on Wake Island. If you don't have the stomach for it, then the next time we see Perth, feel free to get off."

The exec stared down at the deck. "Yes, sir," he said. "I've got the attack plans for both routes once those tankers come out."

"Very well. Brief me in the morning, and then we'll get the department heads in for a strategy session. That is all."

They submerged at dawn, but not before a single sweep of the air search radar revealed multiple contacts behind them that appeared to be searching the waters west of Brunei Bay. Malachi elected to stay out offshore for one more day, but then he knew he'd have to close the coast to get into position once that convoy came back out. He could only hope that he'd been correct in his estimate of how long it would take to load the oil.

TWENTY-FOUR

For the next three nights they crept into the Brunei Bay approaches and took a radar look. All the tankers seemed to still be there. Most of the pips were fuzzy, indicating that there were barges alongside. Strangely, there didn't seem to be any patrols along the coast or in the approaches, so Malachi felt he could assume there'd been no survivors from the Kawanishi. Otherwise all those destroyers would have been out there looking for him.

Relations with his exec had settled into a chilly formality. Malachi realized that Marty knew his time aboard *Firefish* was growing short. Once they got back to Perth, *if* they got back to Perth, this would have to be settled, one way or the other. They'd held the briefing for the attack plan the morning following the exec's declaration. Even by then, the department heads were aware that something had gone wrong between CO and XO. Marty gave the brief, and Malachi approved the plan with one major change.

"If they come out at night I'm going to do this on the surface, with both guns and torpedoes. If they come out during the day, then we need to move the ambush point out to the seaward end of that river delta area, where the water will be so turbid that the Kawanishis can't see us at periscope depth."

"You're talking eighty feet," the exec reminded him.

Malachi knew what he meant. Periscope depth was 60 feet of water beneath the keel. There was no depth evasion possible in only 80 feet of water. "I'm talking lurking in eighty feet at the point where it begins to drop off to six hundred feet," he replied. "We get into trouble, we run for the deep water. Our soundings indicate that happens pretty fast."

A weather front rolled in about midnight of the third night, and by dawn the seas were being whipped up into a medium chop, with frequent rain squalls blowing through. They took a final radar sweep and went back down to the safety of the depths. The radar sweep had revealed no contacts, so Malachi ordered the boat to take up position near the tip of the submerged delta to await developments. The waiting was getting on everyone's nerves and it was showing in sporadic arguments out in the passageway or testy exchanges over minor problems. Sound couldn't hear much above the drumming of rain on the surface, especially when they closed into shallower waters to take a periscope look. The northeast monsoon was coming on, and with it, typhoon season.

At noon, however, Sound reported hearing sonar pinging to the east of them. Pinging meant destroyers. Destroyers hopefully meant the convoy was preparing to sail. Malachi moved the boat to the west and went down to 250 feet. Over the next three hours at least three destroyers or frigates wandered around the approaches to Brunei Bay, sanitizing the obvious submarine ambush points. He wondered if they knew he was out here—they'd used a lot of radar over the past week. Or perhaps the Japanese long-range HFDF stations had picked up his initial report about the convoy. Or, conversely, they were just being careful, especially since they had nothing else to do while waiting for slow, fully laden oil tankers to get under way and organized into some kind of formation.

By nightfall the pinging had stopped and the destroyers seemed to have gone back into the anchorage area of Brunei Bay. Malachi surfaced the boat and went to battle stations, guns and torpedoes. The weather had, if anything, deteriorated. A steady northeast 30-knot wind had raised a decent sea by now, even in the lee of Brunei. Sheets of spray and occasional green water were bursting over the sub's low, sloping bow, to the point where Malachi, dressed out in oilskins and a sou'wester hat on the bridge, had ordered the five-inch crew to get back down below deck but to leave the gun ready to work. The 20mm crew were somewhat protected by the periscope array and the bridge itself. It was almost like being back off Scotland, Malachi thought, except both the air and the water were at eight-five degrees. Visibility was perhaps 500 yards in the noisy darkness. He'd posted four lookouts, who became quickly soaked, so he sent them back down.

Malachi had given one last briefing in the conning tower before going topside. "I want to do this on the surface if at all possible, where we can use our speed to raise hell from *inside* the convoy. I want extra ammo handlers available at the forward hatch to feed the five-inch. I've told the gun captain to shoot at anything he thinks he can hit once the first torpedo goes off and to keep shooting until we have to dive.

"XO, use the surface search to take us right into the convoy. I want to run in the opposite direction they're going, and I will do the conning from the bridge on the bitchbox. I need you to keep constant track of where the nearest deep water is for when I finally need it."

"Yes, sir, got it. Will we shoot from the TDC?"

"Only as regards settings," Malachi said. "These are fully loaded tankers. They'll be drawing twenty feet of water if not more, so set the fish for six feet and contact exploders. They'll run at sixteen feet. I'll basically point the bow at the nearest target and yell fire. You shoot one torpedo at a time—if we can hit six ships, we can come back later and finish them off. If they're full of gasoline, we won't have to."

"And the twenties?"

"I want to save them for the destroyers. In this weather they're gonna have a hard time seeing us, and I'm going to be doing some twenty-knot broken field running once we get into the convoy. If a tin can gets close that twenty-millimeter cannon can tear up his bridge works and his gun crews. We'll save the stern tubes for destroyers in pursuit."

There were nods all around in the red light of the conning tower.

"This will be a melee, boys," Malachi said. "And remember what the Army teaches about combat planning: *no* plan survives first contact with the enemy."

"Do you plan to make more than one pass through the convoy?" the exec asked.

"No," Malachi replied. "We'll make one pass through the convoy and then head for the nearest deep water, which is why I want you to keep track of where that is at all times. Right now, open all outer doors. When you shoot the first fish, order the five-inch crew topside."

Malachi went back to the rain-swept bridge. The wind had come up a bit, and he had to tie his oilslicks to stay dry. The exec called up on the bitchbox and gave him an entry course into the convoy just behind the first ship on the left. There were eight ships running in two columns, separated by about a thousand yards, or half a mile. The radar showed that the destroyers were all out in front of the convoy. Sound could hear intermittent pinging, but the rainfall was masking most useful sounds. He reported that all outer doors, fore and aft, were open and recommended 20 knots now.

"I'm aiming the boat to pass two hundred yards behind the first ship in the left-hand column," the exec said. "I'll call CPA, and then you need to turn right to one six five and slow to twelve knots to drive down between the columns."

"It's raining hard and dark as all hell up here. If I can't see the targets, we'll turn around and come back up from behind."

The boat charged ahead through the four-foot-high waves, blasting spray everywhere. Fortunately, there was no swell to make her pitch, courtesy of the island of Borneo.

"CPA," the XO called. "Recommend come right to one six five."

"Make it so," Malachi responded, and stared hard into the stormy darkness. His binocs were useless in the monsoon rain. He'd just passed right behind a fully loaded oil tanker and hadn't seen a thing. Now he was barreling down between two columns of invisible big ships, and still couldn't see a thing.

This wasn't going to work. Not at all. The same weather that made him invisible to the destroyers made the tankers invisible to him. Change of plan. Go Army.

He yelled at the 20mm gun crew to secure their gun and lay below. He ordered the boat to slow down to five knots, and then ordered the five-inch crew to go up, secure their gun, and lay below. He waited until the gun crews had done what was necessary and then dropped down into the conning tower, the last man closing the forward hatch behind him. The boatswain's mate remained on the bridge as an extra lookout.

"Still can't see a goddamned thing," Malachi called down. "So now we're gonna do a radar attack. Keep me on a course to clear the formation, and once we're clear we'll turn around."

That took another five minutes, at which point Malachi ordered the boat to reverse course. "Get me behind the tail-end Charlie in the right-hand column," he ordered. "Eight hundred yards."

As the boat reversed course she began to run with the wind and the chop, which cut the amount of spray inundating the bridge. The exec took over the conn and drove the boat to a position 800 yards or so behind the last tanker in the *right*-hand column. Malachi fully understood that if he wanted the tactical picture, the conning tower was the place to go. The exec could execute the attack because he had that tactical picture—the radar, the plotting table, the TDC, and access to sonar. All of this was fine with Malachi—his job right now was to drive *what* the boat did, not how.

"The convoy is making ten knots; recommend we change speed to ten knots."

"XO, you do what you have to do: get us stable behind him, shoot when you have a good solution. If we hit him, then drive us over to the other column and do the same thing to the last guy in that column. When the tin cans show up we'll bag ass."

"You still want the five-inch crew to come up when we shoot?"

"Negative; we may have to crash dive. You have permission to fire when ready."

"XO, aye."

The boatswain moved closer to where Malachi was standing. A puff of diesel smoke blew back over them as they ran downwind. The boatswain reached into his raingear's left sleeve and produced a lit cigarette, which he passed to Malachi. Then he bent down behind the windscreen and lit another, hiding the flare of the lighter in a sound-powered phone box.

"There's three hundred rounds still in that twenty back there, Skipper," the boatswain said. "In case someone needs his windows shot out."

"Good," Malachi said. "We may need that, especially if one of these guys goes high order."

They both felt the thump of a torpedo bolting out forward. There was no sign of a wake, even though the rain and wind had diminished a tiny bit. They waited. Nothing happened.

"Check your solution and fire again," Malachi called down.

Three minutes later came another thump forward. Eighteen seconds later there was a red flare ahead of them, followed by a loud booming noise. Immediately the boat began turning left to head for the back of the other column. There'd been no explosion of the tanker's cargo, but she'd definitely been hit. There'd be some noise on the Japs' radio circuits about now, Malachi thought. The escorts would be turning around.

The rain suddenly increased as a squall overtook them. They headed for the back end of the left-hand column. The heavy rain posed a new problem: the surface search radar was always degraded by rain, which resulted in a splotch of fuzzy interference on the scope in the conning tower. Without the radar he could no longer go around flying blind inside the convoy.

"Captain, the radar can't see anything inside of one thousand yards," the XO reported. "Recommend we clear the convoy until conditions improve."

"I concur, XO; get us out of here."

The boat continued to turn, past the bearing of the final ship in the convoy and out to clear water behind the lumbering parade of 10,000-ton steel monsters. The relative wind rose as they headed back east. Between the sheets of spray from the bow and the downpour from the skies, Malachi was totally blind. He nudged the boatswain, and then they both went down the hatch into the conning tower itself. Just opening the hatch had caused a minor deluge within the conning tower, accompanied by curses.

"Set up for an end-around," Malachi ordered as he shucked his soaked oilskins. "Get us five miles north of the convoy's base course and then parallel that course until we can get a better picture."

"*Anything* would be a better picture," the exec noted, pointing to the PPI scope. Malachi saw that the entire scope was just a blotch of dim, white light, no matter what range setting the operator switched to.

"What's an end-around?" the boatswain asked, never having been in the tower during an attack.

"Jap *maru* convoys can only go about ten, twelve knots," the exec said. "If we miss an attack, we drive away from the convoy, then parallel their course and come to twenty knots. Once we get ahead of them, then we sneak back in for another try."

"And right now we're driving away?"

"Right. They're headed roughly northwest. We're headed due north, and then we'll turn to match their course and make our end-around run."

"Pretty neat," the boatswain said.

"Yep, and now it's time for all boatswain's mates to lay below," the exec said. "As you may have noticed, there's not a lot of room here."

"Oh, yes, sir, I'm sorry."

"Once you get below," Malachi said, "you can tell everybody what we're up to."

"Yes, sir, I'll do that." The boatswain dropped down the ladder to the control room.

"As if we could stop him," the exec said, and the attack team all grinned.

"How's the radar?" Malachi asked.

"A little better, Captain, but we need a few more miles of offset before I'll be able to see the formation again."

"Okay, we'll keep going. Is it my imagination or do I feel a swell building?"

"Yes, sir, I believe we're coming out from under the lee of Brunei. This may be a bigger storm than we thought."

They waited, smoking cigarettes and increasingly looking for a handhold as the boat, running at 20 knots, began to roll. *Firefish*, with her pointed bow so close to the water, would cut through waves like butter, but a deep Pacific Ocean swell would roll her like a slick log. By the time the radar operator could again pick up the convoy, the boat was rolling trough twenty degrees in each direction.

"The formation looks like it's coming apart," the radar operator announced. "They're currently at nine miles, bearing one niner zero from us."

"Control, Conn," Malachi called on the bitchbox. "I'm going to open the conning tower hatch. Once the pressure in the boat stabilizes, tell me what the barometer is reading."

"Control: aye."

A plotter went up the ladder and opened the hatch to the bridge. Immediately there was a blast of fresh, if seriously wet air streaming through the hatch and into the boat. As that subsided, Control called back. "Niner seven one millibars, Captain."

"Suspicions confirmed," Malachi said. "There's a typhoon coming." He looked at the fathometer, which read 600 fathoms, or 3,600 feet of water beneath the keel.

"Okay," he said. "This mission is a bust. We'll slow to five knots and head into the swell to stop this rolling. Once the batteries are fully charged, we'll go down and ride this bitch out. *Dammit!*"

All those days of waiting, he thought as he went below. And nothing to show for it except one possible hit on the back end of an oil tanker. Now they'd have to hunker down as deep as they could and ride out what was coming in relative peace and quiet. The tanker convoy was on its own and probably in great danger. What a waste of time.

It took them seven hours to cram as much energy into the batteries as they could hold, which was good, because by that time, the seas were becoming truly monstrous. Malachi had posted an OOD and two lookouts when he'd first turned into the train of swells, but pulled them back down two hours later because they'd had to lash themselves to the periscope shears to keep from being swept overboard. At a depth of 200 feet it was much quieter but still not exactly calm. They could feel the regular pulse of the swells and the sonar gear had been turned off because of all the ambient noise. Malachi ordered the boat into electrical conservation mode, turning off as much gear as they could and running the air-conditioning system for an hour on, an hour off. He wasn't sure how long they'd have to stay down. Just before they had submerged the radioman brought him a weather advisory saying there might be a typhoon approaching his patrol area.

The question now was what to do once the storm passed. Go back to Brunei Bay? The convoy may have turned back to seek shelter there once they realized a typhoon was chasing them. If so *Firefish* would get another chance to do some good work. If not, he still had all but two of his torpedoes. They'd gotten one message off to Perth that they had hit one tanker and were now executing storm evasion just to the northwest of Borneo. The operations officer had some doubts about whether the message actually got out with the atmosphere so badly disturbed. Perth might move them to another patrol area, but the boat's fuel situation might not permit that, and then they'd have to return to base. Malachi could just imagine what the admiral would make of his least favorite skipper turning in an empty-handed patrol.

The effects of the typhoon intensified after twelve hours of submergence. They had rung up three knots and were steering a course into what seemed like the direction from which the storm was coming, but the boat was being pushed around with increasing energy. Malachi ordered them down to 250 feet, which provided some relief. He couldn't imagine what it was like up on the surface. He'd experienced nothing like this in his S-boat, even though the North Atlantic was notorious for savage winter storms. The batteries were down to forty percent and the atmosphere in the boat was beginning to get heavy. He wasn't ready to release air from the ballast system into the boat yet, but he knew they'd have to eventually if they couldn't go back up for another twelve hours.

In the event it turned out to be more like eighteen hours before they could go up to periscope depth and take a look as daybreak broke. The seas were confused and the sky still overcast, with a low scud flying across the sea at about a thousand feet. They put the radar mast up and checked for steel. There was still a great deal of interference from the leaping waves, but no contacts. The relief when they surfaced and opened up the hatch was immense. The giant swells were gone so the boat wasn't moving around so much. The engineers lit off the diesels and took a brief suction on the interior of the boat to draw down the concentration of CO_2. This caused a small tornado in the conning tower until the snipes switched over to the main induction pipe to feed the diesels. The batteries were dangerously low, which meant they'd have to stay on the surface during the day. Malachi was counting on the residue of the typhoon to keep Jap air resources on the ground.

He ordered the boat back to the area where they'd hit that one tanker. If she was still afloat they could finish her off. The radar finally picked up a single, small contact toward the end of the day. Malachi elected to remain on the surface as dusk fell and was finally rewarded by the sight of an overturned ship. She was upside down in the water with only her stern quarter visible. Malachi called the exec to the bridge to get a picture.

"That's the one we hit, I think," he said.

The exec took some pictures as the light dwindled. "How so?" he asked.

"She's missing her rudder and propeller," he replied. "We fired from astern. Without a rudder, the typhoon probably pushed her into the trough and then capsized her."

As if to confirm his theory a sudden wind shift brought the stink of bunker fuel oil streaming over the uneasy sea. Malachi ordered a course change away from the wreck. He didn't need oil fouling his various cooling water intakes.

"Get me a course back to Brunei Bay," he said. "Let's see if they turned around."

By nine that night they were approaching the entrance to Brunei Bay. They'd been navigating by taking hand-cranked radar bearing shots at the coast of Borneo to avoid sending any radar signals into the bay or the surrounding airfields. Finally it was time to paint the bay itself. Malachi came down from the bridge to the conning tower.

"Three contacts," the operator called out. "Pretty good sized, too. They appear to be stationary just outside the bay."

"Anything that looks like a destroyer?" Malachi asked.

"Negative, sir. I'd say tankers."

"Down the radar," he ordered, and then went over to the navigation plot. They were just off the tip of the submerged delta, with mud to the east and deep water to the west. Where was the rest of the convoy, he wondered. Still out there on the track to Japan? Scattered by the storm? He studied the chart.

"Okay," he said. "I want to set up an ambush position five miles northwest of here. I'm assuming these guys will come back out and try again for Empire waters. We'll stay on the surface through the night. If they do come out before dawn, we'll attack on the surface. The seas are subsiding, so we'll use torpedoes *and* guns with incendiaries. I want single radar sweeps in a small wedge centered on that cluster of anchored ships. Once we're in position, shut down three of the four diesels to conserve fuel. We're going to call this the hurry up and wait patrol. I'm going topside."

Back up on the bridge he felt a little better about their situation. The night was clear, but still no moon; the weather was only going to get better. On the other hand, their fuel situation was not going to get better. They had enough to stay up here for another day or so before having to start back to Perth. The Brits had told him that the Germans were using specially configured U-boats to act as mobile refueling ships for the U-boats on distant station. They called them *milch* cows, but it meant that their boats could stay on station instead of having to drive thousands of miles back to base. I'll have to suggest that to the admiral, and then he laughed, a short, sarcastic bark that startled the lookouts. He sent down for a reheated greaseburger and some coffee, and then lit up a cigarette, using the boatswain's technique of lighting it in the sound-powered phone box.

It was the COB who brought him his sandwich. He then went back to the hatch to get the mug of coffee being handed up from below. "Hamburgers are all gone," the COB reported. "So there was a choice of Spam and Spam, so I chose Spam. Mustard, mayo, hot sauce."

"Great choice," Malachi said. He then explained to the chief what they were doing, besides just waiting around for the Japs. Then he waited for the COB to get to what *he* wanted to talk about.

"The XO," the COB began.

"What about the XO?" Malachi asked, as if he didn't know.

"He seems really down. Upset about something. Crew's beginning to talk. They can't get close to you, so he's been the Friend in High Places for them. Now they're worried."

"The Iceman has done something to their friend in court?"

"Something like that."

Malachi explained what the problem was. It was the COB's turn to bend down and light a cigarette in the phone box. He didn't say anything for a minute. Then he did.

"You know, Skipper, if you'd told me about that when it happened I could have grounded out a lot of this static. The guys simply don't get you. *Firefish*'s been the hottest boat in Perth since you came aboard, but you're always up on a mountain somewhere, like God hiding in the clouds.

"I'm the captain," Malachi said. "I *am* God."

The COB grinned in the darkness. "I beg your pardon, your Holiness. But you know what I'm talking about, surely."

"Of course I do, COB," Malachi said. "Consider it a character flaw. I've been this way since I joined the fleet, way back in nineteen thirty. I'm a solitary man. No wife, no family, no relatives. I can't fake it just because I'm in command. I don't sleep—did you know that?"

"Jesus H. Christ, Captain, who doesn't know that?"

"Well, *you* try to convince your brain to shut down when it doesn't want to. I have some melancholy personal history, COB. It's not for publication. It's my business and no one else's. But I hear what you're telling me about the XO."

"He'll be leaving once we get back, then?"

"I think so," Malachi said. Then he turned to face the COB in the darkness. "He's a fine officer. Brave, too. He's in for a Navy Cross for that fire. But that's not me. I'm a killer, Chief Torpedoman O'Bannon. That's why I'm here. I'm going to kill Japs, kill Japs, and then kill *more* Japs, just like Halsey ordered us to. I am what and who I am. I know that captains are supposed to be more than that: a leader, compassionate, fair, encouraging, sympathetic to the crew's problems, a communicator, reassuring in time of danger, protective of the command. I wish I could rise to those standards, but I can't. The crew's got it right. I *am* The Iceman."

The COB stared at him in the darkness.

"I appreciate your candor and your advice, COB," Malachi continued. "Where I can, I will follow it. *Firefish* is a good boat, and the crew is one of the best out here. I'm the flawed one, but there it is."

The chief took a last drag on his cigarette and rubbed it out under the bullrail of the bridge. "I apologize if I upset you, Captain."

"Not at all, COB. I thank you, as always."

"That last part, Captain? This crew being one of the best out here? It would mean something, I think, if you maybe told them that."

Malachi stared out into the darkness for a moment. "Absolutely, COB. You're absolutely right."

The bitchbox transmit light lit up. "Contacts are moving, Captain."

"Battle stations, guns and torpedoes," Malachi replied. The COB hurried below.

TWENTY-FIVE

Malachi went down into the conning tower a few minutes later to take a look at the radar picture. The operator said one contact was definitely standing out to sea; a second had moved from its position toward the bay's entrance. The third was still stationary.

"Nothing else out there?" Malachi asked. "No destroyers approaching?"

"There's a big rain squall out to the west," the operator pointed out. "If there are ships in that thing, we couldn't see 'em."

"Okay, keep an eyeball on that sector. In the meantime, help the plotters set up for torpedo attacks on the ones that are moving."

The exec arrived in the tower to see what was going on. Malachi told him what he wanted to do, which was torpedo the two contacts that were in motion. If the third one stayed behind in the bay, he wanted to go in and use the five-inch to set him on fire. He showed the exec the large white blob returning from the rain squall. "Keep an escape course handy in case *that* spawns a couple of tin cans," he said. "Shortest route to deep water."

"Yes, sir," the exec said.

"I'll use TDTs to feed the computer visual bearings, assuming I can see them. Otherwise, radar track, conventional attack. Two fish per target. Depth set for six feet, speed high, contact exploders."

"Got it, Captain."

Malachi refilled his coffee mug and went back topside. The five-inch crew were out on the foredeck, and the boatswain and his team were lovingly feeding the 20mm cannon. Malachi uncovered the two TDT binoculars on either side of the bridge and then waited for his eyes to adjust to the darkness.

"What've we got, Skipper?" the boatswain asked from the 20mm cannon platform up behind the periscope shears.

"Three tankers who made it back into port after that storm," Malachi said. "Two are under way, coming back out. Number three isn't moving yet."

"Is it true we sank that one we shot at the other night?"

"The storm turned him upside down because we blew his rudder and propeller off, so I guess we can claim him."

"Damn right, we can," the boatswain asserted.

The bitchbox light went red. "Captain, the lead ship is coming straight out of Brunei Bay, course three fifty, speed twenty. Recommend we come to one eight zero, speed ten to intercept for a torpedo attack."

"Speed twenty? That's not a tanker."

"Concur, Captain. Maybe we need to send down the gun teams?"

"Good call, XO," Malachi said. "Set us up for a surface torpedo attack. *You* run the attack. Get into about fifteen hundred yards and let him have it. Then head for number two."

"Aye, aye, Captain," the exec said. Malachi began to scan the darkness through one of the target data transmitter binoculars to see if he could spot the oncoming contact. Another cruiser? He called for a relative bearing to the target.

"One seven five true, three three zero relative," the exec responded. "Range, two thousand one hundred yards."

Malachi strained his eyes to see something, anything in the darkness, training the TDT to the port bow and swinging it through a ten-degree arc. The exec would be focused on the torpedo attack geometry. Malachi's job right now was to make sure the boat didn't drive under the bows of the contact. Suddenly, the boatswain erupted.

"Holy shit, holy *shit*: look at that thing!"

The boatswain had acquired a set of binoculars. Malachi turned to see where the boatswain was looking, and then swung the TDT to the right ten degrees. The unmistakable silhouette of a Japanese battleship filled the optics. Towering pagoda superstructure. Enormous black gun barrels nested forward in two huge steel turrets. A city block wide. Huge, black, silent, and coming on like a moving mountain. He reached for the bitchbox. "XO, it's a *battleship*. Fire all six forward when the solution locks. Change running depth setting to ten feet. Now!"

The exec didn't reply, but instead snapped the talk-switch twice to indicate he'd gotten the message. Fifteen seconds later, the entire load of the six torpedoes forward began thumping out of the front of the boat. It took just over ninety seconds for them to all head out. Malachi stared into the darkness. Then he remembered the ship behind the leader.

"Execute a *left* turn away," he called down to the exec. "Maximum speed."

The boat heeled sharply as the diesels accelerated and began a swing to the left, away from what was about to happen half a mile in front of them. Then the torpedoes began to hit. One. Two. Three. Nothing. Nothing. Four. No visible fire. No giant explosions. Just the sounds of four solid hits, each raising a red pulse followed by a bright white fountain of water high into the air all along the starboard side of the battleship. To Malachi's amazement, the monster kept going as if nothing had happened.

Malachi ordered the gun crews and the lookouts to get below, and they cleared the decks in record time, having seen what was out there. As the boat swung left he watched the behemoth slide on by in the darkness, seemingly untouched. Behind the battleship a searingly bright white light switched on and began to probe the surface of the sea. Then a second one. Malachi took a bearing on the searchlight with the TDT and called it down to the tower.

"Second big one," he said, as *Firefish* began to gather speed in her run to safety. "Mark the bearing. Prepare to fire tubes seven through niner. Enter the same course and speed of the big guy. What's the water depth?"

"Eighty-five feet."

At that moment, one of those sixty-inch diameter carbon arc searchlights found *Firefish*. It passed over, and then swung back, bathing the frantically running submarine in its harsh, blue-white light. Immediately what seemed like a hundred guns opened up from the number-two ship. A firestorm of shells howled in, landing all around them. Long, for the moment, but not long enough. Shell fragments started to snap and whine off the conning tower.

"Plot set!" the exec called.

"*Fire* at will," Malachi said. "Can we dive?"

"Negative, Captain, another mile to go to one hundred feet."

More bits of shrapnel whined over the water, one close enough for Malachi to feel its hot breath. "Start zigzagging then, XO," he called. "They're on us with a searchlight and five-inch guns. Prepare to dive."

He checked one more time to make sure the gun teams were securely back inside and then scrambled over to the hatch just as that blue-white searchlight beam settled on the conning tower. He dropped down and slammed the hatch, completely blinded.

"*Emergency dive!*" he yelled when he was halfway down the ladder. "Take her down to periscope depth. XO, lay below to supervise the dive."

The exec dropped down the ladder to the control room about the time Malachi hit the deck plates in the conning tower. He could barely see. The light from that five-foot-diameter searchlight was the same light created during a welding arc. It was designed to blind. The diesels shut down with a whoosh as the main induction valve was slammed shut. The boat was diving at nearly 20 knots, which meant that plane control would have to be perfect in only 80 feet of water. As water rose over the conning tower they could hear the thumps of near misses around the boat.

Malachi stared at the depth gauge. Periscope depth was 60 feet of water. There would be only 20 feet of water beneath the keel until they got away from the mud banks. "Retract the sound heads," he ordered, hoping the sonarmen could get them up before they got wiped off the hull.

He checked the pit log: they were still doing 15 knots. Good news: they'd get under quick. Bad news: they'd probably overshoot the ordered depth. He also needed to turn the boat as soon as possible. With that searchlight on them, Jap spotters would have been able to determine their course. He wasn't sure what that second big ship had been, but in these shallow waters they could ram *Firefish* with relative ease, even submerged. But not right now: he needed to leave the dive team below alone so they could truly concentrate on maintaining depth control. This was no time to go slamming into the bottom and then broaching in full view of two Jap capital ships. He checked the depth gauge: 50 feet. Then 60 feet. Then 65 feet. The numbers were fuzzy.

The deck under his feet began to level. The pit log read nine knots. Still too fast but better than 15. Nobody in the conning tower said a word. They could hear the exec down in the control room issuing quiet but confident orders to level the dive and get back up to 60 feet without exposing the periscopes.

Seventy feet. Catch her, XO, he thought, knowing there was no point to saying that.

Sixty-five feet. Six knots, almost level again.

Then, without being told, the exec put five degrees of left rudder on to turn away from the last observed course on the surface. Malachi felt a surge of pride. He'd trained them hard, and it was paying off. If they got out of this he'd have to make sure the exec was recognized as CO material. He may not have the killer instinct, but he was savvy and focused. The thumps up on the surface began to wander astern. Then he looked at the fathometer: 15 feet between the bottom and the boat's keel. He thanked God it was dark topside, because in the daylight they would have been clearly visible to any aircraft.

Over the next fifteen minutes the fathometer slowly, achingly slowly, began to show more water beneath the keel as the boat struggled to seaward of those mud banks. Now there was 25 feet beneath the keel. Then 40 feet. He closed his eyes to create the tactical picture: they were headed west northwest, six knots, away from the coast of Borneo. In a few more minutes they could get deeper. Once the depth began to really drop off they'd slow down to three knots to conserve battery. Then what?

Get down to 200 feet, redeploy the sound heads and take a listen. Had the big boys left the area? And where the hell were the destroyers? Battleships didn't go out to sea without a clutch of escorts around them.

"You okay, Captain?" the radar operator asked. Malachi blinked open his eyes. The entire attack team was staring at him.

"Yes," he said. "The searchlights blinded me for a few minutes." He looked at the fathometer: 180 feet and dropping.

"Take us down to one hundred feet, XO," he called down. "Nice job controlling the dive. That was perfect."

"XO: aye." The exec sounded like he thought he hadn't heard right.

"Redeploy the sound heads," he ordered. "Plotters: you had a track on that battlewagon. Assuming he kept going, tell me where he should be now."

"He was going twenty knots, Captain," the senior plotter said. "If he didn't slow down he's long gone."

"We hit him with four torpedoes," Malachi said. "I'm betting that, eventually, he has to slow down. Run the plot." He turned to the bitchbox. "XO, secure from battle stations. Get all tubes reloaded as quickly as possible. We're going to go look for that big boy."

He went below to make a head call and to get some coffee. As he passed back through Control he saw the fathometer reading 110, but it was on the fathoms scale, which meant they had six hundred feet plus beneath the keel. "Make your depth *two* hundred feet," he ordered as he was climbing back up into the conning tower.

"Planesmen," he called over his shoulder. "That was slick wheel-work tonight. Thank you."

The two men at the planes broke into wide grins. The COB, who was standing behind them as the diving officer, cleared his throat and told them to mind their depth in a stern voice.

Malachi smiled. The COB, not wanting big heads on the planes just now.

They came back up to periscope depth thirty minutes later for a radar sweep. Nothing. Malachi checked the time: 0100. If he was going to chase a battlewagon in the dark, it would have to be on the surface.

"What's the battery status?"

"Seventy-eight percent," the OOD replied.

"Okay, let's surface, recharge, and run fast enough to find those guys. We'll give it two hours."

Once on the surface they ran down the last-known course of the big boy, which indicated he was on his way to Singapore. They got out a radio report of having torpedoed a battleship, but without visible effect. They did claim the one tanker. Malachi went back up to the bridge while they ran at 20 knots through a relatively calm sea. There was no moon and a high, thin overcast. They could stay up until dawn, which should allow a full battery recharge.

He ran back through the attack parameters on the battleship. He'd ordered 10 feet, which should have resulted in a 20-foot depth. Maybe that hadn't been deep enough. Maybe the fish had all hit the big guy's armor belt. Or prematured. Or the warheads just weren't big enough. He did know that he'd hit that thing with four out of six fish. Should have done something. He called down and told the radar operator to give it one sweep every fifteen minutes.

Just after one hour of running on the surface at 20 knots the radar operator reported a contact ahead. Three contacts, in fact. One large, the others smaller. Bearing 225, range 12 miles.

"Moving?" Malachi asked.

"I'll need another sweep in three minutes," the operator replied.

"Don't sweep it. Point the antenna down the bearing by hand, crank it by hand, and see what you get on the A-scope."

"Radar: aye."

One large, two others small. A wounded battleship, surrounded by destroyers? And where was that second big guy, the one with those searchlights?

The relative wind was from ahead and it felt good, even at eighty-eight degrees. He had four lookouts posted above him, and the sound of the diesels was actually comforting. The question now was: what do I do when we get there?

Radar called back up after five minutes. "Targets are stationary, Captain."

"I want to get into four thousand yards of them on the surface," Malachi told the radar operator. "Give me a thousand-yard heads up."

"Radar: aye."

"Ask XO to come to the bridge."

A minute later the exec came up through the conning tower hatch.

"Over here," Malachi said, knowing that the exec wouldn't be able to see anything in this darkness.

"Yes, sir?" the exec asked when he'd felt the bullrail.

"I think we hurt that big bastard," Malachi said. "Radar indicates a large contact stopped and surrounded by two smaller contacts. Here's what I want to do: we'll go into four thousand yards on the surface, shift propulsion to the batteries, and see what we can see. Then we'll submerge. This time I want to use the magnetic exploders, contact backup. I don't want to get in close, not with all those tin cans. So I want low speed, a fourteen-foot-depth setting. The way they're running deep, that should get the fish under his keel. No point in shooting at his armored sides. We'll fire three fish on magnetic. If nothing happens, then we'll change to contact only and change the depth setting accordingly."

"And once we shoot?"

"We'll wait and watch. If we don't get results from the magnetics, we'll shoot again on contacts only and then get the hell out of here."

"We don't know where that second big guy is," the exec pointed out.

"Being a big guy, he won't be a destroyer," Malachi said. "If we're gonna get a second chance at this guy, we need to stay hidden from the tin cans."

Malachi waited impatiently as the boat closed in to the cluster of contacts. They had only about an hour and a half until dawn, so they had to get this done before the Kawanishis came up.

"What's the range?" he asked over the bitchbox.

"Four thousand, five hundred yards. Dead ahead."

"Switch to the battery. Prepare for a quick dive."

"Conn: aye."

He ordered the lookouts to go below. If one of those tin cans attending the wounded battleship spotted them, he didn't want to wait for lookouts to get back in the house. Then he had a thought. "Send up the boatswain," he ordered.

A minute later Boatswain McReedie popped up out of the hatch and began feeling his way toward the front of the bridge.

"Over here, Boatswain's mate," Malachi said. "I need you to man up one of these TDTs."

"Can't see shit, Cap'n," the boatswain said. "Even on red light. *Damn*, it's dark."

"I understand," Malachi said. "But you're the only other guy who's seen this battlewagon, so I want you to start looking. You've got a good eye. He should be about thirty-eight hundred yards dead ahead. You take this TDT; I'll go over to the port side. We're headed right for him."

"Aye, sir."

They crept through the dark toward the last reported radar position on the targets. It was the boatswain who finally saw them.

"There," he announced. "I see 'em."

"Bearing?" Malachi asked patiently. "There" didn't tell him anything. The boatswain looked into the dimly lighted dial of the TDT. "Two five one," he replied.

"Visual bearing, two five one," he said over the bitchbox.

"Conn: aye. Two five one. The range is twenty-eight hundred yards."

"All stop," Malachi ordered. Then he started looking hard. His eyes were fully night-adapted, but apparently not as sharp as the boatswain's. Then he saw it: a large, black shape, with smaller gray shapes around it. The boat glided silently forward as it slowly came to a stop.

"He's over, Cap'n," the boatswain said. "Big starboard list. There's a tin can alongside, and another one out front, maybe setting up a tow."

Malachi stared hard at the image in the TDT optics. There was a thin, white column of steam coming from the big guy's stack. He thought he could see red lights on the decks of the two ships. "How far over, Boatswain?"

"Maybe twenty degrees," the boatswain said. "Ain't no lights in that big castle thing, either."

He's lost electrical power, and he's venting steam from his boilers. There was no fire, but there was definitely flooding. As they used to teach in damage control school, if you're facing fire *and* flooding, deal with the flooding first. If you don't, the fire won't matter. Malachi knew what he had to do.

"Come left and reverse course at five knots," he ordered.

"You're not going to shoot?" the exec asked.

"Not yet," Malachi said. "He's listing at twenty degrees to starboard. We need to get around this cluster and attack from his *port* side. That way we're shooting at exposed hull, not armor belt."

"Aye, aye, sir," the exec said. "Dive now or stay on the surface?"

Malachi was torn. He could see better on the surface. But there was always the chance that some sharp lookout on one of those tin cans might see them, too. The boat's speed would be the same either way as long as they were on the battery: slow.

"How much time before nautical twilight?" Malachi asked.

He waited for them to consult the navigator. "Just under an hour," the exec replied, finally.

"Okay, give me full power on the battery. You have a position plotted on the table. I want to stay two thousand yards away from them while we circle around. We'll stay surfaced unless they spot us."

"Conn: aye," the exec said.

Malachi could feel the vibration as the boat came up to eight knots, the max speed they could get from electric motors on the battery. But it was silent, and that was important in these calm waters, especially at night. If he'd lit off the diesels, the Japs would have heard it and come a-running.

It took twenty minutes to slip around behind the group of Jap ships and into a position where they could look at the big guy's port side. It looked a lot like the starboard side to Malachi, but the boatswain said he could see red lead, an antifouling paint used universally by ships who sailed the Big Salt.

"All stop," Malachi ordered. "Visual bearing is zero two five true. Range?"

"Two thousand, three hundred yards."

"Come right to zero two five. Open the forward outer doors. Set running depth for ten feet. Speed *slow*. Contact exploders. I want to shoot *two* fish. If they hit, we're leaving. If they don't, we'll try two fish, magnetic."

"Conn: aye, plot set."

"Fire when ready," Malachi said. "Boatswain, lay below now, and thank you."

"Aye, sir," the boatswain said and scrambled across the bridge to the conning tower hatch.

One thump, then a second. He thought he could see the torpedoes' wake as they streamed out toward the stricken battleship at 33 knots. And then a destroyer came up from behind the big guy and slid alongside.

Shit, he thought. Running depth set for 10 feet ought to mean the fish would run at 18 or even 19 feet. How much did that damned tin can draw? Fourteen? Sixteen? He waited, staring hard through the TDT optics.

A pulse of red light blazed beneath the destroyer, followed by a second one ten seconds later. An enormous waterspout rose into the air alongside the battleship. An even bigger bolus of white fire bloomed into the night air from one of the destroyer's magazines as she broke in two alongside the battleship and capsized.

"Goddammit," Malachi swore. He reached for the bitchbox. "A tin can ate our fish. Prepare for a second attack. Two fish, depth *twelve* feet, magnetic exploders, speed *high*. Fire when ready on the same bearing."

He swung the TDT to the right of the battleship, and saw what he'd been expecting: a Jap destroyer was accelerating out from behind the battleship's other side. In a minute he'd be heading in their direction. He felt the first thump, and then the second of the follow-up torpedoes.

"Emergency *dive*," he ordered. "Make your depth two five zero feet. Steer zero two five." Then he ran for the hatch as the boat slanted down. As he was dropping into the hatch he felt, rather than heard, an underwater explosion in front of them. He waited for a second, but none came. Typical Mark fourteen, he thought.

With the hatch closed and the boat headed down at a fifteen-degree angle, Malachi landed on the conning tower deck plates with a bang. He ordered the exec below to take the dive. "I want to drive right under them," he said. "There's a tin can coming up from starboard."

"Conn, Sonar: active pinging, zero niner zero relative."

"Conn: aye," Malachi responded. Now that he was in the tower, he became Conn instead of the XO. "Make ready tubes niner and ten. Open outer doors aft."

The boat's hull thrummed as she went deep under maximum electrical power. "What was the firing bearing on the big guy?" Malachi asked.

"Zero two five."

"Roger, come to course zero two five; I want to pass close under the stern of the big guy, not directly underneath him."

"Recommend course zero three five."

"Make it so," Malachi replied, glancing at the depth gauge: 130 feet and dropping swiftly. "Sonar, Conn: has that destroyer shifted mode yet?"

"Negative, Captain. He's still in omni search."

With any luck, Malachi thought, he's headed for where those fish came from; we're headed for the opposite side of the action.

"Conn, Control: two hundred feet, leveling now."

Malachi acknowledged, even as the first sounds of a ship breaking up began to penetrate the hull. It sounded like they were coming from the boat's left. Destroyer? Malachi wondered. Or the big guy? That was why he'd come right instead of driving directly beneath the battleship: that destroyer might have sunk right on top of them. The real question was what had that final torpedo actually hit—the wreckage of the destroyer, or the battleship's exposed bottom?

"Conn, Sonar: that destroyer has shifted mode to attack, but he's drifting right pretty quick."

"Probably has contact on the big bubble we made when we dived," Malachi said. Releasing all that air from the ballast tanks would leave a bait-ball of bubbles in the water that reflected sonar pulses quite nicely. Sure enough depth charges began to boom in the distance behind them.

"Okay, Plot, I want to get fifteen hundred yards on the other side of the big guy. If there's no escort noise out there, we'll come to periscope depth and see what we've got."

The noises from the sinking destroyer reached a crescendo of snapping steel plates, drowning compartments opening their last air into the sea, and exploding boilers. Then it diminished into an eerie silence.

"Slow to five knots," Malachi ordered. "Course to observation point?"

"Plot recommends coming left to zero three zero, distance two thousand, five hundred yards."

"Make it so."

He felt the boat coming left. He checked the depth gauge—260 feet. Pretty good for an emergency dive, he thought. The hull wasn't even complaining that much, and certainly not like that destroyer's hull. He smiled and reached for a cigarette.

Twenty minutes later they rose to periscope depth. Plot gave Malachi the expected bearing of the target. He spun the scope around to line up on that bearing. When the scope broke water he was surprised to see that it was daylight. The battleship was still there and still listing, but not as bad as before. Ahead of her was a destroyer with a huge plume of smoke pumping out of her stack as she struggled to pull the much bigger ship in the direction of Brunei Bay. This was his first really clear view of the ship, which he recognized as a prewar, Nagato-class battleship. He gave a visual bearing to the attack team, estimating her course as 110 and her speed at 3 knots. Then he pulled down the scope. Those last two fish must have hit the remains of that destroyer.

The plotting team cranked up the TDC and got an attack solution generating. Malachi rested his eyes for a moment. It had been a surprise to see daylight. The round image of the stricken battleship seemed to be imprinted on the back of his eyes.

There was something he was missing. Something important. Daylight. Had to do with—

A buzzing noise began to penetrate the conning tower. Malachi's eyes snapped open. "Take her *down*," he yelled down the hatch. "Flood negative to the mark. Twenty-degree down-bubble!"

The startled plotting crew was still staring at him when the first of a string of bombs from a Kawanishi float plane went off 200 yards away, administering a powerful punch to the boat's hull. A second one was much closer, even as the boat passed through 100 feet, knocking a cloud of insulation out of the overhead and causing the periscope structure to whip from side to side. Then a third, which hit the boat behind the sail with an ear-shattering clang. It was big enough that it dented in the back fairing of the conning tower. For one eternally long second they all stared at that bulge in the steel and waited for the explosion, but none came. Another bomb did go off, at some distance on the other side of the boat, but *Firefish* was far enough under by now that it wasn't much more than a distant depth-charge explosion.

"Passing one five zero feet," the exec called up. "What was that noise?"

"Make your depth two hundred feet," Malachi replied. "Pump negative immediately. That noise was a bomb which I think is sitting in the twenty millimeter nest right now."

Malachi could feel the boat go quiet as that news penetrated. The battleship forgotten, he now had to figure out how to get out of this mess. If that bomb decided to go off, they'd all get to find out what *Firefish*'s crush depth really was.

The exec caught the dive and got her leveled out just past 220 feet and then brought her back up to 200 as ordered. Once she was stable at depth Malachi ordered a turn out to sea and away from Brunei. He slowed her down to 4 knots, not knowing what it would take to dislodge the bomb so that it could finish its arming routine. He looked at the dent. The bomb had to be almost 20 inches in diameter. *Big* bomb. Goddamned Kawanishi. He should have paid better attention to what time it was. Got fixated on what looked like a sure kill on a battleship even though she was almost an antique. This one's on me.

"Everything is always on you," the exec said, quietly. Malachi hadn't realized that the exec had come up into the conning tower, or that he'd said those last words out loud. Malachi gave him a blank look for a moment before shaking his head. He was more tired than he'd realized.

"What do we do about that thing?" the exec asked.

"We stay down until night and don't make any sudden moves. Any damage down below?"

"Nothing important," the exec said. "And the battery is almost topped off, so as long as they don't send destroyers, we should be able to get away. And the bomb, if that's what it is?"

"We'll have to physically see it. My guess is the plane was so low it didn't have time to arm itself. Any of the torpedomen ex-EOD by any chance?"

"I'll ask the COB," the exec said. Then he saw the pushed-in steel. "Good God," he said.

"Yeah, exactly. Get me a damage report, minor or not. I'll tell you what: if we can get that thing off safely, I'm ready to go back to Perth."

"Just say the words, Captain," the exec said as he continued to stare at the bulge in the skin of the conning tower. "This shit's getting real old."

TWENTY-SIX

They surfaced nine hours later, still only 50 miles from Brunei Bay. The seas were calm but the barometer was falling, indicating that another storm was coming. Malachi, the COB, and the boatswain clambered up to the 20mm nest to see what they had. The gun was mangled, crushed almost beyond recognition in their red flashlight's cones. The bomb was black, finned, with two reinforcing rings around its middle. At the nose was a small three-bladed propeller, with two of the three blades bent back to almost flat. Malachi put his light on that propeller.

"That's the arming mechanism," the COB said. He'd done a one-week course at the EOD school to learn about safing and arming mechanisms in the fleet. "If this is like our aircraft bombs, they load it onto a wing pylon. Then they hook a wire that goes from the pylon to the nose of the bomb. That little propeller is held in place with a pin. Once they drop it, that wire pulls the pin and the propeller spins. After it spins a certain number of turns, the bomb arms. That way, if they drop it really low, they don't blow themselves up."

He shifted his flashlight to the back of the bomb. "Our really big bruisers have two propellers—one at the nose, one at the back end. They both have to work as advertised, or the bomb won't explode. Looks to me like they forgot the one at the back—see this brass plate?"

They all hunched down over the back end of the bomb. The two-inch-diameter plate gleamed back at them. "You unscrew those four screws and install the propeller mechanism, with the pin. Then when they bring it out to the bomber, they attach that wire I told you about."

"Meaning this bomb wouldn't have exploded even if the arming mechanism *had* had time to arm?" Malachi asked.

"It's a Jap bomb, Skipper, so I don't know. But our bombs have a plate just like that. He must have been pretty low for this to happen."

"Low enough that we were able to hear him in the conning tower," Malachi said. "So that thing won't explode unless that propeller gets to spin some more?"

"That's the theory, Captain," the COB said. "But to be sure, we need to get rid of it."

"How much you think that thing weighs?" the boatswain asked.

"Thousand pounds, maybe a bit more," the COB replied.

The boatswain whistled. "We ain't got nothin' that'll lift *that* off," he said.

"First thing we have to do is secure that propeller so it can't move," the COB said. "We don't know how many more turns it takes to arm this sucker."

"What are all those holes for, around the middle?" Malachi asked. The COB just shook his head.

The chief engineer had joined them on the gun platform. "I'll get some monkey shit," he said. "We can pack that propeller thing and immobilize it."

They all nodded and the engineer went below to get a tube of a metallic putty-like substance known throughout the fleet as monkey shit, and used to fix just about any leak temporarily.

The red light lit up on the bitchbox below them "Captain, XO."

Malachi climbed down through the tangled wreckage of the 20mm mount. There was no way they could cut all that away and move a half-ton bomb. "Go ahead," he said.

"I just tried the periscopes. Both are jammed. We can get the surface search radar mast up, although it's pretty noisy. I haven't tried the air search."

"Wonderful," Malachi said looking up at the columns of steel that held the scope assemblies. They didn't look bent, but that bomb was nosed in right at the base of the housings.

"I give up," he said. "Plot a course for Perth."

When they made it back to the harbor entrance at Fremantle two weeks later they were met by a utility boat sent out from the tender. A repair superintendent came aboard and handed them an anchorage assignment. Apparently the tender wasn't taking any chances. Three specialist petty officers—one chief and two petty officers first class—from the explosive ordnance disposal detachment on the tender also came aboard.

"The plan is *Firefish* goes to anchorage and we take everyone off except the EOD people. Once they disarm it, they'll send out a small floating crane barge from the port and lift it off. *Then* you can come alongside."

"Sounds good to me," Malachi told him. "I will stay aboard, though."

"Um, sir, the admiral was specific—"

"It's my boat and my bomb," Malachi said. "Tell him whatever white lies you want to, Lieutenant." He turned to the three EOD men, who were grinning. "Gents, let's go topside and I'll introduce you to your work."

They anchored half an hour later about three miles from the port facilities, in 70 feet of water. The weather was calm, and the disembarkation of the crew uneventful. The exec asked to stay but Malachi said no. "Keep everyone onboard the tender until this is over, one way or another. Then they can come back so we can get her into port. The EOD guys tell me that this doesn't take that long. The only real problem is the possibility they've put anti-intrusion traps in it and it goes off. Then you'll be back where we started—in temporary command."

The exec looked down at the deck plates. "About the only way I'll ever get command, I guess," he said quietly.

"That's not true, XO, not true at all. Now get going."

It took three motor launches to offload the crew and the important papers, such as the logs and the communications codebooks. By the time Malachi had climbed back up to the bridge the EOD people were huddled around the bomb as if praying over it, which possibly they were, he thought. A nice cool breeze had come up from the

northeast, raising little whitecaps all the way back into the river entrance. He wondered if Kensie would be in town.

He'd had time to think about the situation with his exec during the
slow transit back to base. He'd concluded he'd tell the commodore that
it was time for Marty to transfer off and go into the prospective commanding officer pool. He might not have the killer instinct, but he'd
saved the boat a couple of times and more than proved his technical
competence during the attacks. Their disagreement over the Kawanishi attack had been real enough, but now Malachi felt that his cold-
shoulder routine had been overdone. He heard one of the EOD techs
say "Okay, let's do it," and wondered if he should leave the bridge and
go hang out way back on the fantail, or even in the after torpedo room.
That would certainly take care of this Iceman moniker, he thought
with a cold smile. He decided to go up and watch instead.

To his surprise, they were working on the back end of the bomb.
The chief explained what they were doing. One man was working inside the hole underneath the brass plate. A second was speaking into
an Army field radio, describing everything the first tech was doing,
step by careful step, to someone ashore. The chief had laid out what
looked like bath towels on the only flat space available as a place to
lay whatever parts the first tech removed. It almost looked like the
bomb had been draped for surgery.

"Those Japs are sneaky little buggers," the chief tech said. "We've
had reports of them replacing the tail fuse with a booby-trapped time-
delay fuse. So first, we have to take a look."

"My COB said they'd probably been in such a hurry to take off
they forgot or didn't bother with the back-end fuse. We were only
about ten, twelve miles offshore *and* in shallow water. They got buck
fever, maybe."

The chief grunted a laugh. "See these holes right here, next to the
ring? If it was a Kawanishi dropped this thing? Then this baby is a
combo-bomb, built for seaplanes. The fuse assemblies are a safety feature; if the prop doesn't complete sufficient revolutions that fuse
won't work. But these?" He pointed at the holes. "These are to let
water in. Turns this beast into a thousand pound *depth* bomb, which
bypasses the fuse's safety features. Set to go off at two hundred fifty

feet. I know that because both ends of this thing have a blue ring painted on them."

Malachi felt himself go cold. They'd made as much of the transit back from the operating area on the surface as they could, but there were times they thought it safer to be submerged during daylight. For once he hadn't indulged in any deep dives—he'd set the cruising depth for 150 feet.

"Clear," the first tech announced, lifting out a brass cylinder the size of a tennis ball can, with several clipped colored wires extending from ports around its base.

"That's the detonator," the chief said, laying the cylinder gingerly down on one of the towels. "The main explosive is type ninety-eight, pretty stable, so it takes a shot of some stuff like nitro to start the party. Now we gotta see if he's got a brother up front."

"I'll get out of your hair, then," Malachi said, his throat still dry from the realization of what could have happened.

Three hours later *Firefish* was safely alongside the tender, her sail already covered by an anthill of workers disassembling the entire periscope stack and cutting away the remains of the 20mm cannon. A crane barge had come out and lifted off the supposedly harmless bomb and then carted it out to deeper water. There it was lowered to the bottom with a timed explosive attached, released, and after ten minutes, it detonated with a crowd-pleasing geyser of dirty seawater punching its way into the air. Malachi had told the COB what all those holes around the middle had been for, causing that old salt to go pale in the face.

A messenger from the tender appeared on the quarterdeck as the crew settled into the return-to-port routine of refueling, rearming, and receiving stores, food, and mail. The quarterdeck watch called Malachi in his cabin and told him that the commodore would like to see him at his convenience. Malachi finished signing for the torpedoes that were about to be onloaded and the newest book of code keys, which he turned over to the operations officer. As per regulations, ammo and fuel could not be loaded at the same time except at sea, so the boat would refuel first, then load the torpedoes. It was axiomatic in the fleet that the first thing any warship did when she returned to port was to make herself ready for sea. Several years ago he'd asked his department head why "they" would do that to a crew who'd been out on patrol and were tired if not exhausted. "They may be tired," the department head had told him, "but they really want to get ashore. You will notice that the fuel and the ammo will get aboard in record time."

The commodore himself greeted Malachi on the tender's quarterdeck with a warm welcome and congratulations for having made an attack on a battleship. Then they went to the flag quarters for a coffee.

"I'd offer you a whiskey," he said, "but you don't drink, so coffee it will have to be."

"I'd probably accept one if you offered, sir," Malachi replied. He told the commodore what he'd learned about "his" bomb from the EOD people. Even the commodore blanched at the thought. "Well," he said, "that typhoon was unfortunate, but they gave you credit for damaging the battleship, the capsized tanker, and one destroyer. But it was the big boy that got Pearl really excited. She was the *Yamashiro*, an oldie from the thirties with fourteen-inch guns. They got her back into Brunei, where they apparently ran her aground to prevent her from capsizing."

"I hit her with four fish," Malachi said. "Four of six fired. She just drove off. Once again, the Mark fourteen let us down."

"We've made progress on that," the commodore said. "Or, rather, Pearl has. They found out that the contact exploder pin was being crushed when it hit at a ninety-degree angle. BuOrd's working on a new design, but Nimitz has also ordered the magnetic exploder deactivated permanently."

"Well, that *is* progress," Malachi said, remembering the COB's theory.

The commodore smiled wearily. "Yes, and no," he said. "Our admiral doesn't work for Nimitz—he works for MacArthur. He has determined that the Perth boats will still use the magnetic exploder."

Malachi just stared at him for a moment. Then he shook his head. "Well, the problem I saw is that the warheads are just too small to deal with battleships. I'm glad we hurt him, but I think we'd be much better off concentrating on tankers. If their big guys can't get fuel, they're no threat to anybody."

The commodore put his hands up in a sign of surrender. "You're preaching to the choir, Malachi," he said. "In the meantime, how's the boat and the crew?"

"The bomb was my fault," he said. "I'd forgotten that it was daylight topside *and* I'd forgotten we were only forty miles, if that, from a Kawanishi base."

"A battleship in your periscope, even an antique, will do that," the commodore said. "We'll get a damage assessment in the next twenty-four hours. In the meantime, I want you to take some time off. You look like you got rode hard and put away wet."

"To tell the truth, I feel like I got rode hard and then run over a cliff," Malachi admitted. "In that regard—"

"Yes?"

"My XO, Marty Brandquist. He did a superlative job on this patrol. I think he's ready to go into the PCO pool, my former comments not withstanding."

"Changed your mind?"

"He may not have the killer instinct, Commodore," Malachi said, "but he's smart, expert on an attack, and already thinking like a skipper. And always right *there* when I needed him. I think he's ready to go out on a PCO patrol and then get his own boat."

The commodore sat back in his chair. "That's quite a turnaround," he said. "Want to tell me what really happened out there?"

Malachi sighed and slumped in his chair. He told the commodore about their disagreement about making sure there were no survivors from the Kawanishi.

The commodore nodded. "Thank you," he said. "And, yes, he would have to transfer after a conversation like that. I agree with you, by the way. Up to then the Japs didn't know one of our boats was there. You did exactly the right thing, in my opinion. It's not like the Japs don't do that on a regular basis."

"I finally figured out that it wasn't a weakness, but rather a difference in operational opinion. We hit that Kawanishi hard and fast. There may have been no survivors to worry about. But . . ."

The commodore was silent for a moment. "One of our skippers surfaced after sinking a troop transport and ordered the machine-gunning of several hundred troops in the water in lifejackets. *His* XO asked to be transferred when they got back to Pearl. The matter was hushed up because that skipper was, well, let's just say, untouchable in terms of how many ships he's sunk. This matter is small potatoes compared to that, and I'll forward your recommendation to the admiral about Marty Brandquist. Write it up as soon as possible."

Malachi reached into his briefcase. "Did that on the transit back," he said, handing the memorandum over. He then produced his captain's log.

"Does Marty know you're doing this?" the commodore asked.

"As long as you approved, I was going to put a copy of that in his inbasket before I go ashore tonight. That way he won't start cranking on a request-to-transfer letter."

"Yes, good move. Get back to your boat and see how bad the periscope stack's been damaged, but then do get ashore. Maybe call that good-looking doctor friend of yours."

Malachi's brows rose in surprise.

The commodore grinned. "Why are you surprised, Captain?" he said. "We commodores know stuff."

Back aboard *Firefish* the news on the periscope assemblies was mixed. The attack scope was well and truly hammered. The acquisition scope was damaged but repairable. The surface search radar mast needed new suspension bearings, and the air search mast was okay.

"Fortunately," the repair superintendent told him, "the last of our refugee S-boats is being sent back to Pearl next week. We're going to do a little raping and pillaging, since she's going back for de-comm. We'll take her entire attack scope assembly, do a little metal bending, and put it in *Firefish*. We're also going to relieve her of her twenty-millimeter mount, which happens to be a twin barreled set. Your boatswain is beside himself."

"I'll just bet he is," Malachi said. Then he went to find the exec, who was busy in the engine room arguing with a tender engineer. Malachi gave him the high sign and they went back to his cabin.

"What was that all about?" he asked.

"Number four engine needs a new injector rack," the exec said. "They don't want to do it. They're claiming the engine needs a complete overhaul and that's shipyard work, not tender work. BuShips rules."

Malachi sighed. The tail wagging the dog, again. Then he asked about the boat's RFS status.

"We're rearmed and refueled," the exec replied. "Of course without periscopes we're not going anywhere productive, but we can leave port if we have to."

"Excellent," Malachi said. "You know about how they're gonna do the scopes?"

"Yes, sir. Sounds good to me and a whole lot better than a three-week trip back to Pearl."

"Yes," Malachi said. "Okay—I'm going ashore to the hotel. There's a memo you need to read—I put it in your cabin. Basically, it says that I recommend you for independent command and for orders to the prospective commanding officer pool in Pearl. From there you'll make a PCO cruise with another skipper, and then get your own boat, unless you piss him off."

The exec was clearly stunned. "I thought—" he began, but Malachi cut him off.

"You rate it and you're ready," he said. "You've demonstrated that more than once. The incident with the Kawanishi was one of those things they call a command decision. Within the year you're going to learn all about that. I've told the commodore, and he's going to forward my recommendation up the chain. You might begin preps for a turnover with a new XO."

"Do we know—?"

"Hell, no," Malachi said. "But he'll have some big shoes to fill. Well done, Marty. Now I'm going ashore."

"You've almost never called me Marty before," the exec observed. "All this time . . ."

"Well, I guess that's why they call me The Iceman," Malachi said. "For whatever it's worth, Marty, it was never personal."

Malachi got a ride downtown to the hotel, went to his room, ordered in room service, took a thirty-minute hot shower, and went to bed. For once, the killing dream stayed away. The next morning, much refreshed, he had breakfast in the hotel dining room and then took a cab back to the tender and *Firefish*. He spent the day wrangling various repair jobs, going through the three bags of official mail to see what had to be dealt with and what could be "lost" in wartime transit. The supply officer had conducted payday the afternoon before, with the inevitable consequences ashore in the bars and fleshpots of Perth/Fremantle. Through all this, he'd been waiting for the call from the admiral, who had, by now, read his captain's log. It came at 1600, just as the crew was headed ashore for the evening. The tender provided him a car to the admiral's downtown office. The commodore was present for the meeting.

"A most interesting patrol, Captain," the admiral began. "Everything from a seaplane to a tanker to a battleship. *And* a typhoon, for your sins. And then you brought us back a bomb. How are you?"

"I'm tired, Admiral," Malachi said. "We all are. It was interesting, but in the Chinese sense of that word."

The admiral smiled. "Yes, indeed. I know exactly what you mean. Well, Pearl is beyond pleased with your assault on *Yamashiro*. They'll get her refloated and back into operation, no doubt, but it really offends them when we hit one of their capital ships. My congratulations."

"Thank you, sir," Malachi said.

"Your squadron commander has forwarded your recommendation for your exec to go to the PCO pool. I concur, and we'll make that happen. In the meantime, we'll need to find you another exec, but ComSubPac will need to weigh in on that. From what I've been told, your repairs will take a couple of weeks, so we have time. But here's the question: you've done three patrols as CO. Are you up to doing another one? Or do you want to take some time off and then maybe go to new construction?"

"I think I can do another," Malachi said. "Pressing my luck, perhaps, but we've done some damage in *Firefish*."

"You absolutely have," the admiral said. "But recently the force had a case where the CO, who was, apparently, emotionally and physically exhausted, handed over command to his exec in the middle of a war patrol, went to his cabin, and stayed there for the remainder of his patrol. This prompted Pearl to ask the question: how many patrols should a CO make?"

Malachi could only shrug. "Depends on the patrols, and it depends on the age and resilience of the CO, I guess," he replied. "A couple of oh-my-God, this-is-it depth-chargings can make all the difference. I think the fleet's strategy has a bearing on this."

"Yes?"

"As long as we're being sent out to attack carriers and battleships, we're put in the position of attacking heavily defended formations. Personally, I think we ought to be hunting down and destroying their logistics train—tankers, freighters, troop carriers, seaplane tenders, repair ships, any convoy that contains no capital ships. Even tankers alone might do it—strangle their fuel oil supply, the battleships and the carriers will have to stay in port. When you think about it, the Japs are seriously overextended, and Japan has no oil."

The admiral sat back in his chair and thought about that for a minute. "You might be interested to know that that concept is even now being discussed at SubPac headquarters. Your squad dog here tells me he wants you to take some time off, and I support that. You've been successful. *Very* successful. But here's what I want. Go on leave for a week. Get away from the war and the boat, as much as you can. And then come back and tell me you can do another patrol, or not. When you do, don't hesitate to say no, because everybody back at home coming behind you could benefit from what you know and what you've learned. No one will gainsay your decision, okay?"

Malachi didn't know what to say. Did the admiral want him to quit? Was his unrelenting tactical aggression causing more problems than he was worth? The admiral's demeanor had changed from thinly veiled hostility to one of concern. The admiral saw him hesitating.

"Our two most aggressive and tactically brilliant COs have recently been lost," he said. "We have, as usual, no idea of what happened to them and their boats. One was on his fourth patrol; the other on his fifth. The docs in Pearl are telling ComSubPac that command fatigue especially is cumulative. So think about it, please. Now—go get a beer."

Malachi left the office totally confused, and then realized that he might be an example of just what the "docs in Pearl" were talking about. One good, and dreamless, sleep did not a recovery make. The beer sounded good, however.

TWENTY-SEVEN

By seven that evening he was back at his usual corner table in the rooftop bar and lounge, savoring that beer. He'd gone back to the boat to see how Marty was coming with all the crises, and then told him he'd be on leave for a week, most likely in town. He said he'd set the XO up for a similar week off when he got back. Everybody was always concerned about the CO's physical and mental state, but it was his job to do the same for his exec, who did not get to go sit down in the wardroom and have a cigarette and a coffee after the action was over.

There were two other skippers and the usual pretty girls behind the bar attending to their needs, real and imagined. He recognized one, but the other commander was a stranger. They'd been too busy with the bartenders to notice when he'd slipped in and gone to "his" table in a far corner. From there he could overlook the city and just barely make out the harbor in the distance. The air was much less humid now that the northeast monsoon had settled in. He wondered if typhoons ever came here. Probably not, he thought: Perth/Fremantle was about as remote as you could get on this planet. And Kensie was engaged to be married.

He'd called the hospital before coming up and asked if he could speak to her. The operator had taken his message and the hotel number. Ten minutes later her assistant called back and gently informed him that Dr. Richmond was away until tomorrow, having taken a week off to attend some parties at the family's station to celebrate her engagement to Gerald Hightower, the eldest son of the family that owned the sole transcontinental railroad in Australia. It had taken Malachi a few seconds to absorb this news.

"Well," he'd said. "Please tell her I send my sincerest congratulations and wish her every happiness."

"I will certainly do that, Captain," the assistant had said, obviously aware of the surprise he'd just delivered.

Now at the bar he thought back to their times together. She had told him that her father wanted to make a marriage for her that would cement the Richmond family's position as one of Australia's premier industrial magnates. Owner of yet another railroad ought to do it, he thought. Maybe it was his confession that had made her realize that how they felt about each other was painfully vulnerable to the vagaries of this war. He was about as temporary a feature in her life as one could get—the skipper of one of America's submarines in wartime, which had a nasty habit of disappearing without a trace on a regular basis, like the two he'd just heard about. God, he'd miss her, though, he thought. Should never have told her.

Two nights later, unable to sleep, he went out for a late-night walk along the city streets. There were few people about, other than the occasional joint US-Aussie shore patrols keeping an eye out for passed-out drunks along the storefronts now that the pubs had all closed. Two of them were walking ahead of him. The occasional Ute, Australia's ubiquitous utility vehicle, clattered by, but everyone else seemed to have gone to bed. The Fremantle harbor area and the mouth of the Swan River were under a blackout order, but up here in Perth itself the lights were still on. MacArthur's recent victories over the Japanese Army in New Guinea had pretty much dissipated the threat of invasion in Australia. The flow of casualties, however, had not diminished one bit.

He'd been thinking about what the admiral had said: can you do a fourth patrol, or is it maybe time for you to go back to Pearl and help train all the new boats that were streaming out to the Pacific war in increasing numbers. He'd made a big mistake exposing the boat to a Kawanishi and now the specter of fatigue was playing on his mind. If he came off the boat now, he'd be leaving at the top of his game. He could go on to another command, or even to a staff. Maybe the staff right here in Perth. Being able to see Kensie would have been part of that decision, although, realistically, there never had been much chance of any real future with her. She'd alluded to the fact that her father's ambitions for her were somewhat medieval, but it was no surprise that the daughter of a seriously prominent family would be expected to do better than an itinerant American naval officer. Now it seemed her father had clarified that question beyond any doubt.

There was a screech of tires out in the street. One of the Utes had come to a sudden stop and was backing up. Then the driver's side window rolled down, framing Kensie's smiling face. "G'dday, mate— need a lift?"

Malachi was so surprised he failed to answer. The Aussie member of the shore patrol duo turned around and said, sotto voce: the answer is yes, you berk.

Malachi grinned at him and then went out into the street to get in. Then he had to go around the vehicle because the Aussies, like the Brits, drove from the right side of the vehicle . . . on the wrong side of the damned road, too.

He climbed into the boxy vehicle and closed the door. "I guess congratulations are in order," he said.

"Whatever for?" she asked.

"Engagement to somebody Hightower?"

She stopped the Ute in the middle of the empty street. "*What?*" she cried. "Who told you that rubbish?"

"Your ace assistant at the hospital. Said you'd been on a week's leave to celebrate your engagement to—"

"To Jerry Hightower?" she asked, before breaking into peals of laughter. "Oh, God, that's funny." Then she realized he was being serious, and she reached across the front seat to take his hand. "I've done no such thing, dear heart. I've been off for a week because I told them I'd quit if I didn't get some time off. Spent the week at the station. And yes, we were celebrating Jerry's engagement, but not to me, for God's sakes. To a Melbourne heiress named Pamela Carstairs, who's probably the only woman in Australia who'd have him. Jerry's a world-class cad, a serious drunk, and possibly a switch-hitter in the bedroom, but his father owns *the* transcontinental railroad, so there you are. They were out here—the Hightowers and the Carstairs—because Father Time had acquired the coal mines and *their* railroads. The party was secondary. Oh, the look on your face."

"Your assistant is a dead man," Malachi growled.

She put the Ute in gear and asked if he still had his hotel room at the Benbow.

"Yes," he said.

"I'm asking because some of the submarines stationed here are supposedly moving to new bases up north."

"So much for military secrets," he laughed. "Your sources may well be better than mine, but I haven't heard that rumor. To my knowledge there aren't any bases north of here that are ours, anyway. I have a week off, by the way. Admiral's orders."

"*Shit!*" she exclaimed. "I just took a week off. I was on my way to Melbourne House for the night when I saw you. Back on shift at six a.m. sharpish, unfortunately."

"What is Melbourne House?"

"Another requisitioned hotel downtown for the docs and senior nursing staff at the hospital. Pretty plain digs, but by the end of a shift in the OR, we're all ready for a night's sleep and little else."

"And you were on shift today, right?"

"Gawd, yes."

"Damn."

She hooted at that. "Poor thing," she said. "Poor deprived thing."

"Depraved is more like it," he said, before realizing they were at his hotel.

TWENTY-EIGHT

The new exec's name was Sanford Higgins. He was class of 1933 and Malachi thought he looked much too young to already be a lieutenant commander. Higgins and Marty had done a three-day turnover while Malachi was enjoying his nights much better than his days. Marty had then flown to Brisbane in preparation for a ride on a boat going back to Pearl for shipyard work. Higgins was not quite six feet tall, with sandy brown hair and bright blue eyes. He had maintained his football player's physique since graduation, and he appeared to have a positive outlook on most matters. He was friendly with the enlisted and, more importantly, the COB thought he was okay, which was an important vote of confidence. His last duty station had been on a fleet boat out of Pearl as the Ops officer. In their first official CO/XO meeting, Higgins was ready with a thorough status on the boat's repairs, some personnel changes, and news that the boat was going out a week earlier than anticipated when she'd first come in.

"Any idea as to the Op area?" Malachi asked.

"No, sir, sealed orders forthcoming. But we're getting a full load of torpedoes for a change, so somebody's expecting rich pickings."

"What do you think so far about *Firefish*?" Malachi asked.

"Looks and sounds like a good boat," Higgins said, carefully. "Can't argue with all those rising suns on the sail, either. She's got a super rep in Pearl."

Malachi wanted to ask him if he'd heard the name Iceman back in Pearl, but he knew that would put Higgins in a difficult position.

"Okay," he said. "Welcome aboard. I won't bore you with a philo-sophical discussion of how I run things, and I'm sure Marty filled you in. I plan to be aboard during working hours, and at the skip-pers' billet downtown nights until we sail. I have a meeting with the admiral tomorrow morning."

"Do you need any staffing or prep materials for that meeting, Captain?"

"No, XO," Malachi replied with a weary smile. "Just me. That's the usual subject of my meetings with the admiral."

He was shown into the admiral's office downtown the next morn-ing at ten o'clock. The admiral pointed him toward a chair while he finished up with two staff officers—something about torpedoes. When they left the admiral lit up a cigarette, offered one to Mala-chi, who accepted gratefully. He needed one right about now.

"Well, Captain, I'm told that *Firefish* has come back together in fine fashion, so much so that Pearl wants her back on patrol a week earlier than we estimated. How's your new exec?"

"Looks like an upstanding citizen," Malachi said. "I'll know better once we're at sea."

"Right," the admiral said. "So, how's by you?"

"I'm better, Admiral," Malachi said. "Got some time off away from the boat, physically and mentally. Got some good sleep, too."

"Yes, you look better than when you came in from that last patrol. Apparently your doctor friend knows what she's doing."

"Indeed she does, Admiral," Malachi said with a smile.

"God *bless* Australia," the admiral said. "Now, some news. The targeting guidance has been changed. We now are to expand our operations to fold in merchant shipping, especially tankers."

"Ah," Malachi said.

"Yes, I know you favor that, and I agree with the new guidance. Instead of attacking heavily protected battleship and carrier forma-tions, we're going to attack the means by which the big boys can get to sea in the first place. Your attack on that battleship may have fig-ured in this decision."

"Because the only reason he was in Brunei in the first place was to get oil?"

"Precisely. Now, you know what I need to ask you."

"Yes, sir, and the answer is yes, I'm ready to go back out. I'm rested, the boat is getting closer to RFS, I've got a new and fresh XO, and I understand we're getting a full load of fish. That sounds like my kind of patrol."

"Indeed," the admiral said. "It's been eighteen months since Pearl Harbor. The Japs are finished in the Solomon's and it appears they're starting to realize that. In other words, they're shifting to *de*fense. MacArthur is driving, well, maybe creeping, north through New Guinea and Indonesia. Everybody knows his true objective is the Philippines. Nimitz is preparing to drive north through the western Pacific islands with an eye toward getting airfields for the new long-range bombers. Then we'll start to attack the home islands. Basically, the Japs have overextended themselves. We need our best skippers to go out there and demonstrate that to them."

"We'll go do just that, Admiral."

The admiral sat back in his chair and finished his cigarette. "You're a hard case, Malachi Stormes," he said, finally. "I didn't think much of you when we first met. But you've convinced me that you are precisely the kind of skipper we need right now: aggressive, focused, and willing to go in harm's way. The submarine force is going to make *the* difference in this war. Chester Nimitz has said as much. Good hunting, Captain."

TWENTY-NINE

Just after nine p.m. the radar operator called a contact, three of them, actually. Range nineteen miles, bearing northwest. The boat was on the surface recharging batteries, idling along at seven knots and changing course every fifteen minutes as a precaution against a Jap submarine ambush. The night sky was dramatic: a half moon popping in and out of towering cumulonimbus clouds, flickering with occasional lightning. The seas were calm but "uneasy," as the new exec termed it. Malachi and Higgins were on the bridge, with four lookouts posted above them. They'd been in their assigned area, northwest of Palau Island, and had seen nothing at all for three nights and days.

"About time," Malachi said, lighting up another cigarette. Higgins didn't smoke. "So, did Marty tell you how he and I worked attacks?"

"Yes, sir," Higgins said. "He said you prefer surface attacks, with you up here on the TDT and him down in the conning tower, directing the attack team."

"Correct," Malachi said. "As far as we know, the Japs don't have radar, but we *do* think they can detect submarine radars. So we radiate one sweep at a time, just enough to develop a course and speed track on the targets. The attack team recommends courses and speeds to get in position, I send the final bearings down to confirm we have correct track data, and then we fire."

"What about the zigzag?"

"Yes, that complicates things if they change course right as we're trying to shoot. But the base course—the course they have to take to get to their destination—doesn't change. If they zig out of my ambush, then we do an end-around, get back in front of them, and try again."

"Bridge, Radar: there appears to be one big contact and two smaller ones, one ahead, one behind. We'll have a course and speed in three minutes."

"Bridge: aye," Malachi said. "Okay, XO, lay below and assume the attack director watch."

"Aye, aye, sir," Higgins said and then disappeared down the hatch into the conning tower. Malachi turned away from the bearing of the oncoming ships and took a big drag on his cancer stick, concealing the sudden glow in his cupped hands. He liked Higgins, who seemed to be as eager as he was to blow up Jap ships. Now he'd have to wait three minutes for the tracking team to develop the approaching ships' course and speed, and then make recommendations to put *Firefish* in front of them.

One big contact and two small meant two escorts. Those were better odds than the formations of battleships and carriers presented, with up to a dozen destroyers to contend with. The big contact could be anything—a tanker, freighter, maybe even a troop ship. The sealed orders had discussed the fact that the Japs were reinforcing Palau in anticipation of an American invasion, now that the Solomons were going under for them.

"Bridge, Conn: the formation's course and speed is one four zero, seventeen knots on first plot. No zigzag as yet. Recommend we come to zero five five to intercept on their starboard bow at a target angle of zero three zero." The exec's voice sounded confident, a nice change from Marty's eternal worrying.

"Make it so," Malachi replied. "Seventeen knots is not tanker speed. This is something else."

Three minutes later Plot refined the track: the formation was doing 20 knots, not 17. And appeared to be turning to the next leg of a zigzag pattern. "We can't get there from here, Captain. We need to run like hell due east while they go southeast, and hope the next leg brings them back to us."

"Okay, do it," Malachi said, glad now that he'd remained on the surface. It was, as always, a crapshoot when dealing with a zigzag plan. If their next leg took them south instead of east, *Firefish* would be even farther out of position. The attack team was making the best bet they could, that the Japs' destination was Palau, and Palau was east, not south of them. The diesels sprang to life with an authoritative roar as the boat came about and accelerated up to full power and 22 knots. In a few minutes the boat was leaving a broad, phosphorescent wake and twin trails of diesel exhaust behind them. He could actually hear the huge quantities of air being sucked into the induction valve behind the sail.

The new batch of torpedoes they had onboard had just come out from the West Coast and purportedly had new running depth sensors. The magnetic exploder feature was still in doubt, so the Perth skippers had decided to just disable it to prevent its predilection for setting off the warhead 50 feet away from the target. The admiral undoubtedly knew that, but with the rest of SubPac having done the same thing he'd probably decided not to push the issue anymore. The new fish also had stronger contact firing pins in their noses, courtesy of some testing done back at Pearl. The bad news was that if you didn't get a boom now, you couldn't keep blaming the fish. He smiled to himself in the darkness; always a hook, he thought.

"Bridge, Conn: they're still opening to the southeast; we can slow down to fifteen knots and still make intercept position."

The surrounding sea suddenly lit up as the moon came back out from behind the clouds. "Assuming they come back toward us, right?"

"Yes, sir," the exec said. "But they should, if they're going to Palau."

"I agree, and if we can get ahead of them, we'll do this one submerged. The moon is staying out more than it's going in. Slow to fifteen knots. How far away is Palau now?"

"Forty-six miles, sir."

"Any time now, then. I need some coffee."

Again it was the boatswain, who'd taken to standing watch in Control when an attack was shaping up, who brought him his coffee.

Malachi thanked him and then asked how he liked his new twin 20mm guns.

"They're a little on the old side, but they're better built than our other mount. Somebody said they were Swedish made."

"No, actually, they were probably made in Germany before the war. Started in Switzerland, but it was the Germans who brought the quality into them."

"Go figure," the boatswain said. "We chasing something big?"

"One big, two escorts. We don't know what we're going after, but if they turn the right way, we'll soon find out."

"Bridge, Conn: they're turning again, back to the northeast. We'll confirm the track, but it looks like we can submerge anytime and get ready for business. Last range was eighteen thousand yards."

The boatswain put two fingers to his forehead in an ancient naval salute and hustled back down below. Malachi acknowledged the report and scanned the horizon. The seas were dark except for wide wedges of moonlit water pointing in the direction of the moon. The light made the water appear black. At 20 knots the Jap formation would cover one mile every three minutes. Six minutes to intercept. He pushed the diving alarm.

Down in the conning tower he conferred with the attack team. "There's a tin can ahead, and another behind the big guy. The trick is to get into firing position without that lead escort getting contact on us. We got a layer?"

"Yes, sir, layer at two hundred ten feet."

"Okay, when Plot says they're eight thousand yards out, we'll go down to two hundred thirty feet and point the boat at the approaching formation. When we hear the first escort go down-Doppler, we come back to periscope depth and make the attack. I'll want bow tubes, four fish, depth setting fifteen feet, speed high. Remember that I want the boat to be pointed on the firing bearing to reduce the chances for a circular run."

He watched as the exec huddled with the attack team over the plotting table. Gone were Marty Brandquist's what-ifs and what-abouts. Higgins was eagerly focused on the kill.

Minutes passed and then the exec pointed his index finger down. "Make your depth two hundred thirty feet," Malachi ordered. "Trim for a quick return to periscope depth. Open forward outer doors. Make ready tubes one through four."

The boat tilted down as the ballast tanks were adjusted to make her heavy. They were making five knots, which was a good speed to take her down without any drama. The game then passed to Sonar.

"Screwbeats approaching from the southwest, bearing two four zero. Sounds like a destroyer."

"Conn: aye, let me know the moment the Doppler shifts to down." And hope and pray the bastard doesn't detect us, he thought. If he busts our cover, the big guy will simply roar past us at 20 knots.

"Up-Doppler, but he's still pinging in wide band search mode," Sonar reported.

C'mon layer, Malachi thought. The wide search pattern of a sonar didn't have the power of the more focused attack beam. The temperature thermocline should deflect the probing beams up and away.

"*Down*-Doppler," Sonar called. "New screwbeats, something bigger. Multiple screws. Bearing two three seven. Definite *up*-Doppler."

"Come to periscope depth and handsomely," Malachi told Control. He looked over at the exec.

"Firing bearing will be one niner zero if the track agrees with the passive plot."

"Come to course one niner zero, speed four," Malachi ordered, watching the depth gauge. The moment they got to periscope depth he ran the scope up, stopping just short of broaching the surface.

"Stable at periscope depth," Control reported. Malachi ran the scope up another three feet and immediately saw a darkened ocean liner in his picture. "Bearing—mark!"

"Two one zero," the exec announced from the other side of the scope.

"Plot agrees. Fire at any time," the TDC operator said.

"Fire one," Malachi ordered, and then went through the normal sequence of sending four fish out to make the kill. If the plot was correct, this big beast would pass at a distance of a half mile. He kept the scope up. The ship was definitely an ocean liner type, with railed galleries along her sides and two big funnels amidships. She was fully darkened but he could still see the five-inch mounts on her forecastle. Converted ocean liner and armed. Meant she was a troopship. Reinforcements for the Palau garrison.

The first torpedo hit her just behind the bow with a red flare and a satisfying geyser of water shooting up into the air. The second hit amidships with another good, solid explosion. The third hit her just behind the second stack but with a small splash, a dud. He thought that the fourth one missed astern until there was a fearsome blast right under her stern. He swung the scope back to amidships and was pleased to see huge clouds of red steam erupting out of the forward stack.

"Make your depth two hundred fifty feet, full power and close the outer doors forward," he ordered. He intended to go deep right behind the stricken ship and run for a thousand yards or so. All the explosions had been on the transport's port side, so he wanted to get over to the other side before those destroyers came racing in to find him. He turned to the attack team as the scope came down and the boat tilted into her escape mode. "Three good hits, one dud," he announced. "She had a big bow wave on her, so she'll carry forward for a mile or so. Troop transport. Big bastard—twenty thousand tons, maybe even more. Five-inchers fore and aft. Reload forward."

The boat vibrated as they slipped into the depths. There were distant sounds of a ship in big trouble coming through the hull, although the layer was masking most of it. Finally they heard a barrage of depth charges going off way behind them. Now that they knew where the escorts were they could slow down and burn less battery power. Malachi ordered speed of four knots and continued to open the distance between *Firefish* and the escorts, which were still making a racket.

"XO, get us out to five thousand yards from the firing track and then we'll turn east. I want to give those tin cans a chance to quit searching and go into rescue mode if that big guy is what I think he is."

"Aye, sir, and when they do?"

"I'm going to attack them."

It took two hours for them to creep back up on the scene of the transport's sinking. Malachi assumed she'd gone down because the radar revealed only two small contacts that were nearly stationary about five miles from where the torpedoes had done their work. The clouds completely obscured the moon now and the seas appeared to be rising. He was temporarily blinded by a flash of lightning on the horizon, and for a moment he thought the Japs had seen his periscope and opened fire.

"Weather's turning to shit," he announced. "Make this a radar attack on the nearest escort. Use low speed, depth setting ten feet, from a range of fifteen hundred yards. One fish. Start the track."

The plotters went to work as the radar operator gave them a single sweep every three minutes, aimed at the pair of escorts. It looked like the destroyers, or more likely smaller destroyer escort ships, were making bare headway, so they had to force a course and speed of east at one knot to satisfy the TDC. The computer balked. The TDC operator had to report an unstable solution.

"Okay, we'll do this the traditional way," Malachi said. "Down the radar mast. Point the boat at the last-known bearing of the nearest escort. Cease any reloading operations and open the outer doors forward."

Once this was done he slowed to three knots to minimize the periscope wake. "Make ready tube number six. Up scope."

It took thirty seconds before his eyes could pick out the dim shape of a DE, which was broadside to him. He couldn't see the other one at all. There were small whitecaps everywhere, so he left the scope up. "Bearing—mark."

"Bearing is three one zero."

He scanned the range lines engraved on the scope's optics, which basically gave him a stadimeter to work with in estimating the range. He could have used the radar, but two masts up was asking for a sharp-eyed lookout report. He worked the dials until he got the dim image exactly between two horizontal lines. "Range—mark."

The exec read the dial so that Malachi could stay on the target. "Range is eighteen hundred yards."

"We will fire manually. Enter a firing bearing of three one zero, speed low, depth ten feet."

Cutting out the TDC, the operator connected with tube six and made the settings. "Tube six is ready, sir."

"Fire six."

The torpedo went out with a good thump. Malachi kept the scope up, pretty sure that the lessened wake would not be discernible in the growing chop. The escort suddenly bucked up in the middle as a large waterspout lifted above her masts. This was followed by a series of steam explosions as she collapsed back into the sea and broke in half. The sound reached them a second later. "Up radar mast— find the other guy."

The mast went back up while Malachi swung his optical scope around, looking for a bow wave. There was nothing there. He went back to the escort. The forward half of the ship had capsized, and the escort's stern was showing now, the tops of his rudders just becoming visible. Malachi realized they were still closing and ordered a turn away to due south.

"Conn, Sonar: screwbeats bearing zero one zero—high speed, classify as a destroyer type ship. Doppler is—wait." There was a three second pause. "Doppler is *down*-Doppler. He's running away."

Running away or trying to make us think so, Malachi wondered. "Stay on him, Sonar, make sure he doesn't circle back."

"Sonar: aye, starting Doppler tracking."

Malachi turned back to the escort in time to see the back end slip down into the depths, leaving a large cloud of steam and a boil of large bubbles in its place.

"Target sunk," he announced. "A DE, I think. We'll track the other one until we lose his screw noises. Then I want to surface in the area."

It took thirty minutes before Sonar reported no more contact on the escort's thrashing propellers. Doppler had remained down the entire time, indicating she was exiting the area. If she'd turned back, the Doppler would have gone to null and then up, indicating she was headed back in. Malachi ordered Sound to keep a close watch.

After they surfaced Malachi ordered the 20mm gun team to come up, and then set two lookouts and called for the exec to come to the bridge and to bring two rain slickers. Higgins came up two minutes

later after securing the attack party in the conning tower and in-
structing Sonar to remain vigilant. He'd also ordered periodic
single-sweep radar observations. That second destroyer was still on
everybody's minds. It wasn't like the Japs to cut and run like that.
Malachi told Control to stay on the batteries until he told them otherwise, but that the engine room could turn on main induction on low
and suck some fresh air into the boat. He asked for a course back to
where they thought the big ship had gone down.

By now there was a light rain falling, amplified by a lightly blowing spray. A steady breeze from the northeast was raising ever-bigger
whitecaps. There was more lightning now, periodically turning night
into bright, black-and-white day. Malachi ordered Control to insti-
tute a broad weave around the baseline course so as not to present a
steady course and speed in case there was a Jap sub in the area.

"What are we looking for?" Higgins asked.

"I wanted you to see something," Malachi replied.

A bolt of lightning crashed down about a mile away, leaving a boil-
ing cloud of steam in its wake. "Now I can't see a thing," Higgins
complained above the rumble of thunder.

"Were not there yet, XO."

Ten minutes later they entered the area of probability, according
to the plot. Even in the fresh breeze they could suddenly detect the
bright stink of fuel oil in the air. The boat was sliding through the
water in dead silence except for the occasional slap of a wave against
the windward bow. A sudden burst of cloud-to-cloud lightning illuminated the sea for a mile around. Malachi heard the exec gasp at
what he saw.

The boat was slicing through a sea of heads and faces, hundreds,
possibly thousands of them, bobbing up and down between the whitecaps. Malachi could just barely hear faint cries of alarm from the
men in the water. Some were in lifejackets, others clinging to each
other in sodden lumps in the rising seaway. The boatswain asked if
the captain wanted him to do anything; Malachi told him no. "The
sea will take them, Boatswain mate. Save your ammo."

"Wouldn't have enough, anyways," the boatswain replied. "*Jesus!*"

The boat passed through the sea of heads, some turning to look at them, others facedown in the water, kept afloat by lifejackets that were slowly absorbing water until they no longer floated. An occasional scream from out in the darkness told of sharks. It took them fifteen minutes to get through the scene, after which Malachi ordered Control to shift to main propulsion diesels. There were still some hours until daylight, and the batteries, as always, craved their amps.

Once down below Malachi and the exec went to the wardroom for coffee. The exec was still a bit shaken by the scene they'd just driven through.

"They're not just toy boats in the periscope, are they," Malachi said as they nursed their coffee. "That ship might have had as many as a whole Army division onboard, bound for one of the Palaus. They'll all die unless the Japs get some ships out here, so I want to close the islands, which is their nearest base. If rescue ships come out, we'll attack them if we can."

Higgins shook his head slowly. "We sank three ships on my last boat. Not much to brag about. Never gave the crews a moment's thought. You've put down a whole lot more than that. Does it ever get to you?"

"Tonight was exceptional in terms of killing enemy soldiers, but no, it does not get to me, ever. I read an intel report recently saying that they beheaded a hundred navy and Marine aviators held prisoner on Wake Island. That's total war, XO. Tonight was total war as well. That's how I feel about the Empire of Japan. If anything the killing is going to get a whole lot worse, which is why I wanted you to see that tonight. If you're not as dedicated to that kind of thing as I am, tell me now."

"Remember Pearl Harbor," Higgins said. "I'm with you."

"Good," Malachi said. "Now we need to get a sinking report out."

THIRTY

The following night they surfaced 30 miles west of the island of Peleliu, site of the Japanese airbase in the Palau archipelago. They'd reported sinking the troopship and one destroyer escort the night
before. After surfacing they received a report from Pearl that the
troopship had been carrying 2,900 Army troops and over a thousand
tons of guns and ammunition. The ship had formerly been a French
ocean liner, displacing 18,500 tons fully loaded. The Japanese high
command was declaring them all lost at sea because a storm had made
rescue impossible.

Malachi got on the 1MC, the ship's announcing system, and told
the crew what they'd accomplished last night. "That's three thousand
Jap troops who won't be there if the Marines ever have to take that
island," he concluded. "Good work. Really good work."

The storm had passed by the time they came back up, leaving the
same half moon and relatively calm seas. Malachi had them patrol a
barrier line running roughly northeast-southwest, still using a random broad weave so that her aspect kept changing should there be
any Jap subs prowling these waters. After dinner in the wardroom,
Malachi took his customary station up on the bridge, with a pack of
cigarettes and a mug of coffee to keep him company. Four lookouts
clung to various protrusions up on the sail as they scanned their assigned quadrants.

Three thousand troops, he thought. Three thousand Japanese
teenagers, dressed up in Army uniforms, crammed ten to a stateroom

in the elderly liner, headed for a single godforsaken island in the middle of nowhere called Peleliu. All now littering the bottom of the sea, some three miles beneath them. In one night *Firefish* had squared the deal in terms of killing almost as many Japs as they had killed Americans at Pearl.

The war was headed into the winter months of its second year and yet the Marines and the Army were still battling Japs in the Solomons, albeit the northern Solomons now. Guadalcanal had been declared "secured." But it was still only the submarine force that was directly battling the Empire's forces all throughout the western Pacific, even off the shores of Japan itself. Malachi thought that the brass back in Pearl had finally figured out the correct strategy: remove the troops, the oil, the rice, the tankers, and the freighters and that fearsomely armed Imperial Japanese Navy would grind to a halt. He had read that the Japs ended up calling Guadalcanal Starvation Island. Good omen.

The sound-powered phone squeaked. He picked up the handset. "We have a special in radio central," a voice announced.

"Be right down," Malachi said. A special was the term for one of those super-secret messages sent out by the codebreakers. Only the captain could read them. The radioman who decoded them from the transmission code typed groups of letters into a machine. The machine then produced a thin ribbon of yellow tape containing the translation. The radioman never saw the tape, and Malachi would have to memorize the message and then feed the tape into a burn bag. He read the message and then went to his cabin, where he called the exec.

"We've been given a new station," he told Higgins. "Apparently carrier air is going to hit Peleliu two days from now, and they want us to be the rescue submarine if any of our birds get shot down. The station is ten miles west-southwest of the Jap airfield."

"Wow," Higgins said. "Our carriers are gonna start attacking Jap island bases?"

"You mean instead of playing defense and getting torpedoed? Looks like it. That has to be a good sign, though."

"Yes, sir, it surely is," Higgins said. "I'll go find the op-order for rescue submarine."

Two days later they submerged at the designated position, which they'd determined by radar fixes on the island. According to the operations order, the pilots would be briefed as to where the boat would be in relation to the airfield. They'd be instructed to ditch as close to that point as possible if they got hit and couldn't make it back to the bird farm. The sub would come up at night and go looking for rafts, which were equipped with small red-lens marker lights.

Malachi stayed at periscope depth until the attack got going in earnest, just after dawn, when the sound of bomb explosions rumbled across the water from the airfield. The entire island was soon obscured by towering columns of dust and black oil smoke as the invisible bombers dropped 500-pound bombs on the runways, hangars, and fuel storage tanks. He then took her down to 250 feet and put the rudder over five degrees, speed 3 knots. There were several islands in the Palau group, and he didn't know if the Japs had dispersed some Kawanishi flying boats to outlying islands. The waters here were too clear to stay near the surface.

They came back up at 2000 that night, taking a quick radar fix to make sure they were near the designated point. They found their first customer after an hour's searching, a tiny red light broad on the starboard bow. Still on the battery, *Firefish* slid silently alongside the startled airman and took him aboard. He told them there were probably three more rafts out there, based on radio traffic during the attack. They found two more within thirty minutes, but not the fourth, despite searching until 0500, when Malachi thought it prudent to submerge. He reported the three rescues and then took her back down to 250 feet. The pilots were all from the *Enterprise* and were in good shape. This was the first time a sub had been used to rescue downed airmen, and all three had been desperately glad to see their saviors.

At nightfall they came back up and continued searching. Just before midnight they came upon a group of four more rafts, containing three live pilots and one who had succumbed to his wounds. Malachi came down to the foredeck of the boat near the five-inch gun and conducted a quick burial at sea ceremony for the dead pilot, recovering only his dog tags and academy ring. The surviving men were badly dehydrated and sunburned, but the first three rescued pilots quickly took charge of their care with the help of the boat's corpsman.

Then one of the lookouts called down to Malachi from the sail. "Radar contact, inbound," he shouted.

The forecastle crew got rid of the rafts by cutting their sides open, and then cleared the decks. Malachi hustled back up to the bridge and called down to the conning tower.

"Looks like a destroyer-sized ship coming out of the harbor area," the exec reported. "It might be coincidental, but he's coming our way at twenty knots."

"Is he pinging?"

"Negative," the exec replied. "But he's coming on. Range is six miles."

"Battle stations torpedo," Malachi said. Now, he thought—stay on the surface or submerge? The destroyer probably wasn't coming out after them, so if they simply submerged and went deep he might just drive over top of them and keep on going, especially since he wasn't pinging. He hit the dive alarm and dropped down into the conning tower.

"Contact is continuing to close, steady bearing, zero eight five, up-Doppler, no ping," Sound announced as the boat tilted down.

"Make your depth two five zero, come to course zero eight five, open outer doors forward, make ready tubes one and two."

The boat tilted even more as it changed course to the east to line up with the approaching destroyer. No pinging, Malachi thought. No ping, no contact on them, but he still wanted to present the slimmest aspect to the oncoming sonar, should it suddenly go hot. "We have a layer?" he asked

"Negative layer," Sound replied. "Still up-Doppler. From the sound of his screws, he's going too fast to hear anything."

Man on a mission, Malachi thought. Attack him? Or let him go? If he was making 20, maybe even 25 knots, their chances of a hit were small.

As nerve-racking as it was, they simply crept forward toward the increasing propeller sounds, staying deep and slow. After ninety seconds, the thrashing screws passed right overhead and then diminished as the tin can headed west, still in a big hurry.

Once they could no longer hear the destroyer, Malachi ordered the outer doors closed and the boat to secure from battle stations torpedo. He then came back up to periscope depth.

"Radar sweep?" Higgins asked.

"No, let's rely on sound. That guy came right at us, but going too fast for sonar work. There might be a silent partner up there. Let's listen for a while, and then we'll do a radar look before we surface."

He waited for the boat to get back to normal sailing conditions. What had that been all about, he wondered. He looked at his watch: 0115. The battery charge had been cut short. Then he had a thought.

"XO, I wonder if that guy was hauling out to sea to meet something important?"

"Well, with no pinging, he was hell-bent on going *some*where fast," Higgins said. "Him showing up wasn't about us."

"I concur. Wait thirty minutes, then put the radar mast up and make sure there's no one lurking up there. Then we'll surface and head west. We'll follow that guy, see what's got him so excited."

They surfaced just before 0200, the radar having seen nothing at all. Malachi ordered the boat west, down the last sound bearing of the destroyer, and came up to 15 knots, a compromise between saving fuel and actually getting somewhere. They had about four hours before dawn would force them back down to elude scouting Kawanishis. Their patrol area was northwest of where they were headed, but COs had lots of latitude when it came to pursuing a possibly valuable target.

Malachi went back up to the bridge and wedged himself between a pelorus and the bridgewing bulkhead, where he soon dozed off, lulled by the rumble of the diesels. He was rudely awakened by a sudden roar from the diesels as they spooled up to full power and an equally sudden heel to port as the boat changed course sixty degrees to the right. He headed for the conning tower and slid down the ladder just as he heard the exec down in Control order a second course change, thirty degrees more to the right, while calling for more speed.

Malachi went down the ladder into Control, where the entire watch team seemed to be waiting for something.

"What's happened?" he asked in as normal a voice as he could manage.

"Sound heard a single ping," the exec reported. "*Left* standard rudder, steady three three zero."

The boat was vibrating as the engines reached full power. Even a standard rudder turn put her in a ten-degree bank. A submarine. Heads-up ball, XO, he thought, as *Firefish* raced away from danger at 21 knots, changing course every two minutes to foil the enemy's fire-control situation. One of the rescued aviators was hanging around in Control. Malachi heard him ask a watchstander what was going on.

"We got sucked into an ambush, that's what," Malachi said. "They sent a destroyer out and told him to go balls to the wall, much too fast to hear anything on sonar, but fast enough to get our attention. The destroyer ran right over us and then later, probably ran right over a Jap sub that had been called in to find the bastards who'd put the troopship down. Battery status?"

"Ninety-five percent," the OOD reported.

"Slow down and submerge. Once we're under, go down to two hundred fifty feet and plot a course back to our patrol area. Good work, people. Their torpedoes are twice the size of ours. XO, my cabin, please."

In the cabin, Malachi congratulated the exec for his quick thinking. "A single ping is the last thing you do to get a range if you don't have radar. He was ready to shoot."

"Yes, sir, they told us that back in Pearl. If he'd had radar, he'd've had us."

"I think you're right," Malachi said. "You did exactly the right thing. Our enemy is still formidable, isn't he?"

"Yes, sir. Now, we've got to get these flyboys off. The op-order says to call for a Black Cat to come out and pick them up, but I have no idea where they're based or if they can reach all the way out here."

"Surely we will be told where and when," Malachi said. "I'd go up and put up a whip antenna for the broadcast, but not while we're being actively hunted. Tonight will be time enough."

"Yes, sir."

"We got complacent tonight," Malachi said. "Correction: *I* got complacent. *You* saved our asses. Well done."

"Thank you, sir."

After the exec had left Malachi noticed that his hands were shaking just a little. That had been close, much too close, he thought. Marty would not have reacted as quickly as Higgins had. Your fourth patrol, Captain, the admiral had said. Sure you want to do this? Tempt the gods of war just one more time?

Ten minutes before they were about to submerge for the day, radar detected one contact, and then several more. The bearing was in the direction of the home islands, and the range was 15 miles, owing to unusually good radar conditions. Malachi elected to stay on the surface in order to develop a course and speed on the convoy, in case they need to go fast to get into position. Fifteen minutes later it became apparent that the convoy was going to pass them ten miles to the north. Malachi ordered full power and headed northeast to get into an intercept position, but halfway there the air search radar detected an incoming plane and they had to crash dive to escape a Kawanishi. As it was, the float plane delivered a punishing depth-charge attack that scared the hell out of the rescued aviators.

"All in a day's work, gents," Malachi told them with a smile, exuding a confidence he didn't really feel. The cold truth was that the Japs knew they were out there, which meant they'd be hunting them as hard as they could. During the attempted end-around, a message had come in telling them to head south to rendezvous with another submarine, the *Tarpon*, to hand over the rescued aviators.

The join up was conducted at night, after an initially tense exchange of signals between the two boats. The seas were flat calm so Malachi drove *Firefish* close alongside, put out fenders, and then let the grateful aviators leap the gap between the boats in fine fashion. *Firefish* passed a sound-powered phone line over to *Tarpon*. The skipper of *Tarpon* relayed the news that the troopship sinking was the talk of the town down in Perth, with many Aussies saying it was an appropriate revenge for the sinking of their hospital ship, the *Centaur.* He also reported that a Jap submarine had been caught snooping around the entrance to Fremantle Harbour but had escaped. He didn't tell of any more US submarine losses, and Malachi didn't ask. In the time-honored tradition, the two boats exchanged movies and then went their separate ways.

The next seven days were a complete bust. No contacts, no convoys, no nothing. It was as if the Japanese had decided to wait out the submarine operating west of the Palaus. On the eighth night, two hours before dawn, a loud, metallic bang followed by a clattering noise erupted in the forward engine room and *Firefish* slowly lost forward speed. Malachi had been dozing in his usual corner on the bridge and he jumped awake. Moments later a report came up from Maneuvering that number one engine had thrown a rod. There'd been a momentary fire, which had been quickly put out, but they were officially down to three engines.

Malachi could only rub his tired face and shake his head. Hell with it, he thought. This is as good an excuse as any.

"Tell the navigator to set a course for Perth," he ordered over the bitchbox. "And get an engine casualty report out before we have to go back down."

Firefish turned for home with just enough fuel to get there, encouraged just before sunrise by a Kawanishi who'd flown over them and then turned around to see if what their tail gunner was reporting was true. By then *Firefish* was passing two hundred feet and executing a wide turn off her original course. The resulting barrage of depth charges fell comfortably astern, but not without reminding Malachi that perhaps his personal fatigue *was* starting to endanger the boat. He had forgotten to order periodic air search radar sweeps just because it was nighttime. Jap planes were not night-capable, but any seaplane could take off in darkness, as long as it would be light when they came back to land.

He went to his cabin and pulled the curtain. He flopped down in his bunk, noting that the boat was headed south at five knots submerged. In the privacy of the cabin he held his two hands out above his chest, palms down. The shaking was still there. He wondered if anyone else had noticed.

THIRTY-ONE

The morning they were due into Perth/Fremantle dawned sky blue and clear. They'd been running on the surface for the past three days, far enough away from known Jap fleet concentrations to be able to rely on their radars to detect other ships and aircraft. Malachi had heard that the Pearl-based subs ran surfaced almost all the way to Japan now before instituting the day-night routine.

Down below the crew was making preparations for entering port, dumping trash and garbage over the side, pumping out the sanitary tank, consolidating the diesel fuel tanks to facilitate refueling, and bragging to one another about all the upcoming conquests once they got ashore. The engineers had begun to dismantle number one diesel until they discovered that the crankshaft was broken and that three cylinders were damaged beyond repair. This meant a new engine, so there was no point in getting it ready for repairs.

The exec joined Malachi up on the bridge when they were about an hour outside the breakwater. The water had suddenly turned light brown, a sign that they were entering the Swan River delta. A huge flock of seagulls was following the boat, eager for treasures as the trash and garbage went over the side.

"About time to set the navigational detail," Malachi said.

"They're already at work," Higgins replied. "We'll go to sea and anchor detail in about thirty minutes. I'll be glad to get in."

"Me, too," Malachi said, keeping his shaky hands firmly planted on the bullrail. "Hate to bring all those torpedoes back in, though."

"I think the troopship will cover a multitude of sins," Higgins said. "That must have really hurt the bastards."

"Enough that they came after us, which isn't something they usually do for more than about eight hours." Malachi raised his binoculars. He thought he could just make out the tall buildings in Perth center.

"I can't see them being able to sustain what they started back at Pearl," Higgins said. "A group of tiny islands trying to control the entire western Pacific. Yes, they took it handily enough, but now what? It's like that old saw about the pelican, whose mouth can hold more than his bellican."

Malachi smiled. "They still have teeth," he said. "That'll change over time, but right now, we still can't stay surfaced anywhere near a Jap base. In fact—"

The bitchbox came on. "Conn, Sound: I just heard what I think was a single ping coming from zero nine five relative."

As Malachi reached for the talk switch, an enormous explosion lifted *Firefish*'s stern completely out of the water, throwing both Malachi and Higgins to the deck and dropping two of the four lookouts all the way down to the main deck. The bow actually submerged even though the dive planes were fully rigged in, popping back up only to be buried under tons of water from the huge spout that had lifted over the stern and then collapsed in a maelstrom of water, stinking of explosives.

Malachi felt the boat collapsing behind him, everything aft of the sail no longer really part of the entire boat. As he staggered to his feet a warm hurricane of air began whistling out of the conning tower hatch. Higgins got up, fell back down, and then struggled to get to his feet as water swept into the bridge enclosure. *Firefish* was going down. Malachi didn't hesitate.

"You stay topside," he yelled at Higgins, who could only stare at him, his mouth open and his face bleeding. Malachi scrambled through knee-deep water to the conning tower hatch, where the water was already waterfalling over the coaming. He clambered into the trunk and pulled the hatch shut behind him. The roar of air fought back, and finally he had to hang his full body weight on the hatch

wheel to get the hatch to close. He then dropped down into the conning tower, where several men were down on the deck, looking like
they were partaking of a picnic in the woods.

He literally threw his body down the ladder to Control, where
there was already two feet of water and rising. He saw several men
struggling to get the watertight hatch at the back of the Control space
closed. Beyond the hatch coaming he caught a glimpse of several figures in the darkness, dimly lit by battle lanterns, but he couldn't tell
if they were alive or dead in the rapidly rising seawater. Finally the
men got the hatch closed. The stream of air stopped as the remaining forward half of the boat lazily flopped over onto its starboard side,
throwing everybody in the control room up on the bulkhead, along
with a wave of the fuel-laced water. Men struggled frantically to hang
on to anything they could get a grip on. Then everything went quiet,
except for the sound of small leaks spraying into the compartment
and the creaking noises the after hatch was making.

Malachi found himself wrapped around the base of the periscope
assembly, one hand jammed in between some piping and the attack
scope column. Battle lanterns shone brightly around the space,
enough for him to see the depth gauge, which was unwinding steadily,
100 feet, 150, then 180, before the hull thumped down onto what felt
like a mud bottom. No one said a word.

"All right," Malachi spoke up, trying to keep his own voice steady.
"We got torpedoed. I need reports on what we've got left forward."

One man, a planesman, got hysterical. "What're we gonna do?"
he cried. "What're we gonna *do*?"

"Remember the tower in New London?" Malachi said. "We all had
to do the tower, right?"

The men were looking at him now, some with the first vestige of
hope in their eyes.

"We're gonna do the tower, just like we did it in New London.
We're at a hundred eighty feet. We're gonna go out the escape trunk
and up to the surface, just like they taught us. But first we have to
make sure we can *get* to the escape trunk. Someone open the control
room's forward hatch."

"But what if it's flooded?" another young seaman asked.

Malachi looked at him. "I need a cigarette," he announced. "My cigarettes are in my cabin. My cabin is in the next compartment. Open the goddamned hatch."

A couple of more senior petty officers started laughing, which is what Malachi had hoped they would do. Suddenly the crew was back, or what was left of it. He tried not to think of how many had drowned back aft. Three men sloshed through the water toward the forward hatch. They banged on it three times with a wrench. Somebody on the other side banged back. They cracked the hatch. No water poured in. Then they opened it wide. The COB was there, looking pissed off. Unlike everyone in the control room, his uniform was dry. There were faces behind him in the light of more battle lanterns. "Took you long enough," he said. "What the fuck happened?"

Malachi climbed down from his perch. The deck plates were still awash on the boat's tilted side, but so far the water wasn't rising. He tried to ignore what he thought was the first faint whiff of chlorine from the forward battery compartment.

"I think we got torpedoed," Malachi said. "I think the back half of the boat's gone, right aft of Control. That's the bad news. The good news is that we're at a hundred eighty feet. We can get out."

The COB nodded. "Hell, yes, we can," he said. "We're mostly dry forward. But I don't know if the escape trunk is clear—it will be if we're just over on our side."

The boatswain appeared behind him and reported that there were three officers and nineteen enlisted forward, some of them injured from the whiplash effect of the torpedo. Malachi made a quick head count in the control room. An agonizingly few of the engineers plus the chief electrician had made it out before they sealed the after control room hatch, and there'd been six men in the conning tower. The rest were the control room watch along with the sonarman and one radioman. Out of his crew of sixty-eight souls, forty-six men, including himself, had survived the boat being blown in half. Thirty more minutes, he thought, and we'd have made it into shallow enough water.

"Get those leaks plugged so we have time to get organized," Malachi ordered. "COB, let's go check the escape trunk."

They made their way forward, stepping over all sorts of equipment that had been blown off the bulkheads by the shock of the explosion. The only lighting came from the battery-powered battle lanterns, and a thin mist of dust and insulation filled the air. As they passed over top of the forward battery compartment they both could smell battery acid, but not chlorine.

Yet.

As always, it would be the batteries that would decide how much time they had left in the boat. Once seawater began seeping into the cells, they would start generating chlorine gas. Who knew how many hull seams had been cracked open.

The escape trunk was 36 inches wide and cylindrical in shape. There were two hatches—one inside the boat, one topside on the forecastle. Everyone aboard knew the procedure, which they'd had to practice in the 200-foot-high water tank at the sub school in New London in order to graduate from sub school.

The escape trunk worked by providing an intermediate stage between the pressure in the boat and the sea pressure outside. A man would climb into the trunk and close the hatch leading down into the boat. Then he would crack a small valve and begin to admit seawater into the trunk. As the seawater rose in the confines of the trunk, the air above it would be pressurized until the outside sea pressure equaled the inside air pressure, at which point, no more water could get in. Depending on how deep the boat was, the man would be standing in the trunk with about two feet of air between him and the outside hatch. He would then don the submarine escape apparatus, otherwise known as the Momsen Lung, which would provide some oxygen on the way up. Holding a small lanyard in one hand, he would then fully open the outer, weather-deck hatch. He and a bubble of pressurized air would then launch for the surface. The lanyard would be pulled out of his hand, which would trip the latch keeping the upper hatch open. It would drop back into place. As soon as the men waiting below began to drain the escape trunk, the hatch would be sealed by the sea pressure outside.

Once he was away, the men left inside the boat would drain all the water out of the trunk and this time three men would go inside the trunk to repeat the escape procedure. The first man out would take with him two things: a Styrofoam buoy, which had a line attached to the hull of the boat, and the first of three inflatable life rafts stored in the forward part of the boat. As the pressurized air in his lungs began to make his chest swell, he would begin a continuous exhale all the way to the surface. At school they'd called it the ho-ho-ho maneuver. The escapee would repeat that phrase all the way to the surface in order to keep his lungs from exploding. Once on the surface, he would fire the CO_2 cartridge to inflate the life raft, and then climb in. There was a sound-powered phone line wrapped around the buoy line, which terminated inside the boat. The first man out would establish comms with the rest of the survivors down below, and then the process of getting the rest of the survivors up to the surface would begin.

Malachi declared that the COB would be the first man out. He was an experienced and senior crew member who was well qualified to deal with whatever emergencies erupted on the surface as terrified junior crewmen began popping up out of the sea.

"How many SEAs do we have here?" Malachi asked.

A count was made. "Forty-five, sir," the COB said. "The rest are back aft."

"Back aft is long gone, COB," Malachi said. "You and two more go up, and take the second raft with you. I'll run the sequence down here."

The COB looked at Malachi, as if to say: but what about the forty-sixth man? Malachi smiled at him, and told him to get going.

For the next hour, everyone still left alive in the broken remains of *Firefish* ascended, three by three, to the surface. The third cluster of escapees took the last lifeboat with them. The last two donned the last two Momsen lungs, trying not to look at the skipper who was helping them adjust the straps and the mouthpiece before they entered the chamber. One of them pulled the mask aside and asked Malachi if he was going to try a free ascent.

"Hell, yes, I will," Malachi said. "Nothing scares me, right? I'm The Iceman."

The young man, a torpedoman third class, stared at him for a second. Then he touched the facemask. "Thank you for this, Skipper," he said.

"Get going, young man," Malachi said. "I'll be right behind you. Remember to grab that hatch lanyard, okay?"

He then spun the wheel of the lower hatch behind them and then waited for the rush of bubbles, which would indicate they'd launched for the surface. Then he sat down on a pile of lifejackets and looked at his watch. It was just eight-fifteen in the morning. They were going to be up there awhile before the Navy in Perth realized they were overdue. They did have the three rafts. That would provide enough flotation for almost all of them, either in the rafts or hanging along-side. As long as no one was bleeding, the sharks would hopefully take their time.

His ears popped. He knew what that meant: the sea was slowly but inexorably seeping into the remains of his boat. The air pressure was rising. He sniffed the air and detected the first swimming pool taste of chlorine gas. He looked around and saw that the atmosphere was filling with a dangerous mist of carbon dioxide, chlorine, and dust particles. The battle lanterns were burning deep yellow now instead of white. His eyes were starting to sting.

And so it ends, he thought. Sunk by a submarine. A certain justice there. Had to hand it to the Japs: they had to know that the balance of power in the Pacific was shifting against them. And yet a sub skip-per had snuck into Australian home waters and done what a small le-gion of escorts and Kawanishi hadn't been able to accomplish. Their warrior code was called Bushido. He had no idea what that meant, but he now felt that code's sharp, unwavering discipline.

A sudden clang penetrated his thoughts. He opened his eyes, which he hadn't realized he'd closed. He was having trouble breathing. The light from the battle lanterns was dimming rapidly and starting to go green. There was now water up to his waist.

Tired, he thought. I'm beyond tired. The sea will soon take care of that, and maybe this was the final punishment for what he'd done, way back in Kentucky, on that horrible night. Kensie had told him he was not to blame, that his father had essentially killed himself.

Well, not quite. There was still the matter of that rock maple chair leg.

Kensie. He'd promised her father he wouldn't hurt her.

Don't let your mouth make promises your body can't keep, old son. He smiled in the gloom of the dying submarine. An older coal miner had told him that just before clocking him unconscious down in the pit after an argument over . . . what? He couldn't remember. He could remember that fist of iron introducing him to a sheet of stars. Kensie, I'm so sorry.

Another loud clang jerked him back to reality.

Who was doing that? *Why* was somebody doing that? Making noise. He lifted his head and looked at the bottom of the escape trunk.

Wait, he thought. I'm supposed to do something. Like get in the trunk. But I don't have a lung. A free ascent from this depth and my own lungs will explode. Wait. No. That's not true, not true at all.

He lifted himself off the pile of lifejackets and climbed into the escape trunk. Then he closed the lower hatch and cracked the fill valve open. Water began streaming in. The battle lantern in the trunk was at the end of its rope. The air was bad, making it hard to get a real breath. His ears popped several times as the pressure increased. Then the water stopped coming in, even as his chest began to swell.

Gotta go, he thought. Last chance. Gotta go and gotta blow, all the way up. He had a sudden vision of his lungs popping out of his mouth, two pink balloons expanding to a ridiculous size before they exploded. He cranked the hatch wheel with what was left of his strength and then pushed the hatch open. Before he was even ready, his body lifted out of the trunk, bruising his shoulders and his hip as he shot for the surface. An agonizing pain hit him in the chest, and then he remembered. He began to blow and blow and blow. After what seemed like an eternity he shot up out of the water into bright sunlight, still blowing, his jaws aching from the effort to keep his mouth wide open.

There were hands on him almost immediately. He opened his eyes but it was hard to focus. Too much light. Noise. He focused and saw a crowd of boats around him. Fishing boats, harbor tugs, a submarine.

A submarine? Jesus wept, had the Jap come back?

His ears were filled with the sound of crackling paper. He caught quick glimpses of faces, men trying to talk to him, but the crackling overwhelmed everything. He tried to speak but could only blow, trying desperately to ease the swelling in his lungs. He fainted.

When he came to, he was in familiar surroundings. A torpedo room. Six tubes, right in front of him. A forward torpedo room. He was back in *Firefish*. But that couldn't be: *Firefish* was gone, broken in half by a type-93 Jap torpedo. A real torpedo: huge warhead, big fish. A carrier killer, unlike the American's own pathetic Mark 14.

A face appeared in front of him. It was Jay Carney. He tried to speak but there was something wrong with his voice. One side of his face seemed to be paralyzed.

"Malachi," Jay said. "You're gonna hate this. We're gonna load you into a torpedo tube and then pressurize it. It's your only chance. It's gonna be tight, but this is the only way we can beat the bends. Understand?"

Malachi tried to say no, he didn't understand anything at all, except that his lungs were killing him. Jay called for the corpsman.

Another figure appeared from behind Jay. Malachi felt a small sting, and then he was being pushed into a heavily greased torpedo tube. Tight did not describe it. His legs went in just fine, but his hips and shoulders did not. He felt a sharp pain in his neck as they forced his body into the 21-inch tube.

"It's okay," he told them. "I'm not claustrophobic."

A warm cloud came over him as the sedative took effect. They had thoughtfully placed a fresh battle lantern in the tube with him. He heard the steel door close behind him. Then his ears started popping as they raised the pressure back to 80 psi, the equivalent of 180 feet of depth. He opened his eyes and then quickly closed them. The stainless-steel cylinder gripped his arms and his upper body in a greasy vise. He couldn't move a muscle, but his chest had stopped hurting, and his hips and legs were relatively free. He was in a torpedo tube. Well, I'm a submariner. What's wrong with being locked into an empty torpedo tube? Must have done something really bad.

He vaguely understood what they were doing to save his life. He was determined to stay awake as they slowly, slowly, began to reduce the pressure one pound at a time to simulate a diver's proper ascent from depth: go up six feet, grab a knot in the line, and then hang for fifteen or twenty minutes. Then do it again, stage by stage, allowing the diver's body to expel the dissolved nitrogen in his bloodstream that was trying to kill him.

His eyelids were heavy. He didn't seem to have control of the left one. I probably should stay awake, he thought. Or, why not just go to sleep for a while? The one thing he remembered about a decompression chamber was that it took a long time to get back to normal. Suddenly he heard three metallic clanks somewhere behind him. He opened his one good eye. What did that mean? He was groggy now, but then understood. They were checking on him. He was supposed to sound out three beats of his own, but he really couldn't move his arms. And it wasn't like he had a wrench handy. He looked around and saw the arming wire clip at the top of the tube. He got his left arm out over his chest and then reached for the spring-loaded clip. He pulled it out of its recess and then let it go. It made a click. He did it two more times. A single clank came back through the firing flask. Okay. We heard that.

He left his arms lying across his waist. He looked down the length of his body. He could see his hands and beyond that, the greasy expanse of the torpedo tube, illuminated by the battle lantern. He tried to take a deep breath but his lungs instantly informed him that they weren't ready for that yet, so knock that shit off, there, Captain.

He grimaced in the dim light from the battle lantern. Captain. Not anymore. You needed a boat to be a captain. He felt a familiar vibration in the hull around him. The sub was under way, probably headed back into the harbor. He hoped they were watching, because the Japs were fully capable of coming back to work over that gaggle of small, unarmed craft surrounding *Firefish*'s lone buoy. He wondered how they'd found out about her sinking. An image of the admiral's face swam into view in his mind's eye. Hi, Admiral, he tried to say, but then realized that perhaps that wasn't the properly respectful way to say hello. The admiral was wagging his finger at him. You said you could do a fourth patrol, there, Captain. Guess what? Then he slipped away into the competent hands of the sedative.

THIRTY-TWO

He woke up to a brightly lighted compartment. All that sunlight was streaming in through a single porthole in the bulkhead to his left. His left wrist hurt. He focused on it to discover an IV line taped there. His mouth was incredibly dry and he tried to speak. The resulting croak brought a hospital corpsman to his bedside. The corpsman placed a metal straw between his lips, and Malachi greedily sucked in some ice water and then promptly choked. The corpsman waited for the choking to subside and then offered the straw again, advising him to take little sips this time. When Malachi had finished, he asked where he was.

"Sick bay on the *Otus*," the corpsman said. "They brought you in last night after you finished decompression. How you feeling, Captain?"

"Groggy, but no pain," Malachi said. "Except for this." He pointed with his jaw to the IV.

The corpsman grinned. "Everyone says that, sir, but we'll take it out today. Lemme go get a doc. Sir, you need a bedpan?"

Malachi was about to shake his head when he realized, hell, yes, I need a bedpan.

An hour later, having been seen by the *Otus*'s doctor and declared back among the living, Malachi was sitting up in the bed, still sipping on ice water, when the commodore showed up.

"Oh, shit," Malachi said without thinking. The commodore grinned at him.

"And a good morning to you, too, there, Captain," he said. He pulled a metal chair over to the bed and sat down. "You feeling a little better?"

"How many of my people made it out, Commodore?" Malachi asked, ignoring the question.

"Everybody who survived the original torpedo hit made it to the surface," the commodore said. "For once, all our gear worked. They said they ran out of SEAs and that you stayed behind."

"Lost my boat," Malachi replied. "Got careless because we were so close to home port. At the time, staying down there seemed like an appropriate thing to do. Plus, there were no more lungs."

"Oh, bullshit, Malachi," the commodore scoffed. "Yes, there's gonna be an investigation, but I wanted to let you know that politics are already intruding. The Aussie Navy is highly embarrassed by what's happened. They've been patrolling the approaches to Perth for months, and they've repeatedly assured us that there were no Jap subs out there, certainly not that close to the harbor."

"Only took one," Malachi said, suddenly feeling weak. "And unlike us, *their* torpedoes work."

The commodore nodded. "Yes, they do," he said. "Look, you get some rest. You had a close call with the bends, coming up like that. Let me take care of the admin tidal wave that's coming. Your surviving people are being well looked after. My squadron doctor will take over supervising your recovery. Once they determine that your lungs are okay, we'll get you moved to the main hospital in Perth."

"If my lungs are okay, I won't need any more hospital care," Malachi said.

"Except," the commodore said with a smile, "there's a certain doctor there who's insisting that *she* take over your convalescence. Of course, you can always say no."

To his surprise, Malachi began to weep. Kensie was going to "save" him, but no one had saved all those boys in the back half of the *Firefish*, especially him. He recalled the images of the after torpedo room following the fire. Now almost a third of his crew was floating around in lightless flooded compartments aft of the control room. The commodore reached over the bed and covered Malachi's right hand.

"I know," he said. "It's gonna be okay."

Ten minutes later the submarine squadron doctor showed up. He made a cursory check of Malachi's vitals. While he was doing so he managed to attach something new to the IV, and soon Malachi was sound asleep.

The next morning he was transferred by ambulance to the main hospital in downtown Perth. The squadron doc had explained that the bends could often reappear hours or even days after a free ascent from 180 feet, and that his arterial blood gases would need to be monitored for at least the next five days. Plus, he explained, the hospital had a decompression chamber.

He was installed in a private room to reduce his exposure to infection. Kensie showed up an hour after he'd arrived. She was still dressed in bloodstained surgical scrubs, and wouldn't come in any farther than the doorway to talk to him.

"Oh, Malachi," she said. "I'm so *very* bloody sorry. You look absolutely terrible. Where's your IV?"

"I'm not in any pain, at least not physically," he said. "This is supposed to be a period of observation. Mentally, now, I'm not so good. Lost my boat and a lot of my people."

"I can't come in," she said, indicating her contaminated scrubs. "And I'm scheduled in surgery in thirty minutes. But I'll be back as soon as I can. You keep a stiff upper lip, now."

He suddenly realized she was holding back tears. "Kensie, I'm okay, despite how I may look. I've got enough coal dust in my lungs to keep all those bends at bay. But, please, do come back. I need to see you."

She hurried away, more to keep her emotions in check than for any urgent medical reasons, he suspected.

He lay back on the pillows and closed his eyes. Getting out of the sunken boat had been the easy part. By now, the admiral would have directed the commodore to conduct a formal investigation into the loss of *Firefish*. He, as captain, would be named an "interested party," the Navy's quaint term for someone who stood to be blamed for the disaster. It wasn't as if he was suspected of a crime. This was worse: he'd lost his ship. And under a tradition far more ironclad than any secular law, he was responsible for that loss, simply by being the captain. Even though he'd been one of the highest scoring submarine skippers in terms of tonnage sunk, if the submarine service declared him responsible for the loss of *Firefish*, he would be finished as a career naval officer *and* a submariner.

He had accepted submarine command knowing full well that these were the rules. Few submarine captains found themselves in this situation, because when a sub went down, everyone usually went with it. Submarine losses were the ultimate wartime mystery. A boat left port for a war patrol and was never heard from again. Among themselves, submariners referred to a missing boat as being on eternal patrol, and no one criticized the captain. Maybe, he thought, it would have been easier on everyone if he'd just stayed down there with his drowned shipmates.

"Commander Stormes?" a voice asked from the doorway. He looked up. A four-striper in dress khakis was standing there, a briefcase in one hand. Malachi didn't recognize him.

"Yes?" he said.

"I'm Captain Thomas John Byng, ComSubRon Six, based in Brisbane. I've been assigned by SubPac to conduct the investigation into the loss of *Firefish*. May I come in, please? And are you recovered enough to begin the process?"

"Yes, sir, I think I am," Malachi said. This commodore looked older than his own squadron commander, Captain VanBuren. "If I fall asleep on you, please don't take it personally."

"Promise I won't," Byng said. He pulled up a chair and sat down next to Malachi's bed.

"I'm here to conduct what's called a *preliminary* investigation into what happened to *Firefish*," he began. "I'm going to interview several people, including surviving members of your crew and wardroom, Commodore VanBuren, Admiral Marsten, and some of your fellow skippers. These interviews don't constitute legal proceedings. My objective is to establish, as best I can, what sank your boat. I know the common understanding is that a Jap sub ambushed you right outside Fremantle Habour. It is also possible that you had a massive battery explosion."

Malachi started to speak but Byng put up a hand.

"I realize that's not what you think, but if, for instance, in the course of my interviews I find that *Firefish* had become notorious on the tender for having leaky batteries, or if there had been several instances of hydrogen alarms in the boat, or a series of work requests involving the batteries, then that possibility becomes increasingly real."

"You won't find any of that," Malachi said. "Our batteries were tight. Besides, Sound reported hearing a single ping just before we got hit. It surely wasn't ours. You'll need to speak to the ship's boatswain, McReedie. He was on the bridge with me when that report came up."

"McReedie," Byng said. "Okay, I will. But right now I'd like to ask you where you were and what the boat was actually doing at the time of the explosion. Were you at sea detail yet, or still in a wartime transit watch condition? What were the sea conditions and the visibility? Were there lookouts posted and how many? Things like that. I want to get your perspective, your recollections. What you did after the boat got hit. Basically, your version of events."

Malachi lay back on his pillow and closed his eyes for a moment.

"I can come back," Byng said. "They told me you were on surveillance for latent blood gas problems, and that your free ascent was not kind to your innards. And, by the way, I won't take notes. I simply want to hear your side of events."

Before I have to be sworn and then tell my tale in front of a court reporter and a formal Board of Inquiry, Malachi thought. He knew what was happening here. The commodore would talk to everybody and then build a picture of the boat, its captain and crew, its readiness, its professionalism. If he came away with an impression of a sloppy command or any indications of dereliction of duty, he'd recommend that the legal process begin. That would lead to entirely different kinds of interviews.

"Okay," Malachi said. "We were coming back from Peleliu after an aviator recovery mission."

Malachi told his story while the commodore sat back and listened, occasionally asking a question. True to his word, he took no notes. After almost an hour a nurse came in to draw blood. Byng took that opportunity to end the interview, saying that he was going to find the exec and then work his way down the chain of command for the next few days. Malachi nodded and then closed his eyes for a moment. When he woke up it was almost evening and Kensie was now sitting in the chair where Captain Byng had been, just a moment ago, he thought.

"We've heard that the Gestapo has arrived," she said, taking his hand and giving it a little squeeze.

"It's not like that," Malachi said. "I think Byng's a straight-shooter. They just need to know what happened and if anything could have been done differently that would have prevented my losing the boat."

She nodded and then steered the conversation away from his personal responsibility for the sinking. "I talked to my dad earlier," she said. "He said there was a big kerfuffle at Navy headquarters downtown. All hands on deck to deal with outraged inquiries from Canberra. How could a Jap submarine be operating within sight of downtown Perth? Lots more along that line."

"We had a similar experience," Malachi reminded her. "It was called Pearl Harbor."

"Yes, well, you get the picture. Your Admiral Marsten's in the thick of it, apparently.

There was a knock on the door and Sanford Higgins stepped in. He saw Kensie and made to back out but Malachi waved him in and introduced them. Kensie stood. "I'm back on duty in three hours," she said. "Nice to meet you, Commander, but my sore feet and I need a nap."

"My pleasure, ma'am," Higgins said.

Malachi had to hold back a smile when Kensie walked out, beyond Higgins's line of sight, and mouthed the word "ma'am" with a roll of her eyes.

"How's the crew?" he asked. Or what's left of it he wanted to say, but didn't.

"The COB's holding things together until Pearl decides what's going to happen," Higgins said. "But there's been a big development. Apparently someone at the Aussie naval headquarters lit a fire under the Western Australia sea command, and they put everything that could float out this morning, and I mean everything, tugs, those little coastal supply ships, and even a motorized barge into the Fremantle approaches to see if they could find a Jap sub."

"A little late, probably," Malachi noted with a sigh, knowing that that I-boat would be long gone.

"Well, not exactly, Captain, because the first thing that happened was that one of the coastals, maybe a six-hundred-tonner, hit what they think was a goddamned mine just before noon today. Blew it to pieces. No survivors out a crew of twenty-five."

"A *mine*? The Aussies have a minefield out there?"

"They do now, Skipper. Only it isn't theirs. Apparently sometime before we came back from patrol, there *was* a Jap sub out there, and that bastard laid down a minefield. The good news is that we had two boats leaving on patrol tomorrow morning. They've been delayed until the Aussie Navy can get some sweeps in here to clean house."

"You're telling me we hit a fucking mine? That we *didn't* get torpedoed?"

"Yes, sir, that's what it looks like. The net result hasn't changed of course, but that's why the Aussies are so red-faced about what happened. Their HQ had ordered continuous minesweeping operations for both Perth and Brisbane two months ago. Through some snafu, Brisbane got their sweeps, but Perth didn't. I talked to the harbormaster down in Fremantle, and he said some heads are gonna roll over this colossal 'cock-up,' as he put it."

"Well, I'll be damned," Malachi said. "Except—we got a report just before we got hit about a single ping. McReedie was topside with me. He can verify that."

"Don't know about that, Skipper," Higgins said. "But that commodore from Brisbane is huddling with the Royal Australian Navy folks here. He interviewed me yesterday afternoon once he'd come to see you."

"Seem like a witch hunt to you?"

"No, sir, I think he's on the level. Wanted to know what kind of under way watch and matériel condition we'd set while approaching Fremantle. Lookouts. Radar watch. Sound watch. How many engines on propulsion, how many on battery charge. Stuff like that. No trick questions that I could see."

Malachi sighed. His chest hurt. "Yeah, that was my impression, too. I'm stuck here for another day at least. Any messages I need to see?"

Higgins looked at him for a long moment. "Um, no, sir. I don't think anyone's sending messages to *Firefish* anymore."

Malachi wanted to give himself a Polish salute. "Right," he said. "Is Commodore VanBuren taking care of you and the crew?"

"Yes, sir, he and his staff have been great. He told me they're waiting to see what the investigation turns up before making personnel reassignments."

"That won't last long," Malachi said. "At the rate they're launching boats, you guys will be in great demand." Then he smiled. "I, on the other hand, probably won't. You don't have a cigarette, do you?"

"Sorry, sir, I don't smoke. And—" He gestured toward the prominent no-smoking signs on the walls of the room.

"Yeah, I know. That's probably why I'm so jittery. They won't let me have coffee, either."

"That's cruel and unusual punishment, Skipper," Higgins said. "No caffeine or nicotine? Somebody hates you."

Malachi nodded and tried to think of something to say. His chest really hurt now. Then he realized he'd closed his eyes. He struggled to get them open again, but his eyelids weren't responding.

"Skipper?" Higgins said. To Malachi, Higgins sounded like he was shouting down a long tunnel.

It was the following morning when he woke up. There was a mask of some kind covering his nose, and he now had two IV's. His chest no longer hurt, and the air he was breathing was wonderful. There was a note pinned to his hospital gown: when you wake up, press the button. He pressed the button and a nurse appeared thirty seconds later.

"*There* you are, Captain," she said with a bright smile. "Welcome back. How are you feeling?"

"What happened?" he asked.

"The docs think you had an episode of AGE: arterial gas embolism. It's the nastier form of decompression sickness. Tell me, sir, have you been a heavy smoker?"

He nodded, which was difficult because of the mask. It was, apparently, connected to some serious hoses.

"Well, then, that's what's complicated matters. Your lungs were already compromised. They said you did a free ascent from one hundred eighty feet. Whatever toxins you were breathing down there weren't completely removed by your time in decompression, so they got into your arteries. That means those pesky little bubbles got to travel all over your body, which is why you went unconscious last night. You gave Dr. Richmond quite a shock, I must say."

"Fuck," he mumbled.

"Now, now, Captain: there are ladies present. The good news is that the docs think your bloodstream is clearing up, especially with the oxygen treatment."

"What's the bad news?"

A new voice entered the conversation. "You'll be here for at least another few days, Captain," a doctor he hadn't seen before said. Then he realized that this doctor had an American accent. "And," the doc continued, "I might as well tell you now: your submarining days are over, I'm afraid. I'm Commodore Byng's squadron doctor, and you, sir, are lucky to be alive."

"I wonder," Malachi said without thinking.

The doctor, hearing that, nodded at the nurse, who quickly disappeared, then he sat down. He was in his fifties and a full commander. "Listen to me," he said. "I have some idea of what you're struggling with. You were the CO of *Firefish*. Your boat has been lost, along with not quite half your crew. Now, from the scuttlebutt I'm hearing, the RAN was supposed to be mine hunting and sweeping for the past two months. We Americans assumed they had been, mostly because RAN headquarters told MacArthur's staff that the two American sub bases, here and in Brisbane, were being kept safe from mines."

Malachi struggled to follow where the squadron doctor was going with this.

"What I'm telling you is that there is no longer such a sharp interest in condemning the skipper who 'lost' his boat. *Firefish* was a famous boat in sub circles. You and your people hurt the Japs, a lot. The US Navy will be looking for a way to put this bad news to bed, and quickly. And, also, quietly, if you get my meaning."

Malachi closed his eyes and took deep draughts of that wonderful oxygen. Then he opened his eyes. "You're talking a deal of some kind: no investigation, no outcry against the Royal Australian Navy, no court-martial or Board of Inquiry for me as CO. I get medically disqualified from submarine service. Maybe even medically discharged from the Navy, as long as I go gracefully into the night. How'm I doing?"

"Brilliantly, Captain," the doctor said. "Commodore Byng, Commodore VanBuren, and I met with Admiral Marsten last night when the mine theory was confirmed. Admiral Marsten proposed this . . . solution. What do you say, sir?"

"My people *must* be taken care of," Malachi said. "They all go to new construction."

"Absolutely," the doctor said. "Actually, that's what Admiral Marsten wants, too. They're experienced men from one of the hardest-hitting boats in the Pacific. Any precommissioning skipper would kill to get them."

Malachi nodded. "Deal," he said. "And tell the admiral and the commodores that I appreciate their—" He paused, searching for the word.

"Their consideration?"

"Yeah, their consideration. Exactly. How will all this be handled?"

"By senior line officers who know exactly what to do, Captain," the doctor said. "You get some rest now. The submarine force takes care of its own. The fact that you remained below when you ran out of escape devices has not gone unnoticed."

"The reasons behind that might not make good reading, Doctor," Malachi said.

"Then never write them down, Captain," the doctor said as he got up. "Get well."

"One last question, Doctor," Malachi said. "Why did they send a senior medical officer to broker this arrangement?"

"So that no senior line officers would lose face if you happened to turn it down, Captain. That's why they're senior officers."

Malachi grinned from the hospital bed. The doctor grinned back.

THIRTY-THREE

A week later Malachi found himself ensconced in the cottage at Richmond Station, a move set up by Kensie when she found out he was essentially homeless upon his discharge from the hospital. The rooms at the hotel were for commanding officers; technically, he no longer qualified. They'd offered him a berth on the *Otus* while he waited for his medical board review and, probably, medical discharge from the Navy, after which, they'd find a way to send him home. Kensie had told Lambert, who was off on another trip, of these developments and he had immediately told her to bring him to the station for convalescence.

Malachi arrived without any luggage. One of the consequences of losing his ship was that he'd also lost all his personal possessions, including work and dress uniforms, civilian clothes, shoes, his ceremonial sword, and his service and pay records. He'd been able to acquire two sets of work khaki uniforms on the tender, along with a new supply of underwear, socks, toiletries, and uniform shoes. Kensie had then taken him downtown to get some civilian clothes, which, ironically, consisted mostly of more khaki shirts and trousers.

The first night they went up to the big house for dinner with Margery. It was a quiet affair, as if Kensie and Margery were trying hard to show some respect for Malachi's losses. They lingered at the dinner table after dinner was cleared away. Margery, who'd enjoyed a decanter of red wine pretty much all by herself, asked Malachi what he was going to do now that his submarine was sunk. Kensie bristled at the question, but Malachi waved her off.

"Good question, Margery," he said. "It's an unusual situation for the Navy, you see, because when submarines are lost there are rarely any survivors."

"Oh, dear," Margery said, suddenly aware that Kensie was glaring at her. "I shouldn't have—"

"No, no, it's a reasonable question," Malachi said. "I've been told by an American Navy doctor that I am no longer physically qualified for submarine duty. Something called AGE, an arterial gas embolism. The Navy will conduct a formal medical review hearing and then make a final determination. They might send me to a surface ship, or back to the States to a submarine training command, or they might even medically discharge me and just pension me off."

"But Kensie has told us that you and your submarine are famous, that you've been highly decorated and are known throughout the fleet. They can't just . . . discard you like that, can they?"

Malachi smiled. "It's not personal, Margery. I wouldn't be much use aboard a cruiser or a battleship, especially since I'm a commander. I'd be a senior officer but without the experience in the surface ship world you'd expect from a three-striper. And, traditionally, when a captain loses his ship, even in battle, he can be expected to be held responsible for that."

"Why, that's ridiculous," Margery said. "I mean, I understand if there's cowardice or gross incompetence involved, but as Lambert has often told me, no one can predict how a battle will come out. *No* one. He was with the ANZACs at Gallipoli, you see. He should bloody well know."

Malachi nodded. "The Army has perhaps a more practical outlook on failure in battle," he said. "But in the Navy, the captain is responsible for *everything* that happens to his ship, good or bad. You are fully aware of that when you take command. You have the ultimate authority *and* the ultimate responsibility. Those are the rules, and if you don't like them, then you don't become a captain. Personally, I have no problems with that."

"But in this case, there were others who failed in their duties,"

Kensie pointed out. "We've heard that the RAN was supposed to have been minesweeping the Fremantle approaches, but they hadn't done it."

"Well, here's how I look at it," he said. "The mine killed half my crew upon impact. The other half managed to close off the rest of the boat, and then we got them all out, myself included. That was a good thing, and if in overseeing that one good aspect of this mess I lose my own submariner ticket, well, that's just how the cookie crumbles. On the scale of this war out here in the western Pacific Ocean, this is just a minor incident, Margery. Not minor to me, of course, or to the families that I'm going to have to write condolence letters to, but this is a global war. The Navy will salvage what people they can from the sinking, and then press on with the war on Japan."

"And how will you cope with all this, Captain?" Margery asked.

"I'm sad that this happened, but I'm relieved that over half my crew survived. And that *I* survived." He looked sideways at Kensie. "There are things and special people worth living for, I think."

Margery looked at the two of them. "Well said, Captain," she replied. "Well said."

Back in the cottage, Kensie apologized for her mother's intrusion into Malachi's disintegrating professional situation while she changed into a nightgown, but Malachi made light of it. "She knows how we feel about one another," he said. "So she has a right to know how this is going to come out. Come to bed now; I'm running out of steam."

Kensie said she would and then went back outside to her Ute. She came back with the bottle of Kentucky whiskey. She poured each of them a small glass, and then got into bed. They toasted each other, kissed, and then settled into the night in each other's arms.

For the following week, Kensie stayed overnight at the station when her surgical shifts allowed, which was not as often as Malachi would have liked. Lambert was still away and Margery became increasingly busy running the station in his absence. She continued to be gracious, friendly, and even sympathetic about what had happened, even though she appeared to know nothing about the American submarine operation down in Perth. She was in her early sixties, and there were times when Malachi wondered if she wasn't getting a little dotty. He joined her for dinner in the big house each evening except for one night when he'd had some breathing problems.

The house staff treated him as an honored guest, to the point where they told him to stop making his bed each morning. Sanford Higgins had been coming out each morning to report on developments with the crew, such as where they were going next. Several of the men had already begun the long trip back to the States, usually via submarines headed back for overhaul. They'd get a month's home leave, and then report for duty in whichever shipyard their new boat was being built. He also brought along the paperwork that was generated by the loss of a warship, all the fitness reports on the wardroom, and some awards recommendations. Higgins had done all the scut work, so all Malachi had to do in most cases was to sign. He told Higgins that he'd be sent out again as an exec, but that with the fitrep that Malachi was going to write for him, he'd be in the PCO pool pretty damned soon. Then they would indulge in an hour or so of the latest fleet and war gossip.

By the end of the visit Malachi would be surprisingly tired and would often sleep for two or three hours into the afternoon. He would then get up and go "walkabout" as the station staff called it. The first time he'd tried it they'd had to drive him back to the cottage. After a week, he was able to make it back to the cottage on his own power, but not without knowing there was still something wrong with his cardiovascular system.

At week's end, Kensie arrived after a two-day stint at the hospital, bearing a bottle of Scotch whiskey and demanding to be left alone for an entire hour in the cottage bathroom for a hot soak. She came out wrapped in a white terry-cloth robe and plopped down on the bed, a glass of whiskey in hand and her skin wrinkled like a prune.

"Are you getting better?" she asked in her direct fashion.

"Most days, yes," he replied. "Some days, not so much. I start out feeling energetic but then my energy falls off."

"Time," she said. "I consulted with a world-famous pulmonary specialist in Canberra, a Dr. Catlett. Top man in Canberra; member of the Royal Society in London. He said that as long as you didn't pop an infection, your lungs would recover. He asked if you were a smoker, by the way."

"Not anymore," Malachi said. "I lit one off when I was discharged and damned near died from coughing."

"Well, there you are, then," she said, approvingly. "Some of your problems are from the free ascent, the rest probably withdrawal from nicotine, believe it or not. Which means you *will* feel increasingly better as time progresses. Now, the important question: any developments on what you are going to do now that you're no longer a captain of submarines?"

"How's about I come grab you, pull you into this bed, and have my wicked way with you?"

She grinned. "I was talking about the next chapter in your life, you silly brute. But do hold that thought. You know you can stay here for as long as you want."

"Well," he said. "Putting aside all the practicalities, that seems like my best hope for the rest of my life. Marrying you and settling down here, like the guilty bastard I am."

She sat up, eyes wide. "Are you serious, Malachi?"

"I know, I know, it's probably not possible, or even permissible here in Australia. I'm an American, and I have none of the prospects your parents were hoping for you. But, *God*! I wish. Would you think about it? You know I love you."

She stared at him for a few seconds. Then her expression changed. "Well," she said, archly. "Of course, I'll have to think about it." Then she paused, and finally smiled, unable to carry off the fiction. "Okay," she said, as she reached for him. "All done."

"Not by a long shot," he said.

Lambert came back to the station two days later, with big news: the government was a creating a new ministry to direct all war production, especially of raw materials, and they wanted Lambert to head it up. He stopped by the cottage on the way in to check on Malachi. Kensie was at the hospital but due back in time for dinner. Malachi assured him that he was recovering and thanked him for letting him stay there.

After dinner with the family, he and Kensie went to Lambert's study to break the news that Malachi was probably going to be medically retired from the Navy and that they wanted to get married. Lambert was hardly surprised and gave them his immediate blessing. Then he asked a question that was right to the point: will your Navy allow you to do that? Won't they want you back in the States to teach the new submarine crews? Malachi said he didn't know, but since he was being medically *retired* and not just *reassigned*, they probably wouldn't have a problem with it. He then asked a question of his own: would Australia allow him to marry an Australian national? Lambert was about to say of course, but then remembered that Australia had a seriously restrictive immigration program.

"Let's hold off on asking the question until I become a government minister," he said. "Then *I* will ask that question. Much better chances for a yes. Will you have a pension?"

"I suppose so," Malachi said. "I'd expect to get half my active-duty pay."

"That helps," Lambert said. "Tell me, didn't you say you had worked in the coal industry?"

Malachi laughed. "Yes, I did, but not in any management level. I was a hard-rock miner in Kentucky, starting at age thirteen. Ask me about the coal *business*, I know nothing except that the guys who own the mine do much better than the guys who lift the coal."

Lambert smiled at that. "Would you like to see the other side of the coal business?" he asked.

Malachi looked at Kensie, who was nodding her head emphatically. "Well, yes," Malachi said. "My future boss recommends it, I think."

They all laughed at that.

"Very well, Malachi Stormes," Lambert said. "Let me call in some favors."

The next night during cocktails, Lambert told Malachi that he'd made some inquiries and had been made aware of a gentlemen's agreement between the US Navy and the RAN regarding the *Firefish* incident. He'd also found out about Malachi's DSO, which had rung some bells in Canberra. The long and short of it was that Malachi

Stormes, Commander, USN, Retired, was absolutely welcome in Australia.

Kensie was back on shift, but due home the next afternoon. After dinner, Lambert recommended that Malachi break the news to her that their plans to get married were apparently on track. He then asked Malachi to do one more thing: tell Margery.

"You haven't told her?" Malachi asked.

"No, young man, that's going to be the price of admission, I think. I realized that Kensie was her own woman a long time ago, but it was Margery's dream of some fabulous mercantile alliance, a glittering society wedding, and then, well, I'm not sure what. This awful war has affected her more than I'd expected. Both of her brothers went off to fight with the Brits; one is dead, the other is missing in action in Burma."

"Damn," Malachi said. "I didn't know that."

"There's more," Lambert said. "Margery's British, actually. Not one to complain. But her family lived in Coventry. Her father was something important in the Midlands munitions business."

"Coventry," Malachi said. "When I first took my boat to Holy Loch, they were still talking about what had happened to Coventry, even though it had been over a year. Did—?"

"Oh, yes," Lambert said. "We met in London six months after the family had been all but wiped out in the November raid. I was over there for a war-planning conference of industrialists from throughout the Empire right after. She was very pretty but utterly devastated by what had happened. Her entire family was gone and she couldn't have been more vulnerable. On impulse I asked her to come back to Australia with me. She never looked back, our Margery. But now I think it would be good for you to tell her about you and Kensie. And why. Why, especially, would be good, you know."

"I have something of a past," Malachi said.

Lambert just looked at him.

"Kensie told you?"

"Kensie did tell me, and she also said something that resonated with me. That what happened was part of *who* you were, not *what* you were."

"Yes, I remember those words. I'd never thought of it that way. I'd also never told anyone about what happened. Until Kensie."

"This is Australia, Malachi," Lambert said. "We're realists here, down under. Most of this continent is wild, untamed, and even a bit haunted. Look into the eyes of an aborigine elder and you realize that you're an intruder in this ancient place. But if Kensie has chosen you, that's bloody good enough for me. Be gentle with Margery. She's fragile, not dotty."

"Count on it, Lambert," Malachi said. "I can relate to fragile, believe it or not."

"I'd like you to go see her now, Malachi, if you don't mind. I've told her you need to speak to her about something important. She'll be in the salon at this time of day."

Malachi found his way to what Americans would have called the living room. Margery was sitting in a rocking chair, knitting something. She looked up when he appeared in the entrance to the salon.

"Hello, Malachi," she said with a generous smile.

He took a deep breath and then stepped in.